CHINA'S AVANT-GARDE FICTION

CHINA'S AVANT-GARDE FICTION

An Anthology ❋ Edited by Jing Wang

DUKE UNIVERSITY PRESS

Durham and London

1998

Typeset in Quadraat by Tseng Information Systems, Inc.
Library of Congress Cataloging-in-Publication Data
China's avant-garde fiction : an anthology / Jing Wang, editor.
ISBN 0-8223-2100-9 (alk. paper). — ISBN 0-8223-2116-5 (pbk. : alk. paper)
1. Chinese fiction—20th century—Translations into English.
2. Experimental fiction. I. Wang, Jing, 1950– .
PL2658.E8C46 1998 895.1'35209—dc21
97-37349 CIP

CONTENTS

ACKNOWLEDGMENTS

My journey to China in 1987 was a new beginning. I dedicate this anthology to the twenty-two young men and women on the Duke Study-in-China Program who shared that experience with me: Grant Alger, Laura Beasley, Fred Boltz, Gail Ellis, Kate Farrington, Kevin Force, Arianne Gaetano, Chris Galati, Louis Gump, Lisa Haag, Stephanie Hawkinson, Lauren Herbtsman, Richard Hudspeth, Alec Jeong, Saul Kotzubei, Dara Lao, Mary Markis, Donna Marsh, Brandon Meyerson, Michael Roffman, Lily Su, and Nancy Yu.

INTRODUCTION ❊ *Jing Wang*

The 1980s dawned in China with the promise of a new history that would leave ultraleftism behind. But the nation's farewell to Mao's socialist past was accompanied by a contradiction: the cult of Mao disappeared only to return a decade later as a flourishing culture industry that cashed in on remembering Mao. The Mao Zedong Fever of the early 1990s was puzzling to many. But it was not an accident. Memories of Mao's era and obsessions with Maoism lingered throughout the postrevolutionary decade of the 1980s. Nowhere else were those memories registered more deeply than in narrative fiction. The "wounded literature" of the early 1980s served as a paramount example of writers' efforts to recount and recant the heresy of the Cultural Revolution. The exorcism of Mao Zedong and the radicalism he once stood for raged on. Writers of "reform literature" and the "literature of reeducated youths"—which includes the much acclaimed "root-searching" literature of the mid-1980s—continued Chinese writers' historical mission of reevaluating bygone political movements in the manner of enlightenment philosophers. Never mind if their revisit of that moment grew increasingly ambivalent: was the Cultural Revolution an unredeemable trauma or a utopia aborted? Writing as an anxiety-ridden political act, and specifically, writing as a weighty act of resistance to Maoism, was a sublime agenda that was hardly questioned, let alone challenged, until the debut of the Avant-Garde School (*xianfeng pai*) around 1987.

Indeed, as David Der-Wei Wang so aptly summarizes, Chinese literature from 1919 to 1989 is "burdened with writers' heavy concern for the Chinese nation."[1] The avant-garde, sometimes referred to as

1 David Der-Wei Wang, "Chinese Fiction for the Nineties," in *Running Wild: New Chi-*

"experimentalists," wanted none of this. Their penchant for trivial pursuits was unmistakable: "The burden of a nation is truly not as light as that of a singular 'I.'"[2] This remark teasingly captures the spirit of the young rebels' airy flight from anything onerous. The dramatic contrast between the new school and their literary forebears can hardly be made clearer.

Although the avant-gardists did not issue any manifesto, they struck up a concerted tune around 1987 under the aegis of *Harvest* (*Shouhuo*), an upscale literary magazine. They were a cluster of young writers who flaunted the lightness of being as a mere instance of improvisation in narration. Predictably, nothing could be more unbearable for them than the concept of "burden"—whether it was conceived of as a cultural, historical, sociopolitical, existential, or, not the least of all, semantic burden.

The avant-gardists have come a long way since the May Fourth period of the early twentieth century. Theirs was a belated escape from the bondage of anxiety consciousness (*youhuan yishi*)—a Confucian humanist heritage—that nourished generations of Chinese literati in a compulsive desire to play the role of political missionaries and commentators. Ma Yuan, Yu Hua, Ge Fei, to name a few of them, discovered something that May Fourth writers (especially Lu Xun and his cohort of left-wing writers) could never have imagined nor afforded: writing is fun on its own terms. Not only were rational critiques of politics à la May Fourth exiled from these new writings, but also missing was the atavistic call of the cultural original—traditional ethos and aesthetics—a legacy that Shen Congwen passed on, via Wang Zengqi,[3] to the "root-searching" writers of the mid-1980s.

The avant-gardists emerged at a particular historical juncture when the utopian mood of the country was on the decline. The years 1985

---

nese Writers, ed. David Der-Wei Wang and Jeanne Tai (New York: Columbia University Press, 1994), 252.

2 He Xiangyang, "'Shenfu' yu 'lianzu': Jianping xungenhou wenxue wenhua zhuti de liubian" (Fathers on trial and nostalgia for ancestors: Notes on the transformation of literary and cultural subjectivity after the root-searching movement), *Wenxue pinglun* (Literary review) 5 (1992): 41.

3 In 1980, Wang Zengqi published "Shoujie" (Buddhist initiation), a story that inspired A Cheng and many other "root-searching" writers. The story was originally published in *Beijing wenxue* (Beijing literary monthly) 10 (1980): 41–49.

and 1986 were memorable in that they witnessed the intensification of "methodology fever," the massive propagation of the formula for a market economy, and the reiteration, since spring 1986, of the urgency for political reform voiced by Deng Xiaoping and other high-ranking Party officials. The raging nationwide expectations for a more enlightened and wealthier future grew so quickly that the early signs of stalled economic reform in the cities were taken as ominous setbacks, which baffled a previously impassioned public. A succession of dramatic political events—the university students' demonstration in Beijing in late 1986, Party Secretary Hu Yaobang's immediate ouster as a result, the launching of yet another campaign against "bourgeois liberalism" in early 1987—further deepened the public's mood of disillusionment. An increasingly pervasive dystopian mentality spread. In October 1987 it reached an acme as Premier Zhao Ziyang announced at the Thirteenth Party Congress that China still lingered at the threshold of the "*primary* stage of socialism."

The emergence of the Avant-Garde School around 1987 seemed for many a timely response to the exhaustion of the utopian motif of the early 1980s. Indeed, most Chinese critics at home viewed the rise of the new fiction as a direct reflection of the epochal disillusionment with humanism and heroism. To think of the avant-gardists in such historicist terms was to compromise their "experimental" aura and to pare down an invasive aesthetic revolution to an impassive reflection of a social reality gone awry. It is not surprising, then, that the school's eccentric experiment with language was often dismissed as babbling and called a deplorable example of the "depression of creativity" [4] and of the "loss of the sensational [sociopolitical] impact" [5] of literature in the late 1980s.

Such a historicist view, however, even though it smacks of mechanical causality, is not entirely scandalous. The Avant-Garde School was no historical accident. Its irreverent attitude toward history and culture is decipherable only when seen against the historical context from which it emerged. The young heretics' fabrication of

4 Articles on the phenomenon of the "depression of creativity" were common in 1988 and 1989. For one example see Wang Meng and Wang Gan, "Piruan? Huapo?" (Depletion? Sliding down the hill?), *Zhongshan* (Bell mountain) 3 (1989): 148–160.

5 Yang Yu, "Wenxue: Shiqu hongdong xiaoying yihou" (Literature: After losing its sensational impact), *Renmin ribao*, 12 February 1988, overseas edition.

a rootless subject, devoid of memory, was not a mindless pursuit. The making of a subject without a core who narrates without a purpose was a highly subversive act. What the avant-gardists sneered at was the sublime subject construed for a decade by humanist writers and intellectuals. Theirs was a sociopolitically centered and culturally invested subject invigorated with a teleological and utopian vision toward life. Whether the subject is in search of the Chinese modern, cultural roots, or other "authentic" points of origin,[6] it is charged with reasoned drives. The avant-gardists' heroes and heroines, by contrast, drive nowhere; they only drift.

Indeed, what made possible the dramatic entry of the avant-gardists was precisely their remembrance and overwriting of the epochal discourse of the 1980s—nearly ten years of national outburst of utopian fever and fascination with cultural roots. This anthology aims to exhibit that dangerous narrative space opened up by this group of rebels who consciously worked to shatter the myth of "man" and utopia and to shock and alienate the traditional readership at home. Posing as seditious literary elements in the post-Mao era, the avant-gardists adopted an impious attitude toward history. Those who look in their stories for trenchant critiques of the Cultural Revolution will be disappointed. What they display, instead, is a voracious appetite for the clinical depiction of unmotivated violence, which represents a metonymy, rather than just a metaphor, of the historical cataclysm of the Cultural Revolution (Yu Hua's "1986" is a case in point).

It is not difficult to imagine why this avant-gardist attempt at fictionalizing violence risked offending veterans of the Cultural Revolution. The experimental tribute to homicidal instincts and savage compulsions of the most unpredictable kind was a heresy to the older generation of writers and critics for whom violence was a political act and a symptom, albeit an irrational one, of history. The pure consumption of violence as an aesthetic form was inconceivable, and not surprisingly, utterly sacrilegious, to survivors of turbulent historical

6 For a detailed discussion of Chinese intellectuals' search for modernity see Jing Wang, *High Culture Fever: Politics, Aesthetics, and Ideology in Deng's China* (Berkeley and Los Angeles: University of California Press, 1996), chap. 2. An examination of "root-searching" literature can be found in chapter 4, "Mapping Aesthetic Modernity," and chapter 5, "Romancing the Subject."

trauma. The avant-gardists were oblivious to all taboos, of course, having practiced the art of blasphemy to such near perfection that by comparison even Mo Yan's parade of scatological imagery appeared tame. The antihumanist imagination of brutality in a typical scene from "1986" is a hair-raiser by all standards.

Although the core of the school—Ge Fei, Yu Hua, Su Tong, Sun Ganlu, and Bei Cun—came of age during the 1980s, the avant-gardists did not all belong to the post–Cultural Revolution generation. The two pioneers of the school—Ma Yuan and Can Xue (the only female avant-gardist)—were in fact a generation older. Ma Yuan's mischievous construction of the maze of narration began the discursive revolution as early as 1984 with his publication of "The Goddess of the River Lhasa." It was an intriguing coincidence that during the same year, the Chinese translation of Jorge Borges's stories, a literary event important only in retrospect, was published in China. Many indigenous critics traced the foreign lineage of the young avant-gardists to the Argentinean author ("the young generation of writers were mostly bastard sons of Borges").[7] But in fact it was Ma Yuan (a Han Chinese writing about Tibet) whose idiosyncratic adventures into the labyrinths of narrative opened before our eyes the infinity of the inexhaustible form. Today, any historical account of the literary avant-garde has to start with Ma Yuan.

In 1986, just when Ma Yuan's influence began to be felt in avant-gardist circles, Can Xue published "The Hut on the Mountain," "Old Floating Cloud," and "Yellow Mud Street." If Ma Yuan's pure fiction opens up new possibilities of narrating the legendary, Can Xue's world seems closed because of its allegorical similarity to the immediate historical past—two decades of revolutionary violence now turned inward. But Can Xue is far from interested in delivering another antirevolutionary testimony. Her victims are all disembodied and dehistoricized, as is the origin of the violence with which they are afflicted. She draws us step by step to the killing field located in the psyche of anonymous, historically unidentifiable victims. Hers is a vicious narrative circle that always brings us back, after a journey through the savage imagery of schizophrenia and cannibalism,

7 Chen Xiaoming, "Houxiandai zhuyi: Wenhua weiwangren de wan'ge (Postmodernism: The dirge of cultural survivors), in " 'Houxiandai' bitan" ("Notes on postmodernity"), *Zhongshan* 1 (1993): 181.

to the same closure—the cemetery of the mind. Eternity reappears in the form of the blusterous vortex of violence. The dead, of course, are not resting in peace. At the turn of each page, we are deafened by noises (squeaks, howls, and snickers) and confronted with corpses of all sizes and smells. Dead moths, dragonflies, cockroaches, sparrows, cats, and severed human body parts flood the wreckage of the mental battleground. The dominant imagery of animals and animalism in Can Xue's fiction seems ready-made for its appropriation into the critique of the antihumanistic ravage of the Cultural Revolution. Her hysterical mode of narration was indeed often seen as political in various ways—as gender specific and a camouflage of the feminist resistance to "institutionalized patriarchal rule."[8]

Yet Can Xue's contribution to China's avant-garde fiction has little to do with what readers identify as the "final" referent of all those violent signifiers in her texts. Her fiction does not merely serve as a metaphor either for postrevolutionary or feminist politics. Can Xue's distinctly paranoid persona is, within the confines of her nightmarish world, a self-consciously depoliticized and an empty, albeit psychically energized, form without content. This is what makes her distinguishable from the authors of "wounded literature" and other contemporary female writers. Her fictional logic is built on an inversion: violence is disengaged from history and internalized into a mere mental image that is ultimately fictitious. This displacement of the real/historical by the hallucinatory and the contingent as the locale of authenticity constitutes Can Xue's legacy to those avant-gardists who came after her. As the signifier of violence is finally freed from the tyrannical enclosure of history, it gains an autonomous life on its own terms—multiplicable, uncontainable, and without a raison d'être. It was Can Xue's formal turn in the depiction of violence that made possible the appearance of the wicked little Shu Nong in Su Tong's tale "The Brothers Shu" and Yu Hua's self-mutilating madman in "1986."

Several years after Ma Yuan and Can Xue, the core group of the avant-garde—a generation younger than those two trailblazers—began to publish their best works. Sun Ganlu published "I Am a

8 See Chen Xiaoming, "Zuihou de yishi: 'Xianfengpai' de lishi jiqi pinggu" (The last ceremony: The history and evaluation of the Avant-Garde School) *Wenxue pinglun* 5 (1991): 131.

Young Drunkard" in early 1987; in late 1987, Ge Fei's "The Lost Ferry" ("Mizhou") and Yu Hua's "1986" appeared side by side with Wang Shuo's "Masters of Mischief" ("Wanzhu") in *Harvest*.[9] Wang Shuo's anti-intellectualism and his portrayals of street hooligans risked alienating the elite establishment. Naturally, in 1988 and throughout 1989, literary critics like Li Tuo, Zhang Yiwu, and Chen Xiaoming,[10] and literary journals like *Literary Review (Wenxue Pinglun)* and *Bell Mountain (Zhongshan)*,[11] were much more interested in promoting the avant-garde's experiment with language than paying attention to the soon-to-be-popular "Wang Shuo phenomenon." In the following year, *Harvest* published another cluster of the avant-garde fiction that included Ge Fei's "Green Yellow" ("Qinghuang"), and works by Su Tong, Sun Ganlu, Ma Yuan, and Yu Hua.[12]

All these showcases of the avant-garde in 1987 and 1988 brought to the fore the hypothesis about a "new generational logic" and simultaneously, the proposition of "Chinese postmodernism." As the new school came to define itself more and more around a small group of younger avant-garde writers who belonged to the post–Cultural Revolution generation, Ma Yuan's and Can Xue's membership in the club acquired an increasingly symbolic stature. By 1988, they were remembered as mere antecedents rather than as mainstream avant-gardes.

Although the proposition of a new generational logic was ques-

9 See *Shouhuo* (Harvest) 6 (1987).

10 The earliest criticism of the avant-gardist fiction can be seen in Zhang Yiwu's "Xiaoshuo shiyan: Yiyi de xiaojie" (The experiment of fiction: The deconstruction of meaning), *Beijing wenxue* 2 (1988): 76–80; see also Zhang Yiwu, "Lixiang zhuyi de zhongjie: Shiyan xiaoshuo de wenhua tiaozhan" (The end of idealism: The cultural challenge of Experimentalist Fiction) *Beijing wenxue* 4 (1989): 4–11; Chen Xiaoming, "Wubiande cunzai: Xushu yuyan de lingjie zhuangtai" (Borderless existence: The liminal condition of narrative language), *Renmin wenxue* (People's literary monthly) 3 (1989): 109–112; and Li Tuo, Zhang Ling, and Wang Bin, "Yuyan de fanpan: Jinliangnian xiaoshuo xianxiang" (The rebellion of language: The tendency of fiction in the last two years), *Wenyi yanjiu* (Studies of literature and the arts) 2 (1989): 75–80.

11 Between Oct. 12 and Oct. 16, 1988, *Wenxue pinglun* and *Zhongshan* sponsored a symposium on "Realism and the Avant-Garde" at Lake Tai in Jiangsu Province. A summary of the discussions, recorded by Li Zhaozhong, was published in "Xuanzhuan de wentan: Xianshi zhuyi yu xianfengpai wenxue yantaohui jianji" (A summary of the revolving literary field: Realism and the avant-garde), *Zhongshan* 1 (1989): 181–183.

12 See *Shouhuo* 6 (1988).

tioned by some critics,[13] the experience shared by younger avant-gardes was undeniably one that deviated from that of their immediate predecessors in the generation of "root-searching" writers. The "root searchers" were a generation that went through the catastrophic experience of the Cultural Revolution, of "agonies and sufferings that were deeply engraved on the tomb of history."[14] But what did their followers, the avant-gardists, possess? They possessed texts about utopia, discursive critiques of dystopia, and volumes of Chinese translations of classical and modern Western masters.

As latecomers for whom utopia, disillusionment, and patricide were merely oversaturated signifiers derived from texts rather than real-life experiences, the avant-gardists were acutely aware that they had missed the encounter with history—not just the climactic history of the Cultural Revolution and of the nation's crude awaking from it, but also the history of world literature, philosophy, theories, and the arts that now emerged suddenly in all its weightiness as the signifier of absence for the Chinese literary and cultural elite. This sense of belatedness is in the end indistinguishable from the avant-gardes' urge and rage to overtake contemporaneity and their crisis of historical consciousness. Thus for them, the strategy to deconstruct history is a symptom of a lack—a complex too difficult to subvert except through the vicarious experience of committing violence to language and to the concept of history itself.

What the young avant-gardists experienced, in short, was an existential dilemma of a different order than that of the "root-searching" collective. It is here that the proposal of the generational logic came into play. The dilemma that the young rebels (and the heroes they depict) faced on the eve of the Tiananmen Square crackdown can be summarized as follows: "Perhaps we have nothing, and perhaps we have everything."[15] This contradictory mood reveals itself as an

13 Both Li Tuo and Zou Yu critiqued the proposition that the avant-garde fiction foregrounded a logic that can be conceived of as generational. In their view, the "contemporaneity" of the post–Cultural Revolution generation cannot be reduced to the singular experience of elitism voiced by the literary avant-garde. See Huang Ziping, recorded "Wenxue piping: Yuyan yu xiezuo kongjian" (Literary criticism: Language and the space of creative writing), *Jintian* (Today) 2 (1994): 174–175, quoting Li Tuo and Zou Yu.

14 Chen, "Zuihou de yishi," 132.

15 Li Jie, "Lun Zhongguo dangdai xinchao xiaoshuo" (On contemporary Chinese new wave fiction), *Zhongshan* 5 (1988): 138.

epochal orientation, an emotional plight characteristic of the post–Cultural Revolution generation—a crowd that includes not only the high-minded avant-gardists but also Wang Shuo and his hooligans, and those millions of youngsters who chimed in with rock star Cui Jian when he sang "I Have Nothing Whatsoever" ("Yiwu suoyou").

This is a generation that gallops freely in the realm of desires ("perhaps we have everything"), but feels unrequited and restrained in action. The avant-gardists may not deserve the title "spokespeople for the new generation," but their fiction renders the metaphorical situation of this contradiction palpable. The collective persona in the new fiction experiences its own emptiness, or perhaps even more precisely, its own impotence ("we have nothing") before its entry into the linguistic order of fiction making.

The local realities thus constructed in the avant-gardist fiction are conscious of their own fragility and artificiality. Yet paradoxically, at the same time that language provides the avant-gardists with the means of articulating the withering of reality, it also promises its own emancipation from the continuum of sign-representation-reality (a three-tier system of signification that realism and modernism reproduced relentlessly). It is the dramatic breaking down of this continuum, the annulment of the real and the referential, and the ensuing foregrounding of the floating signifiers that called for the critical assessment, from some quarters, of the new fiction as a mere linguistic maze, a pure energy field, and an "aesthetic game of narration." And yet, for others who would consider themselves historically minded, the revolution that the avant-gardists initiated did not merely stop at the discursive level. The proposal of the new generational logic also meant for them the dawning of an epistemological revolution that bid farewell to humanism and the philosophy of representation in pursuit of the cultural logic of postmodernism.

The debate over naming—whether the new fiction is "postmodernist" or not—continued even into the 1990s, long after the avant-gardists lost their creative momentum in the face of the challenge posed by writers of popular fiction.[16] In early 1993, *Bell Mountain* presented an array of oppositional views on this debate in the "Written

16 For a detailed discussion of the late 1980s debate on "Chinese postmodernism" see Wang, "The Pseudoproposition of 'Chinese Postmodernism,' " chap. 6 in *High Culture Fever.*

Exchanges on 'Postmodernity' " contributed by well-known literary critics. The forum did not yield unpredictable results. Zhang Yiwu and Chen Xiaoming, the two most earnest proponents of "Chinese postmodernism," reiterated their earlier argument for the universality of postmodernity. They declared that the West does not own the copyright on postmodernism and that the avant-gardists had already succeeded in appropriating the foreign version into "our" own.[17] Arguing against this position, Sheng Ning and Wang Bin attributed the proposition of postmodernism to some critics' "fin de siècle dreaming."[18] For "without modernism," Wang Bin asked, "how could we even begin to talk about the 'postmodern'?"[19] This written debate, like many other, earlier discussions of "Chinese postmodernism" since 1989, came to a deadlock as contestants on both sides felt compelled to ask a single question (Do we have postmodernism now?) and answer it either in the affirmative or in the negative. What was left unexamined was, on the one hand, the rich history of the textual construction of "postmodernism" in the West, and on the other, the complex agenda of Chinese cultural politics in reinventing Occidental discourses such as postmodernism. In the mid-1990s, it became more and more clear that the debate over avant-garde fiction would redefine itself around a set of questions that highlighted the Chinese project of taming and challenging (on the discursive level at least), rather than reproducing or imitating, Western postmodernism. The gradual articulation of this position—one that stressed the ideology of the alternative post/modern—brought to the fore the issue of cultural locality and subjectivity. The making of this ideology, no matter how problematic it is, was especially significant in the decade of the 1990s, as Chinese mass culture be-

17 Zhang Yiwu was one of the earliest proponents of "Chinese postmodernism," stressing the global applicability of the concept. See his 1989 essay "Lixiang zhuyi de zhongjie: Shiyan xiaoshuo de wenhua tiaozhan" (The end of idealism: The cultural challenge of experimentalist fiction), *Beijing wenxue* 4 (1989): 11. Zhang continued to elaborate his earlier position in "Houxiandai yu hanyu wenhua" (Postmodernity and the culture of Chinese language), in "Houxiandai bitan," 179–181. Also see Chen, "Houxiandai Zhuyi," 181, 182, 199.

18 Wang Bin, "Shijimo de mengxiang" (The fin de siècle dream) in "Houxiandai bitan," 177.

19 Sheng Ning, "Houxiandai zhuyi wenxue shi buke mofangde" (Postmodern literature cannot be imitated) in "Houxiandai bitan," 174.

came more and more susceptible to the homogenizing process of globalization. In fact, one could argue that it is the imminent invasion into the Chinese market of waves of American cultural exports (such as the importation of Hollywood Blockbusters since 1995) that made the agenda of the Chinese alternative—an imaginary localism—meaningful and compellingly persuasive.

In 1989, however, the configuration of the power relationship between Chinese cultural elites and the hegemonic discourses of the West was subtly different. When the controversy over the avant-gardists' hypothetical relationship with postmodernism first broke out, critics were far more concerned with catching up with the newest intellectual fad in the West than with engaging themselves in articulating an ideology of localism. How to justify the postmodernist label formed the focal point of discussion. For a short while, every critical essay on the avant-gardists harped on the theme of the deconstruction of meaning and the end of history. And it was not until later that a more complex reckoning of the avant-gardists' encounter with history would be delivered.

China's young literary rebels have indeed subverted everything that the revolutionary generation held sacred. Their greatest achievement started with the depoliticization of language. In their effort to construct a new fictional subject that has no historical, sociopolitical, or even personal identity, the avant-gardists map out an imaginary subject position that language simultaneously creates and deconstructs. Although their carnivalesque self-exile in the imaginary takes various forms—a realm indistinguishable from the dream state and mirage (Ge Fei and Sun Ganlu), the hyperspace of violence (Yu Hua), the hallucinatory (Can Xue), the tautological mental maze (Bei Cun), the fabulous and the fantastic (Ma Yuan), and the personal historical (Su Tong)—they share with each other a common thematic interest in "the legendary," "the dilapidated spectacle of history," "violent death," an unresolved complex involving the father, the paralogic of coincidence, and for Yu Hua and Ge Fei in particular, the sadistic urge to disembowel the human body (especially a beautiful female body).

Underlying this thematic cluster of the new fiction is an antihumanist position, a rebellion against a morally, historically, and epistemologically centered subject assembled laboriously throughout the decade of the 1980s by the different schools of writers that preceded the avant-gardists. This holistic subject is undone in the new fiction. It reemerges as nothing more than the semblance of a linguistic construct, an unpredictable aleatory confluence of its chance encounters with history. Invariably, Ge Fei's and Su Tong's protagonists always wander into the labyrinth of history and are fated to retrace the footsteps of history (whether it is the legend of the water god or the genealogy of the nine fishing families in "Green Yellow") only to find that it is ultimately unavailable because its decrepit path merges imperceptibly into the trails marked by the pursuers' own footprints. The flimsy boundary between the historical, the fictional, and the real never exists in the first place.

"History" paradoxically only comes into being when the chase for its traces begins "here and now." In Su Tong's, Ge Fei's, Yu Hua's, and Bei Cun's tales, the presence (or absence) of history can only manifest itself when it enters the illusory dialogue with its pursuer and thus triggers his activity of making linguistic simulacra of the missing sign. "History is neither being nor nonbeing. It is in the end no more than a rewriting of reality."[20] This act of discoursing about history leads us to roads that bifurcate, corridors that go nowhere except to other corridors. This merging of reality, fiction, and history—the linguistic construction of the unreality of the unreal—is a familiar configuration underlying all the avant-gardist works. In 1987 and 1988, during the two best years of the school, the writers' formal experiments were pushed to an extreme. Serving as a mere allegory for the impasse of narration, "history" was turned into a blank sign. It is conceivable how their preoccupations with narrating the paradox of narration, a mind game, can empty history of its narrative content even though on the discursive level, the avant-gardes have always been telling tales that took place in early modern Chinese history. It was, however, not until the 1990s, with the appearance of full-length novels (Su Tong's *Rice* (Mi) and Ge Fei's *Enemy*

20 Chen Xiaoming, "Lishi tuibai de yuyan: Dangdai xiaoshuo zhong de 'houlishi zhuyi yixiang" (The allegory of the degeneration of history: The trend of "posthistoricism" in contemporary fiction), *Zhongshan* 3 (1991): 148.

21 *Mi* was published in *Zhongshan* 3 (1991): 4–94. *Diren* was published in *Shouhuo* 2 (1990): 120–195. The English translation of *Mi* (*Rice*) by Howard Goldblatt was published by William Morrow and Co. (1995).

(*Diren*)[21] come to mind as notable examples), that "history" would unfold itself in the avant-gardist fiction as a palpable, albeit dilapidated, human landscape of depth, rather than as a mere signifier of absence. This return to the tropes of historical discourse instigated the emplotting of several humanist themes that the avant-gardists earlier vowed to subvert, among them, the nostalgia for the missing sign of the father—the origin of history. The earlier patricide complex of the avant-gardists—Shu Nong's story—now enters a new phase. As one critic put it, "the fear of being fatherless (without history or without reality) has begun to reveal itself in the subconscious [of the avant-gardists]."[22] The two post-1989 stories collected in this anthology, Bei Cun's "The Big Drugstore" and Ge Fei's "Whistling," address this symptom of bereavement in their poetic revisit of the haunting spectors of the Father and History respectively.

I do not wish to examine the avant-gardists' change of course at the end of the 1980s in the allegorical framework of the political unconscious. On the one hand, it is almost impossible to disregard the historical trauma that the Tiananmen Square crackdown has bequeathed on Chinese intellectuals. And yet the reorientation, or disorientation, of the fictional logic of the avant-gardists seems also part and parcel of the response of the literary elite to the seige of pure literature by rampant popular culture in the 1990s. The ferment of activities that used to characterize the earlier phase of the school is no longer visible in the new era of mass culture. Elitism bit the dust. And the literary vanguard have much more at stake now if they continue to churn out the kind of highbrow experimental fiction that estranged the reading public. Whatever their aesthetic reorientation may yet signify, regression or compromise, the avant-gardists have left the best of their formalist careers behind them. It would not be an exaggeration to suggest that the term "avant-gardism" lost much of its exploratory edge and incentive at the beginning of the 1990s. It is miraculous that some of them are still publishing furiously. However, their persistence (or resistance) in the new decade only attests to the truism—today's avant-garde may become tomorrow's cliché.

This anthology aims at presenting the golden years—the formalist period—of the Avant-Garde School. Most of the stories collected

22 Chen, "Zuihou de yishi," 135.

here were published before 1989. The two stories published in the 1990s—"The Big Drugstore" and "Whistling"—may not be the best specimens of the school in their transitional, post-1989 phase. (Indeed, better examples are the two full-length novels I indicated earlier.) Those two tales were chosen because of the author Bei Cun's own preference in the one case, and because of the editor's partiality in the other.

The project of anthologizing Chinese avant-garde fiction fulfilled a wish I made several years ago. To this day, I recall the electrifying experience of my first reading of Ge Fei and Yu Hua, which left indelible repercussions on the critical scholarship I have pursued since then. As contemporary Chinese literature becomes increasingly an integral part of the academic curriculum of Chinese studies and/or comparative literature across the nation and beyond, there is a need for an anthology of the Chinese avant-garde composed with an awareness of the global debates over the issues of local history, cultural locations, and postmodernity.

For lay readers, the avant-garde showcase may drive home a different lesson. It serves to contradict the prevalent myth propagated throughout the decade of the 1980s by Western media: that Chinese writers were preoccupied with issues of human rights and that their ultimate cause can be defined as championing the principle of liberal democracy against the autocratic regime of communism. The avant-gardists demonstrate eloquently that writers in China could afford to turn an impervious back to sociopolitical consciousness. What is collected in this anthology is, in a nutshell, a dramatic manifesto of the aggressive making of a postrevolutionary literary sensibility obsessed with form and the pleasure of storytelling.

REMEMBERING MR. WU YOU ❁ *Ge Fei*

1

Not until the two middle-aged policemen in white uniforms and their young skirt-clad female partner showed up did the villagers reluctantly recall Mr. Wu You. That bygone episode, like a maiden's lost chastity, stirred the people's emotions. And since their recollections were triggered by the introduction into their lives of the three outsiders, village elders were quick to tell youngsters eager to revisit the painful past, "Time erases all memories."

Thanks to the three uniformed guests, the villagers learned of such things as handcuffs and, so they were told, alarm sirens. A sense of security accrued from the presence of the outsiders, even though they were not above putting on airs at times. One of their favorite pastimes was getting farmers to stop work, either out in the woods or in the shade of high walls, to relate obscure details regarding Mr. Wu You. They failed to get the answers they sought, not because the people were uninformed but because they were so blasé. Nothing excited the people of this village. I, on the other hand, was eager to work with the outsiders. I still recalled how the condemned man was shot that morning.

Mother reacted to the news that I was going to watch them shoot Mr. Wu You at a spot five miles from where we lived by slapping me across the face. "Killing a man is the same as killing a chicken," she said. So I went out back to watch my younger brother do just that. Old K, who was still little then, held the chicken by its neck in one tiny hand and a small penknife in the other. As I walked up to him, he asked me to help. "Killing a chicken is the same as killing a man," I said.

"They're the same thing," Old K replied.

Suddenly, the bird broke loose and flapped its way across a block of stone before soaring over the wall. Old K stood there holding his blood-streaked penknife, mesmerized by the sight of chicken feathers floating above us. I grabbed his hand and dragged him out the gate, telling him we were going to watch them actually kill a man. He was standing beside me when they shot Mr. Wu You. His mouth hung slack, and he was a different boy from the one who was trying to kill the chicken. On the way home, he muttered the only thing he would say for three whole days: "Killing a man is a lot easier than killing a chicken."

I divulged this to the three outsiders, who wouldn't dignify it with a response, would not even record it. But when I told them I was a distant relative of Mr. Wu You's, they smiled and turned real friendly, urging me to go on with my story. My ears rang with their meticulous mandarin in a singsong twang that made my skin crawl. I said Mr. Wu You was shot on the day of the Dragon Boat Festival.

"That's perfect!" the skirt-clad young woman said.

It really was the day of the Dragon Boat Festival. Women, some of whom had stayed up all night, went down to the stream to pick leaves, which they floated home on bamboo rafts, in sampans, even in washbasins, as wrappings for their glutinous holiday treats. A gossamer mist hung in the early-morning air like evanescent steam, heavy with the subtle fragrance of water reeds. Men were washing rice in large sieves. Children played behind their parents as they worked, splashing stream water with stripped willow switches. Just then one of the younger wives took off running from one end of the village to the other, shouting the whole way. And that is how people learned that Mr. Wu You was going to be shot later that day. Everyone watched her run, except for a smattering of young fellows who had no idea what was going on, since they were too busy staring at the fleshy mounds jiggling beneath her pink chemise to worry about what she was shouting. Much later, whenever they discussed the affairs of that morning, they admitted it was the first time they had ever seen a woman run like that, and for them, all other living objects hung in a state of suspended animation.

2

As soon as they heard the clanking noise, the villagers knew that the police were out for a stroll: all manner of brass contraptions in all sizes hung from their uniform belts. Encountering a middle-aged woman out on the street, they decided to question her. One of them casually slipped a brass hoop off his belt and fitted it over the woman's head, telling her it was a high-frequency lie-detector ring, the most advanced of its kind in the world. It shrieks every time you tell a lie. So she clammed up while the hoop was in place. But as soon as it was removed, words gushed from her mouth. Their technology had met its match.

Apparently feeling tension in the air for the first time since their arrival, the outsiders asked me to show them Mr. Wu You's living quarters, in an old, dilapidated, and boxy little ancestral hall. His room had been sealed on the day of his death, and no one had entered it since. Prying open the rusty latch was hard work. When we finally got the door open, we were greeted by a thick cloud of dust. It was stifling inside, and we were sweat soaked in no time. The room was just as its occupant had left it, as if awaiting his return. A coat of fine white dust had accumulated on a pencil sketch tacked to the wall: a black sun sinking into the reedy bank of a black river inhabited by a pair of egrets with crossed beaks. The sketch had been done for him by an itinerant artist. Appearance was important to Mr. Wu You, who could not abide dirt or slovenliness. He shaved with a finely honed straight razor and wore a black oilcloth apron when doing the dishes. Years later, whenever his name came up in conversation, the villagers invariably remarked, "Just like a woman!"

While finding nothing germane to their reinvestigation of the Mr. Wu You case, the police did note that his bookcases were empty. Mr. Wu You had been a lover of books. On the day the village headman ordered the people to move Mr. Wu You's books outside and burn them, it took more than five hours for the flames to consume the whole pile. Villagers watched the curling ashes of all that paper get sucked up a chimney as their faces were turned bloodred by the blaze. Only Apricot wept. A frequent guest at Mr. Wu You's ancestral hall, where she enjoyed his books, she was the only person he ever taught to read, and it did not take her long to learn a hundred and one ways to cure measles.

Unanimity has not been reached on what actually led to the fiery episode: some say the headman was drunk at the time, but they are refuted by others who say he drank very little that day.

3

The villagers found Mr. Wu You's behavior that day shocking, to say the least. Armed with his seven-inch straight razor, he confronted the village headman in the area's largest public square, and people who saw how jumpy he was knew he had been waiting there for some time. The headman stripped to the waist and hung his shirt in the crotch of a nearby tree, exposing a muscular chest tanned the color of bark. Brandishing his razor, Mr. Wu You charged like a crazed jackass, but the headman stepped nimbly out of the way, clenched his fists, and launched a ferocious counterattack. The first blow landed squarely on Mr. Wu You's nose, spraying blood all over the place, as if a rotten tomato had splattered on his face. The second one caught him on the back of the head, and he teetered briefly before thudding to the ground—just as I opened our attic window, which gave me a ringside view of the mayhem. Surrounded by spectators filling the square, Mr. Wu You staggered to his feet, drying clots of blood clinging to his face, and took a few wobbly steps, like a circus clown trying for a few laughs. Then, with a slight churning motion, he hit the ground again.

The three outsiders danced a jig when this incident was related to them by an old man who guarded the woods. The skirt-clad young woman shocked him by planting a kiss on his whiskered cheek. It was he who had lugged Mr. Wu You home afterward, only to incur the wrath of his wife—that day and every day thereafter—for bloodstains on his shirt that wouldn't wash out no matter what she did. Even now, traces of those badges of glory remain on the back of his yellowed undershirt. After the old watchman laid Mr. Wu You on his bed, Apricot opened the door and strode in, obviously having got wind of the fight. As she approached Mr. Wu You's bed, he spat a mouthful of bloody phlegm in her direction, but she merely removed her apron, leaned over, and gingerly wiped the blood from the corners of Mr. Wu You's mouth. The watchman gets all choked up even now when he recalls that incident. "I've never seen a more fetching girl," he says. "Like a pixie."

Mr. Wu You was just another villager, no one special, even taking into consideration the fact that he had once owned a roomful of books. Then some village children came down with what everyone called the sweats, for which the only known treatment was pillowing their heads on oven-dried river gunk. Mr. Wu You tried to convince them that a certain wild herb could cure their children, but no one listened. Nothing could win over the zealous disciples of the pillow treatment until he employed an argument they could understand: bulls seldom get sick because they graze on wild grasses. The villagers decided to give Mr. Wu You's treatment a chance. It worked, and overnight, his ancestral hall became the local clinic.

4

The burning of Mr. Wu You's books shook the people's confidence in his healing arts. But he had committed an astonishing quantity of the incinerated books to memory; it was an extraordinary gift that not only saved the clinic but simultaneously invested him with mystical airs. By then, Mr. Wu You and Apricot had become nearly inseparable, a development that sparked mixed reactions in the villagers. To some, the relationship seemed shady at best, since she hardly ever left the boxy ancestral hall until late at night, in the company of Mr. Wu You. Over time, they wore a path, luminous and white, through the woods between his home and hers. Gradually, the villagers warmed to Apricot. For by then, they nearly worshiped Mr. Wu You, and rather than concern themselves with the rectitude of the relationship, they convinced themselves that an atmosphere of harmony and sanctity prevailed. Naturally, the village headman was never far from their thoughts, since he had secured his position as headman not by grasping the essentials of forest-fire prevention or by practicing the art of divination but by virtue of a robust, muscular body and a broad, menacing forehead. He was a mighty lion, or so the village women said. Later, after the headman had been carried off by dysentery, a village old-timer told me, "They were still moved to tears even when they knew the headman was feeding them a line."

One day, an outsider came to the village. He swept a spot of ground clean of snow and set up a performing-monkey show. Mr. Wu You and Apricot, who were in the audience that day, looked over at the smirking headman, who said deliberately and in full voice, "I'm going to kill you two." People close by were laughing so hard at the performer's antics they didn't hear the headman. But my brother Old K heard him, and he streaked home as fast as his legs would carry him. Long after the incident, he told me he ran like the wind that day, flung open the door, and fell flat on his face. Yet even before he could clamber to his feet, he was shouting, "The headman's going to kill Apricot and Mr. Wu You . . ."

Like so many village women, Mother was off in some lovely dreamland as she stitched soles for cloth shoes, so she may not have heard what Old K was saying. Which is probably why she merely grunted in response.

Many days passed. Green buds popped from willow branches growing wild above crumbling walls at the village entrance; if you looked past the reeds on the riverbank, way off into the distance, you could see new grass in the mountain hollows. Suddenly, the village buzzed with talk that Mr. Wu You had killed Apricot. No one doubted the truth of the story, since he had confessed to the crime. A couple of forensic interns were invited to the village for what would be their first autopsy. They began by laying Apricot's body out on a three-legged Ping-Pong table, then stood on either side of her, butcher knives at the ready. She looked just as she had when she was swimming in the river in midsummer, the way people had so often seen her: ruddy faced and full of life. Not knowing exactly what to do, the two interns commenced cutting and kept at it all day, until it was impossible to tell what was what. Winding up with seven separate pieces of unequal size, they concluded that Apricot had been strangled after being raped.

5

The three visiting police officers really knew their business: the skirt-clad young woman filled every page of her thirty-by-forty-centimeter notebook. One day, she and the others spoke to the person who actually shot Mr. Wu You, a lad named Kangkang. On the eve of the Dragon Boat Festival, after the magistrate informed him he would be Mr. Wu You's executioner, he decided to make some repairs on his double-barreled shotgun, a family heirloom that hung on the wall of his mother's room. A one-time paralytic whom Mr. Wu You had cured, she had just got out of bed when her son came in to take down the shotgun, which had gathered dust for thirty years or more. "Going after wild boar?" she asked. He walked out without a backward glance.

Kangkang painstakingly wiped down the shotgun three times before taking it to the blacksmith to straighten out the barrel, which was thirty degrees off center. Then he loaded it, went down to the river, took aim at a billy goat, and fired, creating a dark hole the size of a man's thigh in the animal's belly. He smiled contentedly.

The next morning when Old K and I sneaked out to watch Mr. Wu You's execution, we encountered a woman with bound feet, moving as fast as those tiny feet would allow, sort of like bouncing along on stilts. A month or so after Mr. Wu You's execution, we learned the facts of the murder from her lips: her husband had suffered a terrible headache that night, so she took some spirit money into the woods to burn at the family grave site. There she saw the headman force Apricot, who had been walking home alone, to the ground. She was no more than twenty paces from them at the time. The night was absolutely still, she said, and the subtle fragrance of reeds along the riverbank drifted over on gentle winds. It was an intoxicating setting, with a milky miasma that hung over the woods and a lovely halo girding the moon. She declared that the sight of the headman ripping off Apricot's clothes and white underpants had moved her to tears.

For more than a month following Apricot's death, she was in the grips of dementia, her eyes vacant and clouded, until she knew she must do something to keep from going stark raving mad. So on the morning the young wife ran shouting from one end of the village to the other, the bound-foot woman, knowing she could keep the truth bottled up inside her no longer, decided to reveal what had happened that night. She ran like a woman possessed to the execution ground.

The onlookers grew impatient as a light rain fell. Kangkang took aim at Mr. Wu You on a signal from the magistrate, who held a red three-cornered flag in his raised hand. He dropped his arm, and Kangkang pulled the trigger. *Blam!* The shotgun misfired, blackening the front of Kangkang's white shirt. He spat angrily and reloaded. There was fear in Mr. Wu You's eyes. He strained to open his mouth, but his tongue had been cut out a month earlier. He was gesturing frantically when Kangkang's double-barreled shotgun roared one last time.

By the time the woman with bound feet hobbled up to the execution ground, mud-spattered from head to toe, Mr. Wu You was already in the ground. A few bloodstains and some bristly hairs were all that remained. A fine rain was still falling as way off in the distance a wedding party of men decked out in reds and greens was on its way to fetch a bride, their horns blaring, their drums banging. They disappeared from view on the opposite bank of the river.

Translated by Howard Goldblatt

GREEN YELLOW ❁ *Ge Fei*

That fleet of fishermen's boats owned by nine fishing families, which served as floating whorehouses on the Suzi River, vanished more than forty years ago. Yet folk stories about them are still being told and retold.

The Gazetteer of Mai Village (1953 edition) has this to say about the boats:

> Persecuted by soldiers and harrassed by local gangs, the Changs, who were the last of the nine fishing families, moved ashore one day at dawn to Mai Village.

This very sketchy entry was the work of the compilers, three teachers of the old-style private schools. Nothing is said about these people's situation after their move, though the entry does describe in some detail the scenery of that day on which they came ashore under "a sky splashed with many colors." A newly published book, *A History of Prostitutes in China*, by Tan Weinian, gives a vague, ambiguous account of the nine fishing families that is simply indiscriminately copied from *The Gazetteer of Mai Village*. In his better days, Professor Tan had earned my silent emulation of his personal style, as well as the seriousness of his writing. And now? His discussion of this topic, Mai Village and the nine families, was riddled with errors, one after another. Amid the uncertain words, the image of the aging and sad professor, looking ridiculous in a pair of loose riding breeches, flashed across my mind; he seemed to be trying to stride across a brazier. On page 427 of his book, Tan Weinian mentions, as many other scholars have, the controversy over the meaning of the term "green yellow." He repudiated the popular proposal that it was the name of a pretty young woman, saying that this was "at the least" a "careless" assumption. As for taking the term to refer to the changing of the seasons, from spring into summer, as some people have proposed, this was even more absurd, he maintained. Based on his instinct and stubbornness, Tan believed that "green yellow" was the title of a work, a year-by-year record of the lives of the prostitutes associated with the nine fishing families on the Suzi River. He also believed that, barring the unexpected, the record was still to be found somewhere among the people.

Enticed by this intriguing assertion, I decided to go back to Mai Village for another visit. Just before leaving, I ran into Professor Tan in a wineshop and brought up the subject of my trip. As in the past, after he had heard me out, he immediately responded in an impatient way and, gesturing his hand in disagreement, said, "You'll find nothing there."

1

Elytis once wrote, "Trees and pebbles cause time to elapse." Yet one may say that nonetheless, people are unlikely to forget things that happened forty years ago.

One evening three days after I arrived at Mai Village, I met an old man by the low hazel bushes along the Suzi River. He was repairing the fence of a sheep enclosure. Like many of the villagers, he did not want to talk about the "shameful events" of the past. Shades of sorrow had etched heavy lines on his face and caused the skin on his face to appear hard as stone. Standing there by the wooden fence of the enclosure, amid the strong smell of sheep, I hesitated for a long while. Finally the old man began to talk to me. He looked as though it required a strenuous effort to recall the past, and he seemed to be trying to revisualize certain scenes, to bring them before his eyes and then stabilize them there. He talked with heavy hissing sounds and turbid guttural noises. These noises caused some difficulty for me, and to take notes on what he said, I often had to ask him to pause or repeat when I could not follow him.

According to the old man, the shabby boat with the awning stretched over it arrived at the riverbank in a drizzling dawn. It was the rainy season of early summer and somewhat cold at dawn. The man Chang had with him a thin and weak little girl. They made their way with difficulty along the muddy, hilly road toward the village, their figures wavering in the strong southeast wind. Almost the entire village saw them coming. Behind them, their wooden boat, moored at the riverbank, was wrapped in flames; its burning bamboo cabin crackled briskly in the drizzling rain. This man from outside was a shrewd one. Perhaps he had burned his boat so that the villagers could not refuse to let him stay.

When Chang and the girl arrived at the village, they were exhausted. Chang found the gates of all the houses shut against them, and so he stood in the rain with his daughter for a long time. About noon, people peering from the cracks in their gates saw that Chang and his daughter were being led away by the ferryman. "Even now," the old man said, "I still don't know Chang's given name. His daughter's name, I think, is Young Green. She is old now and lives by the back of the village. Anyway, she doesn't use the name Young Green anymore."

"What happened after that?"

"I'm not sure. The day they came was three, maybe four days before the Dragon Boat Festival. I remember, because the old ferryman's boat overturned on the festival day, and three people were killed in the accident. The villagers felt that the bad luck was brought by the newcomers. That Chang never did talk or smile much; it was as if he had something on his mind. Maybe he couldn't get used to being in a village."

The old man showed no response whatever to my casual mention of the term "green yellow." An odd impression he gave as he recounted the past was that while he was revealing something he was also covering up something. At the end, as I was leaving, he added something.

"I used to go to the Suzi River every day at dusk," he said, "to fetch water. Sometimes I would see that outsider sitting on a low stool in front of his gate, doing nothing and watching his daughter catch butterflies on the hillside all covered with mugwort. But most of the time their old pinewood gate was closed by the time the sun set. He was probably a good father. Two years later, the daughter seemed suddenly grown up."

The Suzi River flowed silently by my feet, giving off coolness from its surface. Along the riverbanks were scattered shabby abandoned cabins, some with walls tumbling down, some with roofs caving in. It was early autumn, and there was no one working in the fields. Villagers were gathered near the walls, taking in the sun and waiting for the ripening of the cotton crop. The villagers, including the roaming yellow dogs, showed no interest in my visit. As a matter of fact, the first day I arrived at Mai Village it took quite some effort just to give them a vague idea of the purpose of my visit. But they did arrange for me to stay in a flour mill on the east side of the village. The mill's machinery had broken down the previous week and had been sent for repair to a town some dozen kilometers away.

I returned to my room and again smelled the suffocating dust. This village lacked warmth and curiosity, I thought. It wasn't just that poor man Chang—any newcomer from outside the village would feel lonely here. It was still early. I lay down on the bed near the wall. Just as I was dozing off, an incident from the past came suddenly to my mind. It was nothing special, but somehow the recollection of certain things in it made me somewhat uncomfortable.

2

It was at dusk one hot day nine years ago. On the main road to Mai Village I met an old rags-and-malt-sugar man.[1] He was sitting on the embankment of a roadside ditch, shaded by a chinaberry tree. He had the look of an honest working man. Two bamboo baskets, weathered to a dark gray color, lay in front of him. He held a bamboo flute in one hand. His sad eyes looked as though he were expecting something. Across from him was a vast field of jute, turned a lavish vermilion by the setting sun. His manner attracted my attention and made me want to talk to him. For some unexplainable reason, I felt he had been sitting there all day, puffing slowly at his long-stemmed pipe. As I approached and stopped beside him, I could see all the marks on his face left by the years. Only then did I realize how old he must be.

He told me his name was Li Gui and that he was from a town named Heng Tang. I recalled Heng Tang as a place often mentioned in a classical reference book of song lyrics. He said that he had

1. The rags-and-malt-sugar man collects rags and other discarded things from people and gives them malt sugar in return.

been lost, probably since that morning. "It seems that everything's changed here," he said. I sat down beside him under the chinaberry tree, and he handed me his long-stemmed pipe.

"There are no holes in your flute," I remarked.

"But it makes music. Right now I don't have the energy to play it."

He smoothed the flute lightly, staring at the bend in the road ahead and at the village at the far end of the road as though he could hear the sounds from there.

"Do you live here?" he asked me.

"No, I am passing by."

Then, unable to find any suitable topic for continuing our conversation, we sank into silence. To me, the silence was natural. Finally, the old man asked if he could go to the village with me for lodgings that night. I agreed.

It grew dark as we walked toward the village on the deeply rutted road. We passed through a mud-walled courtyard and, stopping at the first lighted house we saw, knocked on the door. The man living there was a medical man. He carefully sized us up and asked some questions. Finally, he reluctantly agreed to let us stay for the night. He took us to a room on the west side of the courtyard, a room filled with hay. He lit the oil lamp on the altar against the wall, and his face showed the worry and alertness that were typical of people in rural areas. Before leaving, he told us he was going out of the village to make a house call to see a woman suffering from eczema.

The old man and I lay down next to the piles of hay. We heard the doctor locking all the other doors and then leaving the house. It was after that that something strange happened.

About midnight, it suddenly began to rain heavily, and I was awoken by the sound of thunder. The courtyard was deserted, and the gate had been blown open and flapped repeatedly and loudly against the mud wall. The window of the west room where I was sleeping was not tightly closed, and traces of raindrops blew in on my face. When I got up to close the window, a flash of lightning produced a sensation that something was wrong. I felt my way to the door and lit the oil lamp. The old rags-and-malt-sugar man was not in the room. The two bamboo baskets, however, were still there beside the door. Probably he has gone to the outdoor toilet, I thought, he can't have gone far. But rain was pouring outside—everywhere was the sound of torrents of water. In the wavering lamplight, I looked at the depression on the hay where the old man had slept; my heart felt a little chilled.

It was probably quite a while later that, half asleep, I heard the door pushed open quietly. The old man appeared at the door, barefoot, his ragged shoes in one hand, his trousers rolled up above the knees. His bare legs, which showed beneath the knees, were very fair skinned, quite at odds with his age and rough life. Covered with mud all over, he leaned against the door and smiled slightly at me, seeming to imply that he did not have to explain what he had been doing. He went back to the place where he had slept earlier and lay down. In the very dim light I saw that one of his toes had been scratched by something sharp like a piece of glass or nail; it was bleeding.

Soon after that, the rain stopped. I remained wide awake the rest of the night. Even now, I often think about this incident. The doctor came back the following morning, with an oil paper umbrella under his arm, looking depressed—the patient had died. I told him I would like to stay on, probably for another couple of days. He agreed. At noon that day, the old rags-and-malt-sugar man picked up his bamboo baskets and said goodbye to me. I watched him step over the threshold and walk onto the narrow wooden bridge that spanned the Suzi River. Over many years time has shrunk and eroded him, as flowing water does pebbles. In my mind, he left the impression of an honest and pitiful man. Events proved my judgment to be correct.

In the winter of 1967 I was at Lezhou, transferring to a long-distance bus for Achuan, when I chanced to notice on a map showing the bus routes that the town of Heng Tang was a stop on the way. I decided to go there on my way back from finishing my business. I did not know why I wanted to see this old man—perhaps to find a certain feeling I had lost to him, maybe to dispel a vague dread in my memory.

I found Li Gui soon after I got off the bus at Heng Tang. He lived in a small river valley behind a bamboo wood. I remember that it was noon on a bright sunny day. A pretty girl was washing his bedding in a pond in front of his house. After that, since I was often in the Lezhou area to learn more about its dialect, I occasionally stopped off at Heng Tang and visited the old man. Gradually the people there, particularly that girl, took me as their close friend.

3

My investigations into "green yellow" had been quite fruitless. The long river of time always silently drowns everything, yet memories will contrarily bring to the surface long-sunken fragments from the bottom of the river, like green grass shooting up from under the snow. During my days in Mai Village, I roamed around, searching for traces of the past, while one by one the nights were lost to imaginings of the distant past.

Early one morning I went to the doctor's house where I had stayed nine years earlier. The room filled with hay plunged me once again into memories of that rainy night. To me it was an incident scarcely worth mentioning, and I could not see that there was any connection with the tales of the nine fishing families. The doctor recognized me after just a short hesitation.

He said he did not know much about that "short man, so like a shadow." He said, "I was very young then. Once when that outsider had scabies, my father went to his shack by the river to see him, and I went with him. The man looked very healthy; no one expected him to die when he did. I remember he was married for a second time to a woman named Emerald. That woman looked quite pretty to me, but she did not make the man happy. The dark shadow on his face never seemed to lift. There was a lot of gossip in the village. Some said he had lived on those whorehouse boats for nearly thirty years and had been with more than one hundred women.

"River fish cannot survive once ashore"—this was how the doctor put it. "One evening in the spring, in the twelfth year after he moved to Mai Village, Emerald appeared at our window, her hair uncombed. I remember my mother gave a long sigh and said, 'That unfortunate man has died.' It was quiet in the night. The woman's cries and moans stirred up a flock of magpies on the trees. The next morning my mother and I went to the shack by the river. When we got there, the lid of the coffin had already been nailed shut. The coffin had originally been purchased by the old ferryman with his life savings, but now someone else was using it. Young Green, the daughter, was sitting on an embankment by the road, her face twisted in a grimace with the shock of her father's death. He was buried hastily at noon that day. It was a drizzly day, typical of early spring, and I remember that the black coffin, wet in the rain, looked very shiny. After the burial, when Emerald was talking about the night of her husband's death, her hands still trembled uncontrollably. She said, 'It seemed like he just stopped breathing suddenly.' "

The doctor was cleaning his wood-handled surgical knife with cotton balls, looking a little distracted. "I never exchanged a word with that outsider. His thinking . . . perhaps . . . his daughter . . . Several times, when my father was returning to the village from his rounds in the evenings and I was with him, we would see that man sailing a small boat around the reeds on the Suzi River, his daughter Young Green with him. Probably he always missed his life on the river."

When I asked him about the various speculations about the term "green yellow," his answer startled me.

He said, "I've never heard the term around here. Still, it may exist. On the boats of the nine families, the prostitutes were generally divided into two kinds, the young and the old. Could the term refer to the two kinds? Women are like bamboos, first green and then yellow."

The doctor walked me to the gate as I was leaving, and as we walked together, he told me, as though he had just remembered, that there was a young man named Kangkang who lived in the ancestral temple of the village. "Maybe he can tell you something else."

4

Standing by the crumbling wall that formed a courtyard, I stared questioningly for a long while at a wooden grain box. It was a very large courtyard. Through the purslane growing on top of the wall, waving in the wind, I could see the faint outline of the green mountain behind the village and the vast expanse of the clean fields about it. The autumn wind, carrying leaves turned partly yellow, blew into the courtyard, bringing with it a chilly message.

"This was the coffin of that man," said Kangkang, pointing to the grain box. He looked like an honest young man. He was squatting on a stone roller beside a well and turning over in his fingers a few pieces from a broken earthenware bowl. He seemed very patient with my roundabout questions.

"That summer, we had heavy rains off and on for more than twenty days. The houses and trees in the village were all flooded, and the villagers all fled to the mountains. A few days later, the rain stopped, and the water level started to drop slowly. One morning at dawn, I was standing on the upper floor of this ancestral temple, staring out at the treetops and roofs that were sticking out of the water. Suddenly I saw a black thing, not far away, floating this way. I went downstairs and waded toward it. It was a coffin. It seemed to be made of good wood and looked very sturdy. The wood was soaked with water, so it had gotten very heavy. My younger brother and I got it home with a lot of work. That evening the village doctor came to my home. He was startled when he first saw the coffin in the yard. He said, 'I thought somebody else had died.'

"At first we didn't know where it came from. I thought it had to be from the graveyard outside the village. The flood must have broken the fence and set the coffins afloat. The graveyard was about one to two *li* away from the village. Strangely enough, the coffin seemed familiar with the roads; like a black dog, it headed straight for the village. The next day, my brother and I went to the graveyard. We did find a grave site on the outer edge of the graveyard that had been washed open by the flood. The opening in the grave mound was large, a deep rectangular hole, like a blooming cotton boll. Much later, we learned it was the grave of that Chang. My brother and I filled the hole with earth and built up the mound to its original rounded shape.

"That night our family argued around the coffin. My brother was shrewd; he was only seventeen, but he already had a sweetheart, a girl in the neighboring village. He insisted he wanted to use the coffin timber to make a big bed for his marriage. In the end, he was only stopped by my mother's tears. She said, 'If newlyweds sleep in a bed made out of a coffin, they will have nightmares.' On this matter, my father, sitting to the side, did not say a word. I knew what he thought. He probably wanted to keep the coffin just as it was; it looked almost like a new one. But in the end we remade it into a grain box. At harvest time, we use it for threshing grain; at other times, we move it into the house for storing grain."

"Did you see anything in the coffin?" I asked.

"No." Kangkang paused a moment and then said, "That doctor also asked me; he asked whether there was money in it."

"I mean, did you see a book?"

"No."

I noticed that he was like a girl in the way his eyes moved about as if trying to cover his feelings. Earlier, when he was telling me about the flood, I had already noticed this.

"There must have been something in the coffin," I said. "That man died only a few decades ago. Not everything would have rotted away."

Kangkang's boyish face showed uneasiness. The pieces of broken earthenware clinked noisily in his hand. After quite a while, he stepped off the stone roller, walked to me, and lowered his voice: "Nothing, I mean absolutely nothing; not even human bones."

I was stunned.

"At first I wondered too. How come not even a bone or a hair of that bastard was there? Maybe his grave was robbed a long time ago. Only my brother and I know about this; nobody else. I feel a bit afraid. Sometimes I just want to cut up the box and burn it as firewood."

The box lay motionless in a corner of the courtyard. A morning glory vine from the vegetable patch had climbed up the brownish yellow side of the box. It was like a faint trace from a life long perished. It was like a proverb—the finest part preserved from among the sayings of the people.

5

On the ninth day of the ninth month by the lunar calendar, I found Young Green, Chang's daughter. She was squatting by the side of a round pond and looked to be about fifty years old. The pretty face had vanished like a song, like a bird flown away forever from its nest. Age was like a black screen, separating her from the past years.

Squatting on a dry spot sheltered from the wind, she was putting creases in a stack of yellow paper on her lap and then lighting the crumpled papers.[2]

"I saw you a few days ago," she said to me.

I said I would like to talk to her about something. She raised her head and gave me a look. "Do you want to buy rabbits from me?"

I shook my head.

She smiled. "If you want to buy a bed or a few chairs, you better talk to my husband." I knew her husband was a carpenter.

"Whom are you burning the papers for?" I asked.

2. A traditional way of remembering the dead, burning the yellow papers symbolizes sending money to the dead.

No answer.

"Why don't you take this paper over to your father's grave to burn?"

No answer.

I handed her a cigarette. She took it and put it in her mouth expertly. The pile of yellow paper had finished burning. Dusting off a flat rock, she sat down. This kind-looking woman was not as hard to approach as I had first thought. Perhaps she was used to letting her memories die and the roots of misery grew only in the deep, arid part in her heart. In silence she drew on the cigarette deeply again and again. To me, her manner, her black silk clothes, her heavy breasts, all sank in the mist of the past. After finishing her third cigarette, she started to tell me about an incident that had occurred the previous winter.

It was a snowy morning. As usual, she was cooking in the kitchen. Her husband was sitting in a room filled with timber and wood shavings. His ink liner was frozen in the chill, so he was waiting to thaw it once his wife had lit the fire for cooking. It was the heaviest snow they had had in a long time. Through the half-closed door, she saw her only son playing in the deep snow in the yard. Because snow seeping in from the cracks of the roof tiles had dampened the straw for the fire, the fire was very hard to light, and thick smoke billowed, filling the kitchen.

Through the smoke, she saw her son, covered with snow, push open the door and come in. He seemed to whisper something to his father, but the father, who had tears in his eyes from the smoke, just pushed the boy away. When Young Green finished cooking and came out of the kitchen, the boy pulled at her clothes and said a thin old man was outside their gate, walking back and forth. Young Green went out with the son, but in the snow and wind, they saw nothing, not even the shadow of a bird. She thought it must have been an old beggar and let it go. At lunch the boy again talked about it and said the old man was very strange. Then he described in detail how the old man looked.

"What my son described was exactly like my father, even to the clothes he was wearing. My father has been dead for many years." She continued, "Though I felt something was strange about it, I didn't give it much thought. Yet I was uneasy all day. That day at dusk my son was drowned in the pond in front of our house. He fell in while he was playing on the ice. There must be something in this. When I told the villagers, nobody believed me."

The strong wind rustled the leaves in the woods and blew the ashes of the burned yellow paper in all directions. She looked at me seriously, but numbly, as though she had left this world. I remembered a book titled *Totem and Fire*, which dealt with incidents of dead people's spirits reappearing in some of China's southern provinces. In rural areas, people often blame "heaven" for disasters, I thought. I did not know how much of this woman's account was reliable, but clearly her confusion and misfortune immediately affected me. All the things that happened in this isolated hilly village were like icicles hanging from the eaves—they were changing silently every second.

"When your father brought you to this village, where was your mother?" I asked.

"She probably died a long time before that. I've never seen her. Anyway, my father might not be my real father—that's what the villagers thought."

"Your father never got used to the village."

"That's right. The day I came to Mai Village with my father, it was the rainy season. Every door in the village was shut in our face. We were left out in the rain. Then an old boatman let us stay in his house, and he went to stay on his boat. At first we were not used to anything here. When I slept in his room at night, in my dreams the bed felt like it was still rocking on water. There are very few girls in this village, and at sixty the boatman still hadn't gotten a wife . . . On the second day after we came on shore, he called me to his boat . . . He bit me until I was bloody all over. I ran a high fever as soon as I got back. Father loosened my clothing and washed my wounds with salt water . . . Later on, the old guy's boat overturned."

6

I stayed that night in the flour mill, and sitting on the cold weighing scales, staring out through the window at the fast-moving dark clouds and the gleaming shapes of trees, I didn't sleep at all. I had lost interest in the term "green yellow," which I now felt might even have been a fabrication by Professor Tan. By contrast, bits of the stories that had been told to me—a thin row of run-down houses, a stand of willow, a stretch of empty land—these mixed with my childhood memories and invaded my dreams.

The next day at midday, on a street corner in the village, I came across a man whose job had been to act as watchman in the orchards. I found him crouched in the doorway of a shabby store, selling tea. His saliva dripped on to his sleeves as he kept his eyes set on the yellow clouds pressing down from the sky, but his ears seemed to remain alert to the various sounds around him.

"Things last longer than people," said the watchman. Scenes from forty years ago were still very clear to him, for he could remember "the look of every medicinal tree in the village and the shape of pebbles on the riverbed." It was the seventeenth day of the first lunar month, the watchman remembered, that Chang, the outsider, had set for his wedding. Early that morning, people had seen him squatting on the shore of the Suzi River, where he had opened a hole in the frozen surface. He was shaving himself with the icy water. At that time, the orchard watchman and his mother were at work on the other side of the river, spreading topsoil in a loquat orchard. About noon, he saw a sedan chair coming from the foothills, swaying and going slowly toward the village. The sedan chair must have come quite a distance, for the carriers, all wearing leg wrappings, showed fatigue in their steps. The watchman's mother shaded her eyes against the sun and looked toward the village. "Somebody in the village must be taking a wife," she said.

A little later, they saw the sedan chair stop in front of the shack by the river's edge. The village matchmaker, with her bound feet and gesturing hands, talked with the sedan chair carriers. Behind her, Chang's daughter, Young Green, was pasting a piece of red paper onto the frame of the muddy window. The sedan curtain lifted, and a tall woman came out. Across the foggy Suzi River, the watchman could not get a clear look at the woman's face. How had this outsider gotten this woman to marry him? The watchman put down his spade and prepared to go back to the village to watch the excitement. His mother muttered behind him, "Poor man, making the wedding look like a funeral."

The people of Mai Village were not the kind to dwell on the past. In the few years since Chang had moved there, people's attitude toward this quiet newcomer had gradually become more friendly. Now on this day, some women brought him mountain-grown dates and grains. Old people went to his hut and helped him get things ready. Chang himself also began to look more pleasant and softer.

The manager of the village ancestral temple even suggested adding a tablet for Chang's ancestors so that "the young couple" could have a formal wedding ceremony in the temple hall. But Chang silently refused the offers. He stubbornly thought his ancestors were not in the temple but in the water. Pulling the tall woman to the shore of the Suzi River, he knelt down facing the broad surface of the river and kissed the muddy riverbank.

The bride was very pretty.

That evening, the door of the watchman's log cabin in the orchard was torn loose by strong winds. The watchman decided to go into the village to get some nails for it. Carrying a lamp, he walked on the hard, frozen dirt road toward the village. As he crossed the narrow wooden bridge over the Suzi River, he saw that the light in the shack was still on. In the quiet night, the light turned the trees an orange yellow. His heart began to pound fiercely. "Whenever I remember the moonlight that evening, I get a feeling of uneasiness I can't explain," the watchman said. The woman's appearance flashed again and again across his eyes, and then, he said, "a wild idea" came into his mind. He walked toward the lighted shack, treading more and more lightly until he reached the adobe window. He squatted down and, moistening a finger, poked a hole in one of the paper windowpanes.

It was the first lunar month, already more than twenty days into the spring, but the temperature was as harsh as in midwinter. A bone-cutting wind blew through the bare treetops and whistled through the eaves and tile cracks. Peeping in, the watchman saw the woman sitting on the edge of the bed and the man staring at her from the other side. A little later, he heard the noise of the woman using a toilet in an inner room. Then the watchman saw her lift the curtain and come out from the inner room. While she was tying the drawstring on her pants, the man dashed to her and grabbed her hands—her loose black pants slipped down to the floor.

"I've seen a woman's body only once in my life. My heart jumped into my throat," the watchman said. "The way I see it now, woman is something one can live with or without." He took up the teacup in front of him and sipped a mouthful, then wiped the thin white beard that covered the corners of his mouth and repeated his words, "Yes, it's true, with or without—maybe you'll understand when you get old."

That night, the young watchman squatting outside the window watched as, in the wavering lamplight, the man stripped off all the woman's clothes and kissed her from her toes upward, slowly. She was trembling and looked as though something was wrong. Her pitiful eyes, like those of a mouse, seemed afraid of what might happen next. The man began to act more and more rough, and the woman began to tremble more and more. Then he lifted her up and laid her on the bed. The shabby bed squeaked noisily, and the woman's body shook like a cup of water. The watchman heard Young Green coughing just then from the next room; it must have been in her sleep. The man hesitated a moment, then he began to take off his own clothes, baring his skinny and snakelike back.

"Then I saw something puzzling," the watchman continued. "The man climbed behind the bed curtain, but then soon after that, he came out. He looked beaten. He put on his clothes and went to sit at the table near the wall. I never saw a face as terrible as that. He lit his pipe and puffed slowly. The woman was sobbing softly in the bed. I wondered what had happened. At first I thought probably the man didn't know how to do it. Later on, I heard from people that that woman Emerald had something wrong with the way she was made."

The man, Chang, sat on in the room till daybreak. Sometime in the night, the wind died down; the oil in the lamp dwindled. Outside the window, the watchman fell asleep and was only woken by the warmth of the morning sun.

7

The cotton in the fields was ripe for harvest, and the autumn colors deepened. One morning I went to the round pond again. There were withering yellow leaves and a thin layer of frost on the grass. Some birds had not yet left for the south, and amidst their lonely cries, the air seemed to have become drier.

In a dark room, Young Green was skinning a dead rabbit; her black cotton shirt was stained with rabbit blood.

"Last night two rabbits were killed by wolves. In late autumn, more wolves come to the village."

A little later she asked me whether I would light the stove for her. I said yes.

"I know you've been going around the village asking about my father. He's been gone more than forty years. I don't understand what his life has to do with you."

I just gave a smile.

"Where are you from?" she asked.

"From the city."

"There must be many people who do that in the city too."

"Do what?"

"I mean prostitutes."

"In the past, yes."

"On our boats it wasn't a big deal, but on land it was, a very big deal. I've been here more than forty years, but very few villagers are willing to talk to me. I hear that people even try to avoid passing our place. In the beginning, the families on the boats were decent fishing people. Our ancestors helped some bandits led by a man named Chen Youliang, and so when Emperor Zhu came to the throne,[3] he banned us from going ashore. One year there was a very bad famine, and some women on the boats began to do that. And so gradually some of the boats got to be the way they were."

"After your father died, where did that woman Emerald go?" I asked.

"She died."

"Died?"

Young Green remained silent for quite a while. She washed the skinned rabbit in a pan and then put it in an iron pot on the stove. She returned to her earlier place and sat down.

"Emerald was a kind-hearted woman. She died for me. After my father died, her own family took her back to their home, which was in the foothills about twenty *li* away. One summer, she came to visit me and brought me a few pieces of clothing. She stayed for a few days, and that was when it happened. That evening, she and I were sitting at a table cutting shoe patterns. We heard dogs barking at the edge of the village. Emerald said that some stranger must have come to the village. After a while, the dogs quieted down, and we thought that probably everything was all right. Then the lamp that was in the shrine on the wall suddenly went out. At first I thought the wind had blown it out, but as I was trying to relight it, a black shadow came in. In the dark we couldn't see the shadow clearly. I felt a pointed

3. In 1368.

thing sticking against my waist. That shadow forced me to a corner against the wall. Finally I realized what he wanted. He put his hands on my clothes and tore a hole in the shoulder. I could smell liquor. He pressed his mouth to my breast . . ."

The old woman crossed her arms in front of her chest as though she felt cold or remembered that terrible moment in the past. She looked frightened. I stared at the guts of the rabbit laid on the ground and felt a chill sweep through me.

"Emerald seemed frozen in shock for a long time," Young Green continued. "When she came to life again, she ran over and knelt down on the floor, holding tight to the man's leg, and begged him, 'Let the girl go. She is just a little girl, not married yet. If you want a woman, take me . . .' The man sounded like he was laughing, and he turned his body a little. I could feel him taking away the knife and waving it in the air, and Emerald's hands loosed her grip."

"Thinking back now," Young Green continued, "how I regret that Emerald tried to stop him. She didn't need to. Actually I had seen that kind of thing on the boats. Every evening officers and merchants came to the boats. Sometimes, even before dark, they would spread out the mats in the cabins and clutch the prostitutes and roll about on them. When that man pushed me down on the floor, I was not very scared. In the beginning I just felt pain. I heard the chirping of crickets, and I heard Emerald's breath becoming shorter and shorter. When the man left, her body had already turned stiff. After that, a village matchmaker came to me and asked me whether I would like to get married. I said yes. A few days later I married this carpenter. He is an honest man."

"Everything passes, but once a person dies she can't come back," she added.

Young Green went to the stove and fanned the fire through the stove opening. The flames grew bigger, and the room was filled with the tasty smell of rabbit meat. By now, the sun was higher in the sky, lighting up the room. I saw a few village women picking cotton on the far side of the field.

"Did your father ever write a book?" I asked.

"No, he couldn't read or write."

"Did your ancestors have any books, such as books of family trees?"

"I don't know. Even if they had them, they must have been buried with my father," she said. "Maybe my father knew, but he died so early. No one expected it. If he were still alive, he would be over eighty. I can never forget his face. In those years I often went to a market that was quite far from here to sell flowers—chrysanthemums in autumn and cape jasmines in spring. Every time I came back, he was waiting for me, sitting under the mountain elm in front of our door."

She wiped her eyes with the back of one hand and stared at the thin smoke rising from the stove.

"Even now I still miss him." She continued, "Once I was taking a bath—"

Her husband came in. She stood up and helped him take his tools off his shoulder, a plane and a saw, and put them on the chicken coop. The carpenter went to the water vat, scooped up a ladle of cold water, and drank it all in one draught.

Then he said, "The cotton in the field is ready to pick."

8

Time passed swiftly, one dusk after another, without leaving any trace in the flat and slanting sky above the village or on the expanses of mountains and wilderness stretching beyond the fences and windows. Day and night, I puzzled myself with the poor man's riddlelike life. Then, when I decided to leave the village, I suddenly felt a sense of unreality. This village—its quiet river, the red sand on the riverside, the people rushing around and their shadows—seemed to have been created from nothing. Or they were like scenes and characters often seen in sketches.

The day I returned to the city from Mai Village, a letter was waiting for me on the front porch. It was from a girl, the girl I saw in Heng Tang in the winter of 1967 when I went there to visit the old man Li Gui. She was the one washing Li Gui's bedding in the pond in front of his house. In the letter she told me Li Gui was seriously ill and probably would not live much longer. He hoped, for the sake of our friendship formed when we met years ago, to see me once more before he left this world. That evening I reread the letter under a lamp. I saw that the postmark on the envelope, though not clear any more, was still readable. It showed that the letter had been mailed a month earlier. The high cheekbones of the old rags-and-malt-sugar man and the dimples of the girl simultaneously flashed across my mind. The next morning I was on the northbound train.

When I found the hut behind the bamboo wood, it was noon, three days later. The old man was sitting against a wall, dozing in the warm sunshine. He immediately saw me, and supporting himself with a hand on the wall, he stood up and moved forward a few steps.

"I knew you'd come," he said. "A few days ago, the death god played a joke on me. I lay on top of my coffin for a whole day and in the evening I woke up."

We sat down at the foot of the wall. When the old man talked he seemed to me to be a perfect machine: internally, every part was rusty, but it was still functioning slowly out of habit. He did not look sick. It was only the natural process of aging that was bringing him to the final edge of life.

"My niece was talking about you all day long. She said you might not come because of being too busy. I thought you would come for sure."

The girl was hanging laundry on a wire; she turned our way and smiled to me.

"I was on a trip to Mai Village, so I didn't see your letter until I came back," I replied.

"Mai Village?"

"That's where I met you."

He nodded. His gray eyes, dull and deep in their sockets, were set on a few birds swooping down in the sky, as though he was trying to focus his sight.

"There is something I've been wanting to ask you ever since," I said.

"What is it?"

"Do you remember that night in Mai Village?"

"Yes, I do. We stayed somewhere like the house of a doctor."

"Later that night, it rained heavily."

"That's right."

"It seems that you went out that night."

The old man was a little startled and then began to cough violently. The girl came over to him and pounded his back for a little while. He turned to one side and spit some phlegm into the grass at the foot of the wall. He curled up the corners of his mouth and said with a smile, "I've had sleepwalking trouble ever since I was a child. I don't know anything about what you say. I thought I slept very well that night."

"You did go out once."

"That's possible. Once I got up and walked out in the fields all night. The next morning my niece found me in the wheat field."

That afternoon, I lay down to rest for a while. The girl opened the door and came in. She asked whether I could help her do some roofing work. With the weather getting cold, the dark and thin hay of the roof needed to be replaced by new thatching. I promised I would help her do the rethatching, even though I had never been on a roof.

I was very slow at the job. When evening came, the old man, with an extra shirt thrown over his shoulders, held a lamp in one hand and stood under the eaves. His appearance reminded me of a walnut shell hollowed inside by worms. A trace of sadness crossed my heart.

I stayed there for three days. As I was leaving, the old man insisted on walking me part of the way through the bamboo wood. A dog followed us. The old man stopped when we came to a dry tributary of a stream.

"There are very few people in this part of the woods. I come here for a walk every evening before dark," he said. "Green Yellow always keeps me company."

"Green Yellow?"

"The dog. It's a very good breed. The hair color is very unusual. The back is greenish blue and one side of its stomach shows a yellow dotted circle, a bit like a plaster."

I looked up and saw the dog sniffing the dirt in the field and going farther, its tail wagging.

9

A few years later, on the second floor of the city library, I happened to come across the term "green yellow" as I was turning the pages of the *Dictionary of Terms*. The dictionary was compiled in the Tianqi reign of the Ming dynasty, and on page 971, I saw the following entry:

> Green yellow. Perennial herb of the figwort family; plant is entirely covered with fine gray hair; stemlike root is yellow in color; flowers in summer.

Translated by Eva Shan Chou

WHISTLING ❋ *Ge Fei*

Everything lay in tranquillity.

Day after day, Sun Deng slumped in the misshapen rattan chair, keeping watch over the passage of time. Dilatory May evoked in him an ineffable feeling. After all, an old man who expected nothing and who faced the shadows cast by the corner of the wall and the soaring eaves in the enchantingly radiant sunlight of high noon could think of something or could think of nothing whatsoever.

One really couldn't find fault with the weather.

It is a common occurrence for a hoary-headed old man who is

The term *hushao* (whistle) refers to a type of shrill whistle produced by placing a couple of fingers in one's mouth and expelling the breath with great force. The sound can carry enormous distances, and hence such whistling is often mentioned in traditional Chinese short stories and novels of the Ming and Qing periods as a kind of remote signaling or calling. From a still earlier period, however, whistling of this sort functioned as a yogic, transcendental exercise or expression. It is best described in the "Rhapsody on Whistling" of Chenggong Sui (231–273). The two main characters in the present story, Sun Deng and Ruan Ji, are based on historical figures who were contemporaries of Chenggong Sui and who were presumably proficient in this kind of whistling. The former (fl. 260–265), famous for his taciturnity, was a recluse who for a long time lived in a cave perched high among the hills. The latter (210–263), one of the eccentric Seven Worthies of the Bamboo Grove, was a noted introspective poet and talented musician. Both men are featured in *A New Account of Tales from the World* (*Shishuo xin yu*), compiled in about the year 430.

An old legend of the celebrated encounter between the two men has Ruan Ji visiting Sun Deng in his hermitage but not receiving any responses to his questions. Thereupon, he withdraws and, halfway up a distant mountain, lets out a loud, piercing whistle. This is followed by Sun Deng's magnificent whistled reply, which inspires Ruan Ji to write the "Biography of Master Great Man," an encomium in praise of the Taoist "true man" that also satirizes the conventional Confucian "gentleman."

not cautious to break a porcelain bowl. Just as the scorching heat or chilling cold of the air yesterday evening disturbed your restless sleep, it seemed as though there were no reason to let those painting fragments accumulate too long at the bottom of the riverbed of memory. Generally speaking, nearly everyone sleeps well in the tranquil nights of late springtime. All you have to do is hold your breath, and you will be able to hear distinctly the sounds of snoring from the rooms along the corridor joining in a chorus (sometimes they are covered up by the calls of crickets and other insects, by the sound of the wind, and so forth).

The sounds of snoring obviously include certain ostentatious elements, just as when a gorgeously dressed young girl brushes shoulders with an old man who supports himself on a cane and she turns around to look at him with a smile as she passes, or they seem like an unceasing discourse that compels you to sink into silence.

This kind of by-no-means-connected discourse, furthermore, could sometimes extend into the sunlight of high noon. It would make the flower buds of sleep that you had so carefully cultivated rapidly wilt. The sounds of snoring, by swift turns, were long or short and were interspersed with some unpremeditated choking and whimpering that seemed like the gasping of a water clock whose flow of water had been obstructed. They were completely without any rhythm to speak of, just like the crying of a little child, suddenly erupting and then fitful. Judging from the sound, it seemed to go on unceasingly just when there was a pause.

"Now you should know."

"What?" Sun Deng asked.

"A precautious person mastered various skills when he was young, but he neglected only the skill of sleeping."

The man was sitting opposite Sun Deng, toying with the go piece in his hand. This go game had already been going on for a long time, but at the moment it still didn't look as though it would soon be concluded. Beneath the dim rays of light, his face appeared rather indistinct (the evening sun sinking in the west caused the light in the room to become weaker and weaker). His foot lightly tapped on the floor and he hummed an ancient melody. Any person's face (whether young or old) is a mirror. All you have to do is scrutinize it and it won't be difficult to discover your own appearance in it. Of course, the things you see in the face of a beautiful woman will be slightly distorted (women always bring about errors in a man's sight, and vice versa), however, there isn't much difference.

This moment was the time right after noon. In that brief instant, the picture of spring that remained was very well preserved. Almost no shadows could be seen in the atrium that was paved with bluestone. The cracks in the stones had been etched long ago and most of those cracks were due to days and years of vigorous scrubbing by rainwater or through exposure to the sun. They spread out like a spiderweb and were as dense, random, and casual as the lines of a palm print.

Perhaps because the distance from the courtyard wall to the pond outside was too close, Sun Deng was only able to see a portion of the pond when he gazed past the half-opened door leaf, but he could more or less determine its size from the tree branches hanging over the surface of the water. As he watched the ducks swimming in the water, they appeared to be careful and cautious; most of the time they didn't seem to be very absorbed in finding food but were looking about in all directions.

His gaze shifted from the paddlings of ducks and rested upon a gentle slope opposite the pond.

That was a parcel of land full of rapeseed flowers. Some of the intertwined rapeseed plants had already gone to seed which caused the colors of the field to be considerably paler than before, as though a faded raincloth had been spread out to dry there. Nonetheless, if one looked at the field roughly beneath the burning rays of light that bore straight down at noon, it still appeared to have a lot of vitality. Its jumbledness, disorderliness, and incompleteness could only be discovered when one got closer to it. Such moments were invariably after a big rain at dusk or in the early morning before everything had a chance to spruce itself up.

......

Now, at last, he could see the bridge. From a distance, this old wooden bridge, which had been abandoned long ago and had stood there in the elements for many years without anyone paying attention to it, seemed like a row of fence posts from a ruined sheepfold. If it hadn't been for the sparse clumps of reeds that grew at the two ends of the bridge to remind them, people wouldn't have been able to notice at all the traces of the river that flowed through here in years past.

The bridge abutments were half sunken in the mud. Beyond the bridge was the great expanse of a cotton field. A woman wearing a kerchief stood up straight in the cotton field; it seemed as if she had just finished relieving herself. Because of the separation and obstruction of the bridge abutments (perhaps there was also a glaring light), Sun Deng was unable to make out her face. There was also a cotton field at this side of the bridge, only he couldn't see any evidence of people in it.

The sun had already risen to the middle of the sky, and, by chance, the shadow cast upon the cotton field by the narrow bridge deck formed a straight line.

Sun Deng's gaze lingered in the distance. His feelings about the places nearby, of course, became duller. Only he felt that a dark, reddish mass of shadowy light—like a cluster of fresh flowers that had been blurred by the rain—drifted before his eyes.

What sort of shadowy mass was it? If one thought carefully, it could only be a person, a pedestrian hurriedly walking by in front of the door.

A person who is in touch with the deepest recesses of his innermost being day and night will easily discover the transformations all around him. These sorts of transformations always transpire in the interstices of time, leaving people unprepared because of their abruptness. Fortunately, they bring with them not a shred of happiness, much less may we mention any sadness.

While Sun Deng stared at the big bridge in the distance, he kept his mind on the shadowy image of that fleeting mass. It was like enjoying the sight of rain falling from the sky on a sunny day (such weather conditions were by no means rare in this area), which always gives one a feeling of unreality quite akin to being in a trance.

The shadowy light flickered past the door and vanished from sight along the left side of the pond. It was only after a while that it would reappear straight ahead and walk into his original line of vision.

Unconsciously, because the sun's light had shifted its position a little, Sun Deng could clearly see the clothesline strung across the atrium. One end of it was buried in the green grass that had recently sprung up by the wall pier, and the other end was attached to the trunk of an almond tree (because of the weight of the clothes on the line, the trunk had become bent like a bow with a slight curve).

The clothesline was empty, and, although the passage of time had rendered it fuzzy and frayed, it was stretched tight as a lute string. The grayish-brown swallow that had stopped there to rest in the morning had already flown away. Sun Deng turned the angle of his vision a bit and then saw it on a windowsill.

Swallows seldom perch on windowsills and they never peck at their food like sparrows. Even when they do go through the motions of pecking at their food, it is only as a pretense for peering left and right. Having passed through the long winter season, the swallow had come back here and it would stay at this house until the end of autumn. Now it was only late spring.

The air was suffused with the frightful aroma emitted by fresh plants. As soon as he stopped being careful, he could smell the pure fragrance of bean pods that permeated the wind. There were some scenes that were difficult to imagine; for example, his daughter came walking in through the inner door carrying a bundle of soaking wet bean pods against her breast. . . . . . She walked into the atrium. The dew had dampened her hair, sleeves, and bare ankles. Even the light in her eyes was soaking wet.

Separated by a wooden table, they sat next to the door. One of her legs was askew, its white skin exposed below the knee; some green grass and little bits of bean leaves stuck to it. Sun Deng watched a beetle crawl across her instep. It paused for a moment where the ankle and the calf joined (it seemed to have lost its way, or perhaps it was catching its breath), then proceeded to crawl upward till at last it disappeared inside the opening of her trouser leg. Later, he noticed that some fingernail marks had appeared on her calf where she had been scratching. The color of the marks became deeper and deeper, like a patch of red maple leaves set off by the evening sun.

Her scratching movements increased in frequency and her manner became increasingly crude, but in spirit she seemed as oblivious as always.

Sun Deng knew clearly that his own expression in front of the threshold, with eyes raised and gazing afar, would surely be easily misunderstood by others as indicating that he was waiting for something. To obviate this misunderstanding, he made an adjustment of his seated posture.

"Perhaps you are waiting for someone?" she said.

The tone of her voice made one feel as though her mental powers were entangled in another matter or were immersed in some future plans, an episode from the past.

"Unh, no——," said Sun Deng.

He turned around and his gaze landed on a table surface that was parallel to the bun of her hair. A go game had been laid out on the table. From the looks of it, the game seemed to have been started the day before, or perhaps three days before, or maybe at some still more distant time.

Judging from the number of pieces, the game seemed to be just half over. The man, holding a go piece between his forefinger and middle finger, was about to set it down. From his indecisive attitude, one could imagine the importance of the move (in Sun Deng's opinion it didn't seem necessary to put so much emphasis on winning or losing a game of go). The woman who was sitting opposite him appeared to be somewhat unsettled. Her gaze made it seem as though she were constantly preoccupied elsewhere. Close beside them, a boy was strumming a lute and singing. From this, we may roughly determine that the woman's gaze was certainly attracted by the sounds of the youth's song or his lute. Perhaps the ancient lute was placed at the side of a bamboo grove, because we can see that, next to the legs of the lute stand, several bamboo shoots were sprouting.

. . . . . . Everything is immutable, eternal, ossified. Probably so as not to let the space unoccupied by the human figures and their surroundings be overly large, the upper portion of the painting, from right to left, was densely filled with grasshopper-sized characters. Regrettably, the painting had been hanging on the wall too long, so that the writing had become blurred.

The greatest stylistic feature of this painting was that it had no style to speak of. Judging merely from the human figures and the activity in the painting, there was no way at all to verify the date when it was completed. What's more, such things as a man and a lady playing go together were, it would seem, seldom witnessed in the customary behavior of the scholar-official class (to be more precise, they were unheard of). Therefore, it is highly probable that this painting was from the hand of a folk artist.

A tear in part of the painting was made faintly visible by traces of mounting glue. With exceptional care, Sun Deng used a bristle brush to whisk away gently the dust that had accumulated on the surface of the painting. Owing to incaution, he knocked over a purple porcelain pot on the table onto the ground. . . . . . The thick bouquet of the tea carried with it the scent of pine nuts. This naturally caused him to think of something else. . . . . . He sat down in the misshapen rattan chair beside the table and made no effort right away to begin sweeping away the stains on the floor. He stared inanely at the pieces of the broken pot, feeling a sense of peace and self-contentment.

At noontime, the sunlight lying in wait on the open floor finally shone upon the pile of broken shards (they looked like a fully opened lily). The tea water had long since evaporated, but the shattered remnants of the pot that were left behind resembled the lingering sounds of an unrealizable promise that wound around the rafters of the house without dissipating.

Outside, the number of people in the cotton field gradually increased. Several children who were playing swayed back and forth as they walked on the bridge. When they reached the broken part of the bridge, they stopped and then turned around to walk toward the other end. Now, one could already see a band of dark gray shadows in the cotton field close by the bridge railings. One after another, the farmers walked into the shadows.

A man smoking a pipe was observing the color of the sky. The expression he wore as he vacantly scanned all around made it seem even more as though he were searching for the silhouette of someone familiar. Two women who were leaning against one of the bridge abutments looked as though they were in the midst of a leisurely conversation (the rest of the people, in contrast, were submerged in silence); however, the sounds of their talking seemed to be extremely feeble. Although Sun Deng could occasionally catch a sentence or two, their talk was utterly disconnected, and he had no idea what it signified.

Still farther in the distance, the cotton fields and the wheat fields that lay beneath the burning rays of the sun were virtually fused into a single expanse. The leaves of the commingled plants obscured the outlines of a little path that sinuously wended its way up the slope of a peak on the horizon, until at last it disappeared in a pine forest halfway up. Seen in the distance, the little path seemed to be a gangway ladder suspended from the ridge of the mountains.

Functioning somewhat as signposts, several uneven elms had been planted sparsely along the little path (the part that was submerged in the wheat fields), causing the vaguely visible traces of the road to be fixed among the cultivated lands. As usual, the shadows of the trees lay horizontally across the blanket of dark green leaves of the crops.

The man came walking slowly along the little path in the direction of the entrance to the village, frequently stopping beneath one of the elm trees to look around. Because he was worried about some fearful gossip or discussions with an ulterior motive (there were also various other possibilities), his bearing while walking along the path was, as always, so abstracted that he seemed to suspect that he had lost his way. The stillness and peaceful atmosphere of the open country appeared to have intensified his disquiet. With great effort, he strove to put on a nonchalant attitude, causing his movements to become even more absurd.

"If a person makes up his mind to go and do something," the man said, "then what does it matter even if he does it a bit clumsily?"

"Yes," said Sun Deng.

He turned over a page of the book that was spread open before him, and, perhaps because he didn't grasp the implications of the sentence that the man had just spoken, he raised his head and glanced at him. Most of the time, this is the way they sat there. Even when they uttered a sentence or two, these seemed as easily shattered as sounds carried by the wind, so that it was impossible to catch the gist and there was no meaning whatsoever. The poetry manuscript with a bookmark pressed between its pages remained spread out flat on the table. Every time that he turned a page, Sun Deng instinctively glimpsed outside the window. It seemed that the game on the go board between them had just been played halfway through. . . . . .

Now it was still the time of high noon. No pedestrians were to be seen on the little path. The path wound behind a mound and abruptly disappeared near the pond, or perhaps we may say that it merged with the embankment around the pond.

The dark reddish, shadowy mass finally appeared at the very front of the pond, walking into his original line of vision. It was the silhouette of a woman. The lines of her back and sides (and even her clothing itself) bore a striking resemblance to those of his own daughter. His daughter had not returned home for quite a long time since she was married away.

The woman on the opposite side of the pond, because of the background provided by the field of vivid rapeseed flowers, made an inexpressible impression upon Sun Deng. Perhaps she was a cloistered maiden of the neighbors, or maybe she was a daughter-in-law who had only recently arrived (under normal circumstances, these two were not easy to distinguish). By the time Sun Deng attempted to discern her features more closely, her retreating figure had already traveled far along the road that was lined with elms.

At Sun Deng's present age, it seemed as though he could already *remember* the time of his senility. The situation was just like remembering the fragments of a dream. For a young man who felt relaxed and calm beneath the motionless light of the sun, senility was merely a question of time. Its shadow resembled a gaily colored stage setting that had become a bit older, like a luxuriant tree that with the onset of the cold had shed its once verdant facade beneath one's very eyes.

He sat in a newly plaited rattan chair next to the table, slowly turning the lid of the purple porcelain pot on the table. Some intermittent, muffled sounds were transmitted from outside beyond the pond—these sounds served as the continuation of the thread of his drifting thoughts—into the rooms along the corridor where they hovered for quite some time.

Now it was just at the time of late spring. The smell of leaves and flowers wafted through the air. Perhaps there were some other scents as well. . . . . . the scents of mosses climbing the moist wall and of pine nuts. The trunk of the almond tree in the atrium had already become slightly bent because of the clothesline tied to it. A puff of wind silently blew through the atrium and the petals of the almond blossoms, like flakes of snow, quietly settled on the bluestone paving blocks.

Sun Deng had not swept out the atrium for a long time. Fresh and wilted petals piled up together, covering the fine cracks in the bluestone paving blocks that were like so many spiderwebs.

In the drowsiness of high noon, no one could put up with the disturbance caused by the swallow. Just at that moment, the swallow was building its nest beneath the eaves. Due to the limitations imposed by the position occupied by Sun Deng, he couldn't see all of the swallow. Only when it flew out of its nest and perched on the windowsill or on the clothesline could Sun Deng see it without any effort. It gave one the impression that it was aloof and constantly trembling with fear. The grayish-brown swallow seemed a lot like a sparrow in its physical appearance, but it spent a third of the year in far-off southern places. Sun Deng had no way to determine whether the swallow that flew back before his eyes every year at the beginning of spring was the same one that had gone away the previous year at the end of autumn.

Looking out through the half-opened door of the atrium, Sun Deng could clearly see the river that shimmered beneath the sunlight. The wheat sprouts along its banks were starting to put forth clusters of grain. The inverted reflections of the crops and the reeds on the surface of the water were dimly visible. The broad river meandered into the distance beneath the glaring rays of the sun. As Sun Deng's gaze penetrated more deeply, the surface of the river became increasingly narrow (and the background increasingly chaotic) until, at the horizon, it became a white thread, winding slantedly along one side of the foot of the mountains.

A man smoking a pipe was drying his fishing net on the bank of the river. Perhaps because he saw someone familiar at a spot farther off, or perhaps because he was startled by a mandarin duck that skittered by on the surface of the water, gawking all around him, he grabbed hold of a corner of his net with one hand and shielded his forehead from the sunlight with the other. In any event, his silhouette made one feel that something was happening near him. The wooden bridge stood loftily above the surface of the river, the water forming countercurrents where it flowed past the abutments. Consequently, with the help of the reflected light of the sun, Sun Deng could see clusters of tiny bubbles that were churned up beneath the bridge. At high noon, the shadow formed on the surface of the river by the bridge span was drawn out into a straight line.

To the right of the river channel, a belt of elms was sparsely planted in the great expanse of wheatlands. The young elms fixed the contours of a road that cut through the wheat fields. Because the elm leaves were not yet fully grown, the hue of the silent shadows cast by the trees was extremely fine and faint. If one did not concentrate one's attention and focus one's vision upon them, perhaps they couldn't be seen at all.

The woman came walking zigzag along the little path in the direction of the village. It seemed that a grain of sand that had worked its way into her shoe was hurting the sole of her foot, so she stopped beneath one of the elms and, with restless eyes, peered all around. Her demeanor was invariably flustered, revealing that something was weighing heavily on her heart. Her right hand propped against the trunk of the elm, she hesitantly took off one of her shoes with her left hand and shook it. Because the single, slender leg on which she was standing could not support the weight of her body, she made a couple of hasty hops. Her movement of taking off the shoe and shaking out the sand went on for too long, causing her tottering body to appear quite ridiculous beneath the sunlight. Beneath the afternoon sky, it was soundless. Puffs of light wind stirred the multitudinous wheat florets.

"No promise on earth lasts forever," said the man.

Sun Deng was momentarily stunned when he perceived some other ideas in what the man had said, but they did not the slightest damage to the tranquillity of his innermost being. He pretended not to have heard the sentence and, letting his hand lead where it may, picked up a piece from the go board on the table. Yet, because his thoughts were entangled by the referent of the words that had just been spoken, his movements appeared to be somewhat indecisive.

The murky gray light of the room made it hard to figure out his face. This poet, surnamed Ruan, would always come here early in the morning or toward evening, taking Sun Deng by surprise...... Both his identity and his ambiguous speech were rather suspicious. Fortunately, most of the time the two of them just sat there like this, their eyes either focusing on the go board in front of them or looking askance at the poetry manuscript with a bookmark pressed between its pages that was spread out at the side of the table, seldom saying anything. Of course, this would create other associated, yet unanticipated, results: the prolonged silence would cause them occasionally to utter unforgettable remarks.

...... It wasn't known how long the go game had been going on between them. Judging from the uncertain manner with which she raised the go piece (in one hand she held a piece that she was about to put down), she conspicuously revealed that she was somewhat weary. This made her failure to give an appropriate response to the sentence that Sun Deng had just spoken understandable. Furthermore, Sun Deng's sentence itself was commonplace and vapid; it comprised no special meaning.

The high bun of hair wrapped around at the back of the woman's head had by now already come loose. Her long hair brushed against her well-proportioned shoulders, and, following the frequent inclinations of her body (as though she were considering where she wanted to place the go piece), it would swish around the edges of her shoulders and cascade over her chest.

Her eyes, which were fixed on the go board, seemed all the while to be mindful of something else. The scattering of her power of concentration was mostly because of the excited noises of the children outside, or because of a white butterfly flitting about in the rooms along the corridor. The butterfly had evidently smelled something fragrant in the house (such as the scent of pine nuts in the woman's hair). It lingered momentarily in the vicinity of the windowsill, then flew over the grassy wall surrounding the atrium and disappeared in the sunlight beyond the house.

At the instant when the sunlight vanished, the courtyard and the atrium, as well as the pond and wheatland outside, which had been covered by it, now all became somber and dark; only the slopes and valleys on the left side of the mountain range stretched out in the distance were still bathed in rays of bright light. In the lowlands of the valleys were growing some pear trees (their blossoms thickly heaped), bamboo, and other types of trees...... This kind of weather often occurred during the late spring season, but it didn't last very long. The sunlight, which receded and then came back like a tide, followed along the expanse of slopes and valleys and spread out in all directions, shining upon the mulberry groves, thatch-roofed houses, and pine forests on the other side of the mountain, and on the little path suspended from the ridge of the mountains like a gangway ladder. Flooding over the feet of the mountains, it came swooping along in the direction of the river, the bridge, and the village.

This mountain range was a branch of an even larger mountain system. Its name had long since been forgotten, or perhaps it never had any name from the very beginning.

"There's no harm in calling it Su Gate Mountain,[1] is there?" suggested the poet, Ruan Ji. He probably regretted this sentence, for he was anxious to change the topic and talk about something else.

"Why is it called such a name?" asked Sun Deng.

"Anyway, that's just how it is," said the woman with a yawn. It was evident that she was unwilling to become further entangled in this question.

"It could be some other name altogether," said Sun Deng.

"If, as you just said, it's a branch range of the Taihang Mountains, there's nothing wrong with this name."

Sun Deng said no more. The usual look of impatience showed on her face, but, in a twinkling, it was once again swiftly retracted, probably because the woman realized that it was she herself who had broached the topic, or perhaps she had thought of something else unrelated to this.

But what sort of affair was this? After all, a man and a woman sitting idly in the vestibule beneath the sunlight at high noon could do something. Furthermore, women are never willing to let that sort of gloomy, dismal expression linger on their faces too long. . . . . . This was a beautiful and educated woman; she knew the limits of her thoughts and emotional frailty. Because she was worried that some frightful, irremediable scene might take place, she never overstepped this boundary (or she never overstepped it first); to a certain degree, Sun Deng was clearly aware of this point.

A part of the little path on the mountain was covered by the boughs of pine trees, so—as one looked along it—the path was discontinuous. The sound of the billowing pines came drifting quietly and gave

1 Sumen Shan, in Henan Province, is part of the great Taihang mountain system. According to *A New Account of Tales from the World*, this is where Ruan Ji actually met Sun Deng and failed to receive answers to his questions. Many other hermits also lived on Su Gate Mountain.

one a feeling of coolness. The black shadow of a person (seen in the distance, it was just a black dot) came walking along the little path toward the bottom of the mountain. For a long period of time, Sun Deng kept his eyes fixed on the expanse of the mountain ridge; his desire to distinguish the shape of the person caused his innermost being to be possessed by an indescribable anxiety.

The woman came walking in through the inner door carrying a bundle of wet bean pods. . . . . . She crossed the atrium and walked to one side of the corridor where she sat down on a small wooden bench. The whitewashed wall that connected the atrium with the house hid from view more than half her body. Looking out through the open window in the whitewashed wall, he could see the bun coiled at the back of her head. One of her legs was quite askew, stretched out near the threshold of the door; her trouser leg was rolled up high, exposing her calf below the knee. The sunlight made the bean leaves and bits of grass that stuck to it distinctly visible. Next to her ankle was placed a porcelain bowl with a blue rim. At very short intervals, her hand would stretch toward the rim and deftly put the podded green beans into the bowl.

Her motions precise and uninterrupted, she never made an error. As more and more of the beans accumulated in the bowl, a few of them would occasionally bounce out and land on the empty floor beside the threshold. The woman frequently turned toward the outside to look for something. Perhaps she was listening to the sounds outside. Her body was facing right and inclined toward that side, exposing her skinny shoulder blades by the edge of the door frame.

One really couldn't find fault with the weather. . . . . . At the side of the pond that was drenched in sunlight was a thickset fence of bushes. The spreading branches of weeping forsythia, which had not yet flowered, extended from the bank out over the surface of the water. Starting from the morning, the old man had been sitting beneath the shade of a tree all the while (the brim of his straw hat hid his face). His long fishing pole hovering horizontally over the pond, the man's fishing line with its bobber made of a chicken quill swayed over the water. The old man appeared to be very patient, or perhaps we may say that it was not easy for others to detect his restlessness. Because he had been sitting there idly for too long, occasionally he would lift his empty fishing line above the water (to check whether the bait had fallen off the hook), then he would lightly put it back in the water. At such moments, his affectations were completely revealed.

A farmer woman, supporting herself with a hoe, was standing on the slanted slope on the other side of the pond. She was getting ready to prepare the wasteland for cultivation. Perhaps she would put in some potatoes or would plant some rapeseed next year. Whenever Sun Deng's line of vision fell upon her, she was always supporting herself with her hoe and catching her breath. The moisture of the newly dug soil was entirely sucked up by the noontime sun, so that its original russet color gradually turned white.

Behind her, a man who was repairing his fishing net by the riverside was smoking a pipe and looking at something far upriver. A small boat sailing on the river reduced its speed as it passed through the wooden bridge.

The sounds of snoring began to echo through the rooms along the corridor again, causing everything around to feel sleepy. The woman was lying down in a rattan chair, her chin propped in her palm and one arm resting in the concavity of her waist. An ant lingered at the opening of her collar (as though it were lost). Accompanied by the creaking of the chair in which she was lying, the woman rolled over and lay flat. Some fingernail marks left from where she had been scratching were revealed on her neck. The color of the marks became deeper and deeper until, at the same time when they reached their maximum (dark red), they gradually dissipated. . . . . . Finally the skin regained its original color.

The shrill mutterings of the woman in her dreams were by no means more fearsome and terrifying than her manner when calm (in her even breathing, her chest and abdomen rose and fell slightly); perhaps the two were fundamentally the same. The transient, concealed, impetuous, and irrepressible bodily sediments were fully exposed in her fitful dream mutterings; on ordinary days, these would normally be submerged in the background of her language and behavior, awaiting their opportunity in secret.

"It's like when you let out a whistle. . . . . . You can't find any meaning." The poet, Ruan, glanced at him then continued: "Don't you want to say something? . . . . . . Even if you don't, I can guess: you're waiting for someone."

Sun Deng didn't respond. He had just seen the fleeting silhouette of a man on the ridge of Su Gate Mountain come walking down the mountain. Only when he got closer did Sun Deng realize that he was a woodcutter. . . . . .

It seemed that they had just finished playing half of the go game between them. Letting his hand lead where it may, Sun Deng picked up the poetry manuscript on the table and turned to the page with a bookmark stuck in it. He glanced at it hurriedly, then closed the manuscript up again.

The woody hibiscus flowers,
The hibiscus flowers in the mountains—
Silent, no one in the mountains,
Abundantly they blossom, then fall.

Everything was motionless, without any animation whatsoever, stiff. . . . . . The painting was like a receding and returning moment from the past, preserved eternally on the wall. The inexpressible look of the woman in the painting embodied waiting. In a more exact sense, listening to the sound of singing was only a vain pretense. To an onlooker (a person who was looking at a painting), her real intention and motive were, it would seem, quite clear. The mouth of the boy strumming the lute was wide open, from the appearance of which it was highly probable that he was singing (his entire body seemed to be immersed in the sounds of music), but it also seemed as though he were saying something inconsequential, or that he was yawning (seen thus, the boy was completely oblivious).

To prevent the lower corners of the painting from being lifted by the drafts that blew through the hall, two red strings in the shape of an X held it against the wall. One of the strings divided the woman's face in half, and there was a go piece precisely at the spot where the two strings crossed (it was difficult to tell at once the color of the go piece upon which the strings pressed). Against the dark gray background of the painting, the scarlet string appeared quite dazzling. Judging from the rusty nails around the edges of the painting, it seemed that it had already been hanging on the wall for a long time.

A person can do many things in a lifetime: looking far away at scenery or concentrating on a painting is sufficient for spending the better part of one's life. The secret feelings of a person's innermost being are only associated with some specific objects; once they are produced, there is no longer any way to erase them. For example, when Sun Deng became conscious of the hidden significance behind the figures in the painting, a corner of his innermost being was occupied by a gigantic, ridiculous fable. What sort of fable was it after all? Since the nameless artist had long since withdrawn his traces behind the curtain of the months and years, everything was beyond verification.

Just then it was at the time of late spring. Bending over the edge of the table in the hall, Sun Deng slept for a short while but was awakened by the buzzing of a bee. . . . . . In the period before the arrival of the rainy season, day after day, the brilliant sunlight made one feel as leisurely and comfortable as if one were in a dream. It seemed as though there was no need to expect that time would occasion any change. . . . . . just like expecting someone to come. As he had so often in the past, Sun Deng kept turning the purple pot in his hand. Because he was worried that it would slip out of his hand and break, his demeanor showed that he was somewhat uneasy.

Under its legs, the bee was carrying the fragrance of flowers that blossomed beneath the blue sky. It flew dancingly in front of his eyes for a spell, then at last stopped to rest on the painting. Slowly, it crawled up one of the red strings and stopped where the woman's waist was. It didn't matter whether it were smelling some scent (perhaps it was the odor of the ink from years gone by), it definitely could not have been the aroma of the woman's body because it was, after all, just a painting.

"Do you mean there's nothing that you want to say?"

Sun Deng laughed.

Ruan Ji was at a loss. The famous poet, who usually spent his nights intoxicated amongst the flowers and willows of the gay quarters, gave one the impression of being unconventional and uninhibited. Unexpectedly, his speech and his behavior seemed all the more like those of a delicate woman, and his nervous temperament, like that of a woman who was skilled at making pretenses, was also well protected.

"When you're walking along a little path and you come to the end of it, there's no harm in stopping to have a good cry," [2] said Ruan Ji.

Sun Deng was just then pondering a move he was about to make

2 The image of Ruan Ji crying when he reached the end of a road is one of the most poignant in the lore about the poet.

with one of the go pieces, so he didn't answer. Ruan Ji rolled his eyes equivocally and, placing the thumb and forefinger of one hand in his mouth, dug out a green vegetable leaf (Sun Deng originally thought that, as in the past, he would let out a whistle).

When the whistling sound suddenly arose, Sun Deng was totally unprepared for it. The strange, strident sound, mixed with the sounds of the billowing pines, reverberated through the valleys of Su Gate Mountain for a long while without expiring. Sun Deng leaned against one side of the door leaf, observing far off in the sky above Su Gate Mountain a flock of soaring birds. Ruan Ji's silhouette stood motionless on the peak (he looked like a pine tree), white clouds amassed behind him. Before long, the glaring light caused a dark green shadow to appear before Sun Deng's eyes. By the time the angle of the sunlight had shifted (permitting Sun Deng to fix his gaze on the peak for a longer period of time), the peak had already long since been deserted. At the foot of the mountain, a woodcutter with faggots piled high on his back came walking slowly in the direction of the village along the little path on the ridges through the wheat fields.

Because the water's source had dried up, a great expanse of rounded stones emerged from the riverbed through the diminishing water. Reeds that had been cut down were neatly arranged along both banks of the river. The rotting hulks of some wooden boats were strewn on the riverbanks. They seemed like one snail after another lying quietly at the edge of the wheatland, several magpies resting on top of them. The groups of people who had gathered along the shores in the morning had already dispersed by now (they were transporting large amounts of earth from the foothills of Su Gate Mountain, seemingly with the intention of filling in the river channel and then, after that, planting grains and cotton on top).

As of old, the wooden bridge stood loftily over the river. Several children playing on the bridge were swaying back and forth as they walked on it. They frequently faced the azure sky as though they were looking for something—perhaps it was a magpie that had flown away from one of the overturned wooden boats, perhaps it was a kite. Their shadows cast upon the sand and stones at the bottom of the river and merged with the shadow of the bridge.

. . . . . .

A sudden morning rainstorm scoured the bluestone blocks of the atrium till they glistened. Some gaily-colored flower petals scattered upon them caused the cracks on the stone blocks to stand out more sharply (just as a smile causes facial wrinkles to deepen). . . . . . The clothesline that crossed the atrium was hung full of variously colored clothes. Their lower hems, which were saturated with water, flapped in the wind. The woman was standing beneath the clothesline, her hollow back concealing her tiny movements. It looked as though she were smoothing out some creases on the clothes, then again it seemed as though she were examining a stain on the clothing (a skirt). Each move she made seemed uncertain. Because she had been standing there too long (once she had thought of turning around but then she instantaneously changed her mind again), so that when she left at high noon, Sun Deng thought that she was still standing there.

For several days, the empty bowl with the blue rim had been lying beside the threshold. The leaves of the bean pods on the floor had long since been dried out by the sunlight. Through the paper of the latticed window was reflected a wispy, fluttering shadow. If it was not the spreading locks of his daughter's hair, then it must have been the shadow cast by the almond tree in the atrium (because he was separated from them by the paper of the window, sometimes it was difficult to tell the difference between the tree's shadow and locks of hair). This kind of situation made it much easier for one to attain tranquillity than at some other times. At those times, for example, if the woman stood straight up behind the window and took the podded young soya beans outside to wash by the pond, or if she carried a bamboo basket on her arm and went walking along the little path on the ridges through the wheat fields, her silhouette growing more distant in the sunlight shining against her. . . . . . Of course, more often the circumstances were like this: there was no one at all behind the window or door (that is to say, it wasn't known where his daughter had gone), and the stalk of beans lying on the wooden bench had been podded just halfway. . . . . .

If one were to say that she spent the whole day inside the house, only going out by chance for a short while the entire time, or if one were to say that in a year (perhaps it was an even longer time), her whereabouts were unclear only on a certain midday, then what would the moment when she suddenly disappeared signify for Sun Deng?

"I went out to stroll for a while," she said.

When she said the word "stroll," it gave one the feeling of casualness, as if to declare that the action itself didn't have any real purpose or significance. It was precisely this totally unnecessary and inevitable pretense that exposed the depression hidden deeply in her innermost being.

"I went out to the garden to see whether the eggplants are ripe," she added.

The moment her eyes met Sun Deng's, they rebounded to her feet like a rubber ball. They dispersed like a wisp of smoke blown by the wind.

On a low earthen bank at the western end of the wheat fields were neatly arrayed row after row of beehives. Just at that moment, a beekeeper wearing a mask stepped out from his tent (the tent where he spent his nights appeared to be extremely eye-catching against the hazy, golden background). Perhaps because the sunlight outside the tent hurt his eyes, he stood rigidly outside the tent beneath a chinaberry tree, peering in the direction of the east. Probably because of the swarms of bees that were fighting in the sky above the rapeseed field, he felt that his hands were tied. Otherwise, he certainly must have seen someone walking along the little path on the ridges between the wheat fields (the position where he was standing was only a few steps away from the little path lined with elms).

When Sun Deng finally realized that he was calling a tawny dog, the sun had already shifted slightly to the west—the wheat was already very tall, so that all Sun Deng could see of the tawny dog as it trotted along the ridges through the wheat fields was its curled tail.

—Then, where is the homeland?

—Homeland?

—The homeland where the soul rests.

—People usually find it in the body of a woman.

—If it exists, it has long since been lost or will be lost sooner or later.

—More often, we discover it when we are looking attentively at a flower petal that has fallen on the ground or when we are gazing at a drifting cloud. Of course, in a certain sense, we may say that it is only a game of go, a kite with a broken string. . . . . .

Ruan Ji pulled the poetry manuscript over to him and turned to the page with the bookmark. Because of the crudeness of the printing, the characters in it were already indistinct. Ruan Ji disjointedly recited a few lines, then suddenly stopped and let out a whistle.

Sun Deng had read the poem long ago but had forgotten a few words and expressions in it. Just now, he surprised himself by having said so much in one breath. Overnight, the fences that he maintained around his speech became unbearably dilapidated. . . . . . So that his words and actions would match the tranquillity of his innermost being, Sun Deng proceeded to sink into a lengthy silence.

When a person reaches middle age, the signs of senility are by no means so apparent as people often say. The firmness of the skin and the circulation of the blood invariably go unnoticed by others. It's just that only when he was alone with his own memories, Sun Deng would vaguely feel something.

A layer of green duckweed drifted in the pond outside; a wind blowing from the southeast pushed it into the northwest corner of the pond. Most of the time several ducks were there searching for food. The manner in which they craned their necks to look all around made one feel that someone was walking beside the pond. A girl carrying a vegetable basket passed in front of the doorway with a flash. At the same time Sun Deng was recalling how she was dressed (a blurred mass of dark red color), a shiver shot through him unawares. He stuck a pipe in his mouth and kept his eyes focused on the sloping land on the other side of the pond (an old lady was watering the newly planted potatoes). This time, the village maiden didn't walk around the pond and into his own original line of vision as he had imagined, but followed along another small path and quietly walked into the distance.

"No matter what you say, this is definitely not a good omen," said Ruan Ji. "The reason people can't remember the multitude of strands and loose ends from the past is because of an uncommon situation or because of a woman."

Sun Deng didn't say anything. The absent-minded manner in which he looked at the go game was quite similar to a trance. Acutely conscious of this fact, he shifted his gaze elsewhere.

Several go pieces were scattered on the board between them; Ruan Ji was just about to put down a piece that he held in his hand, which was suspended in midair. Probably because the prolonged indecision made him feel bored, his hand drew several arcs above the board, and then he tossed the piece into the container, got up, and took leave.

Owing to a certain invariable habit, Sun Deng once again heard the sounds of snoring rising from the rooms along the corridor. The doors to each room were thrown open; the sound that made one feel so despondent most likely was coming from a wing-room on the left side of the corridor. Sun Deng picked up the purple porcelain pot and walked slowly in the direction of the wing-room (his bearing while walking might easily have caused one to believe that he was silently reciting a stanza of poetry). When he reached the window that directly faced the clothesline in the atrium, he suddenly stopped. At this moment, another sound that had been covered up by the sound of snoring became clearer—it seemed like the footsteps of someone walking toward the house along one side of the pond.

While Sun Deng was attentively listening to the sounds, he unconsciously turned around and walked back. He passed through the door to the house and walked up to the side of the almond tree in the atrium—it seemed as though the sounds had stopped. Could it be that the person had suddenly halted? Sun Deng walked out to the side of the courtyard gate and saw a woman washing clothes on a dock at the side of the pond. The sound emitted by the mallet as she struck it on a block of bluestone closely resembled the sounds of footsteps.

As before, the little path on the ridges in the wheat fields was deserted.

……

Behind the woodcutter's back, Sun Deng saw her thin silhouette as she came walking slowly in the direction of the village. She always kept a distance of two elm trees from the woodcutter. When the old man stopped to catch his breath in the center of the wheat fields, she too stood still while supporting herself on one of the trees. Perhaps because a grain of sand was hurting her sole, she took off one of her shoes. An unobstructed gust of wind blowing through the fields wrinkled her clothing. The glaring sunlight caused everything all around to become utterly lacking in vitality. The woodcutter lit a pipe and, suddenly seeming to sense her presence, turned around to look at her but didn't say anything.

The troubled look of the woman standing on one foot made one think that she was calculating something. The moment when she stopped to linger beneath the elm, which bent from her weight, gave the woman the opportunity to put her thoughts in order. Either she suspected that she had lost her way or she felt regret over the inappropriateness of her own visit. In a certain sense, the reason she hesitated to move forward was due to the discrepancy between what she wanted to do and the impression her behavior made on an onlooker. This kind of discrepancy could also occur when people looked at distant scenery or stared at a woman's face.

The abandoned bridge in the cotton fields was just like the vestiges left behind by fleeting time, or the empty echoes of a sound, which cause one to be able to grasp fragments from the past in the depths of thought that remains unchanged for an instant: the sobbing river water, the dense clumps of reeds, the fishing net drying on the river bank, the fishy smell of the water. . . . . .

At the moment of high noon, the groups of people working in the cotton fields congregated from the sides of the bridge beneath the rickety bridge railings (even when there were no children frolicking on top of the bridge, the wind from the south would cause it to emit a slight creaking noise). From the looks of it, they were discussing something, perhaps interspersed with arguments.

A young man stood in clumps of reeds at one end of the bridge looking very ill-at-ease. With the lapse of time, he became conscious of the insipidity of his own isolation, so he indecisively approached the group of people beneath the bridge railings. Probably because the people, who were deeply immersed in their furtive, private conversations, didn't pay any attention to him, the aloof man decided to change his direction on the spur of the moment. Bending his body to slip through the bridge railings, he walked off toward the other end of the cotton fields. In his haste, he bumped his head on the bridge abutment, but he didn't raise his hand right away to rub his head. Instead, he walked straight to a distant spot (a spot that was almost beyond Sun Deng's line of vision and where it was impossible to see a person's silhouette), and only then did he touch his forehead as though he were thinking of something.

Spending too much or too little time in a place can similarly induce in one a feeling of isolation. That day, at high noon, when Sun Deng settled himself in the misshapen rattan chair in front of the table as usual, he suddenly became conscious of this fact. Day after day, time etched the wrinkles in his face like a silkworm nibbling on a mulberry leaf. "Time eternally passes more quickly than people are prepared for, until finally it will turn you into a stranger from a foreign land.

Of course, at the very end, you will become a part of the objects that you are now viewing from afar, just like that wooden bridge. . . . . ."

"That's not necessarily bad," said Sun Deng. "Furthermore, people usually can't detect this type of transformation."

"In the morning, a stalk of bean pods may still be studded with spring dewdrops, but in the blink of an eye it will be withered by wintery frosts," said Ruan Ji.

The daughter came walking through the inner door carrying a bundle of soaking wet bean pods. When she walked to a place in the atrium that was exactly opposite the door, she blocked Sun Deng's line of vision for a while.

"It looks as though your friend Ruan won't be coming today," she said.

Sun Deng realized that the expression he wore at that moment while gazing far into the distance surely must have misled his daughter into thinking that he was waiting for someone, so he adjusted his sitting posture somewhat and, letting his hand follow where it may, pulled over the poetry manuscript on the table, glanced at it hastily, then returned it to its original position.

On those drowsy afternoons, nobody would come to this residence. The deserted atrium, the empty clothesline, the swallow that had gone off to parts unknown, and the half-played go game laid out on the table proved this point in a veiled fashion. There was also the painting hanging on the wall of the hall that could confirm this point: a string on the painting (the color of the string had turned from scarlet to ashen) had long since broken because it was stretched too tight. Attached to the side of the painting, it looked just like an inverted steelyard hook. A corner of the painting had been lifted by the wind, causing dust to fly about in all directions. . . . . .

When Sun Deng picked up a bristle brush and tried to dust the painting, he carelessly knocked over a purple porcelain pot on the edge of the table. The teapot rolled over several times on the table, then fell to the ground and broke into pieces. The dripping sound of the water caught on the surface as it flowed through a seam in the table caused Sun Deng to be silent for a long time.

What sort of sound was it?

Starting from midday, the unbearably old angler had been sitting next to the hedgerow along the left side of the pond. The warm May sunlight had time after time led him into the land of dreams, while the calls of the ducks swimming in the pond and the intermittent sounds coming from the cotton fields kept waking him up over and over. On the gentle slope at the other side of the pond, a brocadelike stretch of rapeseed flowers was in full bloom.

People usually regard the flourishing and withering of plants, the rising and falling of clouds, the departure and return of swallows as symbols of the continuity of time—like the cycle of the seasons—but for Sun Deng, the situation was by no means like this. Who knew whether the swallow crying sadly beneath the eaves was the same one that flew away last year at the end of autumn?

Everything lay in tranquillity. All life fled from the sunlight of the present moment of high noon and escaped into dark corners leaving behind for him some fragmentary memories, a yellowing poetry manuscript, a jumbled mass of wilted petals, an unrealizable promise. . . . . .

After his daughter had been married off to another district, she hadn't come back for a long time, yet in recurring reveries, her silhouette finally became clearer before his eyes. . . . . . She came walking toward the village along the narrow, little path below Su Gate Mountain, then suddenly halted in the center of the broad, flat wheatlands.

The woman, utterly immobile, stared at the painting on the wall. Seemingly smelling the scent of pine resin[3] in the tufts of her hair, a blue butterfly fluttered back and forth in the gloomy light behind her. Between the woman and him a go game was laid out; it was impossible for Sun Deng to remember when the game had begun.

The arrangement and number of the go pieces, the melancholy look in the woman's eyes, the manner with which she held one of the go pieces between her forefinger and middle finger, and the thick air in the room all closely resembled the painting on the wall. More than once, Sun Deng felt that the go match between him and the woman, through a certain visual pattern that was difficult to express, formed an exact analogy to the situation in the painting. This absurd analogy brought Sun Deng's distracted consciousness to the margin of the imminent cessation of thought: in the enchantingly radiant sunlight

3 It is essential to note that Chinese ink, from the Han dynasty on, was usually made of soot, obtained by burning pine resin.

of high noon, might an unseen hand quickly paint everything inside the vestibule into a painting?

. . . . . .

Perhaps because of the prolonged and profound silence that made him feel bored, Ruan Ji sighed lightly, then got up and took leave. According to his habit, Sun Deng saw him to the door. Following the little path lined with elms, Ruan Ji's silhouette gradually went off into the distance and dissolved in the dark green background of Su Gate Mountain.

When the sound of whistling rose beneath the sunny empyrean, Sun Deng shuddered as though it were a bolt out of the blue. Shielding his eyes from the strong light with one hand, he saw Ruan Ji standing on the peak of Su Gate Mountain beneath a solitary tree. Against a backdrop of white clouds like thick cotton fleece, he stood motionless, seeming to wait for Sun Deng's answer. Sun Deng looked all around him, then quietly inserted his thumb and forefinger in his mouth—the extreme frailness of his body and the looseness of his teeth caused him to be unable to produce any sound.

The shrill, desolate, plaintive whistle, accompanied by the soughing of the billowing pines, reverberated for a long time in the mountain valleys. It was like the sad wail of the poet who died long ago, penetrating through the barriers of time, continuing up till today, and sinking into the easily awakened dreams of a living person.

Translated by Victor H. Mair

THE NOON OF HOWLING WIND ❁ *Yu Hua*

Through a windowpane free from the slightest cracks and perforations, rays of sun came intruding, intruding nearly as far as the trousers I had thrown over a chair. I lay naked to the waist under the covers, my right hand rubbing at the corner of my right eye to rid it of the crust that had formed while I slept. I felt it was not fitting to leave it there any longer, but it also made no sense to deal with it roughly. So I rubbed it gracefully. But for the moment, my left eye was unoccupied, so I let it look at those trousers. I had taken them off at bedtime last night and thrown them over a chair. Now I regretted having thrown them over the chair so carelessly, leaving them to hang in such a sorry state. The same was true of my shirt. Looking at them now with my left eye, I wondered whether I had shed them like a skin while I was asleep. The pants and shirt really looked like that. By this time, sunlight dappled the legs of my pants, its brightness leading my eye from point to point like a golden flea. And then my body started itching, so I let my unoccupied left hand do the scratching. But soon my left hand had more than it could handle, and I had to let my right hand help it.

Someone started knocking at my door.

At first I thought the knocking was on my neighbor's door, but the sound proved to be clearly directed at me. I was startled by this and wondered who would come knocking at my door. I would have been a likely person to do it, but I was lying in bed at the moment. It was probably a mix-up. So I paid it no mind and went back to scratching myself. I thought of how every time I came back from an excursion, I always knocked on my own door until I was sure no one would open it, and then pulled out my key. At this point the door was banging till it seemed ready to collapse from the banging. I knew the person outside was kicking the door, not knocking on it. Right then, without leaving me time to think of a strategy, the door fell heavily to the floor, making a bang that vibrated through my body.

A hulking, full-bearded man walked to my bed and roared at me in rage, "Your friend is almost dead and you keep lying here."

I had never seen this person before and did not know him from Adam. I said to him, "Have you come to the wrong place?"

He answered firmly, "Absolutely not."

His firmness made me doubt myself. I wondered if I had not gone to bed in the wrong place the night before. Quickly I jumped out of bed and ran outside to see the number on the door. But at this moment my door number was pressed against the floor, so I ran back in and looked for the number plate on the fallen door. On it was written Room 3, Number 26, New Hongqiaoville.

I asked him, "Is this the door you kicked down?"

"Yes," he said.

So there could be no mistake. I said to him, "You definitely have come to the wrong place."

Now my firmness made him doubtful. He looked at me awhile, then asked, "Is your name Yu Hua?"

I said, "Yes, but I don't know you."

Hearing this, he straightaway flew into a rage and roared again, "Your friend is about to die!"

"But I've never had any sort of friend." I too started roaring.

"Bullshit. You're just a low-down philistine." He contorted his features as he spoke.

I said to him, "I am no philistine. All these books piled around my room are proof of that. You might want to push your friend off on me, but I'm not going to accept that. I'm saying that I've never had any so-called friend. But . . ." I drew a calming breath and went on, "But you can go give your friend away at Room 4. That's my neighbor. He has plenty of friends, and I don't think he'll mind adding one more."

"But he is your friend. Don't think you can weasel out of it." He stepped menacingly close and looked as if he would swallow me at a gulp.

"But who is he then?"

He spoke a name I had never heard.

"I have never met such a person," I began to shout.

"You ungrateful, despicable philistine." He reached out an arm as thick as my leg, all ready to yank my hair.

I quickly drew back to one edge of the bed, shouting in desperate panic, "I'm not a philistine. My books are proof of that. If you call me a philistine again, I will ask you to leave."

His hand snapped down and reached under my covers. It was an icy powerful hand that grasped my warm but weak foot. Then he lifted me out bodily from beneath the covers and dropped me on the floor. "Hurry up and get dressed, or I'll drag you out just as you are."

I knew that further argument with this fellow would be meaningless, since his strength was at least five times greater than mine. He would throw me out the window as if throwing a pair of pants. So I said, "Since there's a dying person wanting to see me, of course I'll be glad to go." With that, I got to my feet and began dressing.

And so it was, at noon of that accursed day, the husky fellow kicked down my door and presented me with a friend I did not wish for—a friend on the brink of death at that. Outdoors, the northwest wind was howling with all its might. I had no coat or scarf, nor did I have a hat or gloves. Wearing only a thin suit, I had to follow this large fellow in his coat, scarf, gloves, and hat to see a friend I would not recognize.

On the street, the northwest wind blew me and the tall fellow, like two leaves, to the friend's door. In front of the door were piled many flower wreaths. The tall fellow turned his head and said with limitless sorrow, "Your friend is dead."

Before I could figure out if this development was something to be happy or sad about, I heard a string of piercing wails. The tall man pushed me toward the wailing sounds. At this point, a group of grieving men and women gathered around and said in utterly touching, heartfelt tones, "You must not take it so hard."

I could only nod in pretended sadness, because I no longer intended to say what I felt like saying. I lightly patted their shoulders and lightly stroked their hair to show gratitude for their comforting words. I exchanged long and powerful handshakes with several sturdily built men, promising them that I would not take it too hard.

Then a frail old woman walked over. Her eyes glistened with tears as she grasped my hand and said, "My son is dead."

"I know," I told her. "I am grief stricken, because this all happened so suddenly." I was on the point of saying that her son and I had looked at the sun together the day before.

At this she fell to weeping. Her penetrating sobs raised the hairs on my neck. I said to her, "You must not take it so hard." Then I sensed her sobs were subsiding, and she began wiping her eyes on my hand. She lifted her head and said to me, "You must not take it too hard either."

I nodded strenuously, saying, "I won't. But you have to watch your health."

Again she used my hand as a handkerchief to wipe her tears on. She was rubbing her bleary, steamy tears all over my hand. I wanted to pull back my hand, but she grabbed too tightly. She said, "You've got to watch your health too."

I said, "I will take care of myself. We've all got to take care of ourselves. We have to turn sorrow into strength."

She nodded and said, "My son breathed his last without waiting for you to come. You don't blame him do you?"

"No, I don't blame him," I said.

Again she started sobbing. When she had sobbed awhile, she said, "I only have this one son, and now he is dead. Now you are my son."

I pulled back my hand forcefully and pretended to wipe tears from my eyes. I did not have any tears at all. Then I told her, "Actually, I have thought of you as my own mother for a long time." That was the only thing I could say at this point.

My words stirred her to cry even more brokenheartedly. There was nothing I could do but pat her shoulder lightly. I patted till my hand ached before her crying stopped. Then she led me by the hand to the doorway of a room and said, "Would you go in and keep my son company?"

I pushed open the door and went in. There wasn't anyone in the room, but a corpse was lying there covered with white cloth. Beside the bed was a chair that seemed to have been prepared for me, so I sat down.

I sat next to the deceased for a long time before I pulled aside the white cloth to see what he looked like. I saw a colorless face that gave no indication of its exact age. It was a face I had never seen before.

Seeing this, I covered it up again with the white cloth. I thought to myself, "This is my friend."

So I sat next to the dead person at whom I had looked but forgotten in a moment. I was not here on my own will. There had been no choice but to come. Though this friend I had not intended to meet was already dead, I could not rid the weight from my heart because his mother had taken his place. An old woman I did not know and hardly liked had become my mother. It disgusted me that she used my hand as a handkerchief, but I had no choice but to let her rub her face on it. What was more, anytime she needed it after this, I would have to hold my hand out respectfully, without a complaining word. I knew clearly what I would have to do next. I was supposed to dig out twenty yuan to buy a big flower wreath. I would also have to wear mourning clothes of hemp and keep a vigil at his side. I would have to wail for him and hold his ashes; I would have to go strolling on the streets with his mother on my arm. And after this was all over, I would have to sweep his grave every year during the Festival of Tombs. Also, I would inherit his unfinished business and have to act like a dutiful son . . . The crucial thing for me at the moment was finding a carpenter right away to rehang the door kicked off its hinges by that burly fellow. But for now I had to keep watch beside this damned corpse.

Translated by Denis C. Mair

1986 ❋ *Yu Hua*

Many years ago, a mild and unassuming high school history teacher suddenly disappeared, leaving behind his young wife and a three-year-old daughter. From that time on, nothing more was heard of him. Over the course of several years, his wife gradually began to resign herself to her loss. On a hot, dry Sunday afternoon, she married another man. Her daughter also changed her last name to match that of the new husband, for the old name was inextricably tied up with the pain and difficulty of those years. A dozen years had gone by since that day. They lived a tranquil life. The past receded farther and farther behind them, until it almost seemed to have dispersed like so much mist into the air, never to return.

The husband, of course, was only one of the many who disappeared during the tumultuous years of the Cultural Revolution. When the tumult died down, many of the families whose relatives had been lost began to receive word of their whereabouts, even if it was only to learn that they had died years before. She was the only one who had never heard any news. All she knew was that her husband had disappeared the night he was taken away by the Red Guards. The person who told her was a store clerk who had been among the group of Red Guards who had broken into their home that night. He said, "We didn't hit him. We just took him to his office and told him to write a confession. We didn't even send a guard to watch him. But the next morning, we discovered that he was gone." She remembered that they had come to the apartment the morning after to search for her husband. The clerk had added, "Your husband was always nice to us students, so we didn't torture him."

Not long before, she and her daughter had taken a pile of old newspapers to the recycling station. Standing among the scrap heaps littering the recycling station, she discovered a yellowing sheet of paper dotted with mildew. The writing on the sheet of paper, however, was still legible:

> The Five Punishments: branding 墨, nose-cut 劓, leg-cut 剕, castration 宫, dismemberment 大辟.
>
> Former Qin Dynasty: roasting in oil, disembowelment, beheading, burning at the stake.
> Warring States Period: flaying, drawing and fifthing, halving.
> Early Liao Dynasty: live burial, cannon fodder, cliff hanging.
> Jin Dynasty: skull-crush, death by cudgel, skin-peel.
>
> Drawing and Fifthing 車裂: To tie the victim's head and each of his four limbs to five horse-drawn carts, and by driving in different directions, rend him in fifths.
> Slow Death 凌遲: To mince the victim's body with knives.
> Disembowelment 剖腹: To tear open the abdomen to view the victim's heart . . .

An old man wearing coke-bottle glasses stood by a scale in the middle of the clutter. The daughter, grown up and loath to see her mother tire herself out, carried a heavy pile of wastepaper over to the man and set it down on the scale. She wiped the sweat off her face with a handkerchief as her mother crouched down by another pile of wastepaper behind her. The old man had to bend so close to read the numbers on the scale that she couldn't suppress a grin, but at that moment a sharp cry rang out behind her. When she turned to look, her mother had already slumped unconscious to the ground.

As soon as they took him to his office at the school, they sat him down and told him to write a sincere, honest, and thorough confession. Then they left without even assigning him a guard.

The office was large and lit by two piercingly bright incandescent lamps. The northwest wind whistled over the roof. He sat for a long time at his desk, sat like the building itself, squatting quietly under the bright pale moonlight as the wind whistled around its walls.

He saw that he was washing his feet as his wife sat on the edge of the bed watching over their little daughter. Their daughter had already fallen asleep. The crook of her arm was sticking out from underneath the quilts. His wife hadn't noticed them yet. His wife was staring into space. As always, she wore her hair in two braids. Red silk bows, tied in the shape of butterfly wings, were fastened around the end of each braid. They were just the same as the first time he had ever seen her, the time they had passed each other without a word.

Now he seemed to see those pretty red butterflies floating through the air, towing two shining black braids behind them.

It had been three months since he had first told his wife to stay inside at all times. She had listened intently and done as she was told. He didn't go out very much either. Every time he left the house he saw the women—feather dusters and toilet seats dangling around their necks, half their hair shaved to make a yin-yang pattern on their scalps. He was afraid that they would cut off his wife's braids and ruin the lovely red butterfly bows. That was why he had told her not to leave the house.

He saw snow flurrying through the streets all day long. The snow never fell anywhere else. He saw everyone bend to gather a handful of flakes. He saw them stop to read them. He saw someone slumped beside a postbox. He was dead. The blood was still fresh, still wet. A leaflet drifted through the air and landed on his head, covering half of his face. The people in dunce caps and sandwich boards walked past the postbox. They glanced toward the dead man, but he saw no surprise register on their faces. They looked blank, pitiless, as if they were staring at themselves in the bathroom mirror. He began to recognize a few of his colleagues from school in their midst. He thought, Maybe it's my turn next.

He saw himself washing his feet. The water in the basin had already grown cold, but he didn't notice. He was thinking, Maybe it's my turn next. He was wondering how it was that he had taken to crying out at odd times without even knowing why. These cries were always met by a wooden stare from his wife.

He saw them come in. After they came in, the room was full of noise, full of voices. His wife was still sitting on the edge of the bed, staring woodenly toward him. His daughter had awoken, and the sound of her sobs seemed terribly far away, as if he were walking down the street, listening from outside a tightly shuttered window. It was then that he realized that the water in the basin was cold.

The noise began to settle, and someone holding a piece of paper walked toward him. He didn't know what the paper said. They made him read it aloud. He recognized his own handwriting, remembered something of what he had written. Then they dragged him away, his bare feet clad only in a pair of thongs. The northwest wind blew across the surface of the road, toweling his feet dry.

He shivered when he saw the neat stack of writing paper sitting atop his desk. He gazed at the paper for a moment, fumbled in his pocket for a fountain pen, and discovered that he hadn't brought one. So he stood and looked to see if there was a pen on one of the other teachers' desks. But there were no pens on any of the other teachers' desks. He sat down helplessly and saw two hands imprinted on the desktop. He realized that he hadn't been to the office for over three months. His desk was coated with dust, as were the others. He figured that none of the other teachers had been to the office either.

He saw crowds of people filing through the gate onto campus and knots of people filing out. He saw himself leafing through an old, heavy history book. He had been fascinated by the punishments. Sooner or later, he planned to leave his teaching post and devote himself to their study. In his student days, he had pored through volumes of historical material, taking meticulous notes as he went along. He had also fallen in love for the first time. But the affair did not work out, and his research had come to a premature halt as a result. Just after graduation, he had come across a single page from his notes as he packed to leave. He had intended to throw it away but had somehow forgotten the whole thing in the months that followed. Now he knew that he hadn't thrown it away after all.

He saw that he was washing his feet. He saw himself walking through the teachers college. And he saw himself sitting at his desk. He saw a huge shadow on the wall across from him. The shadow's head was as big as a basketball. He stared at his own shadow. And after he had stared for a long time, he began to think that the shadow was a hole in the wall.

He felt the northwest wind steal into the room and begin to shriek. The wind fastened itself to his clothes and shrieked, slipped into his hair and howled. The sound rubbed against his face, stroked his cheeks, cried out to him. He began to tremble. He began to feel cold. The wind was louder and louder. He turned to look at the door.

The door was shut. He turned to look at the windows. The windows were shut.

He discovered that the windows had been washed so spotlessly clean that they were transparent. He didn't understand. How could the windows be so clean if the desks were coated with dust? He noticed that one of the windows was cracked. The sight somehow seemed terribly desolate. He moved toward the cracked pane, and its desolation mirrored his own.

But when he reached the sill, he realized with a shock that the broken pane was the only piece of glass left in the frame. All the other panes were empty. He absently extended his hand to caress the broken pane. The edge was coarse and sharp under his fingers. He absently rubbed his fingers against it, feeling something warm seep from the tip of his finger. Bits of glass fell from the window to the floor with his motion, shattering crisply on the floor like a broken heart. Soon, only a small triangle of glass remained.

Suddenly, he saw a pair of leather shoes swaying back and forth just in front of him. He lifted his hand to touch them, recoiled, heard his heart pounding and leaping in his chest. He stood motionless, watching the shoes swing slowly back and forth. Then he discovered the cuffs of a pair of pants. They were fluttering just above the shoes. He slammed open the window frame. There was a corpse hanging from the eaves. He heard someone scream. The sound came from his left. Through the darkness he saw a tree, and under its branches, a shadow. The shadow's feet dangled above the ground. Sharp gasps drifted through the air, reaching his ears as feeble whimpers. He stood for a long time, until he seemed to hear the shadow mumble, "It's you," and extend its arms to grab hold of some kind of loop. The shadow's head slipped through the loop. After a second or two of silence, he heard a little stool being kicked over onto the ground, followed by a suffocated whisper. He slumped to the floor, hands gripping the windowsill.

It was only much later that he gradually became aware of the sound of shouting echoing in the distance. The shouts moved closer, dispersing through the night, surrounding the office. They grew steadily louder as they approached, until they seemed to him like a terrible wave of sound welling into his ears.

He leaped from the floor to listen. The school had erupted into a ghostly chorus of wails and brutish howls. It was as if a pack of wild animals had surrounded the office. The noise excited him. He began to pounce around the room, hands waving in the air, drunk with the hoarse bellows escaping from his own throat. He wanted to escape, to merge with the clamor outside, but he didn't know how. As the shouts rang out louder and louder, his own excitement and anxiety only increased. He continued to leap around the room, bellowing. There was nothing else for him to do. Soon, though, he slumped down onto the seat at his desk, exhausted and agitatedly panting for air.

It was at this very moment that he caught sight of his own shadow. He had suddenly stumbled upon a way to escape. There was a hole in the wall. He stood and ran toward the hole, but the realization that the hole had suddenly shrunk to a fraction of its size just a second before stopped him short. Suspiciously eyeing the wall, he retreated to his original position at the desk, hesitated, and charged once more toward the hole. Just as before, the hole began to shrink just as he approached. This time, he held his ground. The hole, he discovered, was precisely the same size as his own body. He stared suspiciously for a few moments. He decided that it hadn't shrunk so much that he couldn't squeeze his way out. He threw himself into the darkness and landed on the floor.

Blown open by a gust of wind, the door began to shimmy against the wall with a series of bone-cracking reports. The wind pounded through the open door and circled the office.

Dazed, he rose and stood for a moment facing the door. He saw a black rectangle cut in the wall, but as he walked stealthily toward it, he was once again assailed by suspicion. This time, the hole stayed the same no matter how close he stood. Instead of catapulting himself into the darkness, he carefully extended a finger toward it. When his finger disappeared into the hole, he extended his arm. He began, slowly and with the utmost caution, to slide through the hole. And when he found himself surrounded by a broad, empty expanse of darkness, he knew that he had escaped.

The shouts that filled the schoolyard were even louder and more stirring than before, and he began to bellow even louder and with even more zeal, leaping off the ground as he ran. And though innumerable shadows—some big, some small, and no two alike—tried to prevent his escape, he managed to evade them all. In a moment, he had reached the street. He paused, tried to determine just where the shouts were coming from, but it seemed as if they pervaded the air, as if they were racing toward him from every possible direction. He stood, at a loss as to where to go. A moment passed. He saw something burning to the southeast, glowing orange like clouds just before dusk. He ran toward the flames, and as he ran, the shouts grew louder.

A huge building was aflame. He saw countless people swaying and twisting amidst the flames. Countless others tumbled from the top of the building to the ground. He stood on the bridge, bellowing, leaping up and down, laughing at how they tumbled and sliced through the air. Flurries of bodies, one after another, rained down from the building until the structure itself vanished, leaving only a glowing tower of flame in its wake. The tower brought his frenzy to an even higher pitch. Watching from the bridge, he shouted and leaped as if his life depended on it. Soon afterward, he heard a string of explosions. The flames crumpled to the ground, but continued to burn across the expanse. He discovered that the flames were flooding toward him across the ground at a breakneck clip. Breathless, he sat on the railing of the bridge, eyes trained on the flames. Gradually, the burning expanse began to break up into isolated piles of flame. The pockets of flame grew smaller and smaller until the fire burned itself out.

When the fire was gone, he slid off the railing and began to walk along the bridge. After a few steps, he turned and walked back to the railing. After a moment, he retraced his steps. He paced back and forth across the bridge for a long time.

It was only much later that the dark sky to the east began to glow. Just before the sun rose, the clouds began to soar into the air, shining red. He saw something burning somewhere in the distance. He began to shout. He ran toward the flames.

When they got home from the recycling station, she started to feel strangely distracted. That night, she heard someone pacing outside the house. There was no moonlight, and the streets were dark and quiet. She heard footsteps approach the house, scraping the ground with an oddly irregular rhythm, as if they were simultaneously slapping the pavement and gliding above the ground. Finally, the footsteps stopped a good distance away from the house without coming any closer. By that time, she had already realized whose footsteps they were.

She heard the footsteps for several nights in a row. The footsteps terrified her. The footsteps made her cry aloud with fright.

Her husband had been taken away on just such a black, moonless night. The Red Guards crashing through the front door, the scrape of her husband's thongs as he left the house for the last time—all of this would always be associated for her with the dark of night. After more than ten years, she still couldn't help being frightened by the dark. With the visit to the recycling station, the darkness she had assiduously tried to bury since that night enveloped her once again.

That day, walking home with her daughter at her side, she had suddenly seen her own shadow lying on the pavement under the sun. The shadow made her cry out. For she now knew that the darkness could pursue her by day as well as by night.

1

The man limped into the small town. It was early spring. One week earlier, a fierce storm had buried the town in spring snow. After a week of sparkling sunshine, however, the snow had almost entirely melted away. A few patches of slush lingered in dark, shady places, but the rest of the town had begun to flower. Soon, the town was enveloped by the sound of dripping water, like a harmony plucked from the rays of the sun. The melting sound lightened the hearts of the townspeople. And with each passing night, the stars burned bright in the sky, promising them another brilliant day when they awoke the next morning.

Windows that had been shut all winter were thrown open one by one, and in them appeared the expectant faces of young girls above pots of sprouting flowers sitting on the sill. The wind no longer blew, cold and bone piercing, from the northwest. Instead, the warm, humid breezes of the southeast stroked their faces. They left their rooms, left their bulky overcoats behind them. They walked into the streets, into springtime. If they still wore scarves around their necks, it was because they looked nice, not because they helped to ward off the wind. They felt their skin, dry and taut in winter, begin to stretch.

Their hands, stuck into pockets or enveloped in gloves, began to sweat. They took their hands out of their pockets, felt the sun moving across their skin, felt the spring breeze sliding flirtatiously between their fingers. And at the same time, the slate gray willows along the river grew tender with green shoots. All of these changes occurred within a week, and on the streets, bicycle bells sparkled as brightly as sunlight and the sound of footsteps and conversation rose and fell and murmured like waves.

It was around that same time that the man came to town. His hair tumbled from his head like a waterfall and dangled about his waist. His beard cascaded down to his chest, obscuring most of his face. His eyes were swollen and cloudy. That was how he limped into town. His pants were tattered, and from the knees down, all that remained were some dangling strips of torn cloth. His upper body was naked save for a piece of burlap thrown over his shoulders. His unshod feet were criss-crossed with deep, callused cracks. The cracks were filled with black grit, and the feet were unusually large, so that each footstep rang out like a hand clap against the pavement.

He walked into spring along with the residents of the town. And though they saw him, they paid him little heed, for as soon as he had been noted, his image had already been cast aside and forgotten. They were walking wholeheartedly into spring, walking happily through the streets.

The girls stuffed their pretty handbags with makeup and romance novels by Qiong Yao. In the quiet hour before dusk, they sat in front of their mirrors making themselves up for an evening out. And only when they had succeeded in making themselves as pretty as could be did they leave the house in search of the hero of the novel, enveloped in the aroma of their own perfume.

The boys' pockets were full of Marlboros and Good Friends cigarettes. They went out into the streets before it got dark and stayed out late. They too were fond of Qiong Yao's novels. They moved through the streets in search of someone who would remind them of a Qiong Yao heroine.

The girls who hadn't stayed home and the boys who weren't wandering the streets had surged into the movie house, crowded into the workers' club, poured into the night school classrooms. Of those who spent their evening behind a school desk, most came not in search of knowledge, but of love, for their eyes were more frequently directed toward the opposite sex than the blackboard.

The old men were still sitting at the teahouse. They had sat there for the whole day, for the last ten years, for the last few decades. And still they kept on sitting. Their time for evening strolls had come and gone, and they were in their own way as content as they had been in the days when they too had promenaded through town.

The old ladies sat at home in front of their color TV sets. It mattered very little if they followed the thread of the drama or not. To sit in comfort and watch as the various characters floated on and off the screen was happiness enough.

Look through the open windows. Walk along the main streets until you get to the narrow residential lanes lined by courtyard homes. What will you see? What will you hear? What will you be reminded of when you get there?

The disastrous years of the Cultural Revolution have faded into the mists of time. The political slogans pasted again and again on the walls have all been painted over, obscured from the view of pedestrians strolling through the spring night, invisible to those for whom only the present can be seen. Crowds surge excitedly down the streets. Bicycle bells sound out across the avenues. Cars leave clouds of dust in their wake. A minivan with loudspeakers mounted on its roof drives slowly by, broadcasting information about family planning and contraception. Another minivan moves slowly through the streets warning of the suffering inflicted on the people by traffic accidents. The sidewalks are festooned with billboards. The residents of the town are attracted by the words and the pictures on the signs. They know full well the perils posed by overpopulation. Many among them have mastered the use of several types of contraceptive devices. Now they understand the dangers posed by traffic accidents. They know that even though overpopulation is perilous, the living must do their best to have a good time and avoid being killed in a traffic accident. They note appreciatively that students from the middle school have volunteered to spend their Sunday directing the traffic that pours across the bridge.

It was just around then that the man limped into town.

He saw a person lying somewhere around his feet. The man's foot somehow seemed connected to his own. He tried to kick it away, but the foot recoiled almost before he had even lifted his leg to strike. When he put his foot down, the other foot shifted back to its original position next to his own. Excited, he stealthily lifted his own foot once more, discovering at the same time that the foot on the ground had once again evaded his own. Sensing his opponent's vigilance, he held his foot motionless in the air until he saw that his opponent's foot was also poised motionless in the air. Then he pounced, landing full force on his opponent's torso. He heard a solid thump, but when he looked down, the prone figure below him seemed unhurt, and his foot was still linked to his own. He closed his eyes and began to spring angrily forward, stomping as hard as he possibly could on the ground. After a moment, he opened his eyes and looked down. The man was still lying on the ground in front of him. He began to feel dejected, to gaze helplessly around. The sun shone on his back, and the coarse burlap bag draped over his shoulders shimmered in the sunlight. He saw a blob of something deep and green somewhere ahead and to the right. A thoughtful smile played sluggishly across his face. He began to creep toward the deep green blob, discovering at the same time that his opponent had shifted into a crouch underfoot. He would have to move even more carefully now. Instead of fleeing, the man was sliding his body along the ground, sliding toward a little pond. And by the time he himself had reached the pond's edge, the man's head slid into the water, followed by his arms, his legs, and finally his whole body. He stood at the edge of the pool watching him float on the surface of the water. He bent to pick up some rocks and began to pelt him, turning away in satisfaction only after the man had shattered into what seemed like a thousand different pieces. Suddenly, he felt a burst of hot sunlight pierce his eyes. His head began to spin. But rather than close his eyes, he looked up through the hot glare and saw a head, streaming with blood, suspended somewhere in the distance above him.

Head held aloft, he began to chase it, but it hid behind a cloud. The cloud began to shimmer like a smoldering cotton ball.

When he looked down, something huge stood in the way of his field of vision. He couldn't see across the fields. He had come to a town.

The thing that had so suddenly blocked his way was like a tomb. He seemed to see drops of sunlight cascade through the air and splatter across its surface. But after a moment, he discovered that the thing in his way wasn't just one thing, but a cluster of things divided by countless cracks and sawtooth fissures. The sunlight drifted down between the fissures as silently as dust.

He lost interest in the chase and began to walk down a road enveloped in pallid shadow by the *wutong* trees lining its flanks, whose densely interlocking branches blocked the intense sunlight overhead. He walked suddenly out of the bright daylight and into what seemed like a dark, gloomy cavern. The road unfolded ahead of him like a carpet of whitened bones. Every few paces, human heads hung suspended from poles on either side of the road. Drained of blood, they too had grown pallid and white. When he began to examine them closely, though, he found that they also looked something like street lamps. He sensed that these heads would begin to churn with gleaming blood at nightfall.

Pedestrians, each as drained and pallid as the heads on the poles, walked by. They all walked in the same monotonous way. He heard a strange noise. Two people approached each other and came to a halt just in front of him. He stopped too. The sound seemed to surround him. But a man with only one leg was limping down the road ahead of him. Compared with the other passersby, there was something terribly interesting, something very vivid, about the way this crippled man moved. He decided to abandon the two people he had seen a moment before and follow the cripple.

Soon, his surroundings grew perceptibly warmer. He was engulfed in a curtain of gold, and the dark gray figures he had seen pass by him on the road just moments before began to gleam. Insensibly, he glanced up once more at the dazzling head. Now he realized that the things in his way were in fact buildings. He recognized them because they were covered with open doors and windows. People filed in and out of the doors. Some of them receded, and some of them approached. He smelled something warm floating from the open window of a butcher's shop. He walked through the warmth, sucking at the air.

He walked to the river. The water was green and yellow in the sun. He saw a thick band of liquid ooze by. Boats bobbed on its surface like corpses. He noticed the willow trees on the banks of the river. Clumps of hair dangled over the water. The hair must have been smothered with fertilizer so that it could grow so unnaturally long and thick. He moved over toward it and held a strand next to a lock of his own hair. Dissatisfied with this initial examination, he tore off a strand from the tree and laid it out on the bank. Then he plucked a strand of his own hair, pulled it straight, and laid it parallel to the willow branch. Once again, he carefully compared the two. What he saw made him feel terribly dejected. He left the willows and walked toward the avenue.

He saw braids swinging in the distance. He saw two red butterflies towing the braids through the air. His chest felt tight and strange, and he moved insensibly toward them.

The fabric shop was thronged by a crowd of people. Spring had awakened their thirst for color. Chatter, as bright and varied as the bolts of silk on the shelves, echoed across the shop floor. Most of the customers were young women, women whose thirst for color was also a thirst for love. Their mothers surged into the store along with them, seeing in the colorful fabrics the youth of their daughters and memories of their own. Here, mothers and daughters could enjoy themselves on an equal footing.

With a friend at her left side, she walked happily out of the store. Her braids swayed as she walked. She usually didn't wear her hair in braids. She usually let it flow loosely down her back. But the night before, she had stumbled upon a beautiful old photograph of her mother. Her mother had looked particularly pretty in braids, and she had decided to try them out on herself. At her first glance in the mirror, she was surprised by just how much the braids had changed her. And when she fastened two red butterfly bows onto her new braids, she was nearly overwhelmed by the transformation. Now, as she delightedly walked out of the store, half of her joy came from the colorful bolts of fabric, and the rest from the sheer pleasure of the braids dangling behind her. She pictured to herself the way red bows would swing back and forth like real butterflies fluttering through the air.

But a madman came walking toward her. She was startled and frightened. And when she saw that he was leering at her, that strings of saliva were dangling from his lips, she gasped and began to run. Her friend shouted and ran after her. They ran for a long time and didn't stop until they had turned the corner onto another street.

Finally, they stopped, looked at one another, and burst into laughter. They laughed so hard and so long that they began to rock back and forth with merriment.

Her friend giggled, "I guess even the crazies come out when it gets warm."

She nodded. They clasped hands, said good-bye, and went their separate ways home.

Her street was just ahead, across twenty paces of pavement awash in sunlight and noise. There was a dilapidated clock shop at the corner. The clocks inside the window glittered. An old bespectacled man had sat in the shop for as long as she could remember. She glanced at him as she turned down the sunny little lane toward her house. After another twenty paces, she could see the glass panes of her building sparkling in the sun. The closer she got to her front door, the heavier her steps became.

Her mother, face drained of color, was sitting inside on a chair. She had been that way for three days now, scared of her own shadow, cowering just inside the door. She hadn't gone to work since it had started.

She asked her mother, "Did you hear the footsteps again last night?"

Her mother ignored her. When she finally looked up, her eyes were full of terror.

"No. I hear them right now," she said.

She stood behind her mother for a moment, confused and annoyed, and then walked over to the window. From the window, she could look out on the avenue and see the happiness she'd left behind just a moment before. But all she saw was the back of a man with hair down to his waist and a piece of burlap slung over his shoulders slowly limping down the avenue. She shivered insensibly, felt a wave of nausea, and turned back to face the room. Footsteps began to sound out in the stairwell, footsteps that resounded with all the familiarity of more than ten years of routine intimacy. Her father was back from work. She ran excitedly to open the door for him. The sound became steadily more distinct as she watched the top of her father's gray head move up the stairwell. She greeted him with a happy cry. Her father smiled and lightly patted her head with his fingers. They walked into the house together.

She felt how gently his fingers touched her hair and thought to herself that this was the only father she had. She remembered when she was seven, a strange man had come to the house and given her a rubber ball. Her mother had said, "This is your father." He had lived with them from that time on. He was always gentle, always nice; he always made her feel good. But a few days before, her mother had told her, "I hear the sound of your father's footsteps walking toward the house after dark." She was confused, and when her mother explained that she was talking about some other father, she felt frightened. This other father was a stranger. She hated him. She wouldn't let him into her heart, because she knew he would take away the only father she had ever had.

She heard her father's footsteps grow heavier as he walked through the door into the house. Her mother looked up at him with frightened eyes. She discovered that her mother's face had grown even paler than before.

2

Dusk was falling and the sky was dim. A sanitation worker wearing a surgical mask was sweeping a pile of garbage by the sidewalk. The broom hissed over the concrete, stirring up heavy plumes of dust from the pavement to drift in the dim light. There were only a few pedestrians on the street, but cooking steam and the distant sound of conversation had begun to pour from the lit windows of the residential buildings. Watery light streamed from the shop windows onto the street, and the languid shadows of listless shop clerks threw themselves onto the sidewalks. The sanitation worker took a book of matches from his pocket and ignited the trash pile.

He saw a pile of blood begin to burn, illuminating the darkness that surrounded it. He moved toward the burning blood, watching as the crackling mass sent little sprays of blood flying at his face. The drops of blood stung his face like sparks. He realized that he was clasping an iron rod in his hand, so he stuck it into the pile, and just as quickly pulled it back. It had taken just a second for the rod to begin to glow red with the heat, so hot that even his hand felt singed. And now those people were stealing toward him, so he began to twirl the rod, to trace glowing red arcs through the air. They continued to advance. They did not run away. They were too scared to run away. He stopped twirling and began to jab at them with the rod. He heard a long and boundless sizzle and saw tendrils of white smoke curl up into the air. He sank the rod into the dark ink, lifted it, and smeared the ink over the wounds he had just inflicted. Seared red welts turned a lush black. They warily stole past him. Elated, the madman bellowed, "墨!"

They had seen the madman as they walked by. They had seen the madman stick his hand into the flames, and then rapidly draw it back out because of the heat. They had seen how the madman twirled his arm through the air, how he had pointed and gestured at them. And they had seen him bend down and bury his fingers in a puddle on the sidewalk before drawing it back out of the water and pointing again. Finally, they had heard his incomprehensible shout.

They saw everything. They heard it all. But they were too busy to pay the madman much attention as they walked past.

It often happens that once everything quiets down after dusk, the movie theater is the first place to begin to liven up after dinner. The little square in front of the movie theater had already been divided up by countless feet into countless little squares, and even more feet were cutting across the pavement as they made their way toward the theater. The show had yet to begin, and those that had tickets in their pockets stood smoking cigarettes and chatting with those that didn't. Those that didn't have tickets had banknotes in their hands, which they waved at the people who had just arrived in front of the theater. A sign reading Sold Out hung from the closed ticket window, but even so, a mob had gathered in front of the window just in case the window were to suddenly open and a few leftover tickets appear. Shirt buttons, popped from their mooring by the crush, fell to the ground under their feet as they squeezed toward the window. A few people took tickets from their pockets and began to stream into the theater, taking care to say hello to those without tickets as they went by. Fissures began to appear in the crowd. The fissures grew until the only people left were people waving banknotes in their hands and stubbornly refusing to leave, despite the fact that the movie had already begun.

He felt the knife twirling in his hands, severing the air around him into fragments. After a spell of twirling, he directed the blade toward their noses. He saw each nose fly up from the knife blade and hover in space. Spurts of blood spouted from the holes where the nostrils had been; flurries of severed noses danced through the air before falling, one after another, to the ground. Soon, the street was engulfed by the noisy clamor of noses leaping and rolling across the pavement. "劓!" he cried forcefully, limping away.

Just at that moment, someone with a handful of tickets was discovered by the crowd. They swarmed into a circle around him. The sound of the besieged man's shouts retreated farther and farther behind the madman.

Pop music pounded through the cafe and flowed out through the open door into the street. A few young men followed the song out of the door, humming through the Marlboros dangling from their lips. They came to the cafe every day to drink a cup of Nescafe before strolling through town until well past midnight, talking loudly among themselves and every so often breaking into raucous song. They hoped that everyone on the street would notice them.

Just as they walked out of the cafe, they caught sight of the madman, who was waving his hands through the air and screaming, "剕!" as he advanced toward them. They burst into laughter, fell in behind the madman, and began to follow him. They pretended to limp like the madman, twirled their hands through the air like him, screamed like him. Whenever a few passersby slowed to look at the spectacle, they screamed even louder. But after a while, exhausted by their pursuit of the madman, they stopped screaming, lit a fresh round of cigarettes, and let him continue on his way.

The chopping knife sliced toward their legs, snapping them off below the knees like cucumbers. Everyone on the street seemed suddenly to have shrunk by at least a foot. Their knees slammed down on the sidewalk with heavy, rhythmic thuds. He saw their knees trample over the severed feet that lay strewn across the ground, pounding them into pieces.

The streets became lush with light. Moonlight splattered across the ground, merging with the lamplight streaming out of the shop windows. Dense patterns of light and shadow blanketed the pavement, like the underside of a leafy *wutong* tree at noon. Countless feet moved across the shadowy filigree, breaking the patterns of light into fragments that only came together again after they had passed. The moist evening breeze carried a cacophony of voices through the air. The windows of the residential buildings were still lit, but now they appeared cold and empty. Only a few people lingered inside, sitting quietly alone or together in pairs. It seemed that the whole town was strolling through the streets, streaming in and out of shops, ambling down the sidewalks.

He realized that everyone around him was naked. The chopping knife flashed toward the lower bodies of each of the men who walked past. All of them had a little tail growing in front. The chopping knife slashed at their tails. Their tails fell to the ground with a ponderous thump, like sandbags. Funny little balls rolled out of the bags after they broke on the pavement. In just a moment's time, they covered the street, careening across the pavement like Ping-Pong balls.

When she walked out of the store, the street made her think of two rivers moving in opposite directions. The few people who swerved into the stores looked like drops of water thrown off to the side by the river's current. In between the streams, she saw the madman. He was limping down the street, twirling his arms, repeatedly bellowing a single word: "宫!" But the people moving to either side of him seemed not to have noticed, caught up as they were in the enchantment of the evening. His hoarse screams were buried amidst the general clamor of voices as he walked past.

She started to walk slowly home. She walked as slowly as she could. For the past few days, she had taken to going out alone and strolling through the streets. She couldn't bear the silence that had enveloped her home. At home, the sound of a pin hitting the floor was enough to startle.

She reached her front door faster than she would have liked. She stood in front, looking up at the stars. The stars suffused the night sky with glowing light. She looked up at the brightly illuminated windows of the other apartments, heard the soft sound of conversation floating through the night air. She stood for a long time before she began to make her slow and hesitant way up the steps to her own house.

Just as she had pushed open the door, her mother cried out, "Close the door!" Frightened, she quickly shut the door behind her. Her mother, hair in disarray, was sitting by the door.

She stood by her mother for a moment. Her mother said, "I heard him screaming."

She didn't know how to reply, so she simply stood in silence for a moment before walking into the living room. She saw her father sitting blankly by the window. She went to him, calling softly, but he continued to stare out the window, replying only with an absent murmur. It was only when she began to move toward her own room that he turned to her, saying, "From now on, I don't want you to go out unless you really have to." Then he turned back toward the window.

She muttered something in reply, walked into her room, and sat down on the bed. The house was silent. She gazed at the window. A few strands of moonlight shimmered across the glass like raindrops. In the distance, the moon looked red. She heard the sound of teardrops falling on her shirt.

3

Flying sparks and the sharp sound of metal hammering metal cascaded through the blacksmith's shop. The smelting furnace cast a reddish glow on the bared torsos of the blacksmith and his assistant. Gleaming beads of sweat snaked down their backs like earthworms.

The madman stood at the door. His sudden appearance brought their hammers to a halt, and a piece of red-hot iron lay on the ground where the startled blacksmith had dropped it from his tongs. The madman walked into the shop, his mouth twisted into a strange smile. He knelt down by the smoking piece of iron, which had already begun to blacken and cool. The madman reached for the iron, and a hiss resounded through the shop. He immediately withdrew his hand and began to suck on his fingers. After a moment, he reached for the ingot again. He lifted it and held it against his face. A few tendrils of acrid white smoke began to disperse through the room. The blacksmiths stood, immobilized by fright and by the extraordinary stench that had filled the workshop. They heard him yell, "墨!" as he limped contentedly out of the workshop, down the lane, and to the street corner, where he paused for a moment before turning to his right. A truck drove by, burying him in a torrent of dust. He walked down the middle of the road and sat down. A few people followed him and began to stare. They were quickly joined by a few more curious passersby.

Her mother hadn't gone to work for almost a month. For the past few days she had sat, silent and immobile, in the front hall. And since her mother cried out in fright whenever she walked in through the door, her father told her not to leave the house at all. She spent every day in her room. Her father still had to go to work, so he left the house early and came home late. He no longer came home at lunchtime. She sat alone, wishing that her friends would come to visit. But when they finally did come and knock on the door, she dared not let them in. Her mother was so frightened by the sound that her whole body trembled. She didn't want her friends to see her mother like that. She could not help but cry as she listened to their footsteps retreating back down the hall.

Now, her mother was afraid even of daylight. Her father had closed all the curtains so that the whole apartment was bathed in darkness. Sitting in her dimly lit room, she felt herself growing distant from the sunlight outside, from the spring, from her youth.

In years past, she had walked through the spring sunshine with her mother and father at her side. And whenever they walked together, arm in arm, they would invariably stop and chat with a few friends of the family. "You still haven't married her off?" they would begin. And her father, with mock seriousness, would reply, "I'm not giving my daughter away to anybody." Her mother, beaming, would add, "How could we give her away? She's the only one we've got."

Many years ago her father had given her a rubber ball, and they had been happy ever since. They had always laughed and smiled when they were together. Father knew how to tell a joke, and Mother learned how to be funny from him. She was the only one who had never got the hang of it. She could hardly count the times when their laughter as they walked down the stairs had made the neighbors exclaim, "What is it with you people? Are you always so goddamned happy?" Father would always proudly reply, "I guess that goes without saying," and Mother would add with a generous flourish, "We're saving some for you, too." She always wanted to contribute something to the ritual, but she could never think of anything interesting, so she simply stood quietly by their side.

But now the house was dark and silent, even when the three of them were together. There had been a few times when she felt she just had to say something to her father, but the sight of him sitting blankly in the living room forced her back into her room. She shut the door behind her, went to the window, stealthily lifted a corner of the blind, and gazed outside. She watched people move back and forth across the street, watched them stand on the corner and chat endlessly about whatever was on their minds. Whenever she saw any of their acquaintances pass by, she couldn't help but cry.

She had spent several days at the window by now. When she lifted up the blind, she felt as if she was walking once more down those sunlit streets.

She was standing at the window watching the pedestrians through the glass. She discovered that they were moving like ants, swarming across the pavement, clustering around a single black spot. The circle around the spot was growing steadily thicker.

He sat cross-legged on the street, hair spilling onto the asphalt like willow branches. The sun had shone on the road for more than a month, slathering it with a layer of golden light, warming the hearts of the passersby. He stretched out his slender arms in front of him. They looked as if they were coated with antique black lacquer that had begun to chip and fade. He held a rusty saw, its blade no more than three inches long, in both hands and began to examine the blade.

She saw a few children shimmy up the trunks of the *wutong* trees that lined the avenue. A few people stood balanced atop their bikes. She wondered if someone was showing off his shadowboxing to promote herbal tonics. But if that was the case, why would he stand in the middle of the road rather than on the sidewalk? The circle kept expanding until the entire street was choked by onlookers. A traffic policeman rushed forward to clear the street. But as soon as he hurried to the other side of the circle, those he had shooed away merely rejoined the throng. She watched as the traffic policeman, realizing the futility of this repetitious task, took up a position on a spot that had not yet been entirely blocked by the crowd and started to wave newcomers around the sides of the circle. The black spot quickly swelled into an oval.

He shouted, "劓!" as he carefully placed the teeth of the saw against the bottom of his nose. His grimy black lips trembled, almost as if he were smiling. His arms began to rock back and forth, and with each spasmodic motion he shouted, "劓," as loudly as he possibly could. The blade worked its way into flesh, and blood began to seep out from under the skin. His dark lips turned red and shiny as the blood dribbled down from his nose. Within a few seconds, the blade hit cartilage with a soft scraping sound. His shouts died down, and he rocked his head back and forth, emitting low rasps. He looked as if he were happily blowing on a harmonica as the saw ate into his cartilage. But after another few seconds, he began to scream. The numbness of shock had passed, and severe pain had come in its wake. His face began to twist with the pain. He continued to work the saw back and forth, but the pain had become unbearable, and he quickly pulled the saw away from his nose and set it down on his knees. He threw his head back and gasped for air. The blood was flowing freely now, quickly staining his mouth and his chin red. Little streams trickled down from his face, tracing a tangle of intersecting lines across his chest. A few drops landed on his head, slid down strands of hair, and splashed on the pavement like little red sparks. He panted for another few moments before lifting the saw once again to the sun and carefully examining the blade. He extended a long and bloodstained fingernail to the blade and began to pick little bits of cartilage out of the teeth. Saturated in blood, they shimmered red in the sunlight. He went about cleaning the blade with extreme care, moving slowly, methodically, and clumsily. When he was finished, he once again lifted the blade to eye level. Satisfied, he pulled his nose away from his face with one hand while positioning the saw blade under it with the other. But instead of setting the saw in motion, he merely shouted for a moment and placed the saw back on his knees. Holding his nose between his fingers, he twisted it from side to side until it dangled loose from his face.

She saw that the oval was gradually dissolving as more and more people streamed away from the center to the edges. It began to look as if someone had accidentally dropped a bottle of ink on the ground. In the center, there was a solid black mass, surrounded on all four sides by splattered drops of ink. The children slid down the tree trunks like cats. There were fewer and fewer bicycles. The street was beginning to clear, and the traffic policeman, instead of standing nervously to one side, was once again moving around the perimeter of the crowd.

He held the saw up to the light for a long time before putting it down. He sat for a few minutes with his hands resting on his knees, as if in repose. Then he began to pick the grime out of the cracks in his feet with the tip of the saw. As soon as he had finished, he proceeded to stuff the grime back in. He slowly and lovingly repeated this process several times. Finally, he set the saw blade on his right knee, looked up around him, let out a great shout, "剕!" and started to saw. The skin broke under the teeth, white at first, but gradually growing lustrously red as the blood began to flow from the wound. With a few more strokes, the saw blade hit bone. He stopped sawing and grinned. Then his hands rocked neatly back and forth until a soft scraping once again issued from the saw. Within a few seconds, though, his face twisted into another scream. Beads of sweat rolled from his forehead. He gasped for air. The rocking slowed, and his scream faded to an almost imperceptible low wail. His arms fell limply to his sides. The saw chimed on the pavement. His neck tumbled against his chest. He sat, softly wailing. A moment later, he looked up, grasped hold of the fallen saw and once again placed it atop his knee, but remained motionless for another moment. Suddenly, as if he had come to a great realization, his lips shuddered into a kind of smile. He removed the saw to his other knee, bellowed "剕" a second time, and began to rock. Seconds later, the blade had cut through his skin and penetrated to the bone. His shouts came to an abrupt halt. He looked up, laughed for a long time, gazed at his leg, and finally produced a throaty rasp. Still rasping, his arms began to rock back and forth. His head bobbed back and forth, and with it, his body. His rasp and the rhythmic sandpapery scrape of the saw sounded together like a pair of cloth sandals swishing through a weedy thicket. A strangely appealing smile lit up the madman's features. Seen from behind, he might have been polishing a pair of nice leather shoes. Suddenly, the saw blade snapped in two with a sharp metallic chime. The broken pieces of the blade fell to the pavement. His body flopped backward and forward as if it had lost its balance. The pain came in waves, and with each wave, his body shivered like a leaf in the wind. He waited a few minutes for the shivers to subside. Then he picked up the two halves of the broken blade and held them up to the light and appraised each one in turn, as if he were trying to ascertain which was the longer of the two. This process was repeated, one blade after the other, again and again, until he finally cast one half of the blade to the side. He continued to saw at his right leg with the one that remained. But as soon as he had managed to make a gentle sawing motion across the bone, he screamed once more in pain. Picking up the piece that he had discarded, he once again compared the blades in the light. He dropped the second half back to the ground and tried the other one. But after only a few strokes, he began once again to compare one blade with the other.

She saw that there were fewer and fewer people clustered together, as if the drops of ink were shooting away, one by one, from the black mass in the center of the spill. The crowd had trickled away until all that remained was a narrow ring. Traffic was moving freely, and the traffic policeman had long since gone on his way.

He compared the two blades for a long time. Finally, he tossed them both aside, inspected each of his legs, and returned to his original cross-legged position. He examined his knees. Then he squinted up at the sun. His blood red lips began to quiver. He stretched his legs in front of him, fumbled at his waist and slowly pulled down his pants. When he saw his tail, his lips curled into a sluggish grin. He appraised it the same way he had examined the broken saw blade. He grasped hold of it with his hand and jerked it up and down. His head began to rock back and forth. He reached behind his back and fumbled for a rock. He splayed his legs out in front of him and lifted the rock above his head. He glared up at the rock for a moment, finally nodding his head with evident satisfaction. Bellowing "宫!" at the top of his lungs, he pounded the rock against the tail as hard as he possibly could. Then he began to roar.

Within a few seconds, the circle disintegrated. She watched as the spectators scattered like a flock of magpies frightened into sudden flight. In the distance, she could see something bloody sitting on the pavement.

4

Just before dawn, she was startled awake by her mother's scream. She heard her mother putting on her clothes as her father murmured something soft and indistinct. Her father would be telling her to stay in bed. She heard the bedroom door open. She heard her mother take up her customary position by the door. The chair emitted a few low, hollow squeaks. She imagined watching her mother sit down in the chair. She heard her father's heavy, helpless sigh. She could no longer sleep. The moon glimmered weakly through her window curtains. She lay under her quilt listening to her father get out of bed. As her father paced across the floorboards, she felt tiny tremors shaking her bed. Her father slumped back down on the bed, which squealed under his weight like a crying baby. After that, the house was so quiet that she could hear herself breathing.

The window curtains changed from pale silver to red. The sun was rising. She climbed out of bed, pulled on her clothes. She heard her father get up from bed and walk to the kitchen. The sounds he made were barely perceptible. He had grown accustomed to the silence. She too had taken to moving silently through the house. As she dressed, she watched the color of the curtains brighten until fiery shafts of light filtered through the cloth and onto her bed.

By the time she appeared in the living room, her father was just leaving the kitchen. Mother sat motionlessly in her chair. She couldn't repress a wave of sadness when she saw her tangled, unkempt hair. She hadn't really looked at her mother for a long time. And now she had discovered that her mother had grown suddenly and unrecognizably old. Unthinkingly, she reached out her hand to touch her shoulder. Her mother started, looked up at her with terrified eyes, and said, "I saw him last night. He was standing next to the bed. He was covered with blood." She too began to shiver as she remembered what she had seen the day before outside her window.

Father walked over and gently squeezed her mother's shoulders. Mother stood up and slowly walked toward the table. They sat and ate a little in silence.

It was time for Father to go to work. He moved toward the front door, and she returned to her bedroom. Her father hesitated by the door, turned, and followed her back inside. She had just begun to lift the curtain to look outside when she heard him whisper, "Why don't you come out and take a walk?" She turned, looked at her father, and then followed him out the front door.

But when they had descended the stairs into the light and he asked her if she was going to go see any of her friends, she could only shake her head in response. She felt lost outside the dim apartment. She felt like going back inside. She had grown accustomed to seeing the world through a square of glass that looked out on the street. But she followed her father out of the lane and into the street, stopping at the corner for fear that someone would come to visit. They would come up the stairs and pound on the door. Her mother would be so scared. She decided to stand guard at the intersection. Her father turned right. It was rush hour, and swarms of bicycles moved down the street to the accompaniment of chiming bells. She watched her father disappear unexpectedly into a shop down the block. When he emerged, he walked back and stuffed a handful of candy into her hand. She watched until her father had disappeared once more, and then looked down at the candy. She put one piece in her mouth and stuffed the rest into her pocket. She heard herself chewing, but no taste came. She watched a young man maneuver his bicycle at breakneck pace down the street until he was swallowed up by the swarming rush-hour traffic.

A friend from school sauntered up, saying, "Where have you been?"

She stared blankly back, then shook her head.

"Then why don't you ever answer the door? Why are the curtains always closed?"

She rubbed her hands together.

"What's wrong with you?"

"Nothing," she said, her eyes searching the street for the bicyclist.

"You look pale."

"I do?" she looked at her friend.

"Are you sick?"

"No."

"You don't seem very happy."

"I'm fine." She braced herself, forcing a smile. "What are you doing today?"

"The commodity fair. Today's the first day." Her friend took hold of her arm. "Let's go."

Her friend's footsteps rang out excitedly beside her. She thought to herself, "Forget about all of that."

The spring commodity fair was on another street. And the fair made people forget about everything else, let them live in the excitement of the moment. Winter was over. Spring had already arrived. They needed to change their lifestyle. They crowded together to browse, crowded together to explore. As they strolled between the makeshift stands that had been erected on either side of the street, they picked out new clothes, chose which household items to purchase, selected the kind of life that was to come. A megaphone hung from the roof of each of the concession stands, and each megaphone was blaring music and pitching products at earsplitting volume. They were buffeted by a chaos of sound at every step. But despite the deafening noise, the dizziness, and the fatigue, they squeezed and pushed their way through the fair, shouting excitedly to each other as they went along. And what with having to shout to be heard, the crowd itself was even noisier and more chaotic than the megaphones. Suddenly, one of the megaphones began to blare out a solemn piece of funerary music, thereby winning the battle for their attention. The crowd, laughing and elated, began to stream toward the stand, for rather than taking the music as an ugly prank, they found it amusing. And together they surged into the humor of the moment.

They had already given up trying to control where they went. There were so many people pushing behind them that the only option left was to keep moving forward. There was no retreat. She clasped her friend's shopping bags in her arms. Her friend bought enough for both of them to carry, but her eyes continued to shuttle hungrily between the various concession stands. She herself hadn't bought a thing. She had merely squeezed through the crowds, gazing all the while at the products on display. That was enough. Buried in the happiness of the crowds and the noise, she could forget all the things she had decided to forget. It was as if she were experiencing once again the way her family used to be. Hadn't her family been something like the fair?

They were driven forward until they were pushed beyond the perimeter of the crowd. The force at their backs suddenly disappeared. She stood there like a boat washed ashore by strong waves. The waves quickly receded, leaving her stranded. She gazed blankly back at the crowds, feeling hollow.

She heard her friend say, "I loved that skirt. Too bad it's too crowded to get back to it."

She too had seen the skirt, but she hadn't liked it as much as her friend had. She hadn't really liked any of the clothes on display.

She very much wanted to squeeze back into the crowds, but not for the skirt.

"Let's try to squeeze back through," she said.

Her companion, instead of replying, nudged her with her hand. She looked over to where her companion had pointed to see the madman.

He was standing a few feet away, spattered with dry blood, his hands twirling through the air. He was screaming something at the top of his lungs. He seemed just as happy and excited as everyone else who had come to the fair.

The boundless crowds of people swarmed toward him, and with a flash of his knife, their heads flew into the sky. Thousands of skulls collided in the air with an incomparably thunderous crash. The crash began to crack into smaller shards of sound until the shards came together once again in a bone-crunching sonic wave. The shattered skulls swirled through the air like broken tiles and began to fall. Blood rained down like sunlight. And at that very moment, a shining hacksaw materialized in his hands. It was soaring through their waists. Headless torsos stumbled across the ground, rolling fat brush strokes of blood across the pavement. The disembodied legs began to walk like automatons along the twisting and intersecting paths they made on the pavement. Every so often, two pairs of legs would collide and tumble helplessly to the ground. A steaming cauldron of hot oil appeared. Those bodies that were still untouched rained into the cauldron. The oil began to sizzle. One after another, bodies popped out of the liquid like flying fish and fell to the side. The sky now emptied of heads, which fell to the ground, carpeting the pavement and burying the severed torsos and legs beneath them. And bodies continued to fry and pop from the cauldron. He reached toward the people who continued to walk toward him and started to peel off their skin. It was like peeling posters off a wall, producing a marvelous tearing sound, as if he were shearing through bolts of silk. After they had been peeled, the subcutaneous fat began to bulge and dribble away from the muscle below. He stuck his hand through the muscle and began to pluck out the ribs. Their bodies slumped. Then he pulled at the chest muscles until he could see the lungs still heaving for air. He carefully tore open the left lung to watch as the heart continued to expand and contract with each beat. Two braids swung somewhere in the distance. Two lovely red butterflies towed the braids through the air.

She saw the madman staring at her once more, saliva dripping unceasingly from the corner of his mouth. She heard her friend cry out in surprise. She felt her friend grab hold of her wrist, and her legs began to pump up and down. She knew her friend was running beside her, pulling her away.

5

The spring snow had long since been forgotten. Peach flowers were slowly beginning to bloom. The willows by the river and the *wutong* trees on the sidewalk were a deep green. And the sun, of course, was sparkling even more brightly than before. Although spring had yet to run its course, they had begun to carry out all the familiar rituals with which they welcomed the arrival of summer. The girls embroidered their dreams with skirts from the fair, imagined the way the silky fabric would flutter around their legs as they walked the summer streets. The boys fumbled through their closets looking for swimsuits, and having found them beneath piles of summer clothes, imagined the way the water would sparkle in the summer sun. They kept the swimsuits on their dressers for a few days. Finally, they tossed them back into the closet. Summer, after all, was still a long way off.

The madman was sitting cross-legged on the street. The sun was splattering across the pavement, and a breeze blew overhead. Dust rose through the air and drifted away like a fine mist. The asphalt was sticky with sunlight. People streamed down the sidewalk, dragging their slanted shadows behind them. Their shadows, in turn, glided happily over the pavement, oblivious to the heat. A few of the shadows slipped under the madman's buttocks. He was single-mindedly assessing the blade of a kitchen cleaver. The cleaver had been picked out of a trash heap, and its blade was rusty and pitted with holes.

He turned the knife over and over in his hands until a sluggish grin of contentment lit his face and saliva dribbled down his chin. The wound on his face had begun to ooze, his face was swollen, and his nose was hugely distended. Pus dribbled down with his saliva.

An extraordinarily strange odor streamed from his body, relentlessly filling the air around him. Pedestrians, smelling this strange stench, felt as though they were moving through a dark place as they navigated past the madman, a place from which they escaped as soon as they moved past him and into the distance.

He set the cleaver on the ground and carefully examined it. He flipped the cleaver over and methodically appraised the other side before flipping it back to its original position. He stretched out his legs in front of him, and gnawed at his lips, his face contorting into a series of grimaces. After a few moments had gone by, he extended his long fingernails toward the sun, as if he were trying to disinfect them. He reached down and began—extremely carefully, extremely methodically—to peel off the dried blood that coated his legs like a thin layer of cellophane. He pulled the week-old film away from his skin, bit by bit. As soon as he had peeled one piece, he placed it carefully to his side and patiently set to work on the next patch. And when he had finished, he once again began to inspect his legs. Having determined that the blood had all been removed, he raised a handful of the dark red film to eye level. He looked through it at the sun. He saw a dark red square of blood. After he gazed at the reddish square for a moment, he moved the little pile to one side. Then, he began to pick up the pieces one by one and gaze excitedly through them at the sun. Another few moments of rapturous examination passed before he collected all the pieces together into another pile and sat on it.

He picked up the cleaver and lifted it to eye level. He saw a black rectangle surrounded by light. He held the cleaver over his lap, testing the blade with his fingers. He brandished the cleaver in the air above his thigh and screamed, "凌遲!" The cleaver pierced his thigh, and he cried out in pain. He looked down to watch the blood begin to seep from the wound. He inserted his fingernail into the wound, and discovering that it was shallow, discontentedly lifted the knife to the sun to examine the blade. After having run his finger along the edge, he smeared it with some of the blood that was dribbling from his thigh. Finally, he began to furiously grind the blade against the pavement. The friction produced a sharp squealing sound. His body rocked until sparks began to fly from the asphalt. The blade, hot with friction, fell from his hands. He bent to examine his handiwork, testing the blade with his finger. Dissatisfied, he set to his task with almost maniacal energy, grinding until beads of sweat began to roll down his torso. A moment later, he dropped the cleaver and teetered forward, panting and exhausted. Having caught his breath, he lifted the cleaver and inspected the blade, running his finger slowly along the edge. This time, he was satisfied.

He brandished the cleaver high above his head, shouted, and brought the knife down onto his other thigh. This movement was immediately followed by a single sharp moan. A second later, he broke into wails as his body began to flutter like a leaf in the wind. His hands fell limp to his sides, shuddering uncontrollably. The cleaver, still embedded in his leg, trembled with the motion of his leg. He trembled until the cleaver jumped from the wound and hit the ground with a dull chime. The blood welled from the wound and dripped to the ground like rainwater falling from the eaves of a house. After a long time, he groped for the cleaver by his side. The knife began to tremble. He hesitated, steadied the handle with both hands, and reinserted it into the wound. Wailing, he slowly cut a piece of flesh from his leg. His body shook violently, and the wails grew louder. These were no longer short and sharp exclamations, but protracted, almost bestial howls.

The pedestrians were terrified by the sound of his howls. The street was empty, but the sidewalks were packed with onlookers. They listened to his grisly howls through a haze of fear. A few brave souls walked toward the madman to get a closer look, only to return to the sidewalk white with fear. A few people tried to move back from the edge of the sidewalk, and those who had just arrived kept well away from the middle of the street.

The sound of his howls began to grow softer, but for some reason, this was all the more frightening. They drifted to their ears from afar, like ghostly wails, piercing and dark. They stood packed together, but each of the spectators felt themselves alone, hurrying through the dark of night, pursued by the sound of howls implacably ringing out somewhere behind them. They felt as if an enormously heavy weight was bearing down on their hearts. They felt their breath come in slow, grudging heaves.

"Someone should get a rope. Someone has to tie him up." A muffled voice broke out from the crowd. It was only then that the spectators began to talk, but the sound of their voices failed to rise above a suffocated whisper. Everyone agreed. A few young men moved quickly away, returning a moment later with a length of rope in hand. But no one would move any closer, and the man who had made the suggestion was gone. The wails were even softer now, mere gasps whistling weakly across the pavement. They could bear it no longer, but they did not leave. They sensed that if the madman wasn't captured now, his howls would keep ringing in their ears, no matter how hard they tried to escape. They suggested that the traffic policeman take care of the problem. It was his job, after all. But he refused to do it by himself. After several minutes of whispered negotiations, four young men offered to accompany him. They armed themselves with sticks to fend off the madman's cleaver and began to advance.

He had stopped wailing. He was no longer in pain. His body was burning, parched. White foam bubbled from his lips as he continued to hack desultorily at his leg. Although he seemed to be gasping for his life, he approached the task with as much earnestness and care as before. But within moments, his hands fell limp to his sides. The cleaver clattered to the pavement. He sat dead still for a long time, sighed, and fumbled for the cleaver.

Five men approached, rope in hand. One of them slapped the knife out of his hand with a wooden baton. The others immediately set to winding the rope around his limbs. He didn't struggle. He simply gazed laboriously up at them.

He saw five executioners approach, somehow managing to walk across the heaps of severed heads, scraps of flesh, scattered bones, and blood underfoot, as if they were on level ground. Behind them, he saw a blood-soaked mob. They had hacked off chunks of their own flesh until their bones lay exposed to the open air. They surged forward, following the lead of the executioners. Each of the five executioners was leading a horse-drawn cart with a rope. The horses' hooves rose and fell without a sound. The wheels of the horse carts rolled noiselessly over the heaps of flesh and bone. As they drew closer and closer, he realized why it was that they had come. He didn't try to escape. He merely gazed quietly in their direction. They were standing just in front of him. The mob of bloody skeletons at their back formed a large circle around him. One of the executioners clasped his neck, while each of the remaining four took hold of one of his limbs. His body rose from the ground, hung suspended in the air. He looked up at the blood red sky. Pieces of dried blood drifted in front of the sun. He felt a length of coarse rope being fastened around his neck. More rope was wound around his arms and legs. The five carts were arrayed around him, pointing in five different directions. The five executioners all climbed atop their carts. His body dangled from the ropes between the carts. He saw the five executioners all raise their black leather whips above their heads. The whips danced, snakelike, through the air, suspending themselves for a moment in midflight before cracking down onto the horses' flanks. Five horse-drawn carts galloped in five different directions. He saw his head, his arms, and his legs separate from his torso. His torso fell with a thud into the heaps already littering the road. His head and limbs hovered behind the carts. The executioners reined in their horses, and then they fell to the ground. The five executioners, followed by the mob of bloody skeletons, led their horses into the distance. Soon, they were all gone. He began to look for his head, for his limbs, for his torso. But he couldn't find them. They were lost among the severed heads, limbs, and torsos that covered the ground.

As twilight deepened, pedestrians were as few and far between as falling leaves. Most of the town was gathered around dinner tables laden with steaming dishes of food. Light streamed out of the apartment windows, brushing past the incandescent rays of the street lamps before merging with the moonlight. The entire town was dappled with slanting skeins of light.

They gathered joyfully around the table to see off the day. There was no reason to hurry, no feeling of being pressed for time. The approach of dusk was delightful. The day was fading behind them, but this was the most marvelous part of the day, because it heralded the liberty and leisure of the night to come.

They cheerfully ate and talked. The dinner conversation was relaxed and happy. Everything made them laugh. After a while they started to talk about the crazy things they had seen, the crazy rumors they had heard going around town. Some of them had seen the madman. Some of them had only heard about him.

They said they couldn't believe he had cut apart his own body with a cleaver. They registered their surprise. Finally, they burst into laughter. They talked about the madman, the one who had sawed through his own nose and sliced his own legs a few days back. They gasped and swore, and having run out of exclamations, were reduced to sighs. Their sighs had more to do with sheer amazement than pity. And as they talked, the terror began to fade. It was something unusual. They always discussed anything unusual that had happened around town. And when the first topic got stale, they would always move on to something else. That was what they did at the dinner table. That was how they passed the time until they were done.

They walked over to the window, stepped out on the balcony. They looked at the moon, felt the evening breeze blowing warm and sweet on their faces. They said to one another, "Let's go out for a walk," and strolled out of the house and into the streets. They knew that a walk after dinner was good for your health. The older people didn't feel like taking a walk. They sat by the TV and began to watch other people lead different lives that somehow reminded them of their own, while their children had already begun to roam the streets outside.

The parents weren't really sure when the kids had gone out, but they vaguely remembered seeing them around the dinner table.

When the young people began to fill the streets, the night grew thick with lively voices. They streamed under the street lamps, disturbing the tranquillity that had reigned moments before. Although they streamed into the movie theater, into the workers' club, toward friends, and toward love, the streets stayed busy. The crowds still poured in and out of the shops like waves, into one place and out of another. They walked for the sake of walking, hurried into the stores just so they could continue moving. Their parents walked for a few minutes to stretch their legs and went home. But the young people continued to walk deep into the night, because they needed to walk, because walking was what made them young.

But evening lasts only so long, and almost before it began, the deep of night arrived. The evening was almost over, they had already said their good-byes. They walked alone toward their respective homes. But they weren't lonely. They had enjoyed the evening to the fullest. There were many more nights to come. They happily made their way home, and the streets once again grew tranquil and still.

The shops were dark, and the windows of the apartment buildings no longer shone. Now there was only the gleam of the street lamps, the light of the moon. They had fallen into slumber. The town went to sleep along with them. But the few remaining hours until dawn would pass quickly, and the morning sun would rise once more.

The madman was still sitting in the middle of the road. The rope was so tight he hadn't moved a muscle since the afternoon. He sat, in a stupor, until the sun was about to rise. The sky to the east shone red. He opened his eyes and saw the red light. He heard the sound of howls echoing in the distance. The howls moved closer, growing louder as they approached, like a pack of wild beasts sprinting toward him. He began to rally, to grow excited. He saw something huge, burning red in the distance. Now he knew where the howls were coming from. He saw countless bodies falling through the flames. He leaped up from the ground and began to run toward the flames.

It seemed that he had just come to from a deep sleep. His chest gradually filled with a strange new feeling. His eyes struggled open. It was dawn. He saw a street lined by *wutong* trees, immobile as a stage set.

It seemed that he had been in a kind of stupor for a very long time. Now he was awake. The swirling mists in his head seemed to drift off into the air. And when they were gone, his mind was an empty room. But peering through a little window, he began to be able to see something, and at the same time, something new began to come into the room.

But now he had no sensation of himself. He wanted to move, but his body wouldn't move. He tried to shake his head, but his head wouldn't react. At the same time, his mind was getting clearer and clearer. But the clearer his mind became, the less he could feel his body. He had the distinct sensation that he was losing his body, or maybe just trying to find it. He started to wonder if you can lose your body. He was startled to find that it was gone.

He started to remember. There were so many things to remember. They were tangled together in a heap. He struggled to put them in some kind of order. He remembered that he was in his office. Two bright incandescent lamps, the northwest wind whistling over the roof. Dust coated the desk top, but the windows were clean. He remembered walking down the street in thongs, a crowd of people at his back. He remembered them breaking through the door. He was washing his feet, his wife was sitting on the edge of the bed. His daughter was asleep.

Now he was wide awake. He realized that it had happened last night. The morning clouds had begun to rise, the sun was on its way. He was certain it had happened last night. He had left his house last night. He was taken away last night. His wife had watched numbly as they took him away. His daughter had started to cry. Why did his daughter have to cry?

But he knew that he wasn't in the office anymore because instead of spotless windows and dust-caked desks, he saw a street lined with *wutong* trees. He didn't understand how he could have gotten here. He desperately tried to straighten his mind, but he still couldn't understand what he was doing here. He decided not to think about it. He felt that he really ought to go home. Maybe his wife and daughter were still asleep. His daughter's head would be cradled in his wife's arm. His wife's head would be resting on his shoulder. But somehow he was here instead. He wanted to go home. He wanted to stand up. But his body wouldn't react. He didn't know where he could have lost his body. He couldn't go home without a body. His heart would break if he didn't go home. Now he seemed to recognize the street. If he walked down the street for a few minutes and turned at the next corner, he would be able to see the windows of his apartment just up ahead. He was certain he was quite close to home. But he didn't have a body so he couldn't go home.

He seemed to see himself walking across campus carrying an armful of heavy books. He saw his wife, hair in braids, walking in his direction. They didn't know each other yet. They passed each other by without a word. He had glanced back to see a pair of pretty red butterflies. It seemed that the street was covered with snowflakes. He saw people pick the snowflakes off the ground and begin to read them. He saw a dead man slumped against a postbox by the side of the road. The blood was still fresh, still wet. A snowflake drifted through the air and settled on his head, obscuring half of his face.

The sun had risen, and hazy light slid silently down from between the clouds. The street began to stir with life. He watched people come in from the wings, appear on stage, talk with one another, strike poses. He was not among them. Something separated him from them. They were who they were, and he was who he was. He felt himself stand up and move toward the edge of the stage. But he remained in place, and instead of moving toward him, the stage simply retreated further into the distance.

She woke as the sun rose. She heard the sound of bowls clanging in the kitchen. Her father was already making breakfast. And Mother was probably sitting in her usual place by the door with the same look on her face. She didn't know how much longer this could go on, or how it might end. She really didn't want to think about it. Instead, she watched as the sparkling morning light began to slide through the curtains. She wanted to open them, to let the sun shine through the clean glass panes onto her bed, onto her body. She climbed out of bed and slowly began to comb her hair by the mirror. The face in the mirror was pale and lifeless. She wondered how she would make it through another day. She walked out into the living room. With a shock, she discovered that the room was suffused with light. The curtains had been thrown open. The sun swarmed through the open windows. Her mother's chair sat empty, one wooden leg bathed in sunlight.

"But where is she?" she thought. Her chest tightened with dread. She ran toward the kitchen. Her father wasn't in the kitchen. Her mother turned toward her and smiled gently. Her hair was neatly combed, and her face, though haggard and pale, had regained its familiar composure. Sensing her shock, her mother explained, "Just after the sun came out I heard him walking away." Her mother's voice sounded so tired, but she couldn't help smiling in relief. Her mother began to busy herself with breakfast, and she gazed for a moment at her back. Suddenly, she remembered something important and turned back toward the living room. Her father was already standing just behind her. Her father's face was as bright as the sun. She realized that her father already knew. Her father patted her gently on the head. His hair was white. She knew why his hair was white.

After breakfast, Mother picked up the shopping basket, asking, "What do you think you'd like to eat?"

She quietly added, "It's been a long time since I cooked you a good meal."

Father looked at her and she looked at Father. Father was at a loss, as was she. Her mother waited for a moment before repeating with a smile, "Come on. What do you want to eat?"

She tried to think of what she might want to eat, but nothing came to mind. She glanced once again toward her father.

He turned toward her. "What do you feel like eating?"

"What do *you* feel like?" she returned.

"I'll have anything."

"I'll have anything too," she said. She thought that seemed like the right thing to say.

"All right then. I'll buy anything."

The three of them chuckled. She said, "I want to come." Her mother nodded. The three of them went out together.

They walked arm in arm. Things were back to normal. They stopped to chat with some friends, who began to chat and joke with them just as they always did. She walked joyfully between them.

When they got to the corner, her father turned right on his way to work. She and her mother stood and watched as her father strolled easily and confidently down the block. After a few seconds, her father glanced back, and discovering that they were still looking his way, he started to swagger down the sidewalk. She and her mother burst into happy laughter.

But as she laughed, something occurred to her. Fearing that he would be too far away to hear, she began to shout his name. He stopped and turned. She shouted again, "Buy me a rubber ball."

Father froze, nodded, and walked away. She began to cry. Mother pretended not to notice. They began to walk forward without a word.

They saw a crowd of people gathered around in a circle. They stood at the edge of the circle to get a glimpse of whatever it was everyone else was looking at. They saw the madman. The madman was bound with rope. The madman was dead. His body, which seemed to have been varnished a deep red, was slumped against a postbox. A pair of sanitation workers were muttering to themselves as they picked up the body and deposited it on top of a bicycle cart. Another, grumbling under his breath, a pail of water in one hand and a broom in the other, approached the postbox. He upended the pail, carelessly swept the broom across the bloodstains on the sidewalk, and left. The cart slid away from the curb and down the street. The crowd began to break up. Mother and daughter continued on their way. Watching the madman's body being borne away by the cart, she felt a sudden surge of relief. As they walked, she began to tell her mother that she had seen the madman twice before, and that she had been so scared she had run away. Her mother couldn't help chuckling as she listened to her story. The sunlight was splattering across the pavement, and as they walked down the street, they were walking through the sunlight too.

6

That was how spring ended and summer took its place. No one saw it coming. They had been waiting for it since early spring, but no one heard its footsteps walking into town. They knew that they had left their jackets at home. But no one saw it coming. Until the very end, they imagined that it was still spring. Each day was as lovely as the next, and the season seemed to extend before them indefinitely. It was only when they began to walk the streets in shorts and skirts that they realized that summer had long since arrived. They began to hear the cicadas hum and the ice-cream carts chime. They began to think it was nicer to sit in the shade than to stand in the sun. And they grew even fonder of nighttime than before. The night breeze blew as cool as fresh water drawn from a well. When night fell, they poured from their apartments into the street. Some of them pushed chairs onto the balcony or set them outside the front door. Some people dragged bamboo cots into the lanes when it was time to sleep. Still more fled to the vast fields outside of town to stroll along the earthen embankments that curved above the rice paddies, savoring the moonlight, the croak of frogs, and the gleaming tracery of fireflies dancing through the air.

She always left the house after sundown, meeting her friend in the lane outside the house just as the evening mist had begun to rise. Her friend was wearing a skirt that was every bit as pretty as her own. They walked onto the avenue shoulder to shoulder. She could feel her skirt brushing against her friend's skirt, and her friend's brushing against hers. The street was awash in skirts. Skirts drifted out of open doors and narrow residential lanes into the street. Skirts merged, separated, and swayed through the streets as if performing some kind of intricate dance.

It was then that a madman came hopping toward them like a flea.

The madman was clean and well groomed. He gazed toward them, crying, "Sister, sister, sister . . ."

They tried to remember who he was. People used to say he had gone crazy during the Cultural Revolution. His wife had left him long ago. His daughter was in their class. People said that when he cried "sister," it meant that he was looking for his wife.

"I haven't seen that one in a while. I thought he was dead," her friend said. A second later she tugged gently on her hand and nodded toward a woman and a girl walking together. "That's them," her friend whispered, "that's his wife and daughter." But she already knew who they were.

She watched the woman and her daughter walk past the madman as if they had never met. The madman kept on hopping down the sidewalk, calling all the while for his "sister." The mother and her daughter kept on walking down the street. They didn't look back. They moved forward with ease and grace.

Translated by Andrew F. Jones

THIS STORY IS FOR WILLOW ✽ *Yu Hua*

1

For quite a long stretch I had been leading a bourgeois life. I lived in a place called Smoke. My dwelling was a bungalow overlooking the river. The structure of the bungalow was an unimaginative rectangle. The rectangle suggested how simple and definite my life was.

I greatly enjoyed the sounds of my footsteps as I went ambling about the small city. These were sounds that could only be made by the shoe heels of a stranger. Though I had been living here quite a while, I succeeded in protecting the pure sound of my footsteps. In the worldly noise of the street, my footsteps would not lose their quality.

I refused all dangerous interactions. Many times I encountered frightening smiles, smiles that doubtlessly conveyed a wish to be acquainted. I ignored them because I saw at a glance the treacherous intent behind the smiles. The smiler wanted to enter my life and possess it. He would use his coarse hand to pat my shoulder, then force me to open the door of the bungalow by the river. He would lie down on my bed, as if he were lying down on his own bed, and would carelessly shift the position of my chairs. On leaving he would sneeze three times in a row, and the sneezes would forever occupy my room. Even if I filled the place with smoke from mosquito coils, that would not drive him out. Before long he would bring along several people whose bodies gave off a dreary, kitchenlike odor. Maybe these people would not sneeze, but their mouths would be full of germs. With their loud talk and laughter they would coat my walls with germs. I would feel that someone had taken over my life, that I had been betrayed.

For this reason I now prefer to go out strolling at night. It is not that I doubt my resolve to refuse everything, but nighttime's obscurity lets me safely feel my detachment from the crowd. I have made a study of all the windows in the residential district and found that no window is without a curtain. This discovery is what gives me a good feeling about the residential district. The curtains separate me from people. But danger remains, and the separation is not made forcibly. While walking down the narrow streets of the residential area, I often feel I am walking the corridors of a hepatitis ward: I cannot give up caution.

Night is when I observe the curtains. That is when the light behind the curtains illuminates them mysteriously. When a breeze shifts one of the curtains, its decorative pattern exhibits a ghostly stirring. This makes me think of the river current outside my lodgings, with its glinting ripples. Its changeable, incomprehensible flow makes countless scenes of drifting snowflakes appear in my dreams. But more often than not, the curtains were motionless as they came before my eyes, and so I had ample time to observe their emanations. Though the differences in lamplight and the range of colored patterns affected my observations, I found that after simplifying away the lamplight and colored patterns, these emanations were identical to the gleaming eyes of a snake coiled in a road late in the night. Ever since this discovery, whenever I walk into the residential district I have a feeling of passing under the gaze of hundreds and thousands of snakes.

A long time after this discovery, on May 8, 1988, a young woman walked toward me. She walked toward me to make my life imperfect, or to make it more complete. At any rate, that is the effect her arrival was to have on me. For instance, on a certain day I would wake up in the morning to find that suddenly there was an extra bed in my bedroom, or that the bed I had slept on had disappeared.

2

In fact I had known the traveler for a long time. The traveler came from a place of thick-growing green grass. This I could tell from the pattern of veins in his skin. The first time I saw him was one summer at noontime. His upper body was naked due to the sweltering heat, and his skin resembled a tree trunk just stripped of its bark.

This was when I saw that the veins under his skin were as profuse as green grass.

I can hardly remember exactly when I got acquainted with the traveler. All I can say is, it seems like a long time ago. But I know that if I think back carefully, I can recall the color of the sky that day and the cry of cicadas in the branches. The traveler sat uprightly in the arch beneath the cement bridge. It was summertime, and the place he had chosen filled me with admiration.

The traveler was one of those people who put you at ease the first time you see them. The incomparably peaceful look of him, sitting straight-backed in that archway, made me walk toward him. While I was still thirty-some feet from him, I knew he would not come knocking on my rectangular door; he would not learn that my bed is a place for sleep and dreams; he would not take any interest in my chairs. While walking toward him I knew this would end in a conversation, but I was clear that the nature of this conversation would distinguish it from what is said between a woman washing vegetables and a man lighting coal briquettes. And so when he smiled at me, my smile also appeared quickly. Then we started talking.

Out of caution I kept standing outside the arch. Then I noticed that he made various gestures as he spoke, signaling that he was a person who welcomed others into the arch. I walked in, and he immediately put aside a few pieces of white paper that were spread on the ground. The pieces of paper were covered with lines drawn in pencil. The lines resembled the gestures he had just made with his hands. I sat down on the spot where the papers had been, knowing this would accord with his wishes. Thereupon, I saw his face smiling one foot away. Of all the smiles I had encountered in the little city of Smoke, that was the only safe smile.

He spoke with me in an even-toned voice that reminded me of the slow-flowing water of the river beneath the bridge. I felt accustomed to this voice right from the beginning. Judging from the way we got acquainted, which was not at all lurid or melodramatic, his even-toned voice seemed fitting. His gestures grew more simple, to let my attention focus on his voice. What he told me had to do with time bombs. The time bombs had to do with a battle that happened decades ago.

Early in 1949 the commander of the Kuomingtang army defending Shanghai, Tang Enbo, decided to give up Suzhou, Hangzhou, and other places to concentrate his forces in defense of Shanghai. The battalion of KMT troops garrisoned in the town of Smoke were pulled out all through the night. Before the withdrawal, a man named Goodman Tan directed his platoon of engineers to bury ten delayed-fuse bombs. Goodman Tan was a graduate of Allsave University, with a major in mathematics. On that starry night he buried the ten time bombs in an undetermined geometric pattern.

Goodman Tan was the last KMT officer to pull out of Smoke. As he left the town and turned his head to take a final look, the town under starlight seemed as quiet as a bamboo grove. Even then perhaps, he had a presentiment that he would stand again on this spot several decades later. This unfortunate presentiment came true on September 3, 1988.

Goodman Tan followed his unit to its posting in Shanghai, but when Shanghai was liberated, the long line that marched into military prison did not include Goodman Tan. Obviously he had left Shanghai prior to this. The platoon of engineers under him had been at Zhoushan. Goodman Tan disappeared around the time that Zhoushan fell. Among the many KMT officers and soldiers who fled to Taiwan, three were once attached to Goodman Tan's platoon of engineers. These three men are in nearly complete agreement that Goodman Tan died at sea, because they personally saw the sailboat he rode in being beaten to pieces by waves.

At exactly five o'clock in the afternoon on September 2, 1988, an old fisherman named Goodman Shen boarded a passenger steamer at Dinghai Harbor in Zhoushan, headed for Shanghai. He lay on an upper bunk of a cabin and passed a rocking night that seemed to last decades. Next day at dawn, the steamer pulled up to Wharf 16 in Shanghai. Goodman Shen disembarked among the crowd of passengers, then caught a trolley to the overland bus terminal in West Xujiahui. At seven that morning he bought a ticket for the bus departing at seven-thirty for the little city of Smoke.

In the morning of September 3, 1988, he boarded the overland bus to the city of Smoke. The passenger in the neighboring seat was a young man from a distant place. The young man had stayed in a certain Shanghai hospital for one month because of an eye disease. For some reason he had not gone directly home after his recovery, but was going to Smoke. While on the bus, Goodman Shen told this young person about a KMT army officer, Goodman Tan, who several decades before had directed his platoon of engineers to leave ten time bombs buried in the town of Smoke.

3

The traveler said, "That was ten years ago."

The traveler's voice was as steady as before, but at this point I perceived a change. I sensed the water beneath the bridge had altered its direction of flow. The traveler's manner clearly told me that he was recounting a different matter.

He went on to say: "Ten years ago, on May 8, 1988 . . ."

I felt that he was making a slight mistake, since May 8, 1988, had not yet come, and so I good-naturedly corrected him: "It was 1978."

"No." He gestured in disagreement and said, "It was 1988." He went on to clarify: "If it had been 1978, it would have been twenty years ago."

4

Ten years ago, on May 8, 1988, a stroke of misfortune had come into the traveler's life. Several months later, this misfortune had drawn him to the small city of Smoke.

Not long after May 8, his eyes began to shed tears continuously, and he was oppressed by a growing difficulty of vision. These developments were known only to him; he told no one else, not even his family. He dimly sensed that the weakening of his vision was related to what had happened on May 8. The incident was an utter secret that he could not bring himself to tell anyone. And so his hands were hopelessly tied as he perceived a cloudy obscurity steal over the scenes around him. This went on till one day, as his father sat on the porch reading a newspaper, he mistook his father for a blanket thrown over the chair; he walked over to the chair and grabbed his father by the collar. Two days later, nearly everyone who knew him knew that his eyes were headed toward darkness. He was sent to a local hospital.

From that day, he did not take responsibility for his own body. He let other people order his body about as they wished, but inwardly he was reliving that completely secret incident. Only he knew why his eyes had gone cloudy. He vaguely felt his body getting on a bus, and then getting on a train. After the train pulled into Shanghai, he was taken to a Shanghai hospital. On August 14, 1988, less than half a month after his admittance to this hospital, a young woman from out of town was on a large street in Hongkou District when she was involved in an accident with a Liberation-model truck that came speeding by. The young woman was quickly taken to the hospital where the traveler was under treatment. Four hours later the young woman died on the operating table. One hour before her death the chief surgeon knew there was no saving her, and so he discussed with her father—a distraught man on a bench outside the operating room—the sale of his daughter's bodily organs. This man, obviously befuddled by such a cruel and sudden blow, gave his permission without fully understanding what it meant.

Following the removal of the young woman's eyeballs, three ophthalmologists performed a cornea transplant on the traveler. On September 1, 1988, bandages were removed forever from the traveler's eyes. It felt to him like a folding fan was waved once before his eyes, and the darkness was gone. The traveler's father standing by the bed looked like a person, and in fact looked like his father.

The traveler kept sleeping in his sickbed for two more nights, and was not discharged from the hospital until September 3. That same morning he went to the overland bus terminal in the west district of Xujiahui, and there he boarded a bus to the small city of Smoke. His father did not travel with him, but saw him aboard the bus before catching the train home.

Instead of going home with his father, the traveler went to a small city he had never heard of, called Smoke. He wanted to look for a man named Yang, who had once had a daughter named Willow Yang.[1] Willow Yang had died at seventeen from an auto accident in Shanghai, and her eyeballs went to the traveler. This was told him by a nurse upon his recovery. He found out Willow Yang's address from the cashier's office in the hospital. She had lived at 26 Roundabout Lane.

A tarry asphalt road led from Shanghai to Smoke. On that gloomy

1 The name Willow Yang (Yang Liu) is composed of a family name, Yang, and a personal name, Willow (Liu). Together, the two characters also form the Chinese word *yangliu* (willow), which has poetic associations alluding to the trees planted by the voluptuary Sui emperor Yangdi.

early-autumn morning, the traveler used the vision restored to him three days before to gaze upon the hazy scenery outside his window. In the seat next to him was an old man who was dressed neatly, but whose skin nevertheless gave off an odor of fish. The old man kept his eyes closed till the bus passed Jinshan, then opened them. The traveler's eyes remained fixed on the scenery outside the window. During the last quarter of the trip, the old man began speaking. He gave his name to the traveler as Goodman Shen, and said he was from Zhoushan. The old man stated emphatically: "I haven't left Zhoushan since I was born."

He did not stop with this but went on to tell of the war of several decades ago. Throughout the conversation the old man was the only speaker, and the traveler listened with the same expression as when he was looking out the window. Like someone sitting at home reminiscing about past events, the old man told the traveler about a KMT officer named Goodman Tan and ten delayed-fuse bombs. As the bus approached Smoke, the old man's story had reached the point where Goodman Tan turned his head as he walked out of the small city of Smoke and saw that it looked as tranquil as a bamboo grove.

The little city approached from the bus had a drab, grubby look on account of the gloomy weather. The old man abruptly cut off his words and looked at the quickly approaching city with eyes like a dead fish. He said no more to the traveler. The incident of Goodman Tan's sailboat being smashed apart by waves was unknown to the traveler till several days later, when the old man encountered him again under the bridge's arch and had a long talk with him. It was during that talk that the traveler learned that Goodman Tan had died in the ocean.

The bus pulled into the station in Smoke. The old man and the traveler were the last two passengers out of the station. A few people were outside of the station to meet passengers. Two men were smoking, and a woman was calling to a passing cyclist. The traveler and Goodman Shen both left the station and walked together for about twenty meters. Then Goodman Shen stopped and viewed the little city in front of him in the noonday light. The traveler kept on walking; for some reason as he walked the scene appeared in his mind—as described moments before by Goodman Shen—of Goodman Tan turning his head as he left in early 1949 to look at the little city that looked as peaceful as a bamboo grove in the moonlight.

The traveler walked straight ahead. He asked a young woman waiting there the way to a hotel. She pointed forward, so he had to keep walking ahead. He was walking on a cement road. The trees on both sides looked dust covered and subdued under the overcast sky. But the walls of the houses seemed to reflect plenty of brightness. Even the old walls stripped of whitewash seemed to brim with white sunlight.

Later he walked to the side of the bridge and halted. At that moment there were thousands of citizen-laborers digging out the riverbed. He walked onto the cement bridge and stood there watching them. While he watched, several citizen-laborers unearthed a delayed-fuse bomb. From that moment, the matter of the delayed-fuse bombs took over his thoughts. But the young woman Willow Yang, who had lived at 26 Roundabout Lane, drifted from his memory like a withered leaf.

1

On the evening of May 8, 1988, I left my lodgings by the river as usual.

I carefully pulled the door shut, making the least sound possible. I did this to distinguish myself from my vulgar neighbors, who always made a sound like wood splitting when they shut the door. Then I walked onto the narrow street, which breathed an air of common life.

It was a night of unusually tranquil moonlight, but there was no light on the street. The moonlight fell on the eaves on both sides and gleamed like rain in the early morning. I walked along the street, which seemed coated with black paint. This street, like all streets in the city, always made me uneasy. Darkness did not make me feel absolutely secure. The common sounds that rang through the street by day only punctuated the silence now and then. They were like unappealing wildflowers raising their vile blooms toward me.

Walking down this street I did not encounter a single person. This was my most pleasant walk ever, so I did not immediately walk ahead to the thoroughfare crossing at right angles, but turned to gaze back into the darkness of the little street under the moonlight. The uneasiness of walking along it was now forgotten. I hesitated some time before walking on, unable to resist the temptation to walk back onto this street.

The hesitation I showed at the intersection did not last long. A man, or to put it precisely, an obscure shadow, showed itself on the small street. His footsteps were unusually clear. He wore shoes that were available at any store, and he had gone to the cobbler on a certain corner to have cleats nailed on. I could not stand the sound he made approaching; it was as if someone were rapping the window of my lodgings with a piece of scrap iron.

In this way, my hesitation at the crossroads was obliterated. I turned right and walked away from the intersection onto the avenue. I did all I could to walk faster, hoping the sound from those horrible shoes would die right on the street. But there was plenty of danger ahead of me as well. While trying to get away from the footsteps behind me, I had to avoid the pedestrians ahead. While avoiding them, I had to pass around roadside parasol trees and garbage cans, along with suddenly appearing pedicabs. This was the kind of tough going I had to deal with almost every night. The dark night offered protection, but moonlight and the lights on both sides of the street reduced this protection to pitiful fragments. When part of my body appeared in the lamplight, right away I would feel rattled and alarmed. Even though I walked along this avenue sometimes by day, the even distribution of light then kept me from feeling too obvious. I felt concealed in the midst of exposure. But nighttime was a different situation, and it was the situation at this moment. I was passing the restaurant that had been redecorated fifteen times. By now the footsteps behind me had disappeared; in fact I was surrounded by a confusion of sounds. According to past experience, I knew I was about to walk toward somewhere quiet.

Before long I came to an intersection leading off into the quiet, but the immediate problem was how to cross over the large street. I walked along so I could get to the little street on the other side. Sometimes it was easy to get across, but sometimes there were unexpected obstacles. Right then, it so happened that two bicycles collided in the intersection I was about to enter. The two cyclists exhibited two quite different postures as they flew from their vehicles, but they ended up falling on the pavement in the same manner. Both of them, after pulling themselves to their feet, let out yells like car engines starting. Their yells made all the people nearby run toward them. The crossing was immediately blocked, as if a mineshaft had collapsed. The way they milled about disgusted me, and they made a sound like a grenade exploding. At this point they began shifting leftward, with a movement like the crawling of a huge toad. This revealed my opening through the intersection, and I went across right then.

Now I was on a street leading to a residential district, a downward-sloping cement street. Up ahead was a crossing that looked empty and idle under a street lamp. It was an intersection made up of two equally narrow streets, and it held forth the quietness of the residential district. I walked through this intersection, and then into the residential district proper.

Houses looking utterly foolish in the moonlight gave hints of countless people's existence with the lamplight in their windows. The houses made me feel good inside: they seemed to imprison all the people I did not like. But the imprisonment was not hard and fast. Walking alongside the houses, I could make out occasional faint footsteps on the stairs inside. Their smug casualness struck me dissatisfactorily. Walking into the residential district, there was no way to avoid other pedestrians, and even bicycles and automobiles. But people on foot made me worry the most. The thought that their shoes might tread where I had walked was agonizing to me.

I wandered as before among the rays of light from the residential district's window curtains. It was a reverie in which my thoughts soared and darted like a bat. My imagination was carrying me toward a place I could not know. I felt that I was far from the residential district, going to a place made up of countless phantasmagorical beams of light. But such a state of affairs was not fulfilled at this moment on May 8, 1988. My gaze rested on a curtain patterned with many arcs and circles. I did not know that my gaze lingered, but I began to realize my thoughts had jumped off their usual track and were heading off like a little path winding in another direction. It was then that I felt a frightening thought come to me. I discovered myself trying to get past the curtain I was watching. I sensed that I was about to betray the curtain. I was thinking that this curtain obviously stood for a room, and inside the room there should be a person, or two or more people. Then what were the people doing? This common thought startled me. To make up for this, I suddenly turned away. I walked fast, hoping I would get out of the residential district quickly. I did not dare to lift my head again to look at curtains, fearing that the mistake of moments ago might overwhelm me. I was not aware as I crossed the intersection. I only felt that I was getting a bit calmer. I walked up the sloping cement road. Before long I had walked onto the broad avenue.

The avenue looked much quieter at this hour. The stores along both sides had closed, and only a few people were out walking. Then I felt I had gotten out of danger. Moonlight was spread over the avenue, and walking on it was like walking on a quiet river.

In this way I walked till I was beside the restaurant. Then I heard a sound that began from within me. The sound was far away but getting closer; at the very beginning it sounded like tree leaves in the wind. Then it seemed something like footsteps, as if someone in my mind were walking toward me. It was a shock I couldn't get over. Having gone ten meters past the restaurant, I could tell these were the footsteps of a girl coming toward me. It seemed that she walked into my heart barefooted. That is why the footsteps seemed so soft. Faintly, it seemed I could make out a pair of small pink feet, and my heart was incomparably warm inside, as if sunlight were shining on every inch of it. As I walked forward, she seemed to be walking toward the same place. When I finished walking on the avenue and turned onto the small, narrow street I had the feeling she was walking shoulder to shoulder with me.

I walked to the front of my lodgings in a daze. Pulling out my key, I heard the sound of her pulling out a key. Then, we put our keys into the lock at the same time, and turned them to open the door at the same time. I walked into my room; she walked in also. The difference was that everything about her happened in my mind. Closing the door, I heard the sound of her closing the door. Her door-closing sound was as soft as the sound of her removing a piece of clothing. I stood awhile in my room, feeling that she too stood there. Her breathing sounds were very faint and made me think of the wrinkle pattern on my face. Then I went to the window and opened it. A slight breeze off the river blew into my apartment. I watched the current sparkling and flowing in the moonlight. I felt that she too stood at the window, and we silently watched the current awhile. Then I closed the window and walked over to my bed. I sat on my bed for five minutes, then stripped off my outer clothes, turned off the light, and finally lay down in bed. I looked at the moonlight shining in through the windowpane, covering my room in silver light. She was lying in the bed too, just as quiet as me. I could not accurately determine whether she was lying on my bed or on another bed. I felt that I, like the moonlight, was immersed in the boundless tranquillity of night. I had never felt everything so suffused with the breath of elusive beauty.

2

My amazing inner experience of May 8 did not disappear with the end of that evening. The next morning upon waking I immediately received an unfamiliar impression. I sensed something different from before in my apartment, as if something had been added or something taken away. This impression made me realize I was not a solitary person. Another persona had brought her part of life and added it to my life. I showed no loss of composure over this, nor did I go wild with delight. Just as I accepted the fact of the river flowing outside my room, I accepted her arrival.

Lying on the bed, I felt she had already gone out of my inner heart. While I was asleep she had gotten out of bed and was now in the kitchen preparing breakfast. I ignored the fact that there was no kitchen. I was clear on this point, but I could not persuade myself there was no kitchen because she was in the kitchen. Her arrival even caused my lodgings to change in appearance.

I felt it was time to get out of bed. It would not do to keep sleeping until she finished making breakfast. Having gotten up, I first drew open the curtains. Since I had been asleep, she had not opened the curtains when she got up. This was the minimum consideration a wife should show. As I went to open the curtains I discovered there were no curtains, and sunlight was pouring in. The river current beneath my window reflected an incomparable brightness. Several barges cruising on the river were casting bright reflections on the surface. A few green vegetable leaves floated beneath my window.

Leaving the window I went toward the kitchen. Even though I knew there was no kitchen, I walked toward it and into it. Owing to the kitchen's narrowness, I brushed against her body on my way to the sink. I seemed to hear the rustling of her clothes. Then I began to brush my teeth. As I brushed she seemed to say something, but it was not clearly audible. The sound of my toothbrushing rudely drowned out talking sounds, so I stopped brushing. I glanced toward her, and she was looking at me. I saw the look in her eyes, and it gave me a start. Up to this point, she had existed within my twilight state, but now I was seeing the very real look in her eyes. Though I could not get a precise look at her eyes, her glance had entered my vision with amazing clarity. Her glance was quite calm, with no irritation at my failure to understand her words moments before. The look in her eyes expressed her anticipation of an answer or further question from me. But I had turned my face away and was at a momentary loss because of the shock I felt. Thus her glance shifted away, obviously not attaching great importance to the words just spoken. As her glance shifted, I seemed to feel her face turning away. Following this, she left the kitchen.

A moment later I too left the kitchen. As I walked into the bedroom, I sensed her standing by the window. I walked over and stood beside her. I looked at her from the side, but was not able to see the look in her eyes clearly. She was staring at the current of the river beneath the window.

3

Several days later in the afternoon I left my lodgings. I decided to go out for a stroll because my lodgings were starting to make me feel ill at ease.

The girl who had walked toward me many days before had given me a look the next day that imposed a flaw on my hitherto perfect life. Her glance moved about my room all day, but I could hardly capture it. She seemed to have been living with me for twenty years, and she seldom looked right at me. She seemed to prefer gazing out of the window at the flowing river. Her glance always drifted beyond my line of sight, uncatchable. I could no longer suppress the mounting frustration this caused me.

One afternoon, many days later, I decided to deal with this by abandoning her briefly. She was standing in front of the window, staring at that accursed river. I walked toward the doorway, and as I did so, the whole room resounded with my footsteps. I had never taken such emphatic footsteps. This was my way of conveying to her that I was leaving. I hoped she would fix her gaze on me, but when I reached the door and turned my head, she was still watching the river. Unquestionably, this reinforced my intention of getting rid of her for a while. I opened the door and walked out, then closed it even more loudly than my vulgar neighbors. I did not leave immediately, but instead threw the door open again. I sensed that she stood unresponsively at the window as before. This time, the door closed with a sound as despondent as my state of mind. Walking forward, I heard my footsteps sounding like dry tree limbs falling on the ground.

Walking onto the street in broad daylight, I lost my normal alertness. This was the first time in a great while that I was not very cautious leaving my apartment. I no longer felt the threat posed by people walking on the street. This was when it dawned on me to what extent she had ruined my earlier life. Now, as I walked on the street, I felt my footsteps were disordered. My glances did not probe tentatively as before: there was a crazed recklessness to them, and they plunged without restraint into the spiderweb of glances from passersby. I wanted to hold back these glances of mine, but I could not conquer my compulsion. As I walked forward, I did not pass up any of the glances in my direction. The avidity with which I took in those glances was astonishing even to me. Some glances met mine timidly, and some were full of antagonism. But I did not show the slightest hesitation at this. Under the thrust of these challenging glances, my own glances demonstrated plenty of self-assurance.

I felt I was swaggering down the street, enjoying the thrill of my brusque forward motion. When turning corners or crossing a street, I no longer gave signs of vacillation, but moved as decisively as a stone thrown into water. I had no idea where I was walking, but I sensed that the glances from others' eyes were getting farther apart. Only when I saw no more glances did I halt my steps. At this point, I realized I had reached the residential district.

I was standing beside an open door, through which I could see a young man in a black jacket talking with an old woman. The woman sat in the doorway shelling peas. The voice she spoke with made me think of an old newspaper in the wind. Her gaze strayed from my line of sight as I watched, and she did not look at the young man either. Her gaze skipped back and forth from the peas in her hands to an electric pole in front of her. She was apparently reminiscing about something that had faded away.

I was ready to leave when something happened. A person behind me made a sound composed of three syllables. The sound obviously represented someone's name. I turned my head and saw an equally old woman. The two old women started talking in voices that seemed preserved in brine, punctuated by laughter like pieces of dried fish slapping together.

The young man stood up, perhaps because the old woman had finished her reminiscing. He was close to me in stature. He stood up and walked toward me, glancing at me a moment. The look in his eyes gave me a shock: it was the look I had seen while brushing my teeth in the kitchen. Walking away, he passed close by me.

My amazement did not last long. As he walked ahead, I knew what I should do next. I too walked forward. The discovery I had just made caused me to follow him without intending to.

His placidness as he crossed the intersection struck me as gracious and familiar. He kept on walking up the slope of the cement road, lifting his legs in the same way as I did. Soon he reached the intersection and stood there hesitating for quite some time. I knew he was preparing to cross the avenue and step onto the sidewalk on the far side, heading either to the right or the left. He was waiting for an opportunity, waiting for an opening so he could cross over. Then he made a sudden dash across; I dashed too, because the opening revealed itself to us at the same time. The anxious helplessness he showed while running filled me with shame. From watching him I saw for the first time my own pathetic appearance the countless times I crossed the street.

After this, his manner grew calm and collected. It was the calmness both of us ought to have. Both of us had stepped onto the sidewalk. He began walking placidly ahead. His quietness made me quite satisfied with my own manner of walking. His bearing while walking could not have been more ordinary, which had always been my attitude when going on the street. He walked this way to let himself disappear among the passersby. His method of concealing himself was exactly the same as mine. Nobody would notice him now, except for me. Watching him was like watching myself walk.

He stopped walking at the bungalow near the river and pulled a gold key from his right pocket. I also had a gold key in my right pocket. He opened the door and walked in. He showed extreme caution as he closed the door, making the same sound I made leaving my lodgings. But I did not walk into this bungalow by the river; I stood outside the bungalow beside a cement electric pole. It was at this moment that my bewilderment began. I no longer knew what to do with myself. Before that I had followed his tracks without thinking, and now that the following was over, I was like a leaf drifting from a branch to the ground, not knowing what to do next. I felt that standing there this way was too noticeable, so I began walking nearby while thinking about what I should do.

Just then he walked out holding a sheaf of white paper and a pen. After closing the door he walked to the left, but did not go far before he turned again. He went around a garbage can, walked down steps to the riverbank, then climbed to an arch in the concrete bridge. He appeared to be at peace with himself as he sat beneath the arch of the bridge.

I did not go down the stone steps, because my bewilderment was not over. I was wondering what had prompted me to follow him, and I kept wondering for quite some time before the answer came to me: the look in his eyes was my reason for coming here. But there was no more need to follow him, now that he was sitting uprightly in the arch of the bridge. What was I to do next? Not knowing put me on edge. I walked back and forth on the concrete bridge, while below me within the arch was the glance I had seen many days before in the kitchen. I began to imagine things about the eyes under the bridge. The glance that had agitated me was perhaps staring at a dirty piece of tile, or lingering on a wisp of moldy straw. When barges passed on the river with a stupid chugging of diesel engines, that gaze would fix itself on the rolling black smoke.

I decided to go down to the arch. I did not think two people in the arch would make it seem cramped. So I walked down the slope along the bridge, then down the stone steps. I stood awhile at the river's edge, with him sitting hardly more than ten meters away. His gaze was fixed on the papers in his hand. This was much better than the image I had just imagined. And so I walked toward him.

He raised his head to look at me. His glance made me feel a bit nervous. In fact, he did not show the slightest trace of surprise. He looked at me with complete calm, making me feel I was not walking toward him presumptuously, but upon his invitation. I climbed in the opening and sat face-to-face with him. Examining the look in his eyes from less than three feet away, I verified that it was much like the look I had seen in my kitchen. But his eyes were quite different from the girl's eyes I had sensed in the kitchen. His eyes were long and narrow, but I had sensed the eyes of the girl were much wider.

I told him: "One evening several days ago a girl came into my mind. In some way that is not at all clear, she spent the night with me. The next day when I woke up she did not leave, and I caught a glimpse of the look in her eyes. Her eyes had the same look that you are looking at me with now."

4

After listening he did not show the suspicion I feared, but made me feel he firmly believed my words. He said, "What you are talking about sounds like the beginning of something that happened to me ten years ago."

"Ten years ago," he told me, "on May 8, 1988, it was a beautiful moonlit night."

He was walking as usual on a street in his hometown. The street-lights of his town were orange, and the moonlight shone on their illuminated circles like soft rainfall. He walked along a street that was as detached as his own mood. For a long time he had liked to go out walking by himself. He liked the far-flung stillness of the outdoors. But that night on his habitual walk something unusual happened. For no reason at all he began thinking of a certain girl. He had been walking on a bridge where he stood quietly awhile to watch the river in its ceaseless flow. He was walking toward the base of the bridge when the girl appeared in his mind, and as he walked down the slope from the bridge his thoughts recoiled from her in alarm. He carefully examined what he was imagining and found that the girl was a total stranger. It was obvious she was nothing like the small number of girls of whom he had an impression. He felt it was inconceivable that he would think of a completely strange girl for no reason. He understood her presence to be his own flight of fancy and was convinced it would be forgotten before long, just as words on a sheet of paper are forgotten. He began walking homeward, and the girl walked along in his imagination. He ceased being alarmed, thinking she would slip away from his imagination before long. Thus it seemed natural, when he opened the door to his house, that she went in with him. He came to his own bedroom, removed his clothes and lay down. It made the corners of his mouth turn up with a smile to feel her lie down as well. He was amused that his flight of fancy had lasted from when he was on the bridge until now, but he knew the next day when he awoke it would certainly be gone. In complete repose he drifted off to sleep.

Awakening early the next morning he was immediately aware of her, and more distinctly than last night. He sensed that she had already gotten up. She seemed to be in the kitchen at that moment. He lay on the bed recalling the previous night's experience and was startled by a discovery: last night he had still been sure she existed in his imagination, but this moment's recollection of last night's experience were completely authentic, as if it had truly happened.

He told me: "I went to the kitchen early that morning to brush my teeth, and I saw the look in her eyes."

The sight of that look in her eyes was only the beginning. For a long stretch of days after that, not only was there no forgetting her, but she grew increasingly distinct and complete in his imagination. Gradually her eyes, nose, eyebrows, lips, ears, and hair appeared as had the look in her eyes, and they were incomparably distinct. Often he was made to feel that she was an utterly real person standing before him. But when he reached his hand out to touch her, there was nothing at all. He worked at drawing her image on paper with a pencil. Though he had never studied drawing, after a month of trying he managed to depict her features with perfect accuracy.

He said, "She was an attractive girl."

He pasted the pencil drawing on the wall before his bed. Afterward, nearly all his time was spent in staring at this picture, right until his father discovered he had an eye disease, and he was forced to leave the pencil drawing.

During his illness he stayed in three different hospitals, the last being in Shanghai. All this time, no surgery was performed on him until the afternoon of August 14, when he was wheeled into an operating room. On September 1 the gauze was removed from his eyes. That same day, he learned that on the morning of August 14 a seventeen-year-old girl had been admitted to the hospital following an automobile accident and had died on the operating table at 3:16 that afternoon. Her eyeballs had been removed, and after that, the doctors had performed a cornea transplant on him. Following his release on September 3 he did not return home; instead he found out the dead girl's address and came to Smoke.

His gaze fixed upon a willow tree on the bank for a long thoughtful spell before a flicker of relief played across his features and he said, "Now I remember. The girl's name was Willow Yang."

But later he did not go knocking on the large, black-painted door at 26 Roundabout Lane, which he had found out was her address. This change in plan was due to his encounter on the overland bus with a man named Goodman Shen. Goodman Shen told him about ten time bombs buried early in 1949 when KMT troops were pulling out from the small city of Smoke, and about highlights from the life of a KMT officer named Goodman Tan.

On April 1, 1949—the day after the small city of Smoke was liberated—five time bombs went off, one after another. The master sergeant of the Fifth Platoon in a certain PLA company and a mess-hall worker named Cui were killed in the explosions; thirteen PLA soldiers and twenty-one citizens (including five women and three children) were injured to a greater or lesser degree.

The sixth time bomb exploded in the spring of 1950, while a public trial was being held on the exercise yard of the city's only school. Three evil bullies were about to receive the death penalty when the bomb exploded beneath a temporary platform in the yard. The three bullies, along with a town mayor and five militia members were blown to smithereens. An old man named Li Jin can recall to this day the huge boom, and how heads, arms, and legs went flying every which way in the smoke.

The seventh time bomb went off in 1960. The explosion occurred in People's Park. The time of the explosion was late at night—after 10:00 P.M.—so no death or injuries resulted. But the park was in a shambles for eighteen years afterward. As an indictment against crimes by Chiang Kaishek, the park remained in a devastated condition until 1978 before being repaired.

The eighth time bomb did not explode. On the very day he and Goodman Shen arrived in Smoke by bus, the young man stood on the concrete bridge. The volunteer workers digging the channel under a gloomy sky covered the riverbed like ants, as if they made up the flow of another river. But their flow appeared to be haphazard. Listening to the clamor that floated up from the riverbed, he seemed to feel it as a sultry vapor rising and spreading in all directions. In it, he discerned a sound of metal against metal, followed by a terrified shout from one of the laborers. The worker ran toward the bank, but the mud seemed to hold him in an agonizing struggle. Right after that, all the nearby laborers dashed away helter-skelter. That was how he had seen the eighth bomb.

A few days later he met Goodman Shen again on the same bridge. Goodman Shen walked toward him in dazzling sunlight, but the look on his face called up thoughts of a dusty old wall. Goodman Shen walked up to him and told him: "I am going to leave."

He looked wordlessly at Goodman Shen. Even as Goodman Shen was walking toward him he had sensed that the old man would leave.

The two of them stood for a long time against the concrete railing, while Goodman Shen told him about the eight time bombs described above.

"There are still two bombs that have not exploded," Goodman Shen said.

Goodman Tan had buried the ten time bombs according to the pattern of an undetermined geometric figure. Goodman Shen made this point clear for the first time, and remarked in addition, "If one more bomb explodes, the position of the tenth bomb can be determined from the position of the nine exploded bombs."

But in fact those two other bombs had not exploded. Therefore Goodman Shen said, "Even Goodman Tan himself will not be able to tell their positions now." Finally Goodman Shen said, "After all, thirty-nine years have gone by."

After this, Goodman Shen had nothing to say. He stood on the bridge gazing at the small city of Smoke. As he left, he said he had seen it bathed in moonlight.

On the evening of September 15, 1971, a furnace at the fertilizer plant had suddenly exploded with a deafening sound. Five eyewitnesses reported seeing the furnace rise into the air and fly apart like a glass bottle. The furnace tender on duty that evening, Wu Dahai, narrowly escaped being blown to pieces. At the time of the blast he was squatting in a restroom close by, and the shock wave knocked him unconscious. Wu Dahai died of a heart attack in 1980; on the night before his death, the scene of the furnace explosion came before his eyes. He told his wife that he had first heard an underground explosion before the furnace flew up and blew apart.

The young man told me: "In fact, that was the explosion of a bomb. The explosion of the furnace covered up the truth. So there is only one last bomb that hasn't exploded."

And he continued, "A little while ago I was in the residential district talking with a woman about this. She was Wu Dahai's wife."

1

The young woman who came to me on the evening of May 8 and who the next morning revealed the look in her eyes to me occupied my life for a long time afterward. From then on, my not-very-roomy life had two people in it.

In the period that followed I sat for whole days at a time, sensing her walk back and forth in the room. On the good days, when her mood was carefree, she would sit on the bed and gaze at me with that intoxicating look in her eyes. But more often she seemed discontented. She liked to walk back and forth in the room, making me feel that a gust of late-night wind was blowing about inside my room. I withstood these acts that ignored my very existence, looking for any excuse that would absolve her. I realized that my room truly was a bit cramped, and understood her ceaseless pacing as a possible way of enlarging the room. But swallowing my irritation in silence did not move her. She appeared not to care how much effort it took to overcome the flames of anger within me. Her unresponsiveness finally set off my anger, and one day, as evening drew near, I shouted at her, "Enough! If you want to walk around go out to the street."

My words doubtlessly hurt her, and she walked to the window. She absorbed herself in gazing at the river, showing her hurt and disappointment. I was also sunken in disappointment. If at that moment she had made for the door and left, I do not think I would have stood in her way. That evening I went to bed early but did not fall asleep until quite late. I did a lot of thinking and recalled the wonderful life I once had. Her coming had shattered the life I had had, and because of this, I burned with anger for hours. She was still standing before the window when I fell asleep. I felt that the next day when I awoke she might be gone. It would be better if she could make this a permanent departure. I would not miss her or long for her. I seemed to see a green leaf falling from a branch, then gradually yellowing in the mud and finally turning to dust. Her coming and her going away would be much like such a leaf to me.

But waking up in the morning, I sensed she had not left. She sat next to the bed regarding me with an occasional flash in her eyes. Something told me she had been sitting that way all night. The look in her eyes was as gorgeous as could be, and being fixed on me, it made me feel nothing had happened. Yesterday's anger seemed quite empty now in retrospect. She had never looked at me so long before, and therefore I could not help feeling apprehensive as I gazed at the look in her eyes. I was apprehensive that she would turn her eyes away. I lay on the bed without moving, afraid that the slightest movement would make her think something was happening in the room and she would turn her gaze elsewhere. For the moment, I needed to preserve this absolute tranquillity. Only in this way would she not turn her gaze away; this way she might forget that she was gazing at me.

Her prolonged gazing made me feel I was gradually able to see her eyes. The look in her eyes seemingly grew into visibility right beside me, and her eyes slowly showed themselves. At this moment a dim haze came across my field of vision, but I could still see her eyes distinctly. With the appearance of her eyes, her eyebrows were also gradually revealed. Now I knew why the gleam in her eyes was so bewitching—it was because of the soulful, limpid eyes that the gleam emanated from. Then her nose appeared. I dimly discerned a droplet falling from the tip of her nose; then I saw her lips, which thrilled me to no end. Her lips looked a bit moist, and a few black hairs grew near their corners like willows on a riverbank. After that, her entire head of black hair came into view, and by this point, her face was distinct and whole. The only thing I did not see was her ears, which were covered by her hair. Her black hair surrounded her face with perfect serenity. I wanted very much to reach out my hand and caress her hair, but I did not dare. I feared that all this would disappear before my eyes. At this moment, I discovered my tears were flowing.

From that day on, my tears ran without stopping. My eyes ached constantly. I was somehow aware of a bunch of green grapes in one corner of the room. I began to sense that a change had come over the room. My bed and chairs gradually lost their solid appearance and seemed puffed up like bread. For more than half a month I had not enjoyed the beautiful sight of moonlight shining through the windowpane at night. In daytime, the sun's light looked dim to me. Sometimes I would stand unmoving by the window, where I could hear the water flowing but could not see the riverbank. I felt that the river had grown enormously broad.

When my tears were flowing all day, she did not walk constantly around the room as before. She began to stay at my side, keeping extremely quiet, as if she knew my agony. She seemed weighed down by constant sorrow.

While all the objects around me grew ever more blurred, she became increasingly distinct. As she sat on the chair I seemed to see the slight lifting of her left foot and the shoe on her foot. The shoe was black and let a small area of white stocking show. She was wearing a long skirt. Her skirt dazzled my eyes, and I could not quite make out its color. But it made me recall the residential district that now was so far away, where the many curtains in lamplight had made me think of her skirt. As time went on, I could even make out that her height was somewhere around 165 centimeters. I did not know how I came to this conclusion, but I had no doubts it was correct.

Two more weeks passed, and the tears stopped running from my eyes. Awakening that morning I could feel the ache was gone, which brought an all-embracing serenity. I sensed that she was in the kitchen. I lay in bed looking at the sunlight that came into the room as dimly as before.

From the river beneath the window came the sound of oars, giving a floating quality to this serene moment. The oar sounds gave me a soothing feeling, as if a major illness were on the mend. I felt that all disturbances were flowing into the distance, and what was to follow would be a space of lasting tranquillity. I realized that my past life had gone on too long, and now it was time for a new beginning. I felt a fresh stream of blood flowing in my veins. She was that fresh blood. Because of her coming, I saw a ravishing flower bloom in a green patch of grass. From this time on, my lodgings would exude the air of two people living together, and I knew ours would be an air of harmony and completeness.

I sensed her coming out of the kitchen. She was overflowing with joy as she walked toward my bed, as if she knew my eyeache was gone and had heard my monologue of a moment ago. She walked over and sat on my bed, as if to express complete agreement with what I had been thinking. Her look told me she wanted to plan together for our life to come. She was completely correct in wishing this; her take-charge attitude was just what I had been hoping for. And so I began a discussion with her.

I asked again and again what her thoughts were. She did not answer, but only looked at me silently. Finally I understood that her thoughts were none other than my thoughts. I proceeded to cast my glance here and there around the room. The first thing I noticed was that my windows had no curtains. It struck me that I ought to have curtains in my own lodgings. My life now was not like in the past. In the past, my personal life had been stripped bare. Now secret things should happen between her and I, and these things should be hidden behind curtains.

I said to her, "We should have curtains."

I sensed that she nodded her head.

Then I asked, "Do you like the color of green grass or the color of flowers?"

I sensed that she liked the color of green grass; I was quite satisfied with her answer, because grass green was my favorite. And so I sat up immediately and told her I would go right away to buy curtains the color of green grass. She stood up as if she appreciated my decisive action, and I could sense her satisfaction as she walked to the kitchen. At this point, I jumped out of bed, pulled on my clothes, and walked out of the lodgings. I seemed to pass through the kitchen and see her from behind. My glimpse of her back was dim and unclear, like lamplight shining on a wall. I quietly went out the door, hoping to return as quickly as possible with the curtains. It would be best to get back to the lodgings before she noticed I was gone.

Thus, as I stepped into the small street outside my lodgings, there was no reason to resume my timid manner of walking from the past. I thought of a bicycle racing along and felt that I too should have such speed. I walked with flying steps along the unbearably blurred street. Frequently, I felt myself bumping into other people, but this did not deter me from my rapid progress. Arriving at a large intersection, I sensed a sudden brightening of the blurriness that shrouded me. I once thought that this was how it would be to open curtains in the morning, once curtains were hung in my room. Although a bright expanse appeared before my eyes, it was still a blur. I could tell that I was walking on the main boulevard. I heard noises surge toward me like tides from all directions. Though everything before my eyes had a veiled look, I could make out streets, buildings, trees, pedestrians, and cars. All these things had changed from their past appearance. They had a puffed-up look, and they gave off a vague, slightly visible light. The body shapes of the pedestrians had become odd, and though they walked separately, the vague light clumped them together. I had to use caution as I threaded my way among them. I could not figure out what on earth the vague light was. I feared I might walk into a huge spiderweb and have no strength to pull free. But I threaded my way among them with perfect smoothness. Except for a few unavoidable collisions, my walking was not interrupted.

Before long I came to the place that had always stymied me in the past. I needed to cut across the avenue to get to the other side and walk along a narrow side street that would take me through an always quiet intersection.

In fact, my movements were not the least bit muddled this time. I walked to the right place and turned. But on reaching the middle of the avenue, I suddenly discovered there was no point at all in cutting across this way: realizing that I was about to walk toward the residential district, I told myself that this time I had come out to buy curtains. I did not criticize myself, but immediately turned to walk back. As I took my second step I felt my body being slammed into by an unyielding automobile and thrown in an arc to the ground. I heard bones snapping in my body and felt my serene blood turn to chaos, as if it were breaking out in a riot.

2

On the afternoon of September 2, 1988, I sat next to a flowerbed in the convalescent ward of a Shanghai hospital, pinching a tuft of grass and watching the unwrinkled face of the nurse who was walking toward me.

Just before that, I had been recalling once again the day I went out to buy curtains. The last thing that happened that day was a traffic accident: I was knocked unconscious by a Liberation-model truck, and immediately sent to a hospital in the city of Smoke. During my convalescence, an ophthalmologist who came visiting the surgeon discovered that my eyes were approaching an incurable darkness. She stated this in no uncertain terms at my bedside. When I was able to move about, they loaded me into a white ambulance. I was sent to this hospital in Shanghai. On August 14, three ophthalmologists gave me a cornea transplant. When the bandages were removed from my eyes on September 1, I found everything around me restored to its past clarity.

By this time the nurse had reached my side. She looked at me with youthful, darting eyes, and sunlight was shimmering on her white robe. She gave off a scent of gauze and alcohol.

She said, "Why are you holding a tuft of grass?"

I did not answer, because I did not understand what she was getting at.

She said, "With all these bright-colored flowers around you, why would you rather hold a tuft of green grass?"

I told her, "I don't know either."

She burst out laughing. Her laughter made me think of a kindergarten I had walked past in the small city of Smoke.

She said, "There was a young woman named Willow Yang who is now dead. The last time I saw her she was sitting where you are now with a tuft of grass in her hand. I asked her that, and she gave me the same answer you did."

Because I did not show much interest in what she said, she added, "The look in her eyes was just like yours."

My conversation with the nurse lasted a long while because she told me about a seventeen-year-old girl named Willow Yang. Willow Yang had been admitted to this hospital with leukemia, and just before her departure from this world I was brought to the hospital. She gave up her organs of sight for me. She died just after 3:00 P.M. on August 14, as I lay on an operating table receiving a cornea transplant.

The nurse pointed at the five-story building in front of us and said to me, "Before Willow Yang died, her bed was next to that fourth-floor window."

My own sickbed was two floors below the window she pointed at.

This let me know that Willow Yang and I had beds in the same position, with only a floor in between.

I asked the nurse, "Who had the bed at the third-floor window?"

She said, "I'm not too clear."

After the nurse left, I remained by the flowerbed holding a tuft of grass. I began thinking of the girl named Willow, and wondering what her movements might have been like when death was near. These thoughts stayed with me, and made me inquire after Willow Yang's address while completing the paperwork in the cashier's office. Willow Yang also had lived in the small city of Smoke, at 26 Roundabout Lane. I wrote Willow Yang's address on a sheet of paper and put it in my left pocket.

3

After being discharged from the hospital on September 3, I boarded an overland bus to Smoke.

On that overcast morning the bus traversed the dim Shanghai streets, where black cloud hung above the few skyscrapers. The scene outside the window brought to my mind's eye a dreary gray-tile roof. I reminded myself that my destination was the city of Smoke, and by noon I would be reaching for my key to put it in the lock at my lodgings. And so, as I sat on the bus, I could not get away from the image of her seated on a chair in the room. My mood was as tranquil as a dry riverbed. My excitement had already flowed away. I knew when I walked into the lodgings she would stand up from the chair, but I did not imagine the way she would express her feelings. I would nod at her, and nothing more would happen. It would not seem I had gone away for long, just gone out to the street. And she was not just a recent arrival, but seemed to have been with me for twenty years. Because of my travel fatigue, I might lie down and sleep soon after entering the room. As I fell asleep she would stand motionless at the window. The silence would be unbroken. I hoped that this unbroken silence could continue a great while.

Once the bus pulled out of Shanghai, the broad fields gave me a view of boundless dark clouds. The clouds floated unhurriedly above the open country. The gloomy colors outside my window kept my mood from brightening.

On the tossing bus many human sounds rattled together like scraps of refuse. I sat in seat 27, next to the aisle. In the window seat, number 25, sat an old man in dark blue clothes, giving off a constant fishy scent. Between us, in seat 26, sat a young man of faraway origin. The scent he gave off made me think of green grass waving in the breeze. We were hemmed in by noisy sounds. The young traveler kept his gaze on the scene outside the window, and the old man closed his eyes in thought.

The bus sped along through the overcast morning. Soon it pulled into Jinshan, then out of Jinshan again. At this point, the old man by the window opened his eyes and turned to look at the young traveler in seat 26. The traveler's face was still turned toward the window, making it hard to say if he was watching the scenery or looking at the old man beside him.

Then I heard the old man say to the traveler, "My name is Goodman Shen."

The sound of the old man's voice continued: "I come from Zhoushan." Following that he said with special emphasis, "I have never left Zhoushan in my life."

Then the old man stopped talking. Though he was not talking, he did not move from his conversational posture of a moment ago. When something like forty minutes had passed and the bus was approaching the city of Smoke, he began speaking again. The old man's voice at this moment seemed different from before.

What he told the young traveler was an incident from several years in the past: in early 1949, a KMT officer named Goodman Tan had commanded a platoon of engineers to bury ten delayed-fuse bombs in the small city of Smoke.

The old man's narrative stretched out like a nonstop highway; his voice traveled off to far-flung past events. He kept talking until the small city of Smoke came hazily into sight, and then stopped his unending story short. His gaze turned toward the window.

The bus pulled into the station at Smoke. We three were the last passengers to leave the station. Outside the station stood a few people who had come to meet the arrivals.

Two men were smoking cigarettes, and a woman called to a man riding past on a bicycle. We left the station and walked about twenty meters together, at which point the old man stopped. He stood still and swept his eyes over the city in an odd manner. I kept walking with the traveler until he stopped to ask something from a young woman who apparently was waiting for someone beside the road.

1

A long time afterward, whenever I thought back to events that began the evening of May 8, 1988, the girl's image would spring to life before my eyes. All the things that had happened seemed so real in my recollections that I came more and more to believe that a girl had appeared in my life, not just in my imagination. At the same time, I clearly realized that these things belonged to the past, and I was left with nothing now. I resumed my life of earlier times. Almost every night I went to the residential district to bathe my eyes in light from window curtains. The only difference was that I also wandered unabashedly in the daytime on streets dominated by crowds. I no longer sensed a threat behind the smiles of others, and, what was more, no one smiled at me any more.

In my fading memory, the only shreds having to do with the girl were from May 8 until that unfortunate accident. The story of my life since the accident had been transformed into memory as a few moonless nights. I walked the streets with the mood of a bereaved husband. As time went by I began to believe I once had such a wife, one who had died long ago.

One day, I happened to catch sight of a yellowed piece of paper bearing the words "Willow Yang, 26 Roundabout Lane."

For some inexplicable reason, I had sat down at the desk that day and opened a drawer I had not looked through for years. Inside it, I noticed this piece of paper.

The words on the paper hinted of an event from the murky past, and I fell into empty ruminations. My eyes were fixed on the sunlight outside my window. I linked this moment's sunlight to all the weak remnants of sunlight in my memory. At last, my attention was caught by sunlight beside a bright-colored flowerbed. A nurse was walking toward me in sunlight that etched the subtle pursing movements of her lips. She told me certain things about a girl named Willow Yang. The significance hinted at by this piece of paper had become clear.

Obviously the appearance of the yellowed paper at this moment was meant as a reminder. Many years before, when writing these words in the hospital cashier's office, I had not known my own mind. It had been a completely mechanical act. Only now, by turning up this piece of paper, did I understand my previous actions. Thus, as I left the sunlight at my window to go out into the sunlight on the street, I was fully aware where I was going.

The paint on the large black door at 26 Roundabout Lane had already come off in spots. Knocking at the door, I heard flakes of paint fall with faint sounds. The sounds continued awhile, until footsteps were audible inside. The door let out a debilitated creak, and a fifty-year-old man stood before me. As he looked at me, an air of astonishment showed on his face.

I was terribly ashamed of my forwardness, but he said, "Come on in."

He seemed to recognize me, though he had not expected I would appear in this manner.

I asked him, "Are you Willow Yang's father?"

He did not answer directly, but said, "Come in."

I followed him into the gate and through a moss-covered atrium; we entered a side chamber facing south. A few old-fashioned chairs were grouped in the chamber. I chose one near the window to sit on, feeling dampness on its surface. He examined me with a look of long familiarity. He was an utterly placid person, as revealed a moment before by his way of opening the door. His placidity helped me to convey accurately my reason for coming.

I said, "Your daughter . . ."

I tried to remember the moving lips of the nurse beside the flowerbed, and I went on to say, "Did your daughter die on August 14, 1988?"

He said, "Yes."

"At that time I was on the operating table in a hospital in Shanghai. It was the same hospital where your daughter died."

I told him this, hoping that his placidity would last another five minutes so I could begin with the accident, then tell of his daughter offering her organs of sight just before her death, then tell of the successful cornea transplant.

But he did not let me finish. He said, "My daughter never went to Shanghai. In the seventeen years that she was alive, she didn't go to Shanghai once."

I could not disguise my puzzlement. I was aware of myself looking at him with disbelief in my eyes.

Still he looked placidly at me and continued, "But it is true she died on August 14, 1988."

He could not forget that sweltering noontime, when he and Willow had finished eating lunch in the atrium and she had said to him, "I feel exhausted."

Seeing that his daughter's face was somewhat pale, he told her to take a rest.

His daughter stood up listlessly and lurched toward the bedroom. In fact, she had been listless like this for quite some time, so he did not pay particular notice to her lurching walk, though he felt a pang of concern.

Willow Yang walked into her room, then called through the window, "Wake me at three-thirty."

He assented, then he seemed to hear his daughter talking to herself: "I'm afraid if I keep sleeping I won't wake up."

He did not pay much attention to this sentence. Only later, thinking back to the last words his daughter spoke in her life, did he feel this sentence had meaning behind it. His daughter's voice had seemed to be floating off somewhere at that instant.

That day he took no noontime nap, but stayed in the atrium reading a newspaper. At three-thirty he went into her bedroom and found she had died moments before. He pointed to the room opposite and said, "That was the room Willow died in."

I had no choice but to believe this. The way I saw it, a father bereaved of his daughter would not make jokes lightly.

After a long silent pause he asked me, "Do you want to see Willow's bedroom?"

His question surprised me, but I indicated this was my wish.

We walked together to Willow Yang's bedroom. Her room was dim, and I saw that the grass green curtains were tightly drawn. He turned on the lamp.

Next to the bed I saw two picture frames, one holding a color photograph of a girl, and the other a pencil drawing of a young man.

I went over to the color photograph and suddenly realized that this was the girl who had entered my mind many years ago on May 8. I gazed a long time at her photograph. The image she had revealed to me years ago in my lodgings now overlapped with what I was seeing before me. Once again I felt how genuine those past events were.

At this moment he said, "Do you see the look in my daughter's eyes?"

I nodded my head. I was seeing the eyes of my departed wife.

He asked, "Don't you think the look in her eyes is like yours?"

I did not quite grasp what he meant. Whereupon he said in a half-apologetic tone: "Maybe in the photograph the look in her eyes is blurry."

Then he pointed to the pencil drawing, as if to make up for this, and told me, "A long time ago, when Willow was still alive, one day she suddenly had thoughts of a young man, a stranger to her. She had never seen him before, but he appeared more and more distinctly in her imagination. This picture is the likeness she drew of him."

I was struck by the correspondence between his account of the drawing and occurrences from my past. Thus my gaze shifted away from the girl's color image and stayed on the pencil drawing. But instead of myself I saw a young man utterly unknown to me.

As the father showed me out the gate he said, "To tell you the truth, I noticed you some time ago. You live in a bungalow near the river. The look in your eyes is just like my daughter's."

2

After leaving 26 Roundabout Lane, I suddenly felt my experience of moments ago was as remote as an event from the past. Thinking back, the middle-aged man's voice seemed to belong to another lifetime. Therefore I betrayed no unrest of feelings as I walked farther from the girl's color image. What had happened seemed the recurrence of an event from the past, just as when I sit by the window in my lodgings and recall the night of May 8. The difference lies in the addition of a gate flecked with black paint, a man in his fifties, and two picture frames. My wife died on August 14, 1988. I repeated this stale old sentence in my mind as I walked forward.

Turning onto the road along the river I noticed a young man coming in my direction. He wore a black jacket that caught the sun's rays with an odd brightness. I do not know why I paid such close attention to him. I watched him walk into a bungalow near the river, then walk out again soon after, holding a pencil and a sheaf of white paper. He walked down the stone steps to the bank and under the arch of the bridge.

For some reason I myself cannot explain, I also walked down the bank. By then he was sitting beneath the arch. He showed no sign of opposition to my approach, so I walked into the arch. He moved sheets of paper out of the way, and I sat down in the space. I saw that the papers were marked with crisscrossed lines.

Our conversation began after a minute passed. Perhaps by then he knew I could listen quietly to his drawn-out narrative, so he began speaking.

"Early in 1949, a KMT officer named Goodman Tan placed ten time bombs underground in Smoke in a random geometric arrangement."

His narrative began in 1949 and came down to the present, including mention of nine bomb explosions. He told me, "The last bomb has not exploded."

He picked up a piece of paper and went on: "This bomb I speak of is buried at ten different spots." The first spot is within what is now the Performance Hall, Row 9, Seat 3. "That seat is somewhat worn, and the springs are exposed." The remaining spots are as follows: at the front center door of the main bank; at the intersection leading to the residential district; beside the crane at the cargo dock; at the hospital morgue (he saw no point to this one); under the second parasol tree outside the department-store gate; in the kitchen of Dormitory Suite 102 at the Machine Tool Factory; in the street, sixteen meters from the bus-station entrance; at the gate of 57 Roundabout Lane; beneath the fifth window on the right side of the Workers' Union Dance Club.

At the end of his prolonged account I asked him, "So you're saying there are ten bombs in this little city?"

"That's right," he nodded. "And they could go off at any time."

Now I understood why I had paid such attention to him. My attentiveness was what had brought me to sit here. It was because he reminded me of the pencil drawing in Willow Yang's bedroom. The person in the drawing was sitting in front of me.

Translated by Denis C. Mair

FLYING OVER MAPLE VILLAGE ❁ *Su Tong*

Well into the early fifties, the area around Maple Village, my ancestral homeland, was still covered with opium poppy fields seldom seen in the south. In the spring, the open country on each side of the river was wantonly drenched in scarlet: red waves of exceptional beauty rose in swell after swell like a boundless stretch of surf, beat upon this remote village, and quickened the sanguinary life breath of my rural relations for generation after generation.

My youngest uncle is still in the country. Everyone says he comes and goes among the bales of straw, opium fields, dry manure piles, and fat women of Maple Village as freely as a stray dog with no thought of going home. From hundreds of miles away, I often think of him. I think of him sitting in a clump of big red flowers in our old Maple Village home with his head turned in the direction of the southwestern cities, a short, sturdy, dark-skinned country fellow with a strange look on his little face as though he wants to sleep, to laugh, and to curse, all at the same time. He sings a diverse jumble of folk songs, among which is one for calling his much-loved dog:

> Little dog, little dog, hurry yourself over here,
> Take me to the bordello to kiss my lady
> dear.

Grandfather lives in the city. He's old and decrepit, but his memory is very clear. Every day as dusk descends, his long, deep sighs fill the house just like dust fills the air. He lingers on, unwilling to go to bed: "Tomorrow I might wake up a blind man." And thus he sits in the gradually darkening room with his eyes open wide—old, strong, and serene like an ancient bronze eagle.

You can see his youngest son, my uncle, in the pupils of Grandfather's eyes, enlarged as they are by memory. Grandfather gets his youngest son and a pack of stray dogs all mixed up together. My uncle used to be a real little devil. He liked to saunter outlandishly through the poppy fields sporting a hat like city folks wear to keep the sun out of his eyes. Then one summer he threw that hat in the river and became infatuated with a pack of stray dogs. When everybody saw the rich man's youngest son playing around with a pack of stray dogs all day, and acting crazy, just like a dog himself, it caused a scandal such as was rarely seen in Maple Village.

"That bastard does not understand the human world; he only knows how to act like an animal," Grandfather cursed his youngest son. "Don't pay him any mind," he said, "let him turn into a dog." My grandfather could not help feeling depressed whenever he thought of that little devil.

Many times in the middle of the night my uncle, bursting with energy, would scramble around everywhere on the raised earthen paths between the fields with that pack of stray dogs. He tread closely behind the dogs' round-shaped tracks, and his footprints spread out to every corner of Maple Village. Sometimes when he burst into a fellow villager's house panting and demanding a drink of water, the dogs would wait in an open field nearby barking ceaselessly. All the villagers living on both sides of the river knew him. They all said that he was the reincarnation of a god or a demon, and they were not certain whether he would bring good or evil fortune to Maple Village.

During the Festival of Tombs when everyone in the clan formed a long line and trooped off magnificently to the ancestral temple to offer sacrifices to the ancestors, my uncle was nowhere to be seen. Grandfather angrily kowtowed toward his ancestors' spirit tablets, knocking over a dish of sacrificial offerings in the process, and asked in a hoarse voice, "Divinely omniscient ancestral spirits, please tell me, has a stray dog seduced my son, or has my son seduced that stray dog?" He gazed despairingly into the future, where he imagined the strange, monstrous soul of his youngest son wildly roaming forever beyond the pale.

Several decades later, he sits in a deep drowsy haze under the roof of his house in the city, wearing out that Maple Village bamboo bed until it's as smooth and shiny as oil, telling his family over and over again how his youngest son was abandoned during a flood.

A big white wooden boat, he says, was packed to capacity with forty family members and their belongings. Just as they were about to lift anchor, my uncle and that stray dog ran up to the bank one after the other. "Where are you all going?" he asked. No one answered him, but many hands reached out to pull him onto the boat. They could not budge him, and at that point they discovered that the little devil had tied a rope tightly around his leg and that stray dog. When Grandfather jumped down to untie the rope, my uncle fought him off by biting and snarling and even scratched his face until it bled. While Grandfather was cursing and looking for the big ax, my uncle, panic stricken, shouted at the dog: "Run, Leopard, run! Run, Leopard, run!" The dog took off running and the rope tightened up and pulled my uncle along behind him. They looked just like a pair of wild animals running away, one behind the other, out of the sights of a hunter's rifle. Grandfather sighed ruefully to Heaven: he knew that the boat had to leave, and that the little devil had to be left behind.

"I can see all the way to Maple Village. As long as I don't go blind, I can see Maple Village every day," Grandfather says. The bottom of his mind is deep and desolate enough to allow field upon field of red opium poppies to grow while his youngest son and his dog run through them every hour of every day.

My youngest uncle died in 1956, the last glorious year for opium poppies. His death was tangled up with a dog, a woman, and some other strange, inexplicable events. After he died, opium poppies disappeared from Maple Village. After that, its dark soil gave birth to big crystalline pearls of rice and bright golden grains of wheat.

In my dreams I have flown many times over my faraway Maple Village homeland. Every day I see myself approaching a muddy, yellow river running from east to west. I wade across the river and climb up the left bank. A powerful dragon-head wind races through the vast fields of red poppies on the left side of the river, picks me up, and hurls me into my shadowy old Maple Village home.

One day white streamers were flying ostentatiously in Maple Village, and a cloud of misty gray smoke rose above every roof in town. Many people were scurrying around here and there in the mist, sobbing and wailing. The atmosphere was one of unbearable anxiety, a scene reminiscent of that time many years ago when the river had inundated the village. Separated by thousands of rolling hills and river valleys, is it possible for me to observe that catastrophe?

That day was the anniversary of my uncle's death. His soul had not found a final resting place, but continued to wander around greatly disturbing the normally tranquil village.

When the villagers made their way through the warm, pungent odor of opium poppies to the Tong family's old house to attend his funeral, they actually heard the deep, resonant sound of a funeral bell. They seemed to see my uncle sitting cross-legged on the millstone in front of the old house. One big foot was kicking up and down, covered with ashes, grass, and dog manure; its five toes, spread wide apart, pointed brazenly toward the sky. He was smiling warmly, but one rough, pimply hand was pulling fiercely on the bell rope tied to an old elm tree.

The dead man was ringing his own funeral bell. The sound came from the heights of Heaven or the depths of Earth and made the villagers tremble in fear. They both loved and feared my uncle. On the anniversary of his death, many women and old people wept as though they would die of grief while they softly implored the sun, moon, stars, mountains, waters, grasses, and trees: "Take him away. Take him away."

In the past in my old Maple Village home, everyone had a spirit tablet of bamboo set up in the clan elder's house at birth. After the person died, they burned the spirit tablet and it was transformed into an auspicious bird that flew the deceased to Heaven. From Grandfather's stories, I learned that my uncle was one of those unfortunate characters who had lost his spirit tablet. And nobody could explain its mysterious disappearance.

One story has it that my uncle had always been so dissolute throughout the village and had so disgraced himself in violation of village morality that one night, after the village elder had a strange dream, he ran to the side of the river with a spirit tablet hidden inside his coat, tied it to a stone, and sank it to the bottom of the river. Another story has it that the madwoman of Maple Village, Suizi, crept into the village elder's house one day, stole my uncle's spirit tablet, ran to a deserted spot in the hills, made a bonfire, and burned it, all the while laughing and wailing like a lunatic.

Grandfather did not believe any of these stories. He looked dejectedly at the ceiling and told me, "Your youngest uncle took the spirit tablet himself. He sold it to a villager who was afraid of dying, then he spent the money on drinking and whoring. That's definitely what happened. He could get up to all kinds of terrible mischief even when he was only fifteen or sixteen."

If my uncle's spirit tablet were still sitting up straight in the village elder's room, I would fly over my far-off Maple Village homeland and bring his soul back to the city he never visited and the relatives he never knew.

A descendant of Maple Village, I am about to enter the Tong family's ancestral temple and meet our venerable ninety-one-year-old clan elder.

The venerable old gentleman's house is situated on the sunny south side of a small artificial hill made of piled-up loam. The windows are closed and a single small black hole of a door sucks me inside. I feel dizzy and disoriented in the dark, fusty air. I automatically reach for the light cord, my hand wildly groping along the wall until I suddenly grab hold of a bunch of dusty slips of bamboo. They are awfully heavy, and I throw them down and keep groping along until my hand finally runs across the clan elder's face. It is very painful, like smashing my hand into the trunk of a hundred-year-old tree. Immediately after that, a small flame appears before my eyes. My ninety-one-year-old clan elder holds up a candle. His house has no electricity. In the candlelight, I can clearly see the clan elder's holy, aloof visage: without a stitch on, his aged, dry, gaunt, naked body looks primitive and vigorous. A bright blue light radiates from his eyes, making him appear much younger than me.

"What are you looking for?"

"Tell me where my uncle's spirit tablet is."

"I do not know when it was lost. When a spirit tablet is lost, it cannot be found again."

In the candlelight the clan elder smiles compassionately at me while I rifle through the bamboo slips in disbelief. In the room I smell an ever more pungent aroma of opium poppies and see that the walls and the floor are crowded with long, rod-shaped bunches of dried poppies. Even the venerable clan elder himself is magically transformed into a huge opium poppy whose stifling, saccharine perfume saturates the peaceful village air. I keep searching until I'm drenched with sweat. In the pile of bamboo slips, I find the names of every single person in Maple Village, including my grandfather and my father, but I do not find my uncle's spirit tablet.

"Who stole my uncle's spirit tablet?"

As I shout my question at the venerable clan elder, his face gradually disappears into the darkness. He blows the candle out with a puff and drives me out the door. As I walk down off the earthen mound in a daze, it comes to me: I am going to look for my uncle's last traces in Maple Village. Relying on my sensitivity to his black plastic shoes, I'm going to sniff out his unique odor, a mixture of strong liquor and sweat.

A factory in our city manufactures those black plastic shoes. On Grandfather's most important, sixtieth birthday, when he saw the torrential rain outside the window, he suddenly thought of something and ran out into the rain to buy a pair of black plastic shoes. Wrapped in three layers of oilcloth and mailed three hundred miles by a roundabout route into my uncle's hands in Maple Village, they were the only present Grandfather ever gave to his youngest son.

People say the first time my uncle wore those black plastic shoes was during the Ghost Festival on the fifteenth day of the seventh lunar month. No one knows for sure when it happened, but in Maple Village the Ghost Festival had evolved into a Flower-Burning Festival. Every time members of the older generation who used to live in our old home describe that Flower-Burning Festival, I feel like I've been transported to an unearthly realm.

They say my uncle stood beside an oxcart wearing those shiny, jet-black plastic shoes. The oxcart was loaded to the brim with dried opium poppies ready and waiting to go. The ox, having been splendidly anointed over its entire body with scented peanut oil and powdered opium petals, looked magnificent tied to the front of the cart.

When my uncle raised his whip, they all said, that was his most impressive moment in Maple Village. He bounded up onto the seat of the cart, gently nudged the underbelly of the ox with one big black plastic shoe, and the whole cart full of ghosts and demons started off under his command. As the kindling began to burn, a cloud of red smoke rose up from the oxcart into the clear blue sky and chased along behind the speeding cart like a meteor tail. In the flames behind my uncle, the ghosts and demons, magically transformed into the buds, stems, and leaves of opium poppies, were stirred up into a wild commotion and filled the air with their shrill, unearthly wailing. But the people heard my uncle laughing for joy. Before the flames sending off the ghosts and demons licked up around his back, he sang and shouted as happily as a young god.

Every year my uncle saw off the ghosts and demons; it was just about the only task he was willing to do in Maple Village. People say that later on, whenever the oxen saw those black plastic shoes, they would low mournfully. "Cattle look up to people." Those black plastic shoes of his were like two malevolent mountains oppressing their spirits. He often told people that when he walked past the cattle pens he heard the oxen cursing him in unison. "That one will come to a bad end," said all the Maple Village oxen.

Those old oxen who pulled the cart bearing away the ghosts and demons have often appeared in my dreams. I've seen many oxen die under my uncle's buttocks. Their animal spirits were knocked unconscious by the smoke from those poisonous flowers and they were driven mad by the frenzied atmosphere of the Ghost Festival. In the end one old bull struggled free of my uncle's yoke, escaped from the flowers and the demons, and finally swam across the Maple Village river. I tried as hard as I could to imagine what that old bull looked like flying exultantly across the water. I hope he escaped every calamity, and I would love to let him wear a huge pair of black plastic shoes.

My grandfather predicted that my uncle would die under the hooves of a bull. He always felt those black plastic shoes would become an instrument of disaster from all the jealousy and hatred they would bring him. In 1956, however, the news from home of my uncle's death said that he drowned in the Maple Village river. He was completely naked when he died except for one black plastic shoe.

I had just been born in 1956. I was a quiet, beautiful baby, but I clearly remember witnessing the three-night vigil beside the coffin.

The sound of autumn cicadas fills the moonlit night air while the mourners crowd darkly around the old millstone. Row upon row of silent shadows stand motionless as mountain tops. A large crowd of old people, women, children, and young men are gathered there, unruly but with a common purpose, to surround and protect the center of a lotus flower—my dead uncle. I hear a young boy with snow-white skin striking a bamboo clapper. Each time a stick of incense burns down, he knocks six times six, or thirty-six times. The sound of thirty-six raps on a bamboo clapper gradually brings on the dark night.

I lie in my cradle sunk in a deep sadness born out of primitive feelings of familial relationship. I have a tearful expression on my face, but I do not cry. The first time I see my drowned uncle, his whole body is blue, his eyes are wide open, and he is lying beside the big millstone in front of our old home. The vigil is three hundred miles away, but it seems to be taking place right beside my cradle. As my tiny little life passes through the encircled Maple Village hills, streams, people, and animals, my face grows red and I pant for breath. The river that drowned my uncle is laid bare before my eyes; the water gurgles in the moonlight. Opium poppies, stretching down the left bank farther than the eye can see, sway back and forth in the wind, giving rise to endless bloodred desires. A moving and tragic sense of birth and mortality pervades the entire world as, moved by something profound, I stand up unsteadily in my cradle, gaze at the moonlight outside the window, and burst loudly into tears. My grandfather, my mother, and my brothers and sisters all run anxiously over to find me standing in my cradle crying like a drunken fool, a row of pure, innocent tears flowing brighter and brighter down my cheeks.

Did I see my uncle's spirit float to the surface of the river, glimmering and fluorescent, drifting from the left bank toward the right bank? Did I foresee that my uncle would be unable to cross that muddy, rushing river, and did I watch in terror a dead soul's harmonious union with the universe?

For many years now I have been trying to find the witnesses to my uncle's drowning: the madwoman Suizi and that stray dog. My grandfather remembered that my uncle was a good swimmer; he could not have drowned even if you tied a lead sinker around his neck. What sort of power did the madwoman Suizi have, then, to drown my uncle when he could swim like an eel? The way the Maple Villagers tell it, they never expected my uncle to drown, but when they saw the madwoman Suizi climb dripping wet up onto the riverbank with one shiny, jet-black plastic shoe in her hand, they knew something was wrong.

Everybody had been at the threshing ground drying opium poppy seeds, and no one paid any attention to the river. Only my uncle's dog saw everything clearly. That dog watched for a long time the foaming surface of the river and the silhouettes of a man and a woman as naked and as silent as fish. No one heard the dog bark. They say if I had flown over Maple Village that day, I would have observed a quiet, uneventful midday scene, but at the time I vaguely felt my uncle's death resulted from some grand conspiracy designed by Heaven and Earth. I have always maintained this belief.

During the three days and three nights that Maple Villagers maintained their vigil by my uncle's coffin, the madwoman Suizi put on hempen mourning clothes and came and went in the vicinity of the millstone funeral area. Her hair was wildly disheveled and she had a strangely demented, yet beautiful, expression on her face. She knelt beside my uncle's corpse and gently stared at his shiny, sapphire blue face. Her legs were buried under the piles of paper money that surrounded the corpse when a gust of wind suddenly blew some of the paper away and the mourners saw that her left foot was bare, but her right foot was wearing my uncle's black plastic shoe.

The other black plastic shoe had disappeared. I do not know when my uncle's last remaining shoe escaped from the sole of his muddy foot and went its own way.

I have heard quite a few stories concerning the madwoman Suizi. In the spring, many of the young men of Maple Village dragged Suizi off into the opium poppy clumps and took their pleasure deep into the night. After the men finished fondling Suizi's rich, full breasts, they ran quickly home, leaving her alone there sleeping soundly on the waves of opium poppies. People entering the fields at dawn often came upon her nude body sleeping there on the ground. Her face toward the rising sun, her lips slightly parted, and with innumerable crystal-clear dewdrops caressing the deepest recesses of her body, viewed at dawn from a distance, Suizi's recumbent body looked like a rudderless ship drifting along on the scarlet waves on the left bank of the river.

People say that the madwoman Suizi became pregnant every two years. No one knew when she was due, but they say that whenever her water broke she would crawl down the riverbank, and the baby would drop into the water and float downstream. Those babies were all extremely beautiful, but the sound of their crying was as bleak and depressing as an old man's.

In the villages downriver from Maple Village many children who drifted there on the water, as if being nurtured on some primal sap, gradually grew up as straight as wild millet. Those dirty black-headed children with their vivid, expressive faces and their agile bodies have appeared many times in my dreams. I have a vague feeling they look just like my dead uncle. Perhaps they represent the crystallization of his seed scattered at will in the black earth where it germinated and came to fruition.

I am about to meet my uncle's dog on the road. I hear the sound of the dog's footpads following behind me, and I smell the stench of its body growing stronger and stronger. I crouch down and look back angrily at it. That dog is terribly large, and its face is cunning itself. It raises its front legs in the air like arms and supports all its weight on its hind legs, standing like a man. I see that the dog's back is covered with the scarlet petals of opium poppies, and even its eyes have been scorched until they resemble two balls of amber.

In life, my uncle and the dog were inseparably close. When he was sleeping soundly, the dog regularly climbed up onto his skinny belly and happily barked his head off. When I come to feel that that dog acted just like a loose woman, constantly clinging to my uncle, ruining him, and then leading him to the river of death, I pick up a stone and square off with him for a long time; but when I raise the stone as if to throw it, the dog lets out a grief-stricken moan from deep within its throat, darts into the security of the poppy fields, and disappears.

> Uncle, uncle, hurry up and kill that dog,
> Kill that dog and come home with me.

As I chase that dog along the riverbank, I clearly remember the poem I sent my uncle when I was eight years old. Today I am in a terrible hurry. I dash wildly around Maple Village like a chicken with its head cut off. I am about to see my uncle's wandering spirit blaze forth, a bright light across the road in front of me, guiding me to complete this impossible trip to my old home.

Throughout the journey, I shall see strange scenery stretching out all along the left bank of the river. The irrigation waterwheel that my grandfather peddled when he was young turns incessantly with a creaking noise. A man and a woman stand astride the waterwheel their ancestors bequeathed to them, but the water in the irrigation ditch is as hard as ice and refuses to flow. On the far side of the field a bull runs for its life; a cloudlike swarm of wasps buzzes in hot pursuit around the bull's bleeding, infected horns, and they all recede in the direction of the river.

When I reach the left side of the river, I see with my own eyes the madwoman Suizi in her mourning clothes. She is wearing one black plastic shoe as she walks slowly into the water. When the water covers her ponderously protruding abdomen, she bends backward so her beautiful face is toward the sky and suddenly lowers her shoulders to allow her hair to hang down onto the water's surface. Holding her hair firmly in her hands, she washes it by dipping it repeatedly into the water. As the water begins to ripple, a great number of red bubbles start to foam, and gradually half the river is suffused with a reddish tint.

Everything will appear as though seen before, exactly the way I saw it in my dreams in the city. Everything except my swarthy, strong, skinny, down-and-out uncle: his wandering spirit, wearing one black plastic shoe, comes and goes without a trace. Is he smiling or is he crying? Oh, uncle, uncle!

On the eighth day of the eighth lunar month in 1956, the day before my uncle was buried, everybody in my far-off old Maple Village was discussing the dead man and his lost spirit tablet. Without a spirit tablet he could not be buried in the ancestral graveyard. The villagers searched every house and empty field in the village and went through the clothing of every woman who ever played around with my uncle, but that bamboo spirit tablet was still nowhere to be found. The village was in an uproar, but my dead uncle just lay there on the millstone patiently enduring the chaotic disturbance he himself had caused. At midnight, the young boy striking the bamboo clapper among the mourners suddenly dropped it and began crying and screaming. He shouted in terror that my uncle had opened his dead eyes, that his eyes were like the spring buds of opium poppies, and that the image of a woman and a dog flashed in his poppy-bud eyes.

Everyone said a woman and a dog appeared in my uncle's eyes. My grandfather said so too. The last night before my uncle was buried, three hundred miles away in the city my grandfather heard him crying. At that very moment, Grandfather was absorbed in the task of carefully carving a slip of bamboo. He fashioned it into the exact shape of the bamboo spirit tablets in his ancestral temple, and then he carved my uncle's name on it. After he finished his work, he laughed, then he sobbed a couple of times and climbed slowly up a ladder onto the roof of our house. Grandfather stood on the roof, looked down at our city, and danced and shouted wildly as if in a crazed shamanistic trance, which shook the roof for some time. People who walked by our house that night all say they saw a ghostly emanation like a spirit fire pour down off our roof, land in the middle of the road, and burst into bright blue flames that rose up over a foot high. The spirit fire danced and sang without restraint there on the pavement, burning right through from twilight until nightfall with an incomparably exquisite fragrance.

Bring my uncle back.

A year ago last spring, my grandfather sat on the bamboo bed from our old Maple Village home gradually nearing death. Thoughts of his long-dead youngest son kept running through his confused mind. He could not stop himself from pulling my despondent head against his chest and whispering in my ear, "Bring your uncle back."

Sooner or later I will fly over my far-away old Maple Village home to bring an end to three generations of my family's unfinished business. But no one has ever told me why they planted such vast fields of red opium poppies on the left side of the river. Or why those red opium poppies that once lived and suffered like human offspring have all disappeared today. When I run away from my ancestral Maple Village homeland with my long-dead uncle on my back, I will see once again those opium fields of days gone by. That will be a sultry, stifling moonlit night; the moon will sink lower and lower, minute by minute, a boiling hot moon that will almost burn us to a crisp. The dark red night vapors of Maple Village, in ceaseless frenzy, combined with the night tide of opium poppies, will surround the escapees in the depths of the night. I'll step on innumerable gray frogs, and they will start croaking loudly as they chase madly behind us on the raised paths between the fields.

I will hear the confused shouting of the villagers as lights spring up on all sides. A pack of dogs will buzz behind us like hornets, and the villagers will chase after us trying to seize back the lost soul of my uncle. "Born here and destined to remain here," they will say. My uncle's dog will just then be wandering around outside the village. The brilliantly flashing light from his eerily scorched eyes will cut like a meteor through the night sky and rush upon us with blinding speed. The sounds of dogs, people, and nature will pursue us; the moon will hang down until it comes to rest upon the peaceful black face of the dead man. The kinsman whom I will carry on my back will one day become a thousand-year volcano.

On the night that I escape, in a far-away field a madwoman will give birth to another child. Everyone will hear the sound of that child's desolate wailing, wailing that recuperates all the vicissitudes of life in Maple Village for the past thousand years. With that sound of life all around me, will I be able to pass by the long, narrow left bank and cross over the river?

Many families who moved here from the villages now live under the roofs of this city of ours. Every night the sound of their snoring is quite uneven because they all have their own particular worries and dreams. If you are like me and have had strange dreams ever since you were a child, then you will see your old homeland, your clan, and your relatives in your dreams. There is a river that flows by you when you are born and you seem to be sitting on a bamboo raft floating down that river: you turn and gaze back upon your old home, far, far off in the distance.

Translated by Michael S. Duke

THE BIRTH OF THE WATER GOD ✲ *Su Tong*

And the Lord said: "I will go before thee."—Matt. 26:32

Ma Sang was an itinerant salt merchant from the grasslands. After becoming separated from his camel caravan, Ma Sang had lost his sense of direction and walked three days and three nights through the Gobi Desert, near death from hunger and thirst. Finally, an ash white dirt road appeared in the distance, and barely visible adobe buildings. The light of a foreign sun angled across his head, casting unfamiliar shadows on the ground. Ma Sang did not realize this was Highway 61, nor that he had reached the village of Mopan, in the middle of an area stricken by drought for a hundred years. This place was over a thousand *li* from his hometown in the grasslands.

Ma Sang was covered with dirt, and his fur jacket gave off a strange rancid odor like dead game. Anyone could tell he was from the grasslands by the copper water dipper hanging from his waist. He saw the dirt road snaking before him with a few scattered stalks of wheat growing alongside it. Men and women of the village with faces the same color as the yellow, withered wheat were hoeing and singing hoarsely. The strange tune heard by Ma Sang was the "Song of Prayer for Water." It had been handed down for centuries in the Mopan Village region, and in the song they repeatedly sang praise of a stalwart hero called "Bro" Gao, who had searched for water.

At first, Ma Sang did not even know that "Bro" Gao was a water god to whom the people sacrificed, but as soon as he appeared on Highway 61 he formed a tie with the god. The people in the wheat fields stared at him, open eyed, and the music of the song of prayer for water rose and fell. Ma Sang had begun to be recognized as the son of "Bro" Gao, the water god.

The small white wooden building of a bar was stuck awkwardly at Seven Kilometer Place, at the junction of three roads. If you go to the village of Mopan, you must pass here. Ma Sang made his way toward the dirty yellow, tattered tavern banner. He saw sitting in one window a listless, white-haired old man, both hands thrust between the crotch of his trousers toying lackadaisically with whatever. A mysterious knife scar shone brightly on the old man's forehead. Ma Sang handed his dipper over to the man across the windowsill. "Please give me some water. I'm dying of thirst."

"Who are you?" The old man's ears quivered for a second, and he threw the copper dipper on the floor, grabbing Ma Sang's hand. "Come closer. I already know who you are."

"Who am I? I'm Ma Sang. I was separated from a camel caravan carrying salt."

But the old man said, "You are 'Bro' Gao's son. You've appeared again; you come through here every year."

Ma Sang now realized that a thick film covered the old man's eyes. The old man lifted an earthenware bowl and respectfully gave it to the salt merchant, saying, "Son of 'Bro' Gao, the scent of water on your body is sweet. Drink this wine before you take to the road again."

"I'm just a traveler passing by, and I don't want any wine. I'm dying of thirst, so could you give me a dipperful of water?"

"Don't you know that the people of Mopan don't have any water stored away? You had better accept your father's kindness and go to 'Bro' Gao's well. After you have drunk the water be on your way. Don't stay any longer."

Ma Sang finally realized that he was ensnared in a labyrinth. This place was a thousand *li* from his home in the grasslands. Utterly exhausted, he propped himself under the window of the small bar and thought of the pure sweet stream water of the grassland. Ma Sang was convinced that he was caught in the invisible web of fate and did not know if he could get free.

From whichever side you looked at "Bro" Gao's well, it looked as if it had been stopped up by small bird nests of great age. It was a ramshackle wooden building singing lonesomely on a mountain ridge. When you were so thirsty you couldn't stand it any longer you headed there. You had to say reverently, " 'Bro' Gao, please give me water, please give me water." An old wooden bucket bobbed on top of the water. This was "Bro" Gao's hand. If you pulled on it, you could get water—"Bro" Gao's well water—with a strong metallic odor.

Ma Sang was terrified by the dull yellow eyes of the Mopan villagers. He was only a salt merchant from the grasslands, and he still did not understand the implications of being the son of "Bro" Gao.

Ma Sang slept in the barren wheat fields at night. Each day at dawn when the cock crowed three times, he would wake up and see three women, clay jugs on their heads, winding their way up a distant mountain ridge. Every day was like the others. Ever since "Bro" Gao dug this well, the water was eight inches deep, just enough for three women to draw water.

Every evening Ma Sang walked up the mountain to drink from "Bro" Gao's well.

He would stand inside the dilapidated wooden building staring at the eight inches of water, his face, blurred and strange, reflected by the water's surface. Hanging over his head were the fiber rope and the metal hoe used by "Bro" Gao to dig the well that gave off the smell of old plants. Ma Sang rubbed them bemusedly. The rope, knotted in a complicated fashion, had hung free in the air for so long that it was covered with mildewed moss. It seemed strange that the rope always swung back and forth. At its tip, a bunch of cowflies continually landed and then flew off, buzzing loudly. Ma Sang slowly realized that the small pearl-shaped drop of water that formed on the end of the rope took an unusually long time to form and fall off. Indeed, the cowflies were drinking from the small water drop.

These water drops, left by "Bro" Gao, dripping today as they had for so many years, fell on the head of the grassland salt merchant, Ma Sang. He saw the water drops as an omen. The dripping water brought him closer to the mystic water spirit, "Bro" Gao.

Many people had described the water god as a middle-aged man with a flushed yellow skin, hawk eyes, and the nose of a fish, and now they were saying that Ma Sang looked just like him. Ma Sang turned hot all over. He felt as if the abundant water of his home had already flowed out of his body, and with it his grassland-bound soul. Then, suddenly, he began to feel that he had spent his whole life in this great desert. He had almost forgotten his old home.

One question began to worry Ma Sang: Who was "Bro" Gao's son?

Was he still alive, or was he dead? People said that "Bro" Gao had children like weeds. They all grew up to have yellowish gray, befuddled faces. Without exception they avoided following in the path of their father; they preferred, for some reason, to stay at the knee of their mother, Lan, nursing at her abundant breast. When these sons grew up they had lusty libidos; it's not known how many maidens they deflowered in the haystacks of Mopan Village.

The villagers despaired over these sons of the water spirit; they could find no way to rouse the descendants of "Bro" Gao to follow the path of their father.

It was said that the blind old man at the bar had once traveled three hundred *li* to invite a wandering shaman to the village. The shaman had said, "Water is born from fire; what about your fire?" It was in this way that the greatest fire in a hundred years started to burn at Mopan. The fuel for the fire came from a large pile of grass accumulated over the years at the entrance to the village; later the fire gradually assumed the shape of a garland of flowers. The fire burned blue turning to purple, purple to red, for exactly one day and one night. It was said that eventually eight sets of fragrant, banana yellow male bones emerged from the ashes. These were the sons of "Bro" Gao. They were born at the right time and they died at the right time. Only "Bro" Gao's youngest son, Red Tiger, escaped, and since then no one has ever found out where he went.

Ma Sang had no way to divine Red Tiger's fate, good or bad. He thought that Red Tiger had fled not just from the great fire but from the supernatural demands of the Villagers of Mopan Village. Free spirits are all the same, and Ma thought that perhaps he really was "Bro" Gao's son. Perhaps he really did want to find his father, "Bro" Gao, the eternal water god. But as Ma Sang stood in the barren wheat fields, looking as far as he could in four directions, all he could hear was the sound of the scorching sun drying the grasses and tassels of wheat, an oxcart squeaking below the eaves of an adobe house, and the desert burning with a hazy dust cloud. Time was dried and compacted until it was as hard as iron, just like the land. "Where has our father, the water god, gone?"

If you travel along Highway 61, it's possible you may run into "Bro" Gao. After becoming the water god, he vanished from the area around Mopan Village. If you travel Highway 61 you may see in the dirt of the road a footprint, neither cow's nor man's, that stretches out in front of you. It takes thirsty eyes to distinguish that footprint. You may also hear, floating in the air, the faint sound of a dog barking. All you have to do is travel Highway 61, and "Bro" Gao will be in front of you.

The mountain people along the way will say, " 'Bro' Gao went to find water. Why are you traveling this way?" You should tell them, "I am going to find 'Bro' Gao."

Is there anyone left who remembers the rain that fell a hundred years ago? It was after it fell that "Bro" Gao left Mopan Village. One autumn night "Bro" Gao was suddenly awakened by a sound in the far distance, a thundering sound like a metal bell being struck, which shook the roof of his house. "Bro" Gao crawled out from underneath the sleeping pile of his wife and children, covered his ears with his hands and said, "Who is ringing the bell?"

His wife, Lan, put her arms around his waist and said, "It's thunder. Good heavens! Is it really going to rain?"

"Bro" Gao ran out of the house, naked as he was, and standing atop a very high mound, he discovered that the sky around Mopan Village was closing in from a distance, and in the time it took to blink, the sky had become a huge snake black river and a fierce wind ripped off thatched roofs and rain poured down like a shower of arrows. "Bro" Gao's black dog barked deliriously and stuck his dry red tongue up at the sky. "Bro" Gao hugged the dog and said, "Dog, Dog. Look, it's raining. Rain at last."

When he heard his wife, Lan, leaning against the window weeping, he also waved his fist and said, "Don't be afraid, Woman. Look. Rain is falling. Rain is falling."

It rained for seven minutes. The whole time "Bro" Gao stood naked on the tall mound. He saw a beautiful yellow mist rising up from Mopan Village. Below the mist, a number of people were gathering, and their cries came from all sides. Carrying pots and pans, dippers and basins, the villagers knelt on the ground to collect the rain. "Bro" Gao couldn't tell whether the sounds of crying were from the men or the women, or whether they were human sounds or sounds of nature. After seven minutes, the yellow mist below the mound gradually lifted. The yellow earth kept erupting with the *chi-chi* sound of someone breathing. In his lifetime, "Bro" Gao had never before heard the yellow earth breathing. He held the black dog tightly, and together they lay flat on the ground to listen. It was not until he lifted his head that "Bro" Gao saw the tableau of Mopan Village after the rain. Each of the eight hundred villagers held some kind of earthenware container and ranged around the old elm tree. It was the only tree in the village, and it had already been dead for many years. Eight hundred villagers, respectfully and without a sound, stared intently as water dripped slowly from the tree into their clay jars. "Bro" Gao watched as the withered tree dripped for seven minutes. After that, there was simply no more. The crowd of water collectors stared at the sky as it turned bright blue again. Their bare skin changed after the rain; it became like the faint incandescent shimmering of a glowworm. After the rain, nothing else happened.

"Bro" Gao began sobbing exactly at that moment. As he cried with the black dog in his arms, Mopan Village was quiet. Only his wife, Lan, saw his grief that night.

Weeping, "Bro" Gao went to the side of the well, which had been empty since it was dug two years earlier. His wife and the black dog circled the well with him. It was no longer dry. Now it held eight inches of water. As "Bro" Gao continued to cry, he stuck his head deep into the well mouth. He said, "Is this well water? Woman, turn the pulley wheel and give the well rope to me. I'm going down into the well."

"What's wrong with you? What do you think you are doing?"

"I don't know. I just want to go down there."

"As soon as it rains, you go crazy. Why are you going down there?"

"I want to soak in the water. I haven't had a bath since I was born. Let me down, Woman."

Lan, shaking her head, guarded the pulley wheel, but "Bro" Gao pushed her away with a sweep of his hand. Breathing deeply, he wrapped the well rope around his wrist, and with a glance at his wife, he raised both arms, like a large bird, and flew into the well. The eight inches of well water scattered a shining spray of water in all directions. After the water had risen again, "Bro" Gao floated on top. He shivered all over, and sounded as if he were talking in his sleep. After his face had been covered by the water, it became glittering and translucent.

The night storm was completely over. Dawn revealed scattered pale gold rays of faint color falling toward the village. Lan had not slept the entire night. She had kept hold of the pulley wheel and held her breath, listening for the sound of any movement. "Bro" Gao stayed at the bottom of the well curled up like a quiet infant. It was as if he had gone to another world.

" 'Bro' Gao, wake up. Don't sleep in the well!"

"I'm not sleeping. I'm listening to the water god speaking to me. He told me to take to the road."

"Where will you go?"

"To find water. I must set out at once."

"What is the water god like? Did you see him?"

"I saw him. He and I look exactly alike. The water god told me that all I have to do is set out in search of water, and I will also be a water god."

Lan finally turned the pulley wheel and lifted "Bro" Gao, the water god, out of the well. The night of the storm had passed, and it was this morning that three women carrying water jugs on their heads came to the well to draw water as "Bro" Gao was preparing to leave.

If you come from a place in the south that is crisscrossed with rivers and streams, you won't be able to find any water. And if you have drunk a great deal of water, there won't be any way for you to approach our water god, "Bro" Gao.

Ma Sang, you just imagined the road "Bro" Gao took to find water. At that time Highway 61 did not exist. "Bro" Gao's sandals tramped the dust of the yellow earth like a cloud-roving immortal. He walked beyond the yellow-green field of vision of mountain pigs. He was just a dot moving horizontally across the history of the Mopan mountain region, searching for an exit to flee through. At that time there was no Highway 61, nor a single locust tree lining it.

From "Bro" Gao's melodious voice sprang many songs that spread through the mountain valleys like newly sprouted tree leaves. The mountain people who lived underneath the slopes heard him sing. Dawn or dusk, his songs could always be heard. The people loved the man who sang, but no one realized that he was the water god, "Bro" Gao, of Mopan Village. Children standing on the backs of the cattle guarding the herds would see a man with a dog appear from all directions at once, and then gradually fade away. Day followed day. Those children had no way of knowing that they themselves were treading out a dirt road that would someday be Highway 61.

Highway 61 is an unusual road, one located beyond any map. If you think of it as the way between Mopan Village and Heartbreak Ridge, you will be wrong; if you think of it as an abandoned mountain road, you will be wrong. The highway forms an endless circle. It may intersect Heartbreak Ridge, but it circles on forever. If you travel Highway 61 you will assuredly miss your destination. When you travel here, remember the water god "Bro" Gao. Heartbreak Ridge won't, after all, be your final destination. The story of "Bro" Gao losing his way at Heartbreak Ridge is, after all, just a tale. For all these years the footprints of "Bro" Gao and his black dog must have crossed Heartbreak Ridge. Walking on the highway is like walking in that night storm many years ago. If you want to find "Bro" Gao, you must seek help from this Highway 61.

"Bro" Gao's descendants never traveled Highway 61. According to what is said, Lan's dying words were, "Don't take that road. It is not really a road, and if you take it you will never be able to return to Mopan Village." As she was dying, she looked at the highway in the distance under the ridge. She was sitting at the side of "Bro" Gao's well. Her children and grandchildren removed the whole eight inches of water in the well and lifted their water jars high to give her a bath as the last rites. As the water flowed over the deep purple furrows on her face, everyone saw that she was pressing her lips together tightly to avoid tasting it. She did not want the water meant to send her off. Her bright eyes remained stubbornly fixed on Highway 61. The last thing she said was, " 'Bro' Gao found the water—he drowned in it."

However, the people of Mopan Village ignored the implications of what she had said before her death. They all believed that "Bro" Gao was still on Highway 61, leaving the footprints that were neither man's nor cow's. All along the road the news reaches you: "If you travel on Highway 61 before dusk, there is a chance that you will see stretching before you on the dirt path a footprint that is neither man's nor cow's. You will also hear the barking of "Bro" Gao's black dog in the twilight. All you have to do is travel Highway 61, and "Bro" Gao will be ahead of you."

Just before dark, Ma Sang saw for the first time a bird flying in the air above the road. It was a dainty, black-feathered mountain sparrow. Carrying a piece of wild grass, it headed swiftly toward a dilapidated thatched hut next to the road and came to roost. Ma Sang suddenly remembered that a bird on Highway 61 was supposed to be the spirit of someone who had died of thirst, flying low along the road looking for water. The old blind man at the bar had told him this. When Ma Sang saw the bird he thought of Lan's words. Did "Bro" Gao find water? Did he drown? What should one think? Could the strange bird possibly be "Bro" Gao, the water spirit?

There was a dilapidated hut along the road every five li. These huts were already built the year that Lan constructed the road itself. The reason she didn't tear down the huts was to prepare them for "Bro" Gao. After the last of "Bro" Gao's sons was born, Lan shut her doors and windows at night and no longer waited for her husband to return. She spent ten years constructing Highway 61 for him. Ma Sang guessed that the meaning of the engineering project was that "Bro" Gao was banished. He went to search for water—he would never return home.

Lan took her eight children with her to see "Bro" Gao off. They slowly descended the mountain ridge to the entrance to Mopan Village. As the child in her arms suckled, Lan shook her dried nipple and told "Bro" Gao, "There will be another child when you come back after finding water. You'll see."

"It will be a boy. I know it."

"Don't kick the dog in the nose. You're always doing that. When you return after finding water, be sure not to get rid of that dog."

"The child is sure to be a boy. If I'm not back by summer, go ahead and name him. Call him Red Tiger."

"After you leave, I won't sleep at night. In fact, I can't sleep at night. In the night I'll build a road. I'm planning to build a road, understand?"

Lan placed the child on her back, squatted down, and held "Bro" Gao's feet. In front of them she drew a line and said, "I will build a road from here. Go now. I will follow the dog's droppings and your footprints and build the road after you."

This is why the villagers of Mopan say that Highway 61 was created by "Bro" Gao's feet and Lan's hand.

Lan took her eight children and went to build the road. She was a tall, thin woman of unequaled strength. She used no equipment other than the farm tools "Bro" Gao had left behind. On her back was a wicker basket that had been made south of the mountains. Inside the wicker she put her infant son, who could not yet walk, and some dry provisions. In this way, Lan followed the tracks of "Bro" Gao and proceeded with her work. The road she built made a regular, snakelike pattern, which represented the ebbing of "Bro" Gao's lifeline. From beginning to end, this lifeline was in his wife's hands. Therefore, the villagers of Mopan also said that as soon as Wife Lan died, Highway 61 ceased to exist. After that, there was no way to help the water god "Bro" Gao and no way for anyone to know his present whereabouts. The villagers further said that Lan was the first to be aware of the circular nature of the road "Bro" Gao had taken to search for water. Late at night, when she would raise the lantern wick to work on the road, she would hear her husband singing, the song coming from far away to gather around the lamp. Lan always told her children that their father would come back soon. "He is only forty *li* away. If he travels one night, he will be back." Wife Lan did not know that after Gao descended Heartbreak Ridge, he had become lost and could no longer find his way home. The Mopan villagers, following her lead, said, " 'Bro' Gao will be back soon. He's only forty *li* away. If he travels one night, he'll be here."

If you reside in Mopan Village for ten days you will learn that every story about "Bro" Gao and Lan is ambiguous. It is important to remember that Lan did, indeed, die. She was "Bro" Gao's wife; her intuitive response to "Bro" Gao's every moment had real significance. Her deathbed revelation was recorded on a piece of yellow paper by her youngest son, Red Tiger. He was illiterate, so he used grass-ash ink and painted a picture. Red Tiger was a startlingly intelligent child. He had never once seen his father, the water god, but the picture he painted of "Bro" Gao's drowning was unusually true to life and stirring.

"Bro" Gao found the water.

"Bro" Gao drowned in the great flood.

Ma Sang, if you continue to travel down Highway 61, you will arrive at Heartbreak Ridge. There is always a time like this, when suddenly in front of your eyes rises the beautiful purple, mountainous form of Heartbreak Ridge. Such moments are profoundly important.

You are not mentally prepared. You always assumed that Heartbreak Ridge was a particular steep cliff on a particular mountain peak. But in the September twilight, when the ridge in silence surges into your vision, you will discover it to be only a composite of innumerable bright red knolls. The highest point is, at the very most, only about a hundred meters higher than the road. Heartbreak Ridge looks strange. Floating back and forth between the various knolls is mushroom-shaped miasma, and according to tradition, the purple color is really caused by the vapors of the haze.

How could you imagine that desert air would produce misty miasma? You stand at the end of the road disappearing into the fog, take off your heavy fur gown, and look all around. You feel that Highway 61 has already lost all meaning for you. Heartbreak Ridge is your destination. Its mazelike structure is a mythology of water. When you travel Highway 61 you will sooner or later enter that mythology.

In just this way Ma Sang heard, faintly lingering on Heartbreak Ridge, the song of "Bro" Gao searching for water. Ma Sang's tired body awakened. He walked toward Heartbreak Ridge. Ma Sang, the mushroom-shaped miasma from the depths of the bright red earth floats up to surround you. You have already entered. You have come to Heartbreak Ridge following the songs of "Bro" Gao. His story by now has become a piece of heavy metal fastened to your canvas bag like a badge, and you have pressed close to the heart of the story. From this time on, you will also become a creator of the water mythology.

In the heartland of Heartbreak Ridge, the world reveals itself in an illusory purple color, and you cannot help but lose your way. When you are lost and unable to return, you will be able to see a sheet of bright water marsh under the cover of the mist. In this way you will perceive water anew. The water below the mist sparkles glass blue, impaling your eyes. Seeing the water, you are seeing the death of the water spirit "Bro" Gao, a middle-aged man with reddish yellow skin, hawk eyes, and the nose of a fish sinking into the water forever. Completely naked, arms spread apart, he is sunken forever. Turning his head and smiling, he looks fixedly at the black dog sunk forever in the water. You will recognize in the water god's eyes the glorious instant when one myth begins just as another one ends. That instant for you is also eternal.

In this way, you will experience the fading away of the song of "Bro" Gao. The story that the Mopan villagers told you is also at an end. Everything agrees with the words of Lan: " 'Bro' Gao is dead; he drowned in the water."

People say that heroes who search for water all take to the road, one by one, but the traces of the water spirit are still deeply concealed. If "Bro" Gao, the water god, walks out of our water-hunting history of a hundred years, then a new water god will appear. The new water god will be born in the midst of fire.

Ma Sang stood under a locust tree on Highway 61 packing his luggage. The harvested land next to the road was empty, a wilderness without people. The setting sun was falling dully into the emptiness above the mud-brick houses. Ma Sang had made a complete circle of the road, but he remembered nothing. He only smelled the scent of water on his fur jacket. The odor confused him.

At Ninety Kilometer Place, the bar run by the blind old man stood just as it had before. Ma Sang approached the greasy bar window from a different direction. The knife mark on the old man's forehead once again burned his eyes. Ma Sang closed them and leaned toward the window. He weakly reached out and grasped the hem of the old man's clothes.

"It's 'Bro' Gao's son, isn't it? You've come back again."

"Yes, it's me, 'Bro' Gao's son. I kept going on and on, straight ahead. I traveled and traveled, and now I'm back."

"That's always the way. There are numberless heroes, but only one water god. If you had found "Bro" Gao, you wouldn't have returned. If you had discovered water, then you wouldn't have returned."

"Tell me how I can see water? I was on the road for ten days and nights, but after all that traveling I ended up here. Tell me where I went wrong."

"You are Red Tiger. How did you escape the great fire in the haystacks? Your brothers have already gone. They have fire. They went with your father's soldiers. Your fire! Where is your fire?"

Ma Sang shook all over. Suddenly he understood that the bar, located where three roads met, was the symbol of a lamp. He felt unbearably hot. Piece by piece, he took off all the clothes he was wearing. Finally, dressed only in a flower-shaped loincloth, he sat in the small bar drinking. He and the blind old man sat face to face, each drinking three cups of liquor. Conversing with their eyes and with grunts, they exchanged opinions about fire. Occasionally they glanced out the window. All they could see was the September night covering Highway 61. The withered locust was motionless and silent. Two or three birds came to the road. Ma Sang saw one of them perched on a dry branch. Suddenly, silently, the man began to smile. Bringing his lips together, he imitated the cry of the bird.

It was before dawn on the second day that Ma Sang burned himself to death.

He lit the straw stack at the entrance to the village and sat on top of it with his legs folded underneath him. His copper water scoop lay abandoned at the bottom of the haystack; it was still half full of water. Ma Sang sat on the burning mountain of fire until daybreak, when the cock crowed three times. Far away, three women climbed the mountain ridge, going to "Bro" Gao's well for water. Ma Sang, his body in the blue flames, saw boundless water moving perpetually upon the earth. He felt the same boundless water moving perpetually within his body. He believed that he was close to "Bro" Gao. He believed that he had become the new water god.

Ma Sang was not, in fact, a Mopan man. He was just a traveling salt merchant from the grasslands. And that is all there is to say.

Translated by Beatrice Spade

THE BROTHERS SHU ❊ *Su Tong*

The story of Fragrant Cedar Street is legendary among people in my hometown. In the south of China, there are lots of streets just like it: narrow, dirty, the cobblestones forming a network of potholes. When you look out your window at the street or at the river's edge, you can see dried meat and drying laundry hanging from eaves, and you can see inside houses, where people are at the dinner table or engaged in a whole range of daily activities. What I am about to give you isn't so much a story as it is a word picture of life down south, and little more.

The brothers Shu Gong and Shu Nong lived on that particular street.

So did the Lin sisters, Hanli and Hanzhen.

They shared a building: 18 Fragrant Cedar Street, a blackened two-story structure, where the Shu family lived downstairs and the Lins above them. They were neighbors. Black sheet metal covered the flat roof of number 18, and as I stood at the bridgehead, I saw a cat crouching up there. At least that's how I remember it, fifteen years later.

And I remember the river, which intersected Fragrant Cedar Street a scant three or four feet from number 18. This river will make several appearances in my narration, with dubious distinction, for as I indicated earlier, I can only give impressions.

Shu Gong was the elder son, Shu Nong his younger brother.

Hanli was the elder daughter, Hanzhen her younger sister.

The ages of the Shu brothers and Lin sisters can be likened to the fingers of your hand: if Shu Nong was fourteen, then Hanzhen was fifteen, Shu Gong sixteen, and Hanli seventeen. A hand with four fingers lined up so tightly you can't pry them apart. Four fingers on the same hand. But where is the thumb?

Shu Nong was a timid, sallow-faced little devil. In the crude and simple classroom of Fragrant Cedar Middle School, he was the boy sitting up front in the middle row, dressed in a gray school uniform, neatly patched at the elbows, over a threadbare hand-me-down shirt with a grimy blue collar. The teachers at Fragrant Cedar Middle School all disliked Shu Nong, mainly because of the way he sprawled across his desk and picked his nose as he stared up at them. Experienced teachers knew he wasn't listening, and if they smacked him over the head with a pointer, he shrieked like splintered glass and complained, "I wasn't talking!" So while he wasn't the naughtiest child in class, his teachers pretty much ignored him, having taken all the gloomy stares from his old-man's eyes they could bear. To them, he was "a little schemer." Plus he usually smelled like he had just peed his pants.

Shu Nong was still wetting the bed at fourteen. And that was one of his secrets.

At first, we weren't aware of this secret. It was Hanzhen who let the cat out of the bag. Devoted to the act of eating, Hanzhen had such a greedy little mouth she even stole from her parents to buy snacks. One day when there was nothing to steal and she was standing outside the sweetshop looking depressed, Shu Nong happened by, dragging his schoolbag behind him. She stopped him: "I need twenty fen." He tried to walk around her, but she grabbed the strap of his bag and wouldn't let him pass. "Are you going to lend it to me or not, you little miser?" she demanded.

Shu Nong replied, "All I've got on me is two fen."

Hanzhen frowned and casually slapped him with his own strap. Then, jamming her fists onto her hips, she said, "Don't you kids play with him. He wets the bed. His sheets are hung out to dry every day!"

I watched her spin around and take off toward school, leaving Shu Nong standing motionless and gloomy, holding his face in his hands as he followed her pudgy figure with his eyes. Then he looked at me—gloom filled his eyes. I can still see that fearful look on his fourteen-year-old face, best described as that of a young criminal genius. "Let's go," I said. "I won't tell anybody."

He shook his head, jammed his finger up his nose, and dug around a bit. "You go ahead. I'm skipping school today."

Shu Nong played hooky a lot, so that was no big deal. And I assumed he was already cooking up a way to get even with Hanzhen, which also was no big deal since he had a reputation for settling scores.

On the very next day, Hanzhen came into the office to report Shu Nong for putting five dead rats, some twisted wire, and a dozen or more thumbtacks in her bed. The teachers promised to punish him, but he played hooky that day, too. On the day after that, Hanzhen's mother, Qiu Yumei, came to school with a bowl of rice and asked the principal to smell it. He asked what was going on. Qiu Yumei accused Shu Nong of peeing in her rice pot. A crowd was gathering outside the office when the gym teacher dragged in Shu Nong, who had sauntered into school only moments earlier, and flung him into the corner.

"Here he is," the principal said. "Now what do you want me to do?"

"That's easy," Qiu Yumei replied. "Make him eat the rice, and he'll think twice about doing that again."

After mulling the suggestion over for a few seconds, the principal carried the offending bowl of rice over to Shu Nong. "Eat up," he said, "and taste the fruit of your labors."

Shu Nong stood there with his head down, hands jammed into his pockets as he nonchalantly fiddled with a key ring. The sound of keys jangling in the boy's grimy pocket clearly angered the principal, who in plain view of everyone, forced Shu Nong's head down over the rice. Shu Nong licked it almost instinctively, then yelped like a puppy, and spat the stuff out. Deathly pale, he ran out of the office, a single kernel of rice stuck to the corner of his mouth. The bystanders roared with laughter.

That evening, I spotted Shu Nong at the limestone quarry, wobbling across the rocky ground, dragging his schoolbag behind him. He picked an old tree limb out of a pile of rubbish and began kicking it ahead of him. He looked as gloomy and dejected as always. I thought I heard him announce, "I'll screw the shit out of Lin Hanzhen." His voice was high pitched and shrill but as flat and emotionless as a girl saying to a clerk in a sweetshop, I'd like a candy figurine, please. "And I'll screw the shit out of Qiu Yumei!" he added.

A male figure climbed onto the roof of number 18. From a distance, it looked like a repairman. It was Shu Nong's father. Since the neighbors all called him Old Shu, that's what we'll call him here. To members of my family, Old Shu was special. I remember him as a short, stocky man who was either a construction worker or a pipe fitter. Whichever, he was good with his hands. If someone's plumbing leaked or the electric meter was broken, the lady of the house would say, "Go find Old Shu." He wasn't much to look at, but the women on Fragrant Cedar Street liked him. In retrospect, I'd have to say Old Shu was a ladies' man, of which Fragrant Cedar Street boasted several, one of whom, as I say, was Old Shu. That's how I see it, anyhow.

Let's say that some women doing their knitting see Old Shu on the roof of number 18. They start gossiping about his amorous escapades, mostly about how he and Qiu Yumei do this, that, and the other. I recall going into a condiments shop once and overhearing the soy sauce lady tell the woman who sold pickled vegetables, "Old Shu is the father of the two Lin girls! And look how that trashy Qiu Yumei struts around!" The condiments shop was often the source of shocking talk like that. Qiu Yumei was walking past just then but didn't hear them.

If you believed the women's brassy gossip, one look at Lin Hanzhen's father would strengthen your conviction. What did Old Lin do for a living? you ask. Let's say it's a summer day at sunset, and a man is playing chess in the doorway of the handkerchief maker's. That will be Old Lin, who plays there every day. Sometimes Hanzhen or Hanli brings his dinner and lays it next to the chessboard. Old Lin wears thick glasses for his nearsightedness. He has no special talents, but once after losing a chess game, he popped the cannon piece into his mouth and would have swallowed it if Hanli hadn't pried open his mouth and plucked it out. She knocked over the chessboard, earning herself a slap in the face. "You want to keep playing?" she complained tearfully with a stomp of her foot. "I should have let you swallow that piece!"

Old Lin retorted, "I'll swallow whatever I want to swallow, and you can just butt out!"

People watching the game laughed. They got a kick out of Old Lin's temper. They also got a kick out of Hanli, because she was so pretty and had such a good heart. The neighbors were unanimous in their appraisal of the sisters: they liked Hanli and disliked Hanzhen.

Now all the players in our drama have made an appearance, all but Shu Gong and his mother, that is. There isn't much to be said about the woman in the Shu family. Craven and easily intimidated, she padded like a mouse around the downstairs of number 18, cooking meals and washing clothes, and I have virtually no recollection of her. Shu Gong, on the other hand, is very important, since for a time he was an object of veneration among young people on Fragrant Cedar Street.

Shu Gong had a black mustache, an upside-down V sort of like Stalin's.

Shu Gong had delicate features and always wore a pair of white Shanghai-made high-top sneakers.

Shu Gong had been in a gang fight at the limestone quarry with some kids from the west side, and he had had a love affair. Guess who he had the affair with?

Hanli.

In retrospect, I can see that the two families at number 18 had a very interesting relationship.

Shu Gong and Shu Nong shared a bed at first and fought night after night. Shu Gong would come roaring out of a sound sleep and kick Shu Nong: "You wet the bed again, you wet the goddamned bed!" Shu Nong would lie there not making a sound, eyes open as he listened for the prowling steps and night screeches of the cat on the roof. He got used to being kicked and slugged by his brother since he knew he had it coming. He always wet the bed, and Shu Gong's side was always clean as a whistle. Besides, he was no match for Shu Gong in a fight. Knowing how reckless it would be to stand up to his brother, Shu Nong let strategy be his watchword. He recalled the wise comment someone made after being beaten up one day on the stone bridge: a true gentleman gets revenge, even if it takes ten years. Shu Nong understood exactly what that meant. So one night after Shu Gong had kicked and slugged him again, he said very deliberately, "A true gentleman gets revenge, even if it takes ten years."

"What did you say?" Shu Gong, who thought he was hearing things, crawled over and patted Shu Nong's face. "Did you say something about revenge?" He smirked. "You little shit, what do you know about revenge?"

His brother's lips flashed in the darkness like two squirming maggots. He repeated the comment.

Shu Gong clapped his hand over his brother's mouth. "Shut that stinky mouth of yours, and go to sleep," he said, then found a dry spot in bed and lay back down.

Shu Nong was still mumbling. He was saying, "Shu Gong, I'm going to kill you."

Shu Gong had another chuckle over that. "Want me to go get the cleaver?"

"Not now," Shu Nong replied. "Some other day. Just don't turn your back."

Years later, Shu Gong could still see Shu Nong's pale lips flashing in the dark like a couple of squirming maggots. But back then, he could no longer endure sharing a bed with Shu Nong, so he told his parents, "Buy me a bed of my own, or I'll stay with a friend and forget about coming home."

Old Shu was momentarily speechless. "I see you've grown up," he said as he lifted his son's arm to look at his armpit. "OK, it's starting to grow. I'll buy you a real spring bed tomorrow."

After that, Shu Nong slept alone. He was still fourteen.

At the age of fourteen, Shu Nong began sleeping alone. He vowed on his first night away from his brother never to wet the bed again. Let's say that it's an autumn night forgotten by all concerned and that Shu Nong's dejection is like a floating leaf somewhere down south. He lies wide awake in the darkness, listening to the surpassing stillness outside his window on Fragrant Cedar Street, broken occasionally by a truck rumbling down the street, which makes his bed shake slightly. It's a boring street, Shu Nong thinks, and growing up on it is even more so. His thoughts fly all over the place until he gets sleepy, but as he curls up for the night, Shu Gong's bed begins to creak and keeps on creaking for a long time. "What are you doing?"

"None of your business. Go to sleep, so you can wet your bed," Shu Gong snaps back spitefully.

"I'm not wetting my bed anymore." Shu Nong sits up straight. "I can't wet it if I don't sleep!"

No response from Shu Gong, who is by now snoring loudly. The sound disgusts Shu Nong, who thinks Shu Gong is more boring than anything, an SOB just begging to get his lumps. Shu Nong looks out the window and hears a cat spring from the windowsill up to the roof. He sees the cat's dark green eyes, flashing like a pair of tiny lamps. No one pays any attention to the cat, which is free to prance off anywhere in the world it likes. To Shu Nong, being feline seems more interesting than being human.

That is how Shu Nong viewed the world at fourteen: being feline is more interesting than being human.

If the moon is out that night, Shu Nong is likely to see his father climbing up the rainspout. Suddenly, he sees someone climbing expertly up the rainspout next to the window like a gigantic house lizard. Shu Nong experiences a moment of fear before sticking his head out the window and grabbing a leg.

"What do you think you're doing?" That is exactly how long it takes him to discover it is his father, Old Shu, who thumps his son on the head with the sandal in his hand. "Be a good boy, and shut up. I'm going up to fix the gutter."

"Is it leaking?"

"Like a sieve. But I'll take care of it."

Shu Nong says, "I'll go with you."

With a sigh of exasperation, Old Shu shins down to the windowsill, squats in his bare feet, and wraps his hands around Shu Nong's neck. "Get back to bed, and go to sleep," Old Shu says. "You saw nothing, unless you want me to throttle you. And don't think I won't do it, you understand?"

His father's hands around his neck feel like knives cutting into his flesh. He closes his eyes, and the hands fall loose. He sees his father grab hold of something, spring off the sill, and climb to the top floor.

After that, Shu Nong goes back and sits on his bed, but he isn't sleepy. He hears a thud upstairs in Qiu Yumei's room, then silence. What's going on? Shu Nong thinks of the cat. If the cat's on the roof, can it see what Father and Qiu Yumei are up to? Shu Nong thought a lot about things like that when he was fourteen. His thoughts, too, are like leaves floating aimlessly somewhere down south. Just before dawn, a rooster crows somewhere, and Shu Nong realizes he has fallen asleep—and has wet the bed. Mentally he wrings out his dripping-wet underpants, and the rank smell of urine nearly makes him gag. How could I have fallen asleep? How come I wet the bed again? His nighttime discovery floats up like a dream. Who made me go to sleep? Who made me wet the bed? A sense of desolation wraps itself around Shu Nong's heart. He slips off his wet pants and begins to sob. Shu Nong did a lot of sobbing at the age of fourteen, just like a little girl.

Shu Nong asked me a really weird question once, but then he was always asking weird questions. And if you didn't supply a satisfying answer, he'd give you a reasoned reply of his own.

"What's better, being human or being a cat?"

I said human, naturally.

"Wrong. Cats are free, and nobody pays them any attention. Cats can prowl the eaves of a house."

So I said, "Go be a cat, then."

"Do you think people can turn into cats?"

"No. Cats have cats, people have people. Don't tell me you don't even know that!"

"I know that. What I mean is, Can someone turn himself into a cat?"

"Try it, and see."

"Maybe I will. But I have lots to do before that. I'm going to make you all sit up and take notice." Shu Nong began chewing his grubby fingernails, making a light clipping noise: *chuk chuk.*

As for Hanli, she was one of Fragrant Cedar Street's best-known lovely young things. And she had a heart as fragile and tender as a spring snowflake. Hanli couldn't watch a chicken being killed, and she never ate one. The sight of a bloody, dying creature terrified her, and that trait became the keystone of her character. As youngsters, Shu Gong and Shu Nong often sprinkled chicken blood on the stairs to menace the sisters. It had no effect on Hanzhen but drained the blood from poor Hanli's face. Her terror evoked cruel fantasies in the minds of the Shu brothers. "So?" you say. Well, years later, mixed feelings would characterize Shu Gong's recollections of the girl Hanli, since he was always brutally punished by Old Shu for his cruel pranks: first Old Shu would pin him to the floor and gag him with a wet rag to keep him from screaming; then he would smack him across the face with his shoe until his arm tired. Old Shu would then drag himself off to bed and leave Shu Gong lying half-dead on the floor, his battered face looking like an exploded red windowpane. By then, the wet rag would be chewed into a tight little wad. "How did that come about?" you ask. Well, Shu Gong had considered Hanli his private plaything from a very early age. She was like a katydid he held in his hand as it screeched helplessly; he had her in his grip and wouldn't let go. What I find strange is that the people in my hometown never figured out the relationship between Shu Gong and Hanli, simply writing it off as bad karma.

Let's say spring is giving way to summer, and Shu Gong is washing his face at the tap when he hears someone walk down the stairs behind him. He turns to see Hanli standing at the foot of the stairs with a patterned skirt in a washbasin, her just-washed, shoulder-length hair a shiny black. Discovering Hanli's beauty for the first time, he looks at his reflection in his own basin. The whiskers on his upper lip are like a dark patch of weeds floating on the water. But just as he realizes that he, too, has a certain charm, he detects an indescribable stink and knows it is rising from his underpants, which he has put on that morning without washing them first. He looks up at Hanli, who averts her eyes. Can she smell it, too? A tangle of fantasies whirls around Shu Gong's head and tickles his sex like grassy filaments, invigorating it. He dumps the water from his basin and puts the basin back under the tap, stalling to give his brain time to sort out his feelings and desires. He hears water spill over the rim of the basin and splash on the ground; the basin is full again, but he still doesn't know what to do. Obviously, he wants to do something to Hanli but doesn't know how to go about it. What do I do? An idea forms. Draping the towel over his shoulder, he walks over to the little storeroom beneath the stairs, where he closes the door, takes off his underpants, and examines the whitish stains in the crotch; then he puts his trousers back on. Outside again, he carries his soiled underpants over to the tap and crams them into Hanli's basin; water-soaked, they quickly sink to the bottom. A shocked Hanli stops washing her face and hops away.

"Wha——?" she shrieks, a curtain of hair covering her face.

"Don't have a fit. Just wash them for me," Shu Gong says as he picks them out of the water.

"Why should I? I'm going to wash my skirt."

"Do as I say if you know what's good for you."

"You don't scare me, never did. Wash your own stuff."

"Really? I don't scare you?" A grin forms on Shu Gong's lips as his eyes bore into Hanli's face, in which an uneasy anger resides. He sees spurts of pink blood rise from the recesses of her body to just beneath the skin; he is always seeing Hanli's pink blood. That's why everyone says she is so pretty. With that thought on his mind, he picks up the washbasin and flings the water in Hanli's face. *Whoosh!* The strange thing is she doesn't scream. She stands there, soaked to the skin, and looks straight into Shu Gong's face. Pretty soon she wraps her arms around her shivering shoulders. Crystalline beads of water drip from her hair.

"Pick them up!" Shu Gong kicks the pair of blue underpants that have landed on the ground.

Hugging herself tightly, Hanli glances over at the stairs, but she doesn't move.

"No need to look. There's no one there. Even if there were, so what? I dare anybody to get me mad," Shu Gong says.

Hanli bends over and picks up Shu Gong's blue underpants, then tosses them into the basin.

"Wash them!" Shu Gong demands.

Hanli turns on the tap, closes her eyes, and scrubs them tentatively. Then she opens her eyes. "Soap. I need soap." Shu Gong hands Hanli a bar of soap. He grabs her wrist as she takes the soap from him and squeezes it hard. Not fondles, squeezes. On Fragrant Cedar Street, they say that was when the love between Shu Gong and Hanli was kindled. That may sound far-fetched, but to this day no other explanation has risen to challenge it. So let's keep the faith with Fragrant Cedar Street and move on.

The people's nostalgia for the river that flows through our southern city can last a hundred years. Our homes were built along the river until the banks were black with dense rows of them. It was a narrow riverbed, and the rocks on the sloping banks were covered with green moss and all sorts of creepers. As I recall, once the water got polluted, it never turned clear again: it was black and stank horribly. The river might as well have been the city's natural spillway, the way it carried rotten vegetable leaves, dead cats and rats, industrial oils and grease, plus a steady supply of condoms.

Typical southern scenery. So why were there people who sang on the banks of the river? Why did people see tall-masted ships sailing at night? Fragrant Cedar Street didn't know; Fragrant Cedar Street, which ran along the banks of the river, had no idea.

Late that night, Shu Nong climbed onto the roof for the very first time. He prowled the dusty roof catlike in his bare feet, not making a sound. The world, having lost its voice, allowed Shu Nong to hear the wild beating of his heart. He walked to the edge and squatted down, holding a clothes pole to keep from falling. He could see into Qiu Yumei's second-story room through the transom.

Simply stated, Old Shu and Qiu Yumei were in bed, making love.

In the weak light of the bedside lamp, Qiu Yumei's naked, voluptuous body gave off a blue glare; that was what puzzled Shu Nong. Why is she blue? Shu Nong watched his father ram his squat, powerful body against Qiu Yumei over and over, shattering then congealing the blue glare with lightning speed, until his eyes seemed bombarded with an eternal light. They're killing each other! What are they doing? Shu Nong saw his father's face twist into a grimace and watched Qiu Yumei squirm like a crazed snake. They really are killing each other! Darkness quickly swallowed up their faces and abdomens. The heavy, murky smell of river water seeped out from the room, and when it reached Shu Nong's nostrils, he was reminded of the filthy river flotsam. With the river flowing beneath their window, the one nearly merging with the other, the smells from the window polluted the river, and both created a barrier against Shu Nong's thought processes. He felt as if the world around him had changed, that he really and truly had become feline after falling under the spell of darkness and rank, puckery odors. He mewed and sought out something to eat.

That was the night Shu Nong began spying on his father and Qiu Yumei while they were carrying on.

Shu Nong the voyeur screeched like a tomcat.

Thinking of himself as a tomcat, Shu Nong screeched as he watched.

After each time, a little white object came flying out the second-story window and landed in the river. Shu Nong knew the things belonged to his father but couldn't tell what they were. So once he climbed down and headed for the river, where he saw the thing floating on the surface like a deflated balloon. He plucked it out of the river and onto the bank with a dead branch. It shone glittery white in the moonlight and lay in his hand like a little critter: soft and slippery. Shu Nong slipped it into his pocket and went home to bed. But soon after he lay down, a brilliant idea popped into his head. He took the sheath out, wiped it clean, and, holding his breath, stretched it over his little pecker; he was struck by a sensation of vitality that seized his consciousness. Shu Nong slept like a baby that night, and when he awoke the next morning, he was overjoyed to discover that for some reason, he hadn't wet the bed. Why was that?

The story goes that the sheaths Shu Nong fished out of the river solved his problem, but you needn't buy into that argument if it seems too far-fetched.

Shu Nong's night prowls atop number 18 went undetected for the longest time. Then one day, Old Shu found two yuan missing from his dresser drawer, so he searched his sons' pockets. In Shu Gong's pockets, he found one yuan and some change and a pack of cigarettes; in Shu Nong's pockets, he found three condoms. Needless to say, the unexpected discovery of condoms shocked and enraged Old Shu.

The first order of business for Old Shu, whose methods of punishment were unique on Fragrant Cedar Street, was to tie Shu Gong to his bed. Then he removed a cigarette from his son's pack, lit it, and puffed it vigorously. He asked the hog-tied Shu Gong, "Want a puff?" Shu Gong shook his head. "Here, try it. Don't you want to be a smoker?" Before waiting for an answer, he shoved the lit end of the cigarette into Shu Gong's mouth, and Shu Gong screamed bloody murder. Old Shu clamped his hand over his son's mouth. "Stop that crazy screaming. It won't hurt long. The cigarette will burn out in no time. You can have another one tomorrow if you want."

Shu Nong's punishment was a touchier matter since Old Shu wasn't sure how to handle the situation. When he called his younger son into the little storeroom, he could barely keep from laughing as he held the three condoms in his hand and asked, "Do you know what these are?"

"No."

"Where did you get them?"

"The river. I fished them out."

"What did you have in mind? You're not making balloons out of them, are you?"

Shu Nong didn't answer. Then Old Shu saw flashes of deep green light in his son's eyes as he answered in a raspy voice: "They're yours."

"What did you say?" Suddenly, Old Shu knew he had a problem. He wrapped his hands around Shu Nong's neck and shook his puny skull for all he was worth. "How do you know they're mine?"

Shu Nong's face was turning purple, but rather than answer, he just stared into the strangler's face, then let his gaze slide down past the brawny chest and come to rest on his father's fly.

"What are you looking at?" Old Shu slapped Shu Nong, who flinched although his gaze stuck stubbornly to his father's fly. He was given another glimpse of the blue glare, which made him light headed. Old Shu grabbed his son's hair and banged his head against the wall. "Who were you spying on? Who in the hell have you been spying on?" Shu Nong's head banged into the wall once, twice, but he felt no pain. He was watching blue specks dance before his eyes like a swarm of wasps. He heard the screech of a cat on the roof; he and the sound merged into a single entity.

"Cat," Shu Nong said weakly as he licked his torn gums.

Old Shu wasn't sure what his son was talking about. "Are you saying the cat was spying?"

"Right, the cat was spying."

Some Fragrant Cedar Street neighbors passing beneath the window at number 18 stopped to gawk as Old Shu beat his son mercilessly. People living on Fragrant Cedar Street considered boys well raised if they were beaten often, so there was nothing unusual here. But the victim's behavior perplexed them. Instead of screaming and carrying on, Shu Nong appeared determined to bear up under the punishment, which was a big change from before.

"What did Shu Nong do?" one of the window gawkers asked.

"Wet the bed!" Old Shu replied from inside.

No one had any reason to suspect any different, since Shu Nong's bed-wetting was well known up and down Fragrant Cedar Street. The neighbors were sensitive, alert people but not particularly adept at digging beneath the surface to get to the heart of a matter. When Shu

Nong's destructive tendencies first began to manifest themselves, the people were too tied up in their belief that he was still fourteen and still wet the bed to spot the differences.

Shu Nong had stopped wetting the bed at the age of fourteen, but no one would believe it. Or better put, people found Shu Nong's bed-wetting interesting, but not the cessation of his bed-wetting. Take Shu Nong's mortal enemy, Hanzhen, for instance: she chanted the following when she jumped rope:

One four seven, two five eight,
Shu Nong bed-wets at a nightly rate.

Hanli, who rarely spoke to her mother, told a schoolmate, "My mother's a slut, and I despise her."

Folks assumed that Hanli was aware of her bloodline. Since half the women on Fragrant Cedar Street feuded with Qiu Yumei, any one of them would have happily let her in on the secret. But more to the point was Hanli's precociousness. She didn't need to be told what was what. You can't wrap a fire in paper, after all.

Hanli had not spoken to Old Shu for years. He bought her a scarf for her seventeenth birthday, but deaf to his entreaties, she cut him dead at the foot of the stairs. So he gave the scarf to Qiu Yumei, who tried to drape it around Hanli's shoulders. Hanli tore it out of her hands and flung it to the ground, then spit on it. "Who needs it? Who knows what you're up to?"

"Old Shu gave it to you only because he likes you. Don't be an ingrate."

"Who asked him to like me? Who knows what you're up to?"

"What do you mean by 'what we're up to'?"

"You know what I'm talking about."

"No, I *don't*. You tell me."

"I'm ashamed to." Suddenly burying her face in her hands, Hanli burst out crying. Then, with tears still streaming down her face, she began combing her hair before the mirror. In the reflection, she saw her mother bend over to pick up the scarf, her face frightfully pale. Hanli wished her mother would rush up and pull her hair so they could have a real fight and get some of that hatred out of their systems. But Qiu Yumei just stood there, wordlessly twisting the scarf around her fingers. Threads of pity settled over Hanli, who said through her sobs, "I don't want it. Give it to Hanzhen."

So Qiu Yumei took back the scarf, and the next day she wore it outside. Eventually it was Hanzhen who went to school with Old Shu's scarf draped around her shoulders. When asked, she said her mother had ordered it from Shanghai and that her mother loved her and not Hanli.

It was a different matter with Old Lin, whom Hanli treated with fatherly respect. In fact, this alone was the source of at least half the praise Hanli received on Fragrant Cedar Street. Whenever Old Lin was in the middle of a neighborhood chess game, she brought him food and tea, and back home she drew his bathwater. She even trimmed his nails for him. Qiu Yumei told people Hanli was trying to be an elder sister to Old Lin, treating him like a little boy.

"And what about you?" they would ask. "How does that make you feel?"

"It's fine with me," Qiu Yumei would say. "It makes my life easier."

Let's say it's a blustery day and that the rain is pounding the sheet-metal roof of number 18, turning everything wet and forsaken at dusk. A frustrated Old Lin is searching for an umbrella beneath the stairs. He never knows where the family umbrella is kept. He opens Hanli's door. "Where's the umbrella?" Hanli looks at him but says nothing, so he tosses things around until he finds an umbrella with broken ribs and torn oil paper, which he can't open, no matter how hard he tries.

"Chess," Hanli says. "That's all you think about even when it's pouring rain. Don't come running to me if you catch your death of cold."

Old Lin flings the broken umbrella to the floor. "Don't tell me there isn't a working umbrella anywhere in the house!"

"There is," Hanli says, "but *she* took it when she went out. Would it kill you to stick around and pass up one chess match?"

Old Lin sighs. "Shit, what's there to do on a day like this *except* play chess?" He sits down and arranges the pieces just to keep busy, and Hanli surprises him by sitting down across the table.

"I'll play a game," Hanli says.

"Don't be silly, you don't know how to play."

"Sure I do. I learned by watching you."

"All right." Old Lin reflects for a moment. "I'll hand over one of my pieces. What do you want, cart, horse, or cannon?"

Hanli looks down at Old Lin's hands without answering. She's acting strange today.

"You can have two carts and a cannon. What do you say?"

"Up to you."

Old Lin removes two carts and a cannon and lets Hanli open. But she just moves her vanguard cannon and stops. Obviously, her mind isn't on chess.

"Papa, why don't you two sleep in the same room?"

"Just play, and no foolish questions."

"No. I want some answers."

"She doesn't like me, and I don't like her, so why should we sleep in the same room?"

"But I hear noises in her room at night."

"She walks in her sleep. She's never been a sound sleeper."

"No, I heard Old Shu from downstairs — "

"Keep playing, and stop with all that nonsense."

"Everyone says she and Old Shu — "

"You're getting on my nerves!" He picks up a chess piece and bangs the board with it. "What you people do is your business."

"What do you mean *our* business? It's your business, too. Do you know what people call you?"

"Shut up! Now you're really getting on my nerves!" He stands up, grabs the chessboard, and dumps everything on Hanli. "You bastards won't let me live in peace!"

Old Lin scoops up the broken umbrella and runs downstairs. Rain beating down on the sheet-metal roof has turned the dusk wet and forsaken. Hanli is on her knees, picking up the chess pieces, biting her lip to keep from crying out loud. She tries to figure out what's up with her father. What's up with this family? She can tell by the sound that the rain is picking up, and before long she fantasizes that it is about to innundate Fragrant Cedar Street. From where she sits on the floor, she feels as if the whole building were sinking. With darkness settling around her, she gets up to turn on the lights. Nothing happens, which scares her. Rushing over to the window to look downstairs, she sees Shu Gong poke his head out his window to pull in the line on which his blue underpants have been drying. Darkness claims Fragrant Cedar Street, all but a single bright spot on the crown of Shu Gong's head. Hanli runs downstairs, her flying feet making the stairway shake and creak. In the grip of a vaguely despairing thought, she hears her heart murmur, People should leave one another alone. I'll leave you alone, and you do the same for me.

Hanli bursts into the little room in the Shu flat and plops breathlessly into a wicker chair. Shu Gong eyes her suspiciously. "Who's after you?"

"Ghosts," Hanli says.

"The electricity is out, probably a downed wire."

"It's not the dark I'm afraid of."

"Then what is it?"

"I'm not sure."

"You don't have to be afraid of anything while I'm around." Unable to see Hanli's face in the darkness, Shu Gong grabs hold of the wicker chair and leans down to look more closely; but she turns away from him, the tip of her braid brushing his face.

"People should leave one another alone," Hanli says. "I'm not going to get involved in their affairs anymore, and they'd better not get involved in mine."

"Who's involved in whose affairs?" Shu Gong stops to ponder. "People should try to take care of themselves."

"I'm not talking to you," Hanli says.

"Then who are you talking to?" Shu Gong lifts a strand of her hair and tugs it.

"To myself." She slaps at his hand but misses, which he finds exciting.

"You're something, sure as hell." He yanks the hair out by its root. "It sure is long," he says, mesmerized by the strand of hair. "And really dark." A pulsating desire wraps itself around him; suddenly materializing, it emanates from Hanli, her natural scent making him limp all over. It is more than he can stand. He can hardly breathe. The time has come to inject life into the fantasy that visits him at night. Without warning, he throws his arms around Hanli, sticks out his tongue, and licks her lips. She screams and struggles to get out of the wicker chair, but the frantically licking Shu Gong covers her mouth with his hand. "Don't scream! Keep it up, and I'll kill you!"

Hanli recoils like a little bunny and lets him lick her face as much as he likes, calming herself by staring at the curtain of rain outside the window. "This isn't so bad," she says, sensing the time has come to see what it's like to be with a boy. She can show Qiu Yumei that she knows a thing or two about being shameless, too. This isn't so bad. People should leave one another alone. Hanli smiles and gently pushes Shu Gong away. "We need a real date," she says in the darkness, emphasizing the word *date.*

"How do we do that?" Shu Gong asks, holding her hand and not letting go. He is breathing hard.

"Leave it to me, I'll teach you," she says. "Now let go."

"If you're playing games with me, I'll kill you." Shu Gong shoves her away. He is already very, very wet.

"I'm not." Hanli gets to her feet, puckers up, and gives Shu Gong a peck on the cheek. "I have to go upstairs. We'll do it. Just be patient."

In his search for some wire to make a toy gun, Shu Nong went into the storage room beneath the stairs. The latch was broken, so all it took was a good shove to open the door. Shu Nong found it strange that the room was deserted except for the cat sitting on an old slatted trunk, its eyes flashing. He wondered if the cat was up to no good, since cats are such inscrutable animals. When he walked over to pick it up, the cat sprang out of the way, leaving a pair of plum-blossom paw prints on the trunk. Shu Nong recalled this trunk as a place where his father stored all kinds of odds and ends. Maybe he'd find the wire he needed inside. He raised the lid and nearly jumped out of his skin. Two people were coiled up inside, and they were as frightened as he was.

Shu Gong and Hanli tried to make themselves invisible inside the trunk. He was naked, so was she. His face was scarlet, hers was ghostly white.

"What do you think you're doing?" Shu Nong nearly shouted.

"Playing hide-and-seek." Hanli covered her face with her hands.

"Liar," Shu Nong said scornfully. "I know what you're up to."

"Don't tell anybody, Shu Nong." Hanli grabbed his arm. "I'll give you anything you want."

"We'll see how I feel."

Shu Nong slammed the lid down and turned to leave. By then, the cat was outside, so he walked toward it. Shu Gong jumped out of the trunk, grabbed him from behind, and dragged him back into the storage room. He easily knocked Shu Nong to the floor, then walked over and shut the door. "What are you doing here?"

"Looking for some wire. Nothing to do with you."

Shu Gong removed a piece of wire from the trunk and waved it in front of Shu Nong. "This it?" Shu Nong reached for it, but Shu Gong pushed his hand away and said, "I'll hold on to it for now. If you breathe a word of this, I'll seal your mouth with it, and you can spend the rest of your life as a mute."

Shu Gong was buck naked. Shu Nong noticed that his pecker was as stiff and big around as a carrot, with threads of purplish blood on the tip. As he stared at the bloodstains, his curiosity turned to fear. He looked over at the trunk. Hanli was sitting up, her face bloodless, her arms crossed over her breasts. Still, he detected the radiance of her body, the familiar bluish glare that characterized the bodies of Lin women. It stung his eyes. Shu Nong was feeling bad, real bad. He walked to the door again. By now, the cat was crouched on the first step. As soon as he was outside the room, Shu Nong threw up, the contents of his stomach spilling out in oceanic quantities. He had never thrown up like that before and had no idea why he was doing it now or why he couldn't stop. In the ensuing dizziness, he saw the cat hop up the stairs, one step at a time, until it disappeared from view.

One morning, Shu Nong instinctively knew that he had become Shu Gong's mortal enemy. At home, in the neighborhood, in school—wherever they were, Shu Gong gave him a glacial look out of the corner of his eye; Shu Nong had begun to cast a dark shadow over Shu Gong's secret happiness. Knowing that he was an obstacle in his brother's way, Shu Nong consciously avoided Shu Gong's stony gaze. It's not my fault, he reasoned. I'm a cat, and cats see everything. You can't blame a cat.

"Did you tell anybody?" Shu Gong grabbed Shu Nong's ear.

"No."

"How about Papa, did you tell him?"

"No."

"Watch out. Keep that mouth of yours shut." Shu Gong held up the piece of wire to show Shu Nong.

Shu Nong sat at the table, shoveling food into his mouth with his hand, a reprehensible habit with a long history. Old Shu could not get him to change, not even with his fists. No one knew he was just being catlike. That behavior symbolized Shu Nong's increasing inscrutability, but no one in the family realized it.

"If you tell anybody, I'll seal your mouth with this wire, understand? That's a promise, not a threat," Shu Gong said in measured tones before slicking down his hair with vegetable oil, putting on his white sneakers, and heading outside.

Shu Nong knew where he was going, and his thoughts turned to his father, who threatened him the same way when he was caught climbing the downspout. Who said I can't tell? If I feel like telling somebody, I will, and if I don't, I won't. They can't do a thing about it. They weren't fated to really shake people up, he reasoned; that was left to him. He followed people, seeing everything, and seeing it first. Is there a soul alive who can hide from the eyes of a cat?

They say Shu Nong followed lots of people, not just his brother and mortal enemy, Shu Gong.

As the sound of whistling faded away, Shu Nong calculated that his brother had passed the storage room and jumped to the street from the windowsill. Pinching his nose closed, he hugged the wall and followed Shu Gong to the limestone quarry, where Hanli waited. It was always the same: Shu Gong and Hanli hid between a wall and a waist-high stack of bricks, the space between stuffed with a battered bamboo basket, like a sentry.

Without a sound, Shu Nong flattened out on the ground and watched them through the gaps in the woven basket. Sometimes he saw their feet float and bob like paper boats. Shu Nong didn't think he could control the urge to screech like a cat, but somehow he managed. Afraid of being discovered, he lay on his belly and held his breath until his face turned purple.

Fragrant cedars are long gone from Fragrant Cedar Street, replaced by acacias and parasol trees. Let's say the acacias are in bloom. When the first winds blow, we see a light purple haze shimmer above the eaves of the dark building, illusory somehow; the air is heavy with the redolence of fauna. It's the outdoor season, so we all troop outside. Nineteen seventy-four, if memory serves, early autumn, late afternoon.

The boys gather in the courtyard of Soybean's yard, around a pile of stone dumbbells. Most boys on Fragrant Cedar Street can lift a hundred-pound dumbbell. We see Shu Nong push open the gate and stand on the threshold, wondering if he should go in or back out. He seems to be in a trance, standing there, picking his nose with the pinky of his left hand.

"Get the hell out of here, bed wetter." One of the boys runs up and shoves him.

"I just want to watch," he says as he leans against a gatepost. "Can't I even watch?"

"Come tell us what the young lovers Shu Gong and Hanli do."

"I don't know."

"Don't know or won't say? If you won't tell us, then get the hell out of here."

Shu Nong stays put, his free hand sliding up and down the post. After a moment, he says, "They hide in a slatted trunk."

"A slatted trunk?" the boys hoot. "Doing what?"

"Fucking," Shu Nong says maliciously. He bites his lip as he jerks open the gate and is gone like a puff of smoke.

Hanli realized it had been a long time since her last period, two months by her reckoning, and she didn't know why. She was nauseated and felt tired, limp, and sluggish all the time. Frequently downcast, she suspected it was a result of what she and Shu Gong were doing. But she couldn't be sure. When she tried to ask her mother, the words rose to the tip of her tongue and no farther. Deciding to ask a doctor instead, she slipped off to the clinic. When the doctor uttered that fateful word, his voice dripping with disgust, Hanli reacted as if struck by lightning; she was virtually paralyzed.

"Lin Hanli, you're pregnant. What school do you go to?" The doctor glared at Hanli, who snatched her sweater off the chair and dashed out of the clinic, covering her face with her sweater so people sitting in the corridor would not recognize her. She emerged into the blinding sunlight of a warm, breezy afternoon. The city and the streets closed in on her as always, but this time she was caught in the fetters of disaster and could hardly breathe. "You're pregnant!" Like a steel band cinched around her neck. How did this happen? What'll I do? Nervously, Hanli walked up to the post office and stopped to let her eyes wander up and down Fragrant Cedar Street. Few people were out and about on that peaceful afternoon; the cobblestones shimmered beneath the sun's rays. Hanli didn't dare walk down Fragrant Cedar Street since now it was an enormous pit waiting to claim her.

Hanli sat on the post office steps, her thoughts chaotic. She considered going to Shu Gong, who would be home asleep, but was afraid to enter Fragrant Cedar Street. Maybe she could wait till nightfall, when no one would see her. Where is all this sunlight coming from? How come the afternoon is so long? As hope faded, she felt like crying. But no tears came, for some strange reason. Maybe she needed to escape the eyes of Fragrant Cedar Street residents. Sometime after four o'clock, she spotted Hanzhen walking home with her schoolbag over her shoulder. She was eating candy. "Hey, what are you doing here?" Hanli grabbed her sister's bag and wouldn't let go. There was madness in her eyes as she looked into Hanzhen's round, ruddy face.

"Say something! What's wrong?" Hanzhen was nearly shouting.

"Not so loud." Like a girl snapping out of a daydream, Hanli clamped her hand over her sister's mouth. "Tell Shu Gong I need to see him."

"What for?"

"Just say I have to talk to him about something."

"No. You shouldn't have anything to do with boys like him."

"That's my business." Hanli pulled a handful of peanuts out of her pocket and stuffed them into Hanzhen's hand. "Hurry, and don't tell anybody."

Hanzhen finally agreed, and as Hanli watched her run toward the dark building at number 18, she breathed deeply to calm herself. This wasn't her problem alone—it was Shu Gong's, too. Would he know what to do? She'd wait for him there. The afternoon seemed endless. Later that day, Hanli and Shu Gong walked single file to their love nest, the limestone quarry, where Hanli sat down and hugged herself tightly as Shu Gong rested on his elbow. This was one of Fragrant Cedar Street's better-known love scenes a decade or so ago.

"What'll we do?" Hanli asked him.

"How should I know?" Shu Gong replied.

"Can we get rid of it?"

"How?"

"Don't you have any idea?"

"Who knows things like that? I can barely keep my eyes open. Let me get some sleep."

"No sleeping. You're the original sleeping dog."

"Who do you think you're talking to? I could beat the shit out of you."

"I'm talking to you. Why can't you figure a way out of this mess instead of always thinking about sleeping?"

"How should I know what the hell's wrong with you? Other guys play around with girls without getting into trouble."

"I don't know what happened either. What if we try to beat it out?"

"Beat it out? With what?"

"I don't care. Try one of those bricks."

"Where should I hit?"

"Here, and pretty hard."

"OK, here goes. It's going to hurt."

Hanli closed her eyes as Shu Gong swung the brick, really putting some arm into it and drawing shrieks of pain from Hanli. "Not so hard, you coldhearted bastard!"

"You're the one who said to hit hard. Do it yourself then."

Shu Gong jammed the brick up against Hanli's belly. He was mad, and it was her fault. He brushed the dirt off the seat of his pants as he turned to leave.

But Hanli wrapped her arms around his leg and wouldn't let go. She dug into his pant leg and held on for dear life. "You can't leave just like that." She looked up at him.

"Then what should we do?" Shu Gong asked.

"Kill ourselves," she blurted out after a thoughtful pause.

"That isn't funny."

"I mean it, we die together."

"You're crazy."

"Neither of us lives. We'll jump into the river."

"I can swim, so I won't die."

"No. We tie ourselves to a rock. That'll do it."

"Screw you. I'm not ready to die."

"I'll report you. That's a death sentence. You choose how you want to go."

"I'm not afraid, I'm just not ready to die."

"One way or the other, you're going to. Don't think I won't say you raped me."

Shu Gong sat down and scratched his mussed hair, giving Hanli a look of malignant hostility. On that afternoon, Hanli was cold and detached, like a woman rich in the ways of the world and familiar with the tricks necessary to get by. Shu Gong broke into a sweat on his back and felt nearly paralyzed. When he looked into the weakened sun's rays over the limestone quarry, he saw millions of dust particles spiraling lazily downward. Shu Gong snapped off a wolfberry twig and broke it into pieces, which he crammed down the sides of his high-topped sneakers. Then he rubbed the sneakers. "Whatever," he said. "If you want me to die, that's OK with me. So I die, so what?"

"So what?" Hanli sneered. "What does that mean? I didn't get into this mess alone."

"Don't be stupid. When are we supposed to go out and die?"

"Tomorrow. No, tonight."

Hanli took Shu Gong's hand. He shook her off. She threw her arms around his neck. He pushed her away. Shu Gong looked at the patch of skin revealed beneath the collar of Hanli's sweater, a piece of floating white ice. He pounced on her, pushing her to the ground and tearing the buttons off her coat, which he held in his hand to see clearly before throwing them behind the pile of bricks and pawing at Hanli's purple sweater. He heard the subtle sound of snapping threads.

Hanli was staring wide-eyed, her eyes taking on the subdued purple of her sweater, not a trace of fear in them. "Yes, it'll be dark soon." She appeared to smile when she said that, then obediently let Shu Gong have his way with her.

Shu Gong gasped as he ripped off her chemise: Hanli's small, firm breasts were covered with purple blotches, her nipples dark and enlarged. Shu Gong sensed that her body had undergone subtle changes. He had done what he had set out to do the past few months: he had fixed Hanli real good. "It doesn't matter to me," he said. "If you want me dead, then that's what you'll get."

Not far from the limestone quarry, a cat screeched mournfully, but they didn't notice.

The cat was Shu Nong.

After the curtain of night fell, Shu Nong followed Shu Gong and

Hanli to Stone Pier, which is at the southern end of Fragrant Cedar Street but hasn't been used for years. It was Shu Nong's favorite spot from which to watch people swim. But this was not the swimming season, and he wondered what they were doing there. He climbed onto a broken-down derrick to observe them through the cracked windshield. From that vantage point, he could look down on the river that flowed through town, although when there was no wind, the water lay heavily, like molten bronze. A motley assortment of lamps were lit in homes along the banks; a new moon reflected in the surface of the water was a luminous oval of goose-down yellow. The two people sitting on the river's edge looked like disconnected marionettes. Not sure what they were doing, Shu Nong observed their movements. First they tied themselves together with a rope, then rolled a large rock up to the river very, very slowly, waddling like geese. Shu Nong assumed it was some sort of game. They stopped at the river's edge. A cat on the opposite bank screeched. Shu Nong heard Shu Gong announce to the river, "So we die, what's the big deal?" Then they wrapped their arms around each other and jumped in with a thud and a splash that sent silvery spray in all directions. The moon splintered.

Die? Finally, Shu Nong reacted. Shu Gong and Hanli are drowning themselves in the river! He jumped down off the derrick and made a mad dash back to number 18. His flat was quiet, deserted, so he ran upstairs and banged on Qiu Yumei's door. "In the river! Drowned themselves!" Shu Nong screamed at the dark red door. He heard rustling noises inside.

Qiu Yumei opened the door a crack. "Who drowned themselves?" she asked.

"Hanli and Shu Gong!" Shu Nong stuck his head inside to look for his father. He spotted a shaky hand resting on a shoe under the bed. He knew the hand belonged to his father. With a squeal, he tore downstairs, shouting to the steps, to the accumulated junk, to the window:

In the river!
Drowned themselves!

To this day, if I close my eyes, I can see them fishing the bodies out of the dark river at the end of Fragrant Cedar Street as if it were yesterday. Every man who knew how to swim dived into the black, foul-smelling water. People thronged the neglected Stone Pier, where a single street lamp lit faces that shimmered like the surface of the water. The Shu and Lin families from number 18 were central figures in the drama, and folks took particular notice of Old Shu, who dived to the bottom, came up for air, then dived again, over and over, while Old Lin stood watching on the bank, a chess piece in his hand. Some said it was a horse. Qiu Yumei leaned against an electric pole and sobbed into her hands, hiding her face.

Shu Gong was first out of the water. Old Shu flung his son over his shoulder and ran up and down Fragrant Cedar Street. Black, foul-smelling water spewed from the boy's mouth. Then they fished out Hanli, and Old Shu did the same with her. She looked like a lamb rocking back and forth on Old Shu's shoulder, but no water emerged from her mouth, not even when he had run all the way to the upstairs flat at number 18. She didn't even twitch. Old Shu laid Hanli's body on the floor and felt her pulse. "Nothing," he announced. "She's past saving."

Shu Nong elbowed his way up through the crowd to see what the drowned Hanli looked like, oblivious to the noisy babble all around him. Instinct told him that Hanli was dead. He looked down at her water-soaked body, still dripping as it lay on the floor, each drop the same blue color as her glossy skin. Hanli's staring pupils were more captivating than cat's eyes poking through the darkness. She was really, really blue, and Shu Nong was struck by the realization that all the females he peeked at were blue, even the dead ones. He assumed there was something blue about women and death. What was going on here?

Hanli's death became *the* topic of conversation on Fragrant Cedar Street's lanes and byways. People still loved her, even after she was dead, and they told anyone who would listen that like a tender flower growing in a dank cellar, she was fated to die young. This, you must realize, effectively captures the complex and veiled relationships among the people at number 18. The residents of Fragrant Cedar Street were incapable of glossing over the influence of Old Shu and Qiu Yumei on their children, so the suicide pact of Hanli and Shu Gong was overlaid by a film of tragic romanticism.

From then on, the black lacquer gate at number 18 remained shut to outsiders. Milk deliveries were placed in a small wooden box outside the gate, and if you peeked through a crack, all you saw was a dark building. It was just a feeling, but number 18 seemed off-limits in the wake of the Lin girl's premature death. By looking up, you could, if you were observant, see a change in Qiu Yumei's upstairs window: now it was sealed with sheet metal, which made it look from a distance like the door of a pigeon cage.

Sensitive folks tried to guess who had sealed the window, thereby forcing the trashy Qiu Yumei to spend her days in darkness. "Who did it?" they asked Hanzhen. She said she didn't know, adding, "Go away, and leave my family alone." So they asked Shu Nong, but he wouldn't answer, although his crafty eyes said, Oh, I saw, all right. Nothing gets past me. I see it all.

Let's say it's the night of Hanli's death, and Old Lin drags some used sheet metal and his tool pouch into Qiu Yumei's room, without knocking first. He bangs his hammer against the windowsill three times: *bang bang bang*.

"What do you think you're doing?"

"Sealing up the kennel door."

"Damn it, you'll block out the light."

"It has to be sealed up, and you know why."

"No. Have you gone mad?"

"Keep your voice down. I'm doing it for your own good."

"I'll suffocate in here. No one seals a southern window."

"I'm worried that Hanli's spirit will come looking for you. The river is right outside that window."

"Don't try to frighten me, it won't work. I did nothing to offend Hanli."

"I'm worried you might sleepwalk your way right out that window to your death."

Qiu Yumei climbed out of bed, then sat back down. She buried her head in the quilt and sobbed. "Go ahead, seal it," she said in a muffled voice, "if that's what you want." But Old Lin was too busy nailing up the sheet metal to hear her. He was so good with his hands that in no time the window was sealed airtight. Like I said, from a distance it looked like a pigeon cage in the dark.

How does it feel to return from the dead? To Shu Gong, the attempted suicide was a bad dream from which he awoke drenched. His family stood in the doorway, gawking at him. He felt terrible. "Bring me some dry clothes," he said to his mother. "I want to change." But Old Shu pushed Mother outside. "No changing. Since you didn't drown, you can just dry out on your own. Being wet shouldn't bother someone who can defy death. Go on, dry out, you turtle-egg bastard!"

Shu Gong lay there spent, thinking back to when they were sinking to the bottom of the river, to how Hanli's fingers groped frantically for him and how he pushed her away. He didn't want to die strapped to Hanli, whose finger reached out like a slender fish to peck him on the face before slipping away. Hanli was well and truly dead. He was still alive. Loathing and contempt lay in his father's eyes and in his as well, as they were reflected in the old-fashioned wall mirror; he also saw in them a cold enmity and guardedness. "Get out of here, all of you," Shu Gong demanded. "We have no use for one another, dead or alive." He jumped up and slammed the door shut to remove them from his sight. Slowly, he took off his wet clothes and opened his dresser.

Creak. The door opened, and Shu Nong slipped into the room. He leaned against the door frame to watch Shu Gong change clothes. "I saw the two of you," he blurted out.

"Get the hell out of here." Shu Gong modestly held up his clothing to cover his nakedness.

"I saw."

"Saw what?"

"Everything."

"So you went and told everybody?" Shu Gong walked over to the door and bolted it, then grabbed Shu Nong by the hair with one hand and clapped the other one over his mouth to keep him from shouting. He slammed his brother up against the wall and heard it give and then snap back. Shu Nong's frail little body slumped to the ground as if it were made of sand. *Whoosh!* The breath escaped from Shu Gong's mouth all at once. This was the way to handle things now that something lost had been restored to him. This is how to do it: flatten that disgusting Shu Nong.

I saw Shu Nong out walking one cold early-winter day. He was dragging his schoolbag behind him; with his long, spiky hair, he looked like a porcupine. He was kicking dead leaves on his way home. Whenever there was some kind of commotion, he headed toward it, stood on the perimeter for a moment to see what was going on, then walked off. Once it became clear that there was nothing much to see, he was gone. Hardly anything captured his interest.

Shu Nong was being chased down the street, cradling an air rifle. His pursuer was the man who shot sparrows. "Grab him!" he shouted. "He stole my rifle!" The weapon was nearly as tall as Shu Nong, who finally got tangled up in it and fell in a heap in front of the stone bridge, where he lay rubbing the wooden stock for a moment while he caught his breath; then he tossed the rifle aside and crossed the bridge.

"Don't chase him," someone at the bridgehead teahouse said. "That boy's not all there."

If you knew Shu Nong, you'd realize how wide of the mark this comment was. Shu Nong was all there, all right, and if you have ever been to Fragrant Cedar Street, you know that this is the story of a very clever boy.

Shu Nong noticed a pair of new white sneakers, just like Shu Gong's, on his bed next to his pillow. He picked them up and examined them from every angle.

"Try them on." His father was standing behind them.

This was another major occurrence in Shu Nong's fourteenth year: he had his own white sneakers. "Are these for me?" Shu Nong turned around.

"They're yours. Like them?" Old Shu sat on Shu Nong's bed and inspected the sheet.

"I didn't wet it."

"That's good."

Shu Nong laced up his shoes almost hesitantly, as a result of lingering doubts. He kept glancing over at his father. Shu Nong never dreamed that his father would actually buy him a pair of shoes like this. Normally he wore Shu Gong's hand-me-downs.

"Can I wear them now?" Shu Nong asked.

"You can wear them anytime you like," Old Shu said.

"New Year's is still a long way off," Shu Nong said.

"Then hold off till New Year's," Old Shu replied.

"But that means I have to wait a long time," Shu Nong said.

"Then wear them now." A note of irritation crept into Old Shu's voice. "So wear them now." He began pacing the floor.

The shoes made Shu Nong spry and light on his feet. After bounding around the room, he turned to run outside, but his father stopped him with a shout: "Don't be in such a hurry to go outside. You have to do something for me first."

Shu Nong froze, his mouth snapping open fearfully. "I didn't wet the bed!" he screamed.

Old Shu said, "This isn't about bed-wetting. Come over here." Shu Nong grabbed the door frame, lowered his head, and stayed put as he dimly sensed that the new shoes were a sort of bait. Old Shu raised his voice: "Come over here, you little bastard!" Shu Nong walked over to his father, who grabbed his hand and squeezed it. "I'll be sleeping in your room at night," Old Shu said.

"Why? Did you and Mother have a fight?"

"No. And what I mean is, sometimes. Like tonight."

"That's OK with me. In my bed?"

"No, I'll sleep on the floor."

"Why do that when there's a bed?"

"Never mind. I'll strap you to the bed with a blindfold over your eyes and cotton in your ears. We'll see how you do."

"Are we going to play hide-and-seek?"

"Right, hide-and-seek."

Shu Nong took a good look at his father, holding his tongue as he rubbed the tops of his new sneakers. Then he said, "I know what you're going to do. The upstairs window has been sealed."

"All you have to worry about is getting some sleep. And don't make a sound, understand?"

"I understand. You can't climb in with the window sealed."

"If your mother knocks at the door, just say you're in bed. And not another word more. The same goes for anyone else who knocks at the door. Understand?"

"I understand. But why not do it in the slatted trunk. Isn't it big enough for you two?"

"Don't tell a soul about any of this. You know what I'm capable of, don't you?"

"I know. You'll choke the life right out of me. That's what you said."

"That's right, I'll choke the life right out of you." Old Shu's bushy eyebrows twitched. "What were you mumbling just a minute ago?"

At this point, father and son had flat, expressionless looks on their faces. Old Shu crooked his little finger; so did Shu Nong. They silently hooked their fingers, sealing this odd pact.

Thus began the process that led to the most memorable nights of Shu Nong's youth. He recalled how the black cloth was put over his eyes, how he was tied to the bed hand and foot, and how his ears were stuffed with cotton. Father and Qiu Yumei made love beside him. He was in the same room with them. He saw nothing. He heard nothing. But he sensed their location and movements in the dark; he could tell who was on top and who was doing what to whom. A powerful blue radiance pierced the leaden darkness and touched his eyes, making sleep impossible and rendering movement out of the question. He gulped down large mouthfuls of the musky sweet air, then exhaled it in large puffs. He was getting uncomfortably hot, which he attributed to the dark blue lights baking him as he lay strapped to his bed; the desolate howl of a rat lugging flames on its back emerged from his anguished soul. "I'm hot," he said, "I'm burning up." When Old Shu finally got around to untying the ropes, Shu Nong sounded as if he were talking in his sleep.

Old Shu felt his forehead; it was cold. "Are you sick, Shu Nong?"

Shu Nong replied, "No, I was asleep." Old Shu removed the blindfold. Shu Nong said, "I saw." Then Old Shu took the cotton out of his ears, and Shu Nong said, "I heard."

Old Shu grabbed his son's ear and barked, "Who did you see?"

Shu Nong replied, "She's very blue."

"Who's very blue?" Old Shu pinched the ear hard. "What kind of damned nonsense are you spouting?"

Shu Nong was in such pain he thumped the bed with both feet. "I mean the cat," he screamed, "the cat's eyes are very blue."

Old Shu released his grip and whispered in Shu Nong's ear, "Remember, not a word to anyone."

Shu Nong curled up under his comforter and, with his head covered, said, "If you hit me again, I'll tell. I'm not afraid to die. I'll just turn into a cat. Then nobody will have anything to say about what I do from now on."

Here is the kind of girl Hanzhen was: flighty, sneaky, and headstrong. She loved to eat and was extremely vain. Plenty of girls like that lived on Fragrant Cedar Street, and there isn't much you can say about their lives outside of an occasional newsworthy episode that materialized out of the blue.

It might have been Hanzhen you saw out on the street, but it was Hanli who was on the people's minds, a girl who had died too young. When women took Hanzhen aside and asked, "Why did your big sister want to kill herself?" she replied, "Loss of face." Then when women asked, "Are you sad your sister died?" Hanzhen would pause before saying, "I inherited her clothes." If they kept pestering her, she grew impatient and, arching her willowy brows, said, "You're disgusting, the whole lot of you. All day long you do nothing but keep your eyes peeled for juicy tidbits!" The women compared her with her sister right to her face. "Hanzhen is no Hanli," they would say, "the living is no match for the dead."

To the surprise of all, three months after Hanli's death, Hanzhen herself became the talk of Fragrant Cedar Street. Seen in retrospect, it had nothing to do with the real-life vicissitudes of Fragrant Cedar Street. What the incident actually reflected was the tragic significance of our story. Tragedy is an enormous closed box; once it is opened, people inevitably get shut back inside. If not Hanzhen, it would have been someone else. Can you understand what I'm getting at?

It started with the sweetshop. One day as Hanzhen was passing the sweetshop on her way home from school, she noticed a jar of preserved fruit in the window. As she entered, Old Shi was hanging out a sign that said Closed for Inventory. Hanzhen checked the money in her pocket—she had just enough for a bag of dried plums. She thought she could make the purchase before Old Shi began the inventory. After closing the door, he asked, "What would you like, Hanzhen?"

She tapped the jar. "Dried plums," she said. "I want some dried plums." She was unaware that he had closed the door. She watched him walk around behind the counter, sit down, and start working his abacus. "I want a bag of dried plums," Hanzhen repeated.

"Wait a minute, I'm nearly finished."

As she waited for him to finish, she stared at the jar of dried plums, oblivious to the fact that the door was closed and that she was alone in the shop with Old Shi. Finally, he laid down his abacus. "Dried plums?" he said. "Come back here. I'll give you a special weighing, more than your money's worth." Hanzhen smiled bashfully and ran behind the counter, where she handed Old Shi the money in her hand. He looked at the crumpled bill, then wrapped his hand around hers. "I don't want your money," he said. "My treat."

"Why don't you want it?" Hanzhen asked wide-eyed.

"We'll work a swap," Old Shi said. "I'll give you the dried plums, and you give me something in return."

"Tell me what you want, and I'll go home and get it."

He scooped a big handful of dried plums out of a metal box. "Open your mouth, Hanzhen," he said. She did. With a giggle, he tossed in a dried plum. "Good?"

"Yum," she said.

Altogether, Old Shi flipped five dried plums into Hanzhen's mouth. "Now it's your turn," he said. "Let me see your belly button, that's all I want."

Unable to speak with all those dried plums in her mouth, Hanzhen just shook her head. The strange look on Old Shi's face was one she had never seen before, but the realization came too late, for Old Shi had wrapped his arms around her and was forcing her to the floor, where he crammed the rest of the dried plums into her mouth so she couldn't make a sound. The next thing she felt was Old Shi's sweaty hand pushing her undershirt up and rubbing her exposed navel. Then the hand pulled down her underpants and slipped between her legs. Hanzhen was shocked nearly out of her mind. She wanted to scream but couldn't, with all those dried plums in her mouth.

Old Shi said breathlessly, "Don't scream, don't make any noise. I'll give you ten bags of dried plums and three packages of toffee. Don't scream, don't you scream."

Hanzhen nodded and shook her head as if her life depended on it. She didn't know what he was doing to her; all she could see was

Old Shi's gray head resting against her breasts. Then she felt a sharp pain down below and thought Old Shi was trying to kill her. She grabbed his gray hair with both hands and screamed, "Shame on you! Shame on you!" But there was no sound; it seemed like a fantastic, bizarre dream.

It was nearly dark when Hanzhen walked out of the sweetshop. She hugged the wall as she walked slowly, the schoolbag dangling from her hand, chock-full of preserved fruit that Old Shi had nearly forced her to take. "If you don't tell anybody," he had said, "you can have any treats you want." Hanzhen sucked on a dried plum as she walked. The place where Old Shi had done it felt as if he had left something sharp in there. Hanzhen looked down and was horrified to see a trickle of blood running down her pant leg and onto her shoes and the ground. *Whoop!* The dried plum came sailing out of her mouth as she gaped at the crimson blood. She sat down, hugged her bulging bag to her chest, and started to cry. Passersby ignored her. Sometime later, Old Shu walked by, pushing his bicycle home from work. He asked what was wrong. Hanzhen looked up and bawled, "Shame on Old Shi! Shame on Old Shi!"

The only resident of Fragrant Cedar Street ever thrown into prison was Old Shi from the sweetshop. They dragged him to the local school in chains to be publicly villified. We sat beneath the stage, gazing up at Old Shi's gray head and the look of dejection on his face. Hanzhen was sitting up front, where everyone could gawk at her, though she was oblivious to their looks. She stared blankly at Old Shi, trussed up and on display above her.

Her mortal enemy, Shu Nong, walked up and slyly felt her pocket. When he returned, he said, "She hasn't stopped eating those dried plums. She's still got some in her pocket!" He said Lin Hanzhen was trash, just like her whole family; none of the other neighborhood boys gave him an argument on that score since they had written her off as a worn-out shoe—damaged goods. Under their breath, they called her "a little worn-out shoe." Someone even made up a stinging nursery rhyme for Hanzhen, whose mother, Qiu Yumei, accused Shu Nong of authorship.

If you walked down Fragrant Cedar Street, the one thing you could not escape was the smell of the river that flowed beneath our windows. As I indicated early on, it was like a piece of rusty metal eroding the life of Fragrant Cedar Street. You could not overlook the river's influence, for the street's time was also the river's time.

The residents of Fragrant Cedar Street were tired of putting up with their river. It had taken on the color of its pollutants, and boats from the countryside no longer plied it. One day, an old-timer hooked a rotting sack with his bamboo pole and dragged it up onto the bank. Inside he found a dead infant curled up like a shrimp, a newborn baby boy with a wrinkled face that made him look like a sleeping old man.

The residents of Fragrant Cedar Street had arrived at a point where they didn't know how to deal with their river. It could drown them, but they couldn't do anything to it in return.

One day, Shu Nong had a brilliant idea: he spread a layer of flour over a spot beneath the bridge, then dropped in his fishing line. The minutes lingered until there was a violent tug on his line. He jerked it out of the water. On the end was a worn-out leather shoe—dainty, T-shaped, made for a woman. An onlooker recognized it as one of the shoes Hanli was wearing when she jumped into the river. He threw it back in and murmured, "What cursed luck."

Why Shu Nong got into trouble isn't all that clear.

Let's say it's an ordinary winter morning and Shu Nong is searching for his schoolbag after breakfast. He can rarely find his schoolbag before departing for school. So when he spots it under Shu Gong's cot, he gets down on his hands and knees to get it. But a sleepy Shu Gong presses down on him. "Quit goofing off."

"Who's goofing off? I'm getting my schoolbag."

Shu Gong pins him to the floor and says, "Put a bowl of porridge on the stove for me before you go." A simple request.

"That's not my job," Shu Nong replies. "Do it yourself."

Shu Gong narrows his eyes. "You're really not going to do it?" he asks.

"No," Shu Nong says. "Get out of bed, and do it yourself."

Shu Gong snaps into a sitting position and throws off the covers. "OK, I'm up." He gets out of bed, grumbling, and takes the bowl of porridge over to the stove; then he gives Shu Nong a long look out of the corner of his eye. He jumps up and down to keep warm, bouncing straight into Shu Nong's little room. "You're a lucky bastard I don't feel like pounding you right now," he says as he pulls back the covers on Shu Nong's bed to feel the sheet. It is dry. With a grin, he undoes his pants and relieves himself on Shu Nong's sheet. When he is finished, he snaps his fingers. "Father will come in pretty soon and see you've wet your bed again. I'll let him pound you for me."

Shu Nong stands there stunned, hugging his schoolbag to his chest, his face turning red; instinctively, he runs over to the water vat, scoops out a ladleful of water, and dumps it on Shu Gong's bed. Shu Gong doesn't move a finger. He dresses and says, "Go ahead, sprinkle away. No one will believe I wet my bed, and you'll still be the one to get pounded."

Shu Nong leaves for school after soaking his brother's bed. By lunchtime, he has forgotten the morning's incident—until he sees that Mother has hung out the sheets to dry. Old Shu glared darkly at him.

"I didn't wet the bed, Shu Gong did it."

Old Shu roars, "Liar! You're not only a bed wetter, you're a liar!"

Shu Nong defends himself: "Shu Gong pissed on my bed."

Old Shu jumps up angrily. "Stop lying! Shu Gong was never a bed wetter. Why would he want to piss on your bed?"

"Ask him yourself," Shu Nong says as he sits down at the table and picks up his rice bowl.

Old Shu rushes up and grabs the bowl out of his hand, then picks him up and flings him out the door. "Fuck you, you little bastard!" he bellows. "Nothing to eat or drink for you. Then we'll see if you still wet the bed. And if you still feel like lying!"

Shu Nong sits on the ground in front of the door, looking up at his father and tracing words in the dirt with his finger—*fuck* is one of them. Old Shu slams the door shut, and Shu Nong thumps it a time or two as he climbs to his feet and brushes off the seat of his pants. The cat chooses this moment to spring out through the window. It mews at Shu Nong. It seems to be chewing on a piece of cooked fish.

"Meeow," Shu Nong mews like the cat, then follows it down the street, heading east, all the way to the auto repair shop, where he loses track of the cat. Shu Nong enters the repair shop, where some greasy mechanics are working on cars, their heads hidden under the hoods. Shu Nong squats nearby and watches them work. "What are you doing here?" one of them asks. "Get out right now."

Shu Nong says, "I'm only watching, what's wrong with that?"

A can of gasoline sits on the floor in front of some beat-up cars. Shu Nong is squatting next to it. He sniffs the air to breathe in the gasoline smell. "I know that's gasoline," he says, "and that a single match will light it off."

"You're right," the mechanic says, "so don't play with it. If it goes up, that's the end of you."

Shu Nong hangs around watching them for a long time, and when they realize he is gone, they also discover the missing gas can. They don't associate the one with the other.

Shu Nong walks home with the gas can. People see him, but the problem is no one knows what he plans to do with the stuff. He walks up to the dark building at number 18 and, after hiding the can behind the door, tiptoes inside, where he notes that both his father and Shu Gong are asleep. He softly closes his father's door and jams a toothbrush into the eye of the latch hook. Then he approaches his brother's bed. Shu Gong, whose head is under the covers, is snoring away. Shu Nong curses the covers under his breath: "Watch me even the score, you bastard." He fetches the gas can. The cat has returned home, he discovers, and is perched atop the can, staring with its lustrous green cat's eyes. Shu Nong makes a face at the cat and shoves it off the can, which he carries over to Shu Gong's bed. He pours gasoline on the floor under the bed, smelling its aromatic scent as it spreads silently throughout the room and hearing the dry floorboards soak it up. He walks, and he pours, and he watches the clear liquid seep under the door into Father's room. That should do it, he tells himself. Confident that the gasoline will ignite, he puts the can down and takes a look around; everything is napping, the old, wormy furniture included—all except for the cat, which is watching him with its shiny green eyes. Cat, Shu Nong muses, watch me even the score now. He takes a box of matches from Shu Gong's pocket. His hand shakes; he attributes that to mild fear. So he grits his teeth, lights a match, and drops it to the floor, releasing a brief red flame. The fire takes hold under Shu Gong's bed and begins to spread. He hears the cat screech in agony and watches it streak ahead of the flames.

Shu Nong rushes desperately upstairs, without knowing why. The Lins' door is closed. Qiu Yumei and Hanzhen poke their heads out the kitchen door. "What's gotten into him?" Qiu Yumei asks.

"He's going crazy," Hanzhen says.

Shu Nong ignores them in his race to the rooftop. The first chaotic sounds rise to greet him as he crawls to the roof's edge. He believes he can hear Shu Gong scream as if his soul had left his body and Father trying with all his might to yank open the toothbrush-jammed door. He can even hear bumping sounds as Hanzhen tumbles down the stairs. By then, Qiu Yumei has thrown open a window and is shouting at the top of her lungs: "Fire fire fire fire fire fire . . ."

Shu Nong sees no sign of fire and wonders why. From his vantage point on the roof, he notices a red glow in one of the roof vents, then sees the cat emerge amid a ball of flames. The cat screeches as it burns, giving off a strange charred smell. Its eyes turn from green to purple; it seems poised to pounce on Shu Nong, who contemplates going over to pick it up. But he has second thoughts because of the flames licking its body. How could the cat have caught fire? How could it have followed me onto the roof? Shu Nong watches the cat slink forward a few steps, then crouch down and stop moving. The flames on its body die out, leaving a ball of cinders behind. Shu Nong realizes that his cat is dead—incinerated. He reaches out to feel the corpse—it is hot to the touch. He rubs the cat's eyes. They are still alive—deep purple and shiny bright.

People from all over Fragrant Cedar Street converge on number 18. To Shu Nong, the mob on the run looks like a pack of skittish rats bearing down on his home with loud screeches. He assumes that the building is about to be engulfed in flames, so what possesses them to enter it? He pokes his head over the edge to see what is going on down there. Black smoke pours out of the windows but no flames that he can see. How come? His thoughts are interrupted by a shout from below. "Shu Nong, it's Shu Nong, he's on the roof!" It's Shu Gong down below, brandishing his fists at Shu Nong. He's in his shorts—no sign of flames. Shu Nong wonders why Shu Gong hasn't been burned. Maybe he was pretending to be asleep. Shu Nong sees someone bring up a long ladder and lean it against the building. It's Old Shu. Shu Nong is getting light headed. Things aren't working out as planned. Everything is going wrong. He tries to push the ladder away but can't budge it. Old Shu, his face blackened with soot, is climbing toward him. Shu Nong clings to the top of the ladder. "Don't come up here!" he screams. "Don't come up here!" Old Shu keeps coming, silently, menacingly. Again Shu Nong tries to push the ladder away, but still he can't budge it. He watches his father's smoke-blackened face draw nearer and feels something cold drip from his heart. "Don't come up here!" Shu Nong screams hysterically. "I'll jump if you take another step!" A curtain of silence falls upon the crowd below. Everyone is looking up at Shu Nong. Old Shu stops his advance and joins the others in gazing at Shu Nong for about three seconds before continuing up the ladder. When his cramped fingers touch the roof, he sees Shu Nong leap high into the air like a cat and sail over his head.

With their own eyes, the residents of Fragrant Cedar Street see Shu Nong plunge into the river. Amid shrieks of horror, Shu Nong's voice is the shrillest and loudest of all. It sounds like a cat or, in the final analysis, just like Shu Nong's own voice.

It was an autumn day in 1974 on Fragrant Cedar Street. I think it was some southern holiday but can't recall which one. At dusk, two young northerners were walking from one end of the street to the other. They had stopped off on their way from Shanghai to Nanjing. As they headed down Fragrant Cedar Street, they saw a white ambulance tearing down the narrow street and a crowd of people running toward a dark building. They joined the surging crowd. The building and the area around it were packed with men, women, and children, all seemingly talking at the same time, not a word of which the two northerners could understand. But they detected the subtle odor of gasoline coming from inside the building. "Children playing with fire!" a woman said in Mandarin.

Afterward, the northerners were on the bridge, looking down at the river, its green-tinged black water flowing silently beneath them. When debris from upriver floated under the bridge, it bumped against the stone pilings. They spotted a little white sheath floating past and smiled at each other. One kept silent, but the other said, "Well, fuck me." They were still watching the river when they spotted a charred little animal float by, lying heavily in the water as darkness settled in, making it disappear from time to time. One of the northerners pointed to it and said, "What was that?"

"It looks like a cat," the other one said.

Translated by Howard Goldblatt

THE HUT ON THE MOUNTAIN ❁ *Can Xue*

On the bleak and barren mountain behind our house stood a wooden hut. Day after day I busied myself by tidying up my desk drawers. When I wasn't doing that, I would sit in the armchair, my hands on my knees, listening to the tumultuous sounds of the north wind whipping against the fir-bark roof of the hut and the howling of the wolves echoing in the valleys.

"Huh, you'll never get done with those drawers," said Mother, forcing a smile. "Not in your lifetime."

"There's something wrong with everyone's ears," I said with suppressed annoyance. "There are so many thieves wandering about our house in the moonlight, when I turn on the light I can see countless tiny holes poked by fingers in the window screens. In the next room, Father and you snore terribly, rattling the utensils in the kitchen cabinet. Then I kick about in my bed, turn my swollen head on the pillow and hear the man locked up in the hut banging furiously against the door. This goes on till daybreak."

"You give me a terrible start," Mother said, "every time you come into my room looking for things." She fixed her eyes on me as she backed toward the door. I saw the flesh of one of her cheeks contort ridiculously.

One day I decided to go up to the mountain to find out what on earth was the trouble. As soon as the wind let up, I began to climb. I climbed and climbed for a long time. The sunshine made me dizzy. Tiny white flames were flickering among the pebbles. I wandered about, coughing all the time. The salty sweat from my forehead was streaming into my eyes. I couldn't see or hear anything. When I reached home, I stood outside the door for a while and saw that the person reflected in the mirror had mud on her shoes and dark purple pouches under her eyes.

"It's some disease," I heard them snickering in the dark.

When my eyes became adapted to the darkness inside, they'd hidden themselves—laughing in their hiding places. I discovered they had made a mess of my desk drawers while I was out. A few dead moths and dragonflies were scattered on the floor—they knew only too well that these were treasures to me.

"They sorted the things in the drawers for you," Little Sister told me, "when you were out." She stared at me, her left eye turning green.

"I hear wolves howling," I deliberately tried to scare her. "They keep running around the house. Sometimes they poke their heads in through the cracks in the door. These things always happen after dusk. You get so scared in your dreams that cold sweat drips from the soles of your feet. Everyone in this house sweats this way in his sleep. You have only to see how damp the quilts are."

I felt upset because some of the things in my desk drawers were missing. Keeping her eyes on the floor, Mother pretended she knew nothing about it. But I had a feeling she was glaring ferociously at the back of my head since the spot would become numb and swollen whenever she did that. I also knew they had buried a box with my chess set by the well behind the house. They had done it many times, but each time I would dig the chess set out. When I dug for it, they would turn on the light and poke their heads out the window. In the face of my defiance they always tried to remain calm.

"Up there on the mountain," I told them at mealtime, "there is a hut."

They all lowered their heads, drinking soup noisily. Probably no one heard me.

"Lots of big rats were running wildly in the wind," I raised my voice and put down the chopsticks. "Rocks were rolling down the mountain and crashing into the back of our house. And you were so scared cold sweat dripped from your soles. Don't you remember? You only have to look at your quilts. Whenever the weather's fine, you're airing the quilts; the clothesline out there is always strung with them."

Father stole a glance at me with one eye, which, I noticed, was the all-too-familiar eye of a wolf. So that was it! At night he became one of the wolves running around the house, howling and wailing mournfully.

"White lights are swaying back and forth everywhere." I clutched Mother's shoulder with one hand. "Everything is so glaring that my eyes blear from the pain. You simply can't see a thing. But as soon as I return to my room, sit down in my armchair, and put my hands on my knees, I can see the fir-bark roof clearly. The image seems very close. In fact, every one of us must have seen it. Really, there's somebody squatting inside. He's got two big purple pouches under his eyes, too, because he stays up all night."

Father said, "Every time you dig by the well and hit stone with a screeching sound, you make Mother and me feel as if we were hanging in midair. We shudder at the sound and kick with bare feet but can't reach the ground." To avoid my eyes, he turned his face toward the window, the panes of which were thickly specked with fly droppings.

"At the bottom of the well," he went on, "there's a pair of scissors that I dropped some time ago. In my dreams, I always make up my mind to fish them out. But as soon as I wake, I realize I've made a mistake. In fact, no scissors have ever fallen into the well. Your mother says positively that I've made a mistake. But I will not give up. It always steals into my mind again. Sometimes while I'm in bed, I am suddenly seized with regret: the scissors lie rusting at the bottom of the well; why shouldn't I go fish them out? I've been troubled by this for dozens of years. See my wrinkles? My face seems to have become furrowed. Once I actually went to the well and tried to lower a bucket into it. But the rope was thick and slippery. Suddenly my hands lost their grip and the bucket flopped with a loud boom, breaking into pieces in the well. I rushed back to the house, looked into the mirror, and saw the hair on my left temple had turned completely white."

"How that north wind pierces!" I hunched my shoulders. My face turned black and blue with cold. "Bits of ice are forming in my stomach. When I sit down in my armchair I can hear them clinking away."

I had been intending to give my desk drawers a cleaning, but Mother was always stealthily making trouble. She'd walk to and fro in the next room, stamping, stamping, to my great distraction. I tried to ignore it, so I got a pack of cards and played, murmuring "one, two, three, four, five . . ."

The pacing stopped all of a sudden and Mother poked her small dark green face into the room and mumbled, "I had a very obscene dream. Even now my back is dripping cold sweat."

"And your soles, too," I added. "Everyone's soles drip cold sweat. You aired your quilt again yesterday. It's usual enough."

Little Sister sneaked in and told me that Mother had been thinking of breaking my arms because I was driving her crazy by opening and shutting the drawers. She was so tortured by the sound that every time she heard it, she'd soak her head in cold water until she caught a bad cold.

"This didn't happen by chance." Sister's stares were always so pointed that tiny pink measles broke out on my neck. "For example, I've heard Father talking about the scissors for perhaps twenty years. Everything has its own cause from way back. Everything."

So I oiled the sides of the drawers. And by opening and shutting them carefully, I managed to make no noise at all. I repeated this experiment for many days and the pacing in the next room ceased. She was fooled. This proves you can get away with anything as long as you take a little precaution. I was very excited over my success and worked hard all night. I was about to finish tidying my drawers when the light suddenly went out. I heard Mother's sneering laugh in the next room.

"That light from your room glares so that it makes all my blood vessels throb and throb, as though some drums were beating inside. Look," she said, pointing to her temple, where the blood vessels bulged like fat earthworms. "I'd rather get scurvy. There are throbbings throughout my body day and night. You have no idea how I'm suffering. Because of this ailment, your father once thought of committing suicide." She put her fat hand on my shoulder, an icy hand dripping with water.

Someone was making trouble by the well. I heard him letting the bucket down and drawing it up, again and again; the bucket hit against the wall of the well—boom, boom, boom. At dawn, he dropped the bucket with a loud bang and ran away. I opened the door of the next room and saw Father sleeping with his vein-ridged hand clutching the bedside, groaning in agony. Mother was beating the floor here and there with a broom; her hair was disheveled. At the moment of daybreak, she told me, a huge swarm of hideous beetles flew in through the window. They bumped against the walls and flopped onto the floor, which now was scattered with their remains. She got up to tidy the room, and as she was putting her feet into her slippers, a hidden bug bit her toe. Now her whole leg was swollen like a thick lead pipe.

"He," Mother pointed to Father, who was sleeping stuporously, "is dreaming it is he who is bitten."

"In the little hut on the mountain, someone is groaning, too. The black wind is blowing, carrying grape leaves along with it."

"Do you hear?" In the faint light of morning, Mother put her ear against the floor, listening with attention. "These bugs hurt themselves in their fall and passed out. They charged into the room earlier, at the moment of daybreak."

I did go up to the mountain that day, I remember. At first I was sitting in the cane chair, my hands on my knees. Then I opened the door and walked into the white light. I climbed up the mountain, seeing nothing but the white pebbles glowing with flames.

There were no grapevines, nor any hut.

Translated by Ronald R. Janssen and Jian Zhang

THE BIG DRUGSTORE ❊ *Bei Cun*

I am gone like the shadow when it declineth . . . —Ps. 109.23

Autumn is a very dry season—when the wind buffets the leaves of the Chinese redbud, it can suck them dry of all the moisture stored in them. The people of Zhangban would drop the tasks they were doing when this season began and go swarming up the mountains to gather all the different sorts of medicinal herbs that grow in the early autumn. Before they could wither, these leaves, fruits, and stems were made into various extraordinarily effective herbal medicines, which were used to treat chronic ailments like malaria, epilepsy, and infantile convulsions. The once obscure settlement of Zhangban became known far and wide for these secret formulas.

The big Better Life Drugstore put up its hoarding and went into business a hundred years ago. Beneath its upturned, gold-trimmed eaves, it was well stocked with many varieties of herbal medicine you would be hard pressed to put a name to. The noise of medicine being pounded there would usually start up at the same time as the watchman's clapper sounded the third watch on Shunyi Street. Even the night owls of Zhangban would go to bed when they heard it.

In Huotong, some seven hundred *li* away, Zhangban's reputation grew as the medicinal plants on the hills grew. The inhabitants of Zhangban had been prone to sickness, and had come up with some folk prescriptions to try and counter their endless succession of illnesses. They used steamed and candied redbud leaves, for example, in the treatment of cholera. It was generally reckoned among the herbal doctors in the Huotong area that this medicine had prevented the spread of one terrible outbreak of the disease. According to them, what happened was that when the patients took the medicine, their minds cleared, and once the fever had abated, they were even able to go and work in the fields straightaway, harvesting the early autumn wheat, so they did not get behind with the agricultural cycle.

The people of Zhangban refused to reveal what one ingredient of their medicines was, for if they did, the formulas would lose their value. When people in the mountainous Huotong area got sick, they would come to Zhangban to seek out the doctor at the Better Life Drugstore, and because they looked on it as somewhere they felt very much at home, this increased their reliance on it. With a lot of regulars, Zhangban became quite a lively place.

Among these people was a bone doctor from the area, who brought his own apprentice to study under the master at the Better Life. He said to Dong Yun, the head of the establishment, "He won't be able to learn any skills at my place, because it's the slack season in Huotong at the moment, and there are very few people breaking bones in accidents. Medicines for injuries like falls and fractures are less and less useful, and more people are suffering from convulsions and epilepsy."

The would-be apprentice was a lad from another area whose name was Piao. As soon as he walked into the Better Life Drugstore he saw Dr. Dong, and beside him an apprentice named A Biao, who was pounding medicines.

Dr. Dong said, "It's very easy for people to get ill at this season, it's become quite a habit with the villagers here. They've all gone up into the mountains at the moment to gather herbs for medicines."

The bone doctor said, "There's bound to come a day when the illnesses from Zhangban reach Huotong."

Dong Yun smiled. Patting a wine pot with a steam whistle set into it, he said, "There's no special secret in Zhangban; the key to it is just that, the way people here look at it, even lichen can be used in medicines."

Some time in the late afternoon or early evening, there was a death.

The body was found in an abandoned dock along the River Deepwater. A long time ago, the dock had been used for the covered boats that would anchor here, bringing their cargoes of myrrh and aloes. After the cholera, which drove the people of Zhangban to discover their own secret formulas, the herbal business of this dock gradually died away, and in the end its place was taken by the Shaanxi Horse Gang on Rough Stone Road.

The young man's body had got entangled in the weeds growing in the dock, and was discovered by a woman washing yarn there. At the time, she seemed to smell a strange and unfamiliar fragrance, the smell of a herbal medicine, but she could not tell which one.

When Piao came down to the dock to bleach some *tianqi* root, it was already surrounded by a large crowd of people. Death was a frequent occurrence in Zhangban, but this did not seem to tarnish the village's reputation for medical skills because nobody died of illness; they tended to die from unexpected things like slipping and falling into water, or being poisoned, or being stabbed, or being caught in a fire. To this day, they still remember ninety-year-old Fourth Master Liu, who for no apparent reason choked to death one morning on a mouthful of rice. The people of Zhangban took a great interest in this sort of accidental death.

The woman who had been washing yarn spluttered out an account of how she had seen the corpse with her own eyes: "I smelled something nice, and then I saw the body. He was lying in the water looking as if he was swimming."

Piao pushed his way into the crowd and saw the youth. He had a tip-tilted nose, and his lips were bright red, as if he were in the middle of saying something. His body was black, apart from his face, which was quite pink.

The women were commenting sadly, "Such a pity, he's only a slip of a lad."

"Yes, he's probably not even married. Why did he have to die so soon?" Apparently without any qualms, they poked at his face with reeds. It was red, like a fruit.

"Perhaps he's not dead? He seems to be still breathing."

Piao squeezed to the front and squatted down beside the corpse. He had a feeling he had known the man in the past. Then he smelt a familiar smell, and blurted out, "There's something in his mouth!"

A man gave him a strange look, walked over without a word and pulled open the mouth of the corpse—and some small black balls spilled out, one by one. The dregs of some medicine.

Screaming shrilly, the women scattered like fallen leaves in the wind. Only Piao and the man were left.

"He's still alive," said Piao.

"No, he's dead," said the man. "Aren't you scared of dead people?"

Piao said, "He's not dead."

"You'd be a good doctor," said the man. "But it's not unusual for someone to die in Zhangban. I'll take you to the Better Life Drugstore, if you like, to introduce you to the master. I'm a bonesetter myself, but business is slack at the moment."

Piao stood up and said, "I don't want to be a doctor, and I have no wish to see dead people. I'm just interested in herbal medicines, and I smelt something."

When he described the smell, the man said very firmly, "That was aloe. It hasn't been seen in Zhangban for a very long time."

The body was moved to the backyard of the drugstore the next morning. There were already four corpses there.

Night fell over Zhangban in the twinkling of an eye, owing to the great height of Fox Mountain, and just as this time of peace and quiet was beginning, the noise of the medicine wheel grinding in its trough would become particularly loud. Piao moved back and forth, grinding medicines, his whole body leaning against the wheel. Sweat was dropping from his face, but he was not concentrating. He was thinking about the young man who now lay in the backyard on a slab of granite, and whose mouth was giving off a sweet fragrance.

A Biao looked as though he had gone to sleep, and his head was drooping from fatigue as he tossed the medicines into the trough. Piao thought he heard the sound of Master Dong Yun chewing. One of the old man's foibles was a fondness for eating very hard things, like walnuts and opium husks, and sometimes he would enjoy chewing fresh brown twigs and honeysuckle. He would take a patient's pulse and write out prescriptions while chewing away, and he had cured a number of diseases that were common in Zhangban.

"The guy's not dead, is he?" said Piao.

A Biao's head kept nodding as he supplied him with the medicines. He was almost asleep.

"There's a smell coming from his mouth," said Piao, "as if he was in the middle of saying something."

A Biao suddenly gave a terrible shriek: his hand had been crushed by the wheel. Piao saw him scuttling backward and forward, distraught, in the inner room, holding up his arm, which was dripping with blood, and uttering low cries. Piao thought he looked like someone having an epileptic fit.

In a side room, Master Dong Yun had finished his walnuts and appeared to be snoring softly.

"It's nearly time, nearly time . . .," he said.

Piao did not know what "It's nearly time" meant, but when the middle-aged bone doctor had brought him to the drugstore, he too had said something along those lines. That evening, when the doctor left Zhangban, he had looked very serious. It was the turn of the seasons, and Huotong had a thoroughly depressing air to it. It was sometimes hot, sometimes cold—black clouds lowered over the hilltops but the rain was taking a long time to come. On the main road between Zhangban and Huotong, an oxcart or two would drive past every now and then carrying a load of golden orchids and sending up clouds of dust. At the boundary stone, the doctor had seemed to want to say a few words of farewell to Piao, but his gaze was attracted by Fox Mountain, which was covered with all sorts of medicinal plants. When they flowered, it was quite dazzling, but now it was autumn and the flowers had become fruits. There were things darting about among them like so many insects, and on closer inspection you could make out that they were peasants from Zhangban who had gone into the mountains to gather herbs.

The doctor said to Piao, "I'm going back over the mountains to Huotong. It's nearly time, and when you have got the prescriptions, you can come and find me in the graveyard on the north side of Fox Mountain. Remember, this is all about saving people's lives. I don't want to have to look after those dead people up on the mountain all the time. There are a lot of people in Huotong waiting to be cured."

Then he smiled at Piao, patted him on the head and strode off along the main road. He took the path up Fox Mountain, which was the shortcut to Huotong.

Piao watched his master's receding figure, frail looking in the autumn wind. He could not, for the moment, fully take in what the anxious man had said, because his mind was all the time on the youth who had come floating down the river. He liked the way he looked as if he were sound asleep, and he liked his lips, red as cherry blossoms, from which came the scent of aloe and myrrh that he found so refreshing.

He looked up at Fox Mountain before he went back to the Better Life Drugstore, and in his gaze there was an element of yearning. He was noticing the flowers on the mountain, but he was also thinking of a secluded spot on the southern slope where his mother, who had died in the last outbreak of cholera, was buried. In the painful period after she died, it used to take him four hours to cross Fox Mountain to get there, but now he would only need two hours to climb it and see his mother's grave, hidden like a snow-white tooth between a clump of redbud and some golden orchids.

How happy this made him!

Older people are mostly in the habit of rising early and being wide awake at once, but Dong Yun seemed to suffer from an addiction to sleep: not only did he get up very late, he also gave the appearance of being fast asleep even after he had gotten up. The old man would lie on a yellowing bamboo chair and while away the time, his eyes closed. Whenever the drugstore was buying raw materials, the sound of A Biao haggling over prices with the villagers would suddenly become very loud, but Mr. Dong would sleep through even these afternoon commotions. Occasionally one might see him pop some stamens into his mouth and start chewing, without any change in the serenity of his expression, and only from that could one tell he was actually still awake. In the month leading up to the Mid-Autumn Festival, he liked to chew the stamens of the cotton plant, rather than twigs.

Taking advantage of the fact that A Biao was busy buying raw materials and Mr. Dong was fast asleep, Piao once again left the heavy grinding trough. His secret feelings for the youth were still with him, just as strong as ever. He looked uneasy as he passed Mr. Dong's reclining chair—the old traditional doctor, the possessor of Zhangban's secret recipes, appeared to be fast asleep, and if his faint breathing had not been making some of the hairs in his nose move ever so slightly, Piao might have thought that he was dead and had been lying there for at least a hundred years. Mr. Dong had cleverly relied on this talent to ward off the many doctors who had come to Zhangban from other places to try and trick him out of his secret prescriptions. Having racked their brains trying to combat the sicknesses that were prevalent in the mountain region of Huotong, they thought up all sorts of ruses to get the formulas out of him, some of them even coming to the drugstore masquerading as patients. Dong Yun's somnolent expression would only be swept away when he took such a "patient's" pulse. His eyes would then reveal the keenness of their gaze, and he would turn it on the patient and say, "Your condition is incurable; there is nothing I can do for you—you'd better go home!"

And the doctors, their secrets exposed, would withdraw, shamefaced, and leave Zhangban quietly, under cover of dusk. From then on, they were discredited for having violated the professional code of medicine.

It seemed as if this whole mountainous area of southern Fujian, from Zhangban to Huotong, were filling up with secrets in the same way that some nameless diseases spread. But these secrets did not affect what was going on in Piao's mind. The young man was not interested in studying medicine and had soon forgotten the injunctions of the middle-aged doctor; his interest in that youth far outstripped everything else. There were two questions puzzling him: Why had the drugstore people brought his body back? And why did it give off that strange fragrance?

Piao moved round the soundly sleeping Dong Yun and came to the backyard. At once he saw that the other bodies had all disappeared, and only the youth was still there. He had been dressed in a new dark blue gown and black poplin trousers, and his face was still as ruddy as if he were only sleeping. Piao walked slowly over to him and, sitting down on a stone, studied him closely. The youth's long eyelashes made his eyes look like a pair of rosebuds.

"Why did you come here?" Piao wondered. From the look of him, he must have been terribly tired, coming here by water all the way from Huotong. That must be where he was from; maybe his mother set out one morning on the road to Zhangban and never returned, and the youth got it into his head to go and look for her.

Thinking about such things made Piao feel rather abstracted and sleepy. He was suddenly afraid—it was the same sort of fleeting fear he had felt when he parted from the middle-aged doctor. He recalled that he had said to the doctor, "I'm scared of the Better Life Drugstore—the smell of the medicines there makes me feel ill, and I'm afraid they may kill me."

When the doctor heard that, he smiled and said, "Why on earth should they kill you? Doctors save lives, they don't harm people."

But his words had done nothing to dispel the gloom in Piao's mind. Since his arrival, the heavy work of crushing the medicines had worn him out, and he did not even have time to go up the mountain to see his mother. Before coming across the youth who had come floating downriver, nearly all Piao's thoughts had been taken up with his mother. He missed her more and more each day, and he kept turning over in his mind the circumstances surrounding her death.

He remembered the scenes in Huotong when there had been several hundred deaths from cholera. He woke up early one morning to discover that, out of the blue, people he knew well had died, in the cattle pens, beside the wells, in the stables, and on the ridges between the fields—peasants, shopkeepers, bamboo goods merchants, and medical men. It was late one night when the sickness reached his mother. Piao noticed that she suddenly became extremely weak, and her eyes began to shine dully. She was gasping for breath and he had no idea what to do. He asked her, "Mother, Mother, are you hungry?" She was still gasping, and kept pointing at something, but there was nothing there, and it was only then that he realized she was already very sick. But he had not yet made the link between his mother's illness and the current calamity, because he thought his mother could not die since he was not yet grown up.

At midnight, it was so dark that you could see nothing. But with a sudden burst of energy, his mother sat up in bed, her mouth gaping. Piao asked, "Mother, Mother, do you want a drink of water?" but she shook her head vigorously, staring keenly at a spot behind him, and began to shout in terror. He turned, but there was nothing behind him.

His mother was taken up the mountain, on a gray, wet day, in a plain wooden coffin. The cracks in the coffin had been filled with plaster to stop the noxious fumes from escaping. Following behind the funeral procession, Piao came to the southern slope of Fox Mountain for the first time, and the unusual flowers covering the mountainside attracted his attention.

He was sure that his mother had seen something before she died, and he knew that she had wanted not water, but air. The bone doctor from Huotong said that people in Zhangban probably died of many sorts of illnesses, but when they died, they all felt stifled, and so you could say that virtually everyone died of suffocation.

Whenever he remembered these words, Piao felt strangely scared, as if his heart were being tickled with a goose feather, and his own breathing seemed to become rather constricted. This fear did not go away until the youth was brought onto the bank from the dock along the river, because, although drowned, he did not appear to be dead—he was still breathing deeply, and his breath bore the scent of aloe. Piao liked this smell—it drifted across to him among the smells of all the medicinal herbs used in the big drugstore, and floated in the afternoon sunshine.

The youth seemed to have been roused by the shafts of sunlight, and sat up on the slab of granite. He looked all round the drugstore, his starched collar standing up from his new outfit, and the scent of calamus wound among the building's gold-trimmed beams. He and Piao walked out of the drugstore together, heading for the southern slope of Fox Mountain. As they passed the places where there were water plants, there were butterflies dancing above the water, and on the mountain the brilliant flowers dazzled them, but even so, Piao was able to make out his mother's grave at once.

A bowed old man was standing in front of them, and Piao recognized him as Dong Yun. "What are you doing here?" cried the old man sharply.

"A Biao! A Biao!" Before Dong Yun's words were out of his mouth, A Biao had come up to them with a stick in his hand, and his silent bearing filled them with dread.

The stick struck Piao's body as if it were coming down on soft cotton wool. He did not utter a sound, but bit his tongue. A sickly sweet smell gradually blended into the afternoon air.

The body of the youth on the slab of granite was still particularly striking.

The bone doctor had been living on the northern slope of Fox Mountain for two years. This was the side of the mountain that was closest to Huotong, and it was covered with graves. Here, too, there had been a mass of medicinal plants growing, but Huotong people were evidently not as intelligent as the folk in Zhangban, and they were ignorant about such plants and uninterested in them. During the epidemic of aching sickness, when large numbers of corpses had been carried up the mountain, the herbs had been uprooted, and grave after grave had been dug there instead. Six months later, though, the herbs were growing again, between the graves, their recovery happening in step with the quiet changes of the seasons.

After the cholera, there was nothing for the bone doctor to do, and he came with his simple possessions to the northern slope of Fox Mountain, built a wooden hut there to live in, and became the guardian of the graves. Whatever this man of few words did was noticed by the people of Huotong, and one fairly reliable version had it that the doctor had been so downhearted after the calamity that he had gone to live on the mountain to learn all about the medicinal herbs there and to select a remedy that would counter fatal illnesses in the future. Woodcutters on the mountain would see him fiddling around with the flowers in silence, all day long, and he seemed more like a gardener.

It was early one morning when the doctor discovered the youth, and the air was chilly. The doctor was sitting on a slab of stone outside his wooden hut, gazing at all the different-colored flowers on the slope (they were all laid out regularly, like fields) and further off he saw the youth, toiling up the mountainside.

The doctor was aware that the youth had already been there several times and used to move around among the herbs and flowers after the doctor had finished his day's work. Sometimes he stopped in one place, and through the breeze the doctor could hear the faint, filtered sound of crying.

When the doctor went over to him, the youth looked at him rather fearfully, with an uneasy expression in his eyes. In front of him was a very small grave, at first glance no more than a little mound of earth, with no name on it. This was common enough for the graves on this side of the mountain, for everyone knew that they belonged to the people who had died in the last calamity. Apart from their relatives, only the doctor knew the occupants of these graves, most of whom had been his fellow villagers and neighbors, as well as his patients. He had quietly taken note of their names when their relatives had come to sweep the graves. On his piece of paper, covered with marks, the only one missing was the grave in front of the youth, and in fact he had almost completely forgotten about the unremarkable little mound of earth.

"Is this your mother?" he asked the youth.

The youth nodded. His fear seemed to have gone away now. The doctor asked him, "Why do you always come here after I've gone back to the hut?"

The youth said, "I'm afraid you might drive me away."

The doctor patted him on the head and said nothing. He picked up his spade and turned the soil on top of the grave so that it looked much higher, then he put some pine branches on it. He asked the youth, "Will you still be able to remember the place?"

The youth nodded.

"Come with me." Shouldering his spade, the doctor led the youth over to the little wooden hut. Once inside, he made some soup. The youth was obviously hungry, and drank it all at once. The doctor knew he was on his own at home now.

"Are you here all alone?" The youth was looking round the hut. "Aren't you scared at night?"

"No," said the doctor, cleaning the mud off his spade. "I'm not on my own; there are lots of people on the mountainside."

"But they're dead."

"When people die, it just means they're asleep, that's all." He put the spade back against the wall and said to the youth, "When I was ten, my mother and father were swept away by a whirlpool in the River Deepwater, and when they were found three days later, downstream, it was just as if they were alive. At the time I was rather frightened, but later on I stopped being frightened, because they just seemed to be asleep. They didn't talk any more, but I did the talking for them, and for three days and three nights I talked, because I hadn't had the chance while they were alive."

"And you're still not afraid?" asked the youth, surprised.

"My parents just looked as if they were asleep," the doctor repeated. "Their bodies had not decomposed, their faces looked healthy, and a smell of aloe was coming from their mouths. I still remember that smell, and whenever I smell it I think of them, and how I talked to them. I don't think I had ever talked so much in my life, and I'm still talking. Whenever I want to say something, there they are in front of me."

"Are they here now, in this hut?" asked the youth, doubtfully.

The doctor smiled. He took down a bamboo flute from the wall, went to the door of the hut, and facing the northern slope of the mountain, began to play. The strong, clear notes of the flute always keep close to the earth, and the youth saw that the stems of all the flowers on the mountainside were starting to tremble with the muted flute music.

But the youth could not raise a sound from it. The doctor told him, "You must blow into it gently, neither too fast nor too slow, just as we speak to our dead relatives so that they can hear us."

Three days later, the youth managed to play the flute.

From then on, he often came up the mountain. Each time the sound of the flute penetrated to the bottom of the slope, he would appear in the woods at the foot of the mountain. He helped the doctor to tidy the graveyard and by the spring, when the whole mountainside was covered with azaleas, he had moved in with the doctor.

The day he did that, the youth was still rather hesitant and undecided. He said, "My home is down there, but there's nobody there now."

The doctor said, "This is your home too, and you can see your mother here every day, and there are lots more people to be your friends. When evening comes, you can hear them talking, just as they did when they were alive."

The youth smiled, showing his snow-white teeth.

Piao's mood was easily influenced by the weather, and when black clouds began to build up in the sky his heart felt as heavy as the rain that was threatening.

His careless attitude to his field of study provoked Dong Yun's dissatisfaction, and he took to yelling at him whenever he was awake, using slang expressions that no one understood. At such times, A Biao would just stand meekly on one side. He could gather the gist of it, however: ever since Piao's arrival at the Better Life Drugstore, business had been getting worse, and the herbs hanging from the eaves had gone mouldy.

When A Biao understood this, he glared ferociously at Piao.

"Give him some medicine," Dong Yun said.

Then A Biao lifted Piao up, and Piao felt as though the skin on his neck had been pinched between a door and its frame. It hurt so much that everything seemed to go dark. He was carried off to a slab of stone in the backyard, where A Biao pinned him down with a forceful foot on his back and stuffed a large handful of coptis rhizomes into his mouth. Piao felt his guts rise into his throat, but they were stopped from coming out by another handful of coptis. A Biao was smiling as he forced the medicine into Piao's mouth. "You bastard, all you do is make trouble—you need a good beating! We saw through you a long time ago, but the drugstore won't go under. All the formulas are in Master Dong's head, and no one can take them away unless they kill him. It looks to me as if you wanted to do that, didn't you?"

When he had finished beating him, A Biao went into the front courtyard to sluice himself down. Piao raised his head, almost too feeble to do so. The youth's body was still lying on the granite slab. Piao scooped all the coptis out of his mouth, but there was still a stabbing pain in the tip of his tongue, and the whole of his mouth felt numb, as if it were not there any more. He could not speak. The youth lay on his slab, enduring the heat of the afternoon sun, and to Piao it seemed as if the sun were moving slowly, like a brush, sweeping down from the youth's head along the length of his body. As time went on, the scent of aloe grew noticeably stronger.

There were two strange tears in Piao's eyes.

The changes in the seasons are always accomplished quietly, without one's being aware of them, and so it was with the growth and decay of the flowers and trees on the northern slope of Fox Mountain. With the passage of time, in the rust-filled air, the plants on the slope flourished more and more, and it seemed as if they were so alive they had feet and had walked to every nook and cranny to put down their roots. There were carpets of them, for the moment concealing the graves beneath. As the days came and went, the doctor was gradually transformed into a dutiful gardener, and he not only forgot his position as guardian of the graves, he even lost the medical man's alertness of mind, and his knowledge of herbal medicine deteriorated badly.

Up on the mountain, the youth had learned all about growing

medicinal herbs and how to look after them. He knew when to water them, and when to prune them. When he was not working, he would sit at the door of the hut and play the flute, which by now he was quite at home with. The tunes that he played on the flute were all ones that he had heard the doctor play: he could remember a tune after hearing it only once. He also learned from the doctor the names of all the mountain plants used in making medicines, and the names of the inhabitants of each of the graves.

The doctor said to the youth, "You really are a bright boy. I'm old, and my memory is getting worse all the time. When the folk from Huotong come up to sweep the graves at the next Tomb-Sweeping Festival, the herbs and flowers will confuse them. You will have to take them to where they ought to go."

The youth said, "Are you going away?"

He answered, "No, I have nowhere else to go. I shall always live on the mountain."

He went on to tell the youth more things, teaching him how to loosen the soil round the plants and spread manure, and how to prune them. He wanted the youth to remember the season at which each of them matured, and the names of all the graves on the mountainside and when their occupants had been buried there.

"You'll usually be lonely if you stay on the mountain," he told the youth, "but there'll always be a time when their relatives come back."

A few days later, the doctor fell ill. He lay on his bed, looking at the gray sky outside, divided up by the bars of the window, and he felt as if there were something flowing over him like a river, something that was passing through his joints and the network of channels between the joints, and then returning to its original position. He sensed that he might not have very long to live, that the time to go was getting closer. He looked closely at the drops of water falling from the eaves of the hut, and a wave of excitement swept through his heart like a little stream.

When the doctor fell ill, the youth planted the first aloe tree, because the faint, clear fragrance emanating from its roots drew him to it. He planted it on his mother's grave and felt that his mother's blood was spreading through its roots to its gradually unfolding branches.

The youth said to the doctor, "What medicine from the mountain should you take now?"

The doctor said, "I'm not ill, I don't need any medicine. Those herbs look beautiful, but I'm so tired, it'll have to be you who takes care of them from now on."

"Well, you just lie there," said the youth, "I'm grown up now, and I'm strong. I'll go to the river to fetch some water for the flowers. You stay here."

Then he went out of the hut, carrying a jar for the water.

What happened in the end was unexpected. The doctor must have slept for some two hours after the youth left, but then he was awakened by a sound. When he got up, the hut was deserted. He went out the door and suddenly felt that something was missing from the mountainside. He unfolded the sheet of yellowing paper, and it seemed to echo the scene outside. The doctor still had not found the youth's mother's grave by the time the shadows were slanting.

He took up his flute and headed down the mountain in search of the youth. His cries dispersed over the large area of graves, and the very stems of the herbs shook, but there was no sign of the youth. His sorrowful cries accompanied him to the bottom of the mountain, where there was a wind blowing over the river, and a very conspicuous whirlpool with clusters of redbud leaves and rosebuds turning round and round in it. The jar was on the bank, broken, and the wind was stirring up ripples on what remained of the water inside it.

The doctor did not believe the youth was dead. He stood beside the autumnal river and was aware that on this day, exactly a year since he had laid eyes on the youth, his feelings were much less calm than the water.

He stood on the bank and played a tune on his flute. Just as it was getting dark, he left Huotong and walked up the road toward Zhangban. He hesitated a long time deciding whether to go by the main road or to cut across Fox Mountain by the shortcut.

The youth's corpse had disappeared.

The first person to discover this was A Biao, who was carrying a basket of dwarf lilyturf tubers through to the patio in the backyard, to dry them in the sun. He vaguely noticed someone lying on the granite slab, and at first thought it was the youth, but then he grew suspicious, and when he turned his head he let out a scream of fear, a dull cry of alarm that was particularly piercing in the afternoon stillness and interrupted Dong Yun's dreams. Dong Yun went into the backyard, taking a handful of walnuts, and asked what had happened.

Piao was lying on the slab where the youth had been lying before, apparently fast asleep.

A Biao could not believe that his scream had not woken Piao. He had spilled the lilyturf all over the ground and was just standing there, his face white. Dong Yun gave a cold laugh and said, "His time has come."

When the old man thrust his handful of walnuts down Piao's throat, the boy's limbs began to thrash around, and he started breathing in great gasps. Dong Yun shouted at A Biao, "Why don't you come and help me?"

Piao was put into a cellar in pitch darkness, and everything went according to plan. He felt that the cellar was full of countless hands, which touched him silently but with great strength. Ball after ball of medicine was stuffed into his mouth—medicines he did not know the name of, which were bitter and astringent and made his tongue, throat, and chest feel as if they were being whipped by countless whips. He was vomiting continually, but more medicine kept being forced into his mouth, and his chest felt so hot he thought it might split open. He tore at his own body.

In front of the Better Life Drugstore, while he was taking a short break, A Biao noticed that the villagers looked scared and were whispering to one another, and they seemed different from when they usually came to buy medicines. The news was unpleasant: the corpse of the youth that had come floating down from upstream had suddenly shifted from the dock to the mountainside. A woodcutter had chanced to see him and had mistaken him for someone who had come to sacrifice at the grave of his mother, but when he saw him still kneeling there the next day and went up to him, he realized that it was the strange youth who had drowned some time before.

The fellow said it must have been his mother's soul that drew him up the mountain.

"So Zhangban is haunted!" said one woman, shocked, and this terrified all the people coming in to deliver or to buy medicines, as if it were something they had been warned to expect that was now actually happening.

Dong Yun stepped slowly out of the inner room, and as his gaze swept over the village folk, his face bore an expression of scorn, an expression that had also appeared as he watched Piao carrying the youth step-by-step up the mountain on his back.

The thing happened before Dong Yun had had time to finish Piao off. At midnight, as usual, the watchman's clapper sounded round Shunyi Street. Dong Yun was pondering the main ingredients in the last dose of medicine of that year, and imagining Piao's fate; his mood was relaxed, as though he had been purged. When he had thought everything through, the urge to sleep finally invaded him again.

It was in his bedroom that the fire started.

Zhangban entered the midnight hour slowly and reluctantly, like a clam withdrawing into its shell, until finally it was totally dark. Piao's first wish was extremely simple: in the pitch darkness of the cellar, he wanted to see a little light. With a great deal of effort, he managed to dislodge the stone slab on top of the wooden cover of the cellar, and he got out into the backyard. In the darkness, he found a drum of kerosene and a large amount of rough paper. When he walked into Dong Yun's bedroom he crept silently, like a cat on its padded paws, until the sound of stentorian breathing and the grinding of teeth led him to his quarry.

He set light to Dong Yun.

In the flames, Dong Yun looked like a shining butterfly. Piao's mouth was breathing out the fumes from ball after ball of bitter medicine, but they could not compare with the evil smell that Dong Yun gave off in the flames, a strange smell that Piao had never come across before. He walked a few paces and fainted.

The fire at the drugstore lasted all night. The folk who lived on Shunyi Street all rushed out of their houses, and some worthy fellows tried to quench the flames with buckets of water, but the strange smell emanating from the drugstore almost suffocated them on the spot, and they changed their minds and started running away in fear. The strong ones ran several dozen paces, but the less agile ones fell down dead after only about ten paces.

When morning came, the smell of medicines was still hanging oppressively in the air over Zhangban, and several hundred people had died in the streets of the village, most of them in the area of Shunyi Street. Those who had been lucky enough to escape gathered on Fox Mountain, and even here, when they were almost past the Zhangban village limits, they could still smell the strange smell that came after the fire. Most of the survivors were unable to speak—they had been struck dumb by this singular fire, coming, as it did, right out of the blue.

The bone doctor reached Zhangban when the fire was over. Wearing a loose gown, he walked through the ruins of the village. He was shocked by the crowds of corpses and the collapsed framework of the drugstore. Lifting the hem of his gown, he walked through the still-smoking ruins of the building, utter terror flashing in his eyes. Under a blackened rafter, he found the youth. The boy called Piao was dead, but his body was unmarked.

The doctor began to weep softly beside the youth's body. He sobbed, "I'm an old man; surely you don't want me to dig one more grave for you?"

The youth lay there, like a legacy left by the village for the doctor. When he had finished weeping, he took the youth's body on his back and started off along the road from Zhangban back to Huotong. When he reached the grave of the youth's mother, halfway up Fox Mountain, the doctor put him down. He was old, and wanted to rest awhile. He got out his flute, but his energy failed him and he did not play it.

On Fox Mountain the herbs and flowers were growing in abundance. Even after all the people who died in the fire were buried there, it was still hard to see that it was a graveyard. After the doctor's medical skills gradually deserted him, he became the guardian of this cemetery. In the ensuing long period of waiting, every time midnight approached, he dreamed that the youth was walking up from the bottom of the slope again, and when the sky grew bright with the hazy light of dawn, he would reckon that that day was not too far off.

Translated by Caroline Mason

I AM A YOUNG DRUNKARD ✿ *Sun Ganlu*

PROLOGUE

Do you know who is sizing you up behind your back?

(From RICE WINE COUNTRY)

THE SETTING

Those people have begun climbing the mountain. Grasping ancient beliefs in their hands. In a mountain valley of 1959. They stare at a layer of long-awaited clouds passing overhead. The clouds disappear behind the mountain peak they are about to ascend. Gradually drift into the distance. And wait for them to reach the summit. They stare up at the clouds again from on high. As they disperse, slipping beyond the horizon. And then. This mountain peak is given a name. (i)

The very first thing they discover is that layer sliding toward the valley floor. Of withered leaves. They give them two names. So that when they fall to the bottom of the valley, they can know each other. One of those names enters the land of dreams. Never to be lost. But to send back a painful message. Enchanting yet another. To guard this secret of 1959. (ii)

They decide to conclude the memory. Of the first stone they come upon. They present it with music. And the remaining stones are enriched too. They share in the memory. And wait for the music to save them from falling into the abyss. This happened before 1959. The meditative heroes act out their sacrifice. Between the river and the mountain range. Some desolate plants. Have been painted onto the landscape. (iii)

Those who had thought of crossing the river descend the mountain and cross it. They yearn for the taste of water. They will have no rest. Those on the mountain ponder. As if contemplating sins. One among them begins to grow feeble. Because he wants to outlive himself. Thus shame spreads in every direction. Comforting all those who have descended the mountain. This is the faith of 1959. (iv)

One among them sees the streets below. He searches his soul anxiously. Not planning to tell the others. None of the others. Of course, he comes first. They have lost the pleasure of being occupied by ordinary affairs. The arduous emotions they have experienced will never be revealed. They watch the spring gurgle forth. They do not have the strength to move. Staring silently, they disappear without a trace. This is the offering of 1959. (v)

THE CHARACTERS

Why have I wandered about aimlessly? This is the story I wish to tell you. I am brimming over with poetry tonight; it is not good. I know this. But there's nothing I can do: I am brimming over with poetry. This is just the way I am, tonight. I pretend to be drunk. Actually I haven't had anything to drink. I open a book. Yours. Mine. His. I search for a likeness of myself, but of course I can't find one. In this state, this drunken state, of course I can find no likeness.

My world is nothing more than a well and several lengths of railing. A bottle of cloudy wine and a few muddled sentences.

On a sweltering hot summer evening (the precise time being someday in a hundred years) at the Ostrich Bank (where a wineshop banner once flew), I meet a guest from the north, a self-proclaimed poet who writes sad short stories and has a melancholy demeanor and robust physique, and I complete this ordinary memory of the kind referred to by the blind Argentinean.

THE STORY

Straw mats resembling water, earthenware jugs like ice.

Inside, the bank is very dark and damp, like all the confused thoughts filling my brain.

The square counter is so shiny you can see your reflection in it, and that ostrichlike bartender has a frightening countenance. His expression is somewhere between that of a sage and that of an old bachelor, wallowing in the satisfying loneliness of thoughts and the hostile detachment of one whose once-active sex life is now dead.

The Ostrich abruptly walks over to us and places two earthenware jugs on the table. He suddenly grabs my arm: "Hey! Your color is a bit off! It sure can't be from drinking." Having said this, he withdraws his nose behind the counter and doesn't make another sound.

We haven't gotten the snacks to go with our wine. Judging from the people with dubious expressions sitting at the next table, talk is the drinking snack here. All their heads are bent closely together like chickens pecking at rice as they discuss something at a high pitch. The poet and I perk up our ears attentively to their discussion. But they pause suddenly and then stop talking all together before turning their heads toward us and yelling: "Hey! Talk! Talk! Hey! You! Talk yourselves!" There is a clamor all around, "You two, don't wash down your wine with other people's conversations. Foolish newcomers! A pair of idiots! The both of them! A couple of fools!" Their voices bloated with drunken pride.

"Whether one drinks his fill or not totally depends on whether the talk flows well with the wine, eh!" The person who adds this "eh" to the end of his sentence deftly shuffles a deck of cards on the side of our table as he passes by.

"Shall we give it a try?" the poet asks, lifting his wine jug.

"Well, alright." I shoot a sidelong glance at the Ostrich behind the counter. "What were you doing before you came south?"

The poet raises his nose high above the back of his chair striking a refined pose and says loudly, "I kept myself hidden away at home. You should know, the north is crawling with extraordinary people." Saying this, he looks arrogantly about at the people in the bank.

The Ostrich's neck remains calmly erect.

"Here in the south, folks all hang out on the streets." I whisper. He stretches out his sallow right index finger to drive home his point: "You can't say that just because *you* hang out on the street, *everyone* does."

"Well then, did anyone ever come to find you or pay a visit?" I hastily change the subject. He explains amiably, "If anyone came to the door, we would all turn out in full force. Otherwise, we always keep ourselves hidden away."

"Do you hide together or scatter about in different places?" I assume this must be a popular game in the north at the moment and try to pick up some of the basic rules so that I can be the first to play it in the south.

"There are no rules to our hiding." The poet taps the side of the wine jug with his finger: "Either a few of us form a group, or one carves out a room on his own. Sometimes we hide in a conspicuous place, other times we turn up in very secluded spots. Not hiding is hiding, hiding is not hiding, together is dispersed, dispersed is together . . ."

His intoxicating dreamlike whispers and fleeting expression seem constantly to beg for solace. His enticing melodramatic tone is surprisingly pleasant.

"We move freely in and out of our own lives and the books of others," the poet adds.

I'm not sure what person he is recalling, but figure he's just trying to demonstrate his poetic disposition.

His gaze always passes right through you; even if he loved you dearly, he would still look through you. Like a ship floating by on the current. He has a far away look in his eyes, as if he were always standing proud and aloof.

He is always reciting, his speech like verses from a very colloquial poem. He forever interrupts himself, goes off on unintelligible tangents, or rambles on and on. His conversation is fragmented, not flowing. In short, he is unreal but still unforgettable.

"Did you come south to take part in the seasonal celebrations?"

"No, I'm here to take part in the rites of cynicism."

As we speak, the sarcasm makes the time drag on. The so-called street scene outside the Ostrich Bank is a row of houses that are not very ancient but yet old enough. Some windows closed, some opened; some curtains still, some blowing; some people walking, some standing.

The poet drains his wine jug in one swig. "Between one dream and another are a ceremony and a few rituals. And the rituals and raindrops arrive simultaneously. In legends, this is how eternity manifests itself."

I suppose he is trying hard to reconstruct some poetic atmosphere.

Dipping his index finger in wine drops, the poet forcefully writes words on the table: "Holy water's edge, banana tip border, time of deep sighs, season of pine branch."

"A gift for you!"

His way of expressing things reminds one of people who lead parasitic lives. They are elegant and tiresome. They live in their own fantasies; they are not stingy with time, yet brood over the passing days. They are always wrapped up in the minute details of their emotions, always gossiping behind the backs of others.

"For example," the poet bellows, "the subtle difference between a person who is out visiting all over town from morning till night and a person who roams about spreading gossip and rumors in the lanes of the south or the alleys of the north makes it difficult for them to distinguish one another. If I were wise enough to lightly jest about men who diligently masturbate on little stools behind doors or in courtyard corners, I would fly dreamlike through the extraordinary imaginations of those who, hidden in sidestreets or doorways in the evenings or at midnight, cautiously kiss. If I were in desperate need of poetry to defend those who lazily pass the day away in bed, I would have only to bring up the man whom no one has ever met but who tirelessly plays harmonica in shaded places and street corners, and it would be enough to harmoniously unite those sleep addicts and day dreamers. You may think that women who stay in their homes year after year, sitting before mirrors attending to their makeup, deserve our unflagging attention, but the inner lives of old people who sit in armchairs in the sun reading all kinds of newspapers are even more difficult to figure out. Suppose I were able to appreciate one ten-thousandth of the happiness of a man tinkering with a clock, I would then have enough courage to patiently summarize to a trivial degree the excessive addiction to cleanliness of those people who endlessly tidy their rooms."

The poet speaks animatedly, signaling the Ostrich to bring more wine and methodically pacing around the table.

"Yes, I am immersed in a hatred of an utterly exhausting kind, and my experience appears to tell me that it is hatred alone that exists in such an infinite way. When I first realized this, I was filled with a hatred for hatred. This made me both sad and happy. It was as if I could feel the beauty of standing still and letting the world go on."

"I have seen your ancestors in a film about nomadic peoples." I take advantage of my tipsiness to indulge in a wild fantasy, saying to him cautiously, "Your ancestors wore full body armor; it was really worthless. They rode those rare, lanky work horses similar to that of Luoqian. I remember words like heroism and freedom being mentioned in the footnotes."

"Well then, they must have also mentioned wine, women, and dejected loneliness; these words are naturally related," the poet remarks indifferently.

The drinkers at the table next to ours don't seem to mind the poet's outspokeness. Yet I begin to wonder whether talk like his is suitable for drinking or not. Holding his wine jug in one hand, the poet gesticulates in the air with the other. Has he always been like this? Or is he acting this way because he has recently arrived? Or perhaps all poets have such glib tongues.

"As far as I am concerned, my best years are already behind me; it's too late for bitter memories transformed into eloquent words to soothe the pain of old wounds. The world has left me behind in an artful way, and my poems and I stand alone. I no longer know if the starry night is silent or not, I feel only that I have nothing to do. My years tell me that the wind comes and goes only to tear apart my sentences. My appearance is disappointingly lax, lines of poetry wait, welled up beneath my pen, to depart or reunite, to love once or desire yet again."

"It's always like this when they drink my wine," the Ostrich at the counter says assuredly.

"How sweet, how sweet, how sickeningly sweet!" The cardplayer keeps pacing back and forth, making a constant clamor.

"Look," the poet says confidently and yet resignedly, "I must restrain my free-form way of thinking, I must throw myself into conversation anew as if throwing myself into a dubious understanding. Within this dubious understanding, a boy can never mature. He feels that he is forever mired in a weary and painful memory of maturity. In a rambling discussion such as this, maturity takes on a suffocating feeling that constantly grows closer, faintly making one sense that potential happiness is always accompanied by naïveté. It leads to a rejection of maturity. This type of personality forces one to confront oneself alone for the majority of one's life, and to confront the poetic loneliness of a self-imposed isolation."

"There's reason in this sweetness! There's reason in this sweetness!" The muffled sound of cards being shuffled punctuates these shouts.

"I might as well talk about my father," says the poet. Only then do I notice his obstinacy. "He used what he claimed was a non-influencing method to influence his son's entire life. Father and son argued during strolls together, aggravated each other at the dinner table, and slandered one another as they dozed off to sleep. Only in our feelings about women were father and son surprisingly alike. He instructed me: Women are a lot like books. You feel a familiar strangeness when you read your own book, but a strange familiarity when you read someone else's. As I see it, women and books are the same, both employ mystery to hide their dullness."

"Wine always brings on talk of women, that's a rule, and it looks like the poet won't be an exception today." Even the cardplayer has stopped shouting at this point. With great interest, he presses up against the table.

The poet glances at him disdainfully and goes on, "Of all my meager poems, half of them were written for women, and the other half were written because of women."

"Let's have a look!" the cardplayer interjects.

"As I see it, my poetry is a bit like a pop music concert; there is a certain upbeat and intoxicating feel to it. My real love life, however, is a string of unrelated short stories that begin warmly and end in curses." The poet gives the cardplayer another contemptuous look, stopping him from interrupting again. He then finishes in a conclusive tone, "If one day anyone dares to say he understands women, he will be mistaken."

"Dull, dull." The cardplayer jumps off the bench. "This guy's got no balls, no romance, no sex. He's completely dull! Completely dull." He walks away, accompanied once again by the sound of shuffling cards.

The conversation goes on evasively like this. Words jump about like checkers on a checkerboard. Or like warm rice wine as it flows and twists in one's stomach.

"Shouldn't people speak with themselves more? If they did, would it be possible for a person who understands himself too thoroughly to become bored?" I say, fully drawn into the poet's eloquent words.

"To maintain distance is to maintain feeling. Don't become too intimate with others or with yourself. But I'm different; for someone like me, distance and feeling are both harmful. I want to become close with people. The most important thing to me is closeness. Only later do you come to judgment and reflection, to sympathy and pity, to regret and grief, or anything else. Time has taught me that life must be approached indirectly."

As I sit listening with rapt attention, I suddenly hear the cardplayer by the door shout, "It's raining!"

The crowd grows quiet, and I can clearly make out the sound of the rain, as well as that of the shuffling cards.

I drink and daydream. A piano is playing a melody, and then an orchestra seems to join in somewhere far off. The tune pauses momentarily, then just as a deck of cards is shuffled, the sound of the rain outside the window pours into the room. The string section seems damp as it joins in slowly, and the piano's vibrant tune sounds like raindrops.

"Rain is a temporary thing," the poet's hushed voice interrupts my musings.

"It might be better to say that our impressions are temporary."

"You're so young, yet here you are discussing the temporality of imagination so poetically. What kind of young person are you? How do such heavy words come so lightly from your lips? Isn't it that you rely on the brilliance of your imagination to fly directly to the deepest place in time, while I don't know when I will begin to step nearer to it? Let me grow older more quickly; it is impossible for me to assume the posture of youth to come closer to you, so allow me then to meet you at the deepest place in time."

Listening to the poet, it seems that yet another experience of talking and drinking awaits me somewhere. Only I don't know if the cardplayer will be there or not.

The poet's sallow face makes me realize that he is lost in the chill of deep autumn and the brief moment of warmth when an evening is still filled with light. This is because he is so smug about how often the word autumn or images of it appear in his poetry.

"When I was young, I always imagined dying in an ordinary way in a beautiful garden surrounded by tangled wisteria vines and drooping willow branches. Plants have a certain symbolism for me. If one day I can have my own corpse pressed between the pages of some handbook of plants, then I will be able to find a peaceful resting place amid the decay."

"We've got just such a garden here," the Ostrich behind the counter interrupts suddenly.

"There is one! There is!" the cardplayer joins in at once.

I need to rescue this guest from the north. "Hey!" I get up shouting, "I need to piss!"

"Our bank is built on a slope; piss wherever you like. It will flow downhill!"

The poet stands up abruptly and motions grandiosely to me, "Come with me."

I squeeze my legs together and follow the poet into a narrow corridor leading toward the garden.

"We always have endless corridors and infinite linked gardens. As the years come and go, strolling and walking along like this stirs up certain magical powers like winds blowing up inside a cave, and the intoxicating fragrance of the garden makes one feel he is either sleeping alone surrounded by flowers or floating on water. Walking and dying are equally amazing things."

"But I have to piss!" I urge him.

"No hurry." The poet walks along the road excitedly. "Look," he stops suddenly, "what is this?"

At the end of the corridor, which is covered with carvings and paintings, one can clearly make out a shiny copper coin.

"A rare thing!"

"This is a bank after all!" I shrug.

"I lived in the north for many years, but never once did I see such a thing. I certainly have not traveled in vain." He speaks with great vigor and spirit, as if he had been transformed into a different person: "We should hear an echo." The poet lifts the copper coin and throws it toward the rays of the setting sun that are shining through the jumble of trees in the garden.

We calmly discuss the casting period of the copper coin. The poet concludes that a copper coin able to bounce five feet high on a crushed stone path was certainly cast in the Golden Age. I, however, lean more toward the waning years of the Dream Age.

Just then, the copper coin suddenly flies off toward the bottom of the slope with a clanking sound. I hesitate, but the poet takes off down the slope chasing after the coin.

As the poet runs, his arms swing back and forth as if rowing a lone and resplendent dragon boat in the fading evening light. I begin running rather cautiously—I am still holding in my piss. Before long I fall quite far behind. On this sloped road here in my hometown, the image I am so arduously chasing after moves me as if an illusion.

"Hey, you there! Be humble when you take to the road; don't pass beyond the border of purity." At some point, I'm not sure when, the cardplayer has also come sliding around in the mud left by the rain. He ostentatiously shuffles his cards and spits out sticky sunflower seed shells.

By this time the poet has already run on without a trace.

A quack selling aphrodisiacs uses arms as thin as sticks to wave away the frothy bubbles flying out from his yellow-toothed mouth. At the same time, he casts a handful of copper coins into the air: "For love. This is how you should spend money." He stretches out his neck, blue veins bulging, like some model revolutionary. "Strictly speaking," he insists, "I'm a matchmaker."

"Did you see a poet?" I go forward and ask. "A poet chasing after a copper coin?"

"Did you say a poet? He's no longer chasing after the copper coin; halfway down the road he joined several ascetic monks chasing after a mule in heat!"

I would never have guessed that the poet could give up his goal so easily. I could almost see the mule drawn to the bitter fragrance of the grasses along the flagstone road, and the ascetic monks and the poet plunging into the bamboo forest of December.

I was born into poverty and am certainly not sophisticated enough to stand heroically facing the wind, especially now that the copper coin that had attracted so much attention has rolled to the bottom of the slope. Below neat rows of seductive willow trees, a group of chess players sits engrossed in the middle of a game. The copper coin shoots past a blind chess player. Just then he makes a spectacular move and proudly stretches out his legs, amazingly kicking the copper coin directly into a dark gully by the road.

The poet has gone, never to return. Apparently, I am no more than an insignificant interlude on his trip south.

The evening can no longer hold itself back. I think that I am the only person walking in the moonlight this night. If I were willing, I could face yet another miracle: changing into an empty vessel—for which a fabricated story lacking in tension is the precise symbol.

EPILOGUE

The people on the raft float down the river.
By the water sits a suave young man, an alluring hero.

Translated by Kristina M. Torgeson

MORE WAYS THAN ONE TO MAKE A KITE

❁ *Ma Yuan*

1

The Tibetan New Year falls on the third day of the third lunar month. Some of my colleagues who had come over for New Year greetings first thing in the morning had forced several glasses of highland barley wine down my throat. I felt stupefied and dropped off to sleep by midday. I didn't wake up until dark. When I got up and rinsed my face with cold water, I discovered a blister on the right side of my mouth. No big deal.

Before the week was over, the blister had grown into a huge boil, caked over by a nauseating pus, which looked like a walnut on the corner of my lips. One half of my face was bloated beyond recognition. This was the "delta" area considered vital in popular belief. It was said that from here, the poison could glide through the blood vessels and enter the brain. I wasn't so sure about that, but the pain was something else. I don't mind telling you—scoff if you like—but I actually howled with pain, and more than once, too. This was getting serious.

I started running to hospitals.

In Lhasa, the Tibetan New Year is the major holiday, with big celebrations. My friends were out having fun, while I was all alone in my dorm, crouched over a novel. Single young men like me have a hard time of it: we don't know how to enjoy ourselves; we are doomed to boundless loneliness. But I have my own ways to fight the loneliness. Reading novels is one of them.

Or, I walk out at dusk to look over the pieces of broken pottery strewn along the streets. Or watch the long-haired dogs as they chase each other playfully. Or spend the only fifty-cent coin in my pocket on cups of tea at the sweet-tea house. Or walk to the south of Medicine God Mountain to inspect the offerings left on that holy ground—little clay Buddhist figures? rolls of holy script with illustrations of the Buddha? slabs of slate carved with the scripture?

Or I pull the curtains (my one spare bedsheet, white checkered with blue—you all remember), shut the door, turn on the desk lamp, sit at my desk (the one with the three drawers in a horizontal row), and make up stories for you (interesting stories, of course—or so I hope).

At these times, my imagination soars; stories of all that has happened and has yet to happen rush into my head. Before I put a story down on paper, I am invariably racked by the everlasting questions as to what to write about and how to go about it. If Little Gesang had not popped in and again brought up his own story at the police squad, I really don't know where my imagination might have led me.

He began by asking me whether I remembered the man who sold pinecone-shaped stones. Of course I did. Little Gesang had recently been transferred to the Public Security Bureau; he was absolutely green at the job and was a bit nervous over this particular case. I made him loosen the collar of his uniform and take off his cap with the protruding vizor and relax. I poured him a cup of tea.

"Let me begin with Eight Corners Road, which circles the famous Dazhao Temple. In the maze of streets that crisscross it may be seen people from every corner of the earth. According to informal reckoning, thirty thousand people turn up on this street every day to do business or to worship the gods. And on Sundays, the figure is doubled. Eight Corners Road is, in effect, a buzzing market with a dazzling variety of goods too diverse to imagine. Here you will find the largest antique and jewelry market in China, with business deals running into tens of thousands of yuan every day. Tight-lipped dealers of indecipherable nationality give foreign tourists a glimpse of their wares under the folds of their sleeves. Neither arrogant nor fawning, they bargain coolly, making signs with their fingers.

"It was in this market that I first came across the famous cat's-eye emerald. At a stall on the second turning, I bought a piece of high-quality, jade green, pinecone-shaped stone. It was the size of an unshelled peanut and weighed fifty-two grams. I couldn't tell the quality of the gem, but having taken a fancy to its shape and color, I decided to buy it. The dealer began by asking sixty yuan. I countered by offering thirty. He had been on this spot from time immemorial; his age was undecipherable, anywhere from thirty-five to seventy. Having sauntered into Eight Corners Road every now and again, I was sure we had seen each other before. From the shape of his face, I decided that he was from South Asia—Nepalese? or perhaps Indian or Pakistani. He was quite fluent in Mandarin. We clinched the bargain at thirty-eight yuan. This was on August 12 of the previous year. I made a record on my desk calendar."

2

"Of course you know the shortcut on the southwest side of Eight Corners Road."

To tell you the truth, I didn't; once on Eight Corners Road, I lose my sense of direction.

"Recently they have been paving that street with prefabricated slabs of concrete. You must remember how muddy it used to be in summer."

I nodded—not that I remembered, but to show that I was listening.

"Now the paving is done."

I couldn't make out what this was leading to.

"Nowadays the street is wider than it used to be. When it was being repaved, the courtyard walls of the houses lining the street were torn down by the municipal construction bureau and reconstructed further back to make extra space. In pulling down the wall of the courtyard where a solitary old woman lived, the crew found a male corpse that had not completely decomposed. And yes, it was that man. You may not have noticed that now that stall on the second turning is occupied by a Khampa[1] woman selling furs."

I didn't care to say that I had noticed. I didn't want to interrupt his account.

"The old woman was toothless, with deeply sunken jaws. She said she didn't know the man and had nothing to say. She had no children and no fixed employment and lived by selling old clothes in the neighborhood. She used snuff; otherwise, there was nothing out of

1. A Tibetan people who live in the mountainous rural areas between the upper Yangtse and the Chinese border.

the ordinary about her. According to the neighborhood committee, she had settled on Eight Corners Road after the quelling of the uprising, a good twenty years ago, and nothing was known of her past. The population of Eight Corners Road is ever shifting, hard to make out; even neighbors of many years do not know each other. When we first talked to her, she insisted that she didn't know him, but we finally bluffed her into spilling the beans."

3

She made me think of another old woman who lived alone near Eight Corners Road. She was a bootlegger. She brewed highland barley wine. Her wine wasn't sour, so business was good. One of her clients was my colleague Big Gesang. I don't drink highland barley wine as a rule; it is brewed with unboiled water and always gives me diarrhea. So at Big Gesang's, when he tried to make me down three cups of wine according to custom, I showed him my medical prescription and excused myself. But Big Gesang insisted that this barley wine was brewed with boiled water and would not give me diarrhea. I couldn't hold out against him, and I tried the wine. And that was how I got to know about this bootlegging old woman.

The next time Big Gesang went to buy barley wine, I went along. I wanted to see how barley wine was brewed, and also wanted to know more of this old woman who brewed wine with boiled water when everybody else used unboiled water.

She was wide and comfortable, with plump hands. And very friendly. My image of her had been that of a shrivelled old hag, straight-faced, with dark secrets lurking in the impenetrable folds of her wrinkles. But she was different. I realized I had been wrong. She had no place in any story of mine. Frankly I was disappointed. But let me get back to Little Gesang's story of the other old woman.

4

"She owned that the man had been her lover and that all his goods were stored at her place. She sold anything and everything. She said that he had had a nine-eyed cat's-eye emerald. Now even a five-eyed cat's-eye emerald of fine quality is worth several thousand yuan, so you can imagine how he treasured this nine-eyed one; he always had it around his neck. She said she had asked him for it several times but he always refused; he had fobbed her off with a couple of pinecone shaped stones that she didn't care for. Finally she drugged him with liquor, and with the help of two Khampa itinerant vendors, strangled him with a rope and buried him. She said that she didn't get the emerald after all; it was taken by the two roughs, since she was no match for the two of them, and at the end, it was she, a helpless old woman, who came out with the short stick. She also said that her father was a Muslim and that she herself had been a dealer in jewelry.

"We asked her for a description of the two Tibetans; we asked her three times, and each time she gave a different picture. She added that they had left. We asked her for their names and where they came from. She said that in business one does not ask these personal questions, just as one does not ask about the source of goods or their destination. But she gathered that they were going to the Tibetan part of Sichuan Province. It was hard to say how far she could be trusted. She had been here twenty years, and no one knew anything about her. There she was, with her toothless gums and sagging jaws, a perfect image of a long-suffering martyr. I think there's little truth in what she said."

And then?

"Well, we analysed her confession, and speculated that she may have made up the story about the two Tibetans. Can you imagine how many Tibetans there must be on Eight Corners Road carrying on one kind of business or another? How can one trace the suspects without even a description? Especially when she said that they had left Eight Corners Road and even left Lhasa! But we still decided to send two men into the area she mentioned to take a look."

5

Little Gesang was one of the two men dispatched to Sichuan to follow the trail. He told me he was leaving in a couple of days. I made him promise to tell me the results when he came back. He smiled and said I must be thinking of my novel writing. I was noncommittal. So far, the facts were meager, but who knew what might turn up as the investigation progressed. I had hopes for his findings on this trip.

I suddenly thought of something else and asked Little Gesang whether the old woman was religious. He said that there were a few copper Buddhist figures and some other religious articles in the house, but he was not sure whether they were for sale or for worship. So much for Little Gesang's story.

I am sure you will forgive me; I cannot finish this story. I am tired, and when I am tired, I like to light a cigarette, I don't smoke as a rule.

I lay back on my folded cotton quilt and closed my eyes. I wondered to myself, why is it that old women associated with evil are invariably shrivelled old hags, and why is it that when I heard Little Gesang's story of the murderous old woman, I immediately recalled the other old woman who sold barley wine? And most interesting of all, why is it that my preconceived image of the bootlegging old woman completely merged with the image of the murderous old woman?

6

Knocking at the door.

"Ma Yuan! Ma Yuan!"

It was Xinjian.

"All alone? . . . Good heavens, what happened?"

"A boil. Surely this is punishment for my sins."

"Certainly, your sins. Have you eaten?"

"There's compressed biscuits and canned food."

"Come and stay with me for a few days."

Xinjian was a painter, in charge of designing the decorations for the exhibition hall. So I moved into the exhibition hall. His den was quite spacious. On entering, my eyes immediately lighted on several paper eaglets on his working platform. He had been trained in arts and handicrafts and had moved to Tibet the year before last. His frescoes, sculptures, and oil paintings had all been photographed in color. I have seen them.

Two bachelors' joint housekeeping was quite comfortable, much better than when I was on my own. Xinjian's place was cleaner than mine because a girl sometimes dropped in. The girl was very pretty, flashing white teeth when she smiled. She was Nim, only nineteen. She liked to do her washing by the Lhasa River.

Xinjian also liked to go to the river—for sketching, and to look for and store up inspiration for his art. The Lhasa River in summer is so alluring, he was tempted into taking a plunge. The result was he got a two-inch-long, half-inch-deep gash in one foot. He held his foot and howled, and thus attracted Nim, who was washing clothes at a distance.

The rest can be easily imagined: She found a bicycle to take him to hospital. Then hospital visits, followed by more visits.

She discovered that he was an artist, and after he shaved, that he was actually quite young (he was twenty-nine). She also discovered that his incredibly messy room was his studio. She became his student. She had loved art as a child, and now the two of them spent days together talking about art. He made a bust of her. It was apparent that he was too full of romantic illusions about the coming years. I was more practical, even though I shared his room and board.

She arrived. I left. I might as well take the time to stroll down Eight Corners Road, I decided.

The Buddha might be our eternal idol, I thought to myself as I stood in front of the Dazhao Temple gate. I could not understand the people who were kowtowing their way on a pilgrimage, but I was full of awe. All I saw was their fervor and single-mindedness. As I was dawdling in the temple, I saw her unexpectedly—her profile had the same plump and friendly look. It was unlikely she would remember me, but I observed her as she carefully pasted up four ten-yuan notes on the Buddhist shrine, which was smeared all over with butter. I recalled that occasion when I had drunk her barley wine at Big Gesang's; it really hadn't given me diarrhea.

Spring is the time for flying paper eaglets, which are actually paper kites folded in the shape of eaglets. The paper eaglets of Lhasa might not be unique as kites go, but they soar against the sky, and the sky of Tibet is unmatched in all the world. It is sheer ecstasy to fly a paper eaglet against the bluest sky on earth, or just to watch a paper eaglet flying.

At that moment there were three paper eaglets gliding in the sky above Lhasa, forming a symmetric pattern with three other birds. Nim was probably gone by now. I could return.

Nim was gone when I got back, but there were two other visitors. Zhuang Xiaoxiao was Xinjian's former schoolmate, who needed no introduction.

"This is Liu Yu from the China News Agency."

"This is Ma Yuan from the broadcasting station."

We nodded to each other. Liu Yu told me that a friend in Beijing had asked him to bring me a book; he told me I could get it at his quarters whenever I was free. The friend was a writer, and there was a letter in the book, telling me that Liu Yu was also a writer.

Zhuang Xiaoxiao had completed a brilliant portrait that got him into trouble during an exhibition—a certain leading figure from artistic circles had pronounced that it distorted the image of the Tibetan. Zhuang Xiaoxiao complained profusely. It turned out that the original of the portrait was none other than Nim's grandmother, who lived in the pastoral area of Naqu. Nim came to know Zhuang Xiaoxiao through Xinjian. When she saw the portrait standing in Zhuang's studio, she was struck dumb. The deep furrows on the old woman's face were like cracks in the bark of an ancient elm. The old woman had lived an exhausting life, and time had left its mark on her face. The title of the portrait was *The Years.*

Nim asked Zhuang Xiaoxiao how he had known her grandmother. Zhuang told her that when he was sketching in Naqu, he had lived with her grandmother. The old woman would milk her cow to make fresh butter tea for him, and she told him tales of the prairie. When he asked the old woman for permission to paint her portrait, she agreed. At the beginning, the old woman chatted on cheerfully. Gradually he was absorbed in the painting, and they were silent. The old woman was very patient, but she was evidently worried about her sheep and her cows. She sat there, but her thoughts were far away. At one moment her submerged tiredness surfaced, and he captured it. He brought out all that was contained in that one fleeting moment.

Nim told Zhuang Xiaoxiao that her father had more than once gone to fetch her grandmother to come and join them in Lhasa, but her grandmother always refused on the pretext that she must care for the animals. Granny was over seventy; she had said to Nim that she couldn't last much longer and did not want to die in a strange place. She wanted to stay on the prairie. She was used to the prairie, the sheep, the cows, and the gray eagle.

Zhuang Xiaoxiao decided to submit the portrait for the exhibition of oil paintings to be held during the National Art Exhibition at Shenyang in October. What was Xinjian going to paint? Nim joined Xinjian in planning his next painting.

7

Liu Yu came over to Xinjian's for a chat. I mentioned the topic of novel writing, but Liu was not interested.

Liu Yu expressed some technical criticism of Zhuang Xiaoxiao's *The Years.* He didn't like the artistic expression. He was more interested in young painters from Beijing. All Beijingers like to talk about Beijing, just as all Shanghainese dream of returning to Shanghai.

Then Liu Yu asked Xinjian about his sketch of the painting for the coming exhibition—why had he chosen the Virgin Mary for his subject matter? Xinjian replied that painters all over the world from time immemorial have painted the Virgin Mary, so there was nothing out of the ordinary in his choosing the Virgin Mary for a subject. He conceded that the Virgin Mary is a Christian subject, but at the same time, he added, she is also the embodiment of maternal love: Raphael's *Madonna* would have the same sublime appeal to a twentieth-century Chinese as to any other viewer. Xinjian's sketch showed a woman holding a baby. Her eyes were lowered, and there were two other children, one leaning against her, the other crouched at her feet. It was clear that this was a Tibetan mother with her three children. The background was more abstract: a blurred view of snowy mountains, the Potala Palace, the Great Wall, and flocks of sheep. He actually put the sheep overhead, so I wasn't sure whether they were sheep or clouds.

Our conversation drifted to the problem of censorship at the exhibition. Zhuang Xiaoxiao could speak volumes on the subject; several of his best works have been axed. Now, he says, he has learned how to get things done. He has decided to find a Tibetan collaborator and to put the Tibetan's name in front of his own. He said that this would give him an advantage in terms of either censorship or awards. The censorship board or the selection committee would consider giving special encouragement to Tibetan artists, and thus the work would have a better chance of surviving. Ironically, he could do that because he had complete confidence in his own art, his own intuition, and the genuine hard work—no padding—that he put into his painting.

Suddenly it occurred to me that Xinjian's original for his Tibetan mother was none other than Nim. Did Xinjian have the same idea in mind as Zhuang Xiaoxiao? Perhaps. A novelist friend of mine, Hu Daguang, had done more or less the same thing. His mother was

Tibetan; his father had mixed Han, Mongolian, and Muslim blood. Hu Daguang's pen name was Ping Cuo. He was brought up in the interior; a typical Han Chinese in his everyday habits and his language, he couldn't speak a word of Tibetan, but now he lists himself as a young Tibetan writer.

I am digressing. Let me get back to the subject.

I asked Liu Yu whether he was planning to write something now that he was in Tibet. He was here with a crew to make documentaries, and would be here for a couple of months. He said he was planning to write a short story about an old woman who lived at the foot of the Potala Palace.

8

"It is said that two years ago, there was a campaign to eliminate dogs in Lhasa. Lhasa is really overrun with dogs, but it is said that there were even more in the old days. It is said that the Lhasa dog is a royal breed and would fetch a big price in London.

"The old woman is dead; she lived at the foot of the Potala Palace, not far from your broadcasting station. It is said that she has been dead for several years, but I still want to go and have a look at the place where she once lived.

"She was a devout Buddhist and was single all her life. In her youth, she started the practice of making three daily circumambulations of the outer wall of the Potala Palace with her prayer wheel. You must know that one circuit around the Potala Palace is two thousand meters. And she made three rounds every day. People who often went to turn the prayer wheels all knew her. She made a living by making clay Buddhist figures.

"In the daytime she would sit on some steps in Eight Corners Road, facing the sun. She had fine yellow clay brought from the distant suburbs and several copper molds, and with these she would make clay Buddhist figures with minute care. These figures were of all shapes and expressions: there was the god of happiness, with the thousand hands and thousand eyes; the Tsongkhapa[2] god in an erect sitting position; and most of all, the figure of Sakyamuni, scintillating godliness.

2. The reformer of the Tibetan Church, founder of the Yellow Sect.

"The herdsmen from the pastoral areas who come here on pilgrimages always stopped by her wares. They would choose several Buddhist figures and leave one or two one-yuan notes in the paper container that held her money. And then there were the tourists from foreign parts, who all wanted to take back a souvenir from Lhasa, and they were also her customers. They would ask her for the price, and she would never answer. So they would do as the natives did, take a few figures and leave one or two Foreign Exchange Certificates. On these occasions, she never so much as glanced in their direction, but would remain bent over her molds turning out another figure of Sakyamuni.

"She never took refuge on rainy days, but stared dully as the other vendors hastily put away their goods and ran for cover. She watched the rain wash away the yellow clay that she had brought from the distant suburbs, while the sluggish yellow waters oozed between her feet toward a depression.

"Apparently, she made a good income and offered all her earnings to Buddha. She went at stated intervals to the Dazhao Temple, the Xiaozhao Temple, the Sela Temple, the Zhebeng Temple, and the Potala Palace to worship the gods. Among the cash that she offered the gods could be seen Foreign Exchange Certificates, Overseas Currency Certificates, renminbi notes with different face values, and even Tibetan currency that had long been out of circulation. On every visit, she would give up everything she had; she was completely devoted to the Bodhisattva. She herself never had a decent gown on her back.

"But this is not the story that I was going to tell."

9

"This doesn't sound real, but I believe it is. It made me think of many things. I had not been here two weeks before I heard the story from two sources.

"As I said, there used to be a lot of dogs in Lhasa. This was a couple of years ago; you people had not moved into Lhasa yet. Dogs could move easily in and out of stores and restaurants and public places—an epidemic of dogs, one could say. You know that the Tibetans love dogs, that they would never harm dogs. But at the same time, the dog population was indeed a problem, there had been cases of rabies, and some contagious diseases were suspected of being spread by infected dogs. The number of dogs was out of all proportion to the population of Lhasa, which was only about one hundred thousand. Food became a problem. As well, the swarms of dogs often got into vicious fights and were a nuisance to the neighborhood.

"And so the municipal government of Lhasa launched a campaign to eliminate them, and even set up a spare-time dog-catching squad. People on the government payroll were not allowed to keep dogs.

"Most people could not bring themselves to kill their own dogs; the most they could do was to drive the creatures out. And thus these domestic dogs joined the numbers of homeless dogs, and at one time, the streets of Lhasa were swarming with them. Young fellows would chase them with hunting rifles and small-caliber guns.

"The old woman began to keep dogs. She took in all the dogs that had been frightened out of their wits by the pursuing gunshots and fed them. Now they lay in her courtyard, basking in the sun, undisturbed.

"Evidently dogs have their own language, and they had managed to communicate the news of their good luck to their fellows. Thus the number of dogs under the old woman's protection began to grow. The newcomers would merge with the old hands and try to sneak in through the courtyard gate unobserved, watching the old woman with their accustomed wariness all the while. If by chance she happened to have a stick in her hand, the new arrivals would turn and run, tails between their legs. In the eyes of dogs, there is no difference between a gun and a stick, especially in a time of crisis.

"And thus the old woman's little courtyard became a haven for dogs. She went out every day as usual to make her three rounds of the Potala Palace, and went as usual to make clay Buddhist figures at Eight Corners Road. But she went less often to worship the gods. When people took her clay Buddhist figures without paying enough money, she did not ignore them anymore without batting an eyelid. Now, she would look at the customers mournfully and shake her head from side to side, waiting for them to produce more money.

"The yellow-haired dog with short legs had whelped, giving birth to a golden-haired puppy. When the old woman was out turning her prayer wheel, she would put the puppy at her breast under the folds of her gown. The bitch followed behind, walking in step with the vibrations of the turning wheel.

"People who knew her could see that the old woman was losing flesh: her cheeks sagged, her eyes grew hollow, and her cheekbones and nose stood out starkly. She began to buy milk every day.

"The children who sold milk knew that she never bargained. The going rate for unadulterated milk was forty cents a bottle, but they would charge her fifty cents for a bottle of milk diluted with water. She bought four or five bottles every day, sometimes even more. According to her neighbors, all the milk was fed to the puppies, she never touched any herself; cow's milk or sheep's milk had never been part of her diet. Very soon she had four little puppies under her care.

"Now, with more than twenty dogs slinking in and out of the old woman's little courtyard, the whole lane took on an eerie air. The lane was very narrow; two people passing each other could barely slip by. And the old woman's courtyard was at the very end of the lane. Every evening when darkness descended, the dogs would venture out of the courtyard and move silently in a file along the lane. How effective this would be if the scene could be caught on camera, using a telephoto lens and shooting from a height."

I laughed at him for his professional obsessions. But to be fair, Liu Yu's photos were indeed quite distinguished; I always enjoy listening to the conceptualization of his photographic works.

"To come back to the dogs, first of all the neighbors objected. With so many dogs cooped up together, fights were inevitable, and barking and growling filled the air, disturbing the neighborhood. When the neighbors complained to her, the old woman just smiled in embarrassment. I am sure it was a bitter smile. Now she spent more time with the dogs, letting them get to know her so that they obeyed her orders and didn't fight so much, making nuisances of themselves to the neighbors. The dogs indeed became more manageable, but the old woman herself spent less and less time on Eight Corners Road.

"The old woman's favorite was the golden-haired puppy; it was the only one that literally was born in her courtyard, and it was like her own child to her. It had already grown and could not be held under the folds of her gown when she was turning her prayer wheel. Now she tied a thin string round its neck and held the leash, and the little thing followed her as its mother used to, trotting one step at a time to the rhythmic turning of the prayer wheel. At night it would creep up onto her bed and snooze contentedly on her breast.

"During this period, the old woman often turned up at the grain market. Tibet was not self-supporting in grain, and Lhasa was a city of high consumption, so the price of free-market grain was very high. As a city resident her grain allowance was limited, and there were twenty dogs to feed. How did she cope? All that people could see was that she was getting thinner and weaker by the day. She was occasionally seen pushing a four-wheeled cart to the market and coming back with two full bags of wheat. By the looks of it, it was clear that she was struggling to stay on her feet; she was actually supported by the horizontal bar of the cart, and only kept moving by holding on to the cart.

"She stopped getting butter tea and even saved on barley cakes, as barley was more expensive than wheat. But she actually began drinking the highland barley wine. I forget if I mentioned earlier that she did not take wine or snuff. But now, every day at noon she would sit under the canopy by the roadside and enjoy two glassfuls. Then she would look drunkenly at the gold-haired puppy at her feet, or even mutter something intimate that only the two of them could understand. She was almost at the end of her tether, but she still went on turning the prayer wheel at the Potala Palace, and she still went on making clay Buddhist figures in Eight Corners Road. But look here, Xinjian is falling asleep. We've stayed too long. Let's continue the conversation later."

10

During this period we often went to the Lhasa River. In one stretch of the Lhasa River there is an island in the center of the river. Not long ago, I wrote a story about this island, titled "The Goddess of the Lhasa River."

When I say "we," I mean Xinjian, Luo Hao, and myself. Luo Hao was a professional photographer; he was the little brother of our group, only nineteen years old. It was Xinjian's idea to wash our clothes in the Lhasa River. I daresay he wanted to relive sweet memories. Actually, it was while washing clothes at the midstream island that he told us the story of how he met Nim.

I mentioned Liu Yu's story of the old woman and her dogs and told Xinjian that he had fallen asleep before we could finish the story. Unexpectedly, Xinjian gave another big yawn and said that Luo Hao had told that story a long, long time ago. Luo had been in Lhasa since childhood and naturally knew more about the local legends.

On this particular trip, we had brought a huge bundle of dirty clothes, as well as our bedsheets and blanket coverings. We had also brought a lot of provisions—canned food and other goodies. Luo Hao killed a white leghorn chicken that his brother had reared. So we had cold spicy chicken and beer. At the time, poulet with beer was the ultimate luxury in Tibet.

Two Tibetan girls were washing their clothes next to us. Because neither Luo nor I was looking for romance, we worked next to the two girls silently, each washing his or her own clothes. The water of the Lhasa River was crystal clear; we could see right to the bottom. We first sank our clothes in the stream and put a stone over them. After letting them soak, we would take one piece of clothing at a time and lay it flat on the stone. We then sprinkled washing powder evenly over it and rubbed it with our hands, or trod back and forth on it with our feet. After one piece of clothing was done, we went on to the next piece, and the next after that.

The girls burst out laughing, a wild and unrestrained laughter. They were laughing at our washing; men were so clumsy at these things. While reflecting on this, we also started laughing.

We stood knee-deep in midstream to rinse the soap out. The water was piercingly cold as it rippled over the stones in the shallow riverbed. We stretched out a piece of clothing with our two hands and let the flowing water run through it, rinsing it thoroughly. The water made a pleasant swishing sound as it whirled through the barrier of our stretched-out clothing. The bedclothes were even more alluring as they spread decoratively in their checkered pattern across the surface of the water, their rhythmic undulations tremblingly setting off a string of ineffable associations. Luo Hao was inspired. He retreated a little distance to set up his tripod and pressed the automatic button. Then he waded rapidly across the stream to join us. He just had time to spread out his bedsheet as we had before the shutter snapped. So there we were, three bachelors washing their bedsheets in the Lhasa River, with the Potala Palace in the background.

Luo Hao's second inspiration came as one of the girls untied her heavy plaits to wash her hair. They must have been sisters; they had exactly the same kind of thick black hair. When the younger of the two had untied her hair and was dipping it in the water, she turned up her face to say something to her sister. Luo Hao, ever on the alert, clicked his camera and caught this rare moment. This was the very picture that he later sent to Japan to participate in a photographic exhibition on the theme "Water and Life."

The girls were not shy; Xinjian and I spoke to them in Mandarin and asked them to pose for more shots from different angles. They seemed pleased, and spoke Mandarin pretty well. They left us their names and address and asked for a set of the photographs. They were stout healthy girls. I still remember their hearty laughs and straightforward speech.

Looking at these girls, I couldn't help thinking back to Liu Yu's story of the pack of homeless dogs who found a home, and the old woman who took them in. I was surprised myself at the way the story ran in my head. The girls brought us highland barley wine. We were afraid of diarrhea, but we couldn't say so outright. So we thanked them and invited them to join us. They thoroughly enjoyed the cold chicken, and for our part, we had a pot of their warm butter tea after our beer.

It was the younger sister who discovered the folded-paper eaglet hanging from a bush. She squealed with surprise and delight and kept murmuring words of admiration. After getting Xinjian's permission, with a few deft movements she sent the kite up into the sky.

She prattled on about the two paper eaglets at home: her father had folded them; her father could fold ever such beautiful paper eaglets; when spring came round everybody would beg her father for paper eaglets. He could fold two different kinds, entirely different. Then I remembered that the elder girl, when leaving their address, had mentioned that they lived at the foot of the Potala Palace. I thought this was a chance to ask about the old woman who kept those dogs. The girl was a native and lived in the area; she might have more details about the story.

Regretfully, neither of the girls knew anything about the old woman. It was in fact Luo Hao who was more informed. Luo Hao stated that the old woman had indeed kept dogs, but that it was not a recent development, that she had always kept dogs, yes, as many as twenty at least. Luo Hao also stated that she had never made clay Buddhist figures, had no relatives, and was dead and gone, so much so that the two girls living in the same area had never heard of her. Luo Hao confirmed that she had always saved her own grain allocation for the dogs, and that she herself was emaciated beyond imagination. He said that at the time, many people in Lhasa knew about her and had given her grain out of pity, but whatever she got, she would give it to the dogs. It was also said, according to Luo Hao, that the government had approved an extra allocation of grain above her regular allowance, but even that didn't help. She was so stubborn, she never listened to advice. Anyway, she was always alone and never had anything to do with her neighbors. It was believed that she had died of hunger; some said of disease. Rumor has it that she died of hunger because she was so emaciated. Actually, nobody knew for sure. Perhaps because she spent so much time all day long with those dogs who were always roaming abroad, she caught some infectious disease from them and died of it.

The younger sister was absorbed in the paper eaglet. I happened to look toward the elder sister and saw her turn aside secretly to wipe away some tears. I nudged Luo Hao, and he stopped talking. Xinjian finally gave the paper eaglet to the fun-loving younger sister.

But what was the matter with the elder sister? Perhaps . . .

11

Liu Yu finished his story before leaving Lhasa. I did not interrupt his narration at the time. I felt that Luo Hao's version may be truer to the facts, but Liu Yu's version undoubtedly left more room for philosophical speculation. He was planning to write a short story. His version, as raw material for a story, had more flexibility, while Luo Hao's more down-to-earth version tended to restrict the imagination.

Predictably, Liu Yu would ponder in terms of Buddhism and its innate influence; he was certainly not interested in just running through the plot. Then I discovered that I myself was intensely interested in Liu Yu's story; I wanted to know what the original story had evoked in a fellow writer. Evocation—that is my point of interest.

The third day after Liu Yu left, I found my way to the sisters' home according to the address. I saw that the lane was long and narrow. Just by coincidence, the younger sister was out. I asked after her, and the elder sister said, "She is out flying paper eaglets."

Translated by Zhu Hong

A WANDERING SPIRIT ❊ *Ma Yuan*

He knew that his present task was to dream.
In the middle of the night, he was woken by the mournful cry of a bird.
—Borges, "The Circular Ruins" Qimi the Second

For the sake of the majority of my dear readers, I shall make some slight adjustments to the dates in this story and convert them from the lunar calendar used by the Tibetans to the Western calendar. This may be a short story, but it covers a long period of time. He was the sort of person often seen on Eight Corners Road in Lhasa, out of work and with no intention of looking for a regular job. He is the central character in this story and he was my friend. His name was Qimi. I don't know his real age, but I guess it was somewhere between twenty-seven and seventy-two.

How I met Qimi is another story, which I won't go into here, so I'll just say that we met purely by chance, and that he was very poor—the kind of person you could truly describe as having nothing to his name. He had no wife or family, of course, and he wasn't even capable of working. He was a cripple, with one side of his body paralyzed so that his mouth was crooked, one of his eyes wandered, and he was lame. His left hand—on the same side as his lame leg—was held in front of his chest like a chicken's claw.

He could speak Mandarin, which wasn't that surprising, but what *was* amazing was that he could speak fluent English. He was just one of the many different beggars on Eight Corners Road; he didn't recite the classics and neither, apparently, did he worship Buddha. He was a long-term inhabitant of the street, and according to him, his family had lived there for at least one hundred and ninety years. He said that they had been resident on Eight Corners Road for five generations.

He took me into the second little alley off the Seventh Corner, and after walking some forty paces, we came to the very high gate of a house with a courtyard. He said his ancestor five generations back had bought it for twenty-seven little silver Tibetan coins. It was a two-story stone house, and Qimi had sold it ten years ago for exactly the same amount of twenty-seven silver coins.

"That was the wish my ancestor left in his will. He was called Qimi too, so if we follow the English custom, you ought to call me . . . hee-hee . . . (Qimi was very sweet when he laughed, and his features looked symmetrical) . . . you ought to call me Qimi the Second."

"Qimi the Second." I decided not to spoil his pleasure.

"My family were aristocrats. Do you know what that means? Aristocrats. Don't you believe me? There's something I can show you. Or two things, in fact. Are we agreed?"

"OK, two things," I said.

"That's settled, then. But we mustn't stand here, there's a big dog in that courtyard, a big black dog the size of a donkey. Let's go somewhere else."

"All right, let's do that."

"How about your place? Do you live far away?"

"No, not far. Let's go there, then. But I don't have any barley liquor."

"Do you have any grain alcohol liquor? That would do."

"There's some white grape wine."

He appeared to think this over, weighing its merits, and a minute later he made up his mind. "Fine, we'll go to your folks' place."

"My folks' place?"

"Well, *your* place then, *your* place—OK?"

THE SIXTY-FIRST YEAR OF THE QIANLONG REIGN

When we got to my home, he solemnly undid the top button of his jacket, and I saw, to my surprise, a cat's-eye as long as my middle finger. I knew what the market value of such a treasure would be, but I'd never seen such a large cat's-eye before. Without realizing it, I was stammering as I asked, "Is it . . . is it real?"

"Of course it's real. But it's not every aristocratic family that has such a fine jewel. Look at the quality; it's quite definitely the best."

I know nothing about the quality of gems, but it still gave me pleasure to look at it, and to touch its ice-cold surface.

"How much would it be worth?" I asked.

"It's priceless," he said.

I stood there in the courtyard, examining this treasure closely in the sunlight, and it seemed rather heavy to me, as if there were a connection between its weight and its value.

"Have you been to the new temple of Lobsangka Dalai? You really have to go. The statue of the Buddha in the main hall of the new temple is made of gold, and so is its base, and it's inlaid with lots of precious stones, some of them cat's-eyes as big as this one, or maybe not quite so big."

I had been there, and I had seen the golden base of the statue of Buddha, all inlaid with precious stones. All I can say is that it was the tangible expression of wealth and power combined.

"Now do you believe me?" he asked, with a touch of pride.

He had me confused. "Believe what?"

"That I'm an aristocrat. Only great aristocrats have stones this valuable."

Suddenly I remembered. "Didn't you say you had two things to show me? What's the other one?"

He suddenly looked glum. "There isn't anything."

"Nothing?" On an impulse, I said, "If there's nothing, then that's it. I don't have to believe all your stories. There are crowds of Khampa traders in the streets, all wearing cat's-eyes—are you asking me to believe they're all aristocrats?"

My scorn seemed to have wounded his pride, and there was a rush of blood to his pale face. "Are you comparing them to me? Those people who wear short gowns?"

I knew that aristocrats had worn gowns which came below their knees, and only common people wore short ones. I smiled inwardly, because he had fallen for my ruse.

"All right, I'll let you have a look and meet my precious silver coins. That'll open your eyes, and you'll be so amazed you won't be able to sleep at night. You'll have nightmares, and you won't die a peaceful death!"

His despair at having to do this showed through all the cursing. But what surprised me was that he'd mentioned silver coins, for what was so unusual about silver coins? You could see them on all the stalls in Eight Corners Road, they cost a few yuan each. I didn't know what all the fuss was about.

He fumbled in some inner recess of his jacket and brought out a cloth package, very tightly wrapped. His movements, as he opened it, evinced a quite unusual reverence. I thought he must be acting like this to create an effect, and I have to admit that he succeeded, for the silver coins in the package were by now imbued with more than a hint of mystery.

Twenty-seven small silver coins, engraved with Tibetan on one side and Chinese on the other. I could make out what the Chinese said—it was "Sixty-first Year of the Qianlong Reign."

"So this is the money you got for selling the house?" I asked.

THE SARI

To me, the sixty-first year of the Qianlong reign and the sixteenth year were basically no different. An old Tibetan coin was an old Tibetan coin, and that's all there was to it. Qimi must have been out of his mind to sell a two-story house with a courtyard for fewer than thirty small silver coins. He drank the wine the same way you'd drink beer, finishing a whole glass in one go, and when he'd downed three glasses in a row, all that was left of what had been more than half a bottle of white wine from Qingdao was the bottle.

Wiping his mouth, he said, "That was good. Shame there was so little of it."

I didn't like to say that it had cost more than five *kuai* a bottle, and one bottle could last me a couple of weeks. It was then that I thought perhaps he'd been boasting, and it hadn't been him who sold the house after all. Why would he have done something that was so obviously stupid? He wasn't a fool.

From then on, whenever I strolled along Eight Corners Road, I always paid special attention to the compound that Qimi had pointed out to me. I inquired at a nearby shop as to who lived there, and they told me it was a businessman who had come back from India. They said the family was very rich, of Tibetan nationality, and they were reputed to have another house in India and a car. I also found out that the family usually had only one servant there to look after the house, and the owners often went back to stay in India. They said the servant kept a large dog, a really huge one, which was extremely fierce, and no one from outside had ever dared set foot inside the courtyard.

"And what about now?" I asked.

"The young lady of the family has recently come back from India. She's beautiful, she dresses in a sari, and she puts on makeup, and with those long black eyelashes, she's really lovely."

"And you've got relatives in India too, have you? I see that all the makeup and clothes and things in your shop are imported."

"No, I'm from Lhasa. But this businessman who comes back here from India lets me have these goods at wholesale rates, and there are several other shops that get their stuff wholesale from him too. He's a *big* businessman." The shopkeeper raised his right hand, his pinkie pointing at himself: "And me, I'm just a little guy."

So that's the story.

I thought I would ask him about Qimi, to find out a bit more.

"Do you know Qimi?"

"Qimi? Which Qimi?"

I did an imitation of a half-paralyzed cripple, and he smiled.

"Everyone on Eight Corners Road knows him!"

"He says that that house used to belong to his family, and it was he who sold it to that businessman. Is that right?"

"I can't say for sure. I only moved here a dozen or so years ago, so I don't know much about what happened before that. Qimi does often come and wander along the alley, but I don't know."

I had turned around and was leaving when he called out to me in a low voice, "Hey, hey!"

I turned to look at him. He wasn't looking at me, but had twisted his head in the direction of the alley. I followed his gaze and saw her.

She really was pretty. She had to be the young lady from the businessman's family, the woman who had just arrived from India. She was clearly used to being looked at by strangers, because I, the shopkeeper, and several passersby were all watching her, and she wasn't bothered at all. She held her head quite high, her eyes directed slightly upward, and walked calmly along with great poise. That kind of woman is a natural empress and looks down on everyone else, as if the whole world existed solely for her.

So that was the Indian sari that the shopkeeper had spoken of; it was a glamorous yet quietly elegant shade of soft pink, decorated with flowers outlined in silver thread. She was very tall too, almost as tall as me. I particularly noticed that her leather shoes had a slight heel, and she was half a head taller than the average man. She was absolutely enchanting, and as she walked by, you could catch a sweet breath of fragrance. My gaze, and that of many other men, followed her receding figure, her tight, slightly swaying buttocks.

The next time I saw her was a week later. I was standing on the third corner at Eight Corners Road, talking to Qimi the Second. I saw her first. She was a long way off, just turning into the street by the Dazhao Temple gate. She was conspicuous because she was so tall. I forgot that I was talking to Qimi, and he poked me in the ribs, realizing my mind was wandering elsewhere.

"I know what you're looking at, even without turning round. A woman. It's that woman who's come back from India, the tall one, isn't it?"

"How did you know?"

"Because men all have the same expression on their faces when they look at her. I'm the sixth generation of my family to live on Eight Corners Road, and there's nothing I haven't seen, nothing I don't know. Nothing on this street escapes me; even if I were blind or deaf, things still wouldn't escape me. Is it her?"

Miserably, I had to admit it. "Yes it is." Only when she had come quite close to us did I suddenly think to ask him, "Do you know her?"

He had still not turned his head. "She's that guy's woman."

"Woman?" I didn't understand. Wasn't she the "young lady of the house," the daughter? How could she have become "the woman," the wife?

He went on talking, his voice and manner completely unchanged in spite of the fact that she was by now very close to us and would undoubtedly be able to hear what he was saying, if she could understand Chinese and was paying attention to us.

"When he took her away, she was still a grubby little kid, already tall but skinny with it, skinny as a spring lamb. He took her off to India and fattened her up till she was so fat that I didn't even recognize her. Look at that big pair of boobs, how lovely and plump they are! It's been less than twenty years; things are changing fast!"

She was just about to walk past us, her ample breasts having a very unsettling effect on all the men around. Why was she staring at me?

Qimi, affected by a mixture of emotions, was jerking his crooked face sideways. "Really fast!" he said.

At this point she said something to me, and I shook my head.

With a touch of pride, Qimi told me: "She asked which country you come from. She was speaking English. She's forgotten all her Tibetan."

So in the end, he turned his head and had quite a long chat with her, jabbering away in English. I guessed that most Tibetans abroad must have a lot of cultural contacts with the countries of northern and central Europe and that she might be able to speak German, so I chipped in and in halting German asked her, "Do you speak German?"

Excitedly, she answered me in German at once, "I certainly do."

Qimi, not wanting to be left out, told me that he had told her I was a Han Chinese. He said she said I didn't look like a Han. He said she had asked him to translate for her and me. He had asked her why she didn't speak Tibetan, and she said she had been abroad too long and could no longer speak it properly. He said she hadn't recognized him at all. He said the broad had earned a lot of money from him in the past. She'd been on the game since she was not much more than ten, and was a regular hooker.

She said she was sorry, but I didn't look like a Han, and she had thought I was a tourist. I told her about myself. She said she would like to invite me home for tea. After a moment's hesitation, I agreed to go. The reason I hesitated was that I wasn't too sure how I ought to explain this to Qimi. But then I quickly realized that I didn't need to give him any explanation. I wonder why I felt so guilty, because at the time it had not actually crossed my mind that she might take her pants off as soon as we got to her room. I had absolutely no need to feel guilty, as I was innocent of any shameful intentions.

I said goodbye to Qimi with studied casualness.

It was a heady feeling to set off in the company of this woman. I was aware that the two of us, especially myself, were attracting a lot of attention. Many men were looking at me with enormous envy. I felt particularly superior because I was so tall.

I didn't stay long at her house. We had a conversation that was totally free of erotic overtones. We drank coffee and ate some exquisite little pastries. What impressed me most was the large dog. I also noticed that there was only one room occupied downstairs, which must be where the deaf-mute servant lived. This servant was about fifty, and grew a lot of flowers in the courtyard. Everyone knows that the inhabitants of Lhasa love flowers, but it isn't often that you see such gorgeous flowers as there were in that courtyard. It was a big yard, and very neat. Because of that, my initial impression of the deaf-mute was a favorable one.

As I was leaving, she asked me to come again.

HIS ANCESTOR'S WILL

I was asleep when Qimi came to look for me. It was the time of day when the morning sun is still gentle.

I wasn't able to offer him any green tea, but I brewed up a pot of milky tea for him in my coffeepot. With powdered milk and black tea, it's very simple. I hurriedly washed and gargled, trying to clear up my room a bit as I did so. By the time I sat down, he has slurped his way through half the pot.

Once again, he fished an object out of some deep recess of his jacket. This time it was a yellowing sheet of paper. "Do you know what a will is?"

Of course I did, though I hadn't known that Tibetan people, too, had this sort of procedure for passing on property. "Yes, I do. I think I do."

"That's what this is. My great-great-great-grandfather left it. He was the one who bought the house, so of course he had the final say as to whether it should be sold and how it should be sold. It says—do you know Tibetan?"

"No, I don't. I can't know everything."

"Have you still got any of that sweet wine we had last time?"

"No. Stop prevaricating. What did your great-great-great-grandfather put down for you on this piece of paper?"

"It's in Tibetan. What a shame you don't know Tibetan, a real shame. You know that Tibetan is the world's most remarkable script; it's supposed to have been created by the remarkable king Songtsen

Gampo of the ancient Tibetan Tufan tribe. He married a Han wife, as well as one from Nepal. It's a real pity that you don't even read Tibetan."

"Well, I don't. I can't help it, I don't."

"This milky tea of yours is quite nice. Well, I'll tell you, what's written here is . . ." Very solemnly, he read aloud in Tibetan the writing on the yellowing paper, but I still couldn't make out what it said.

"Now do you understand?" he asked.

"No, I don't," I said.

"I'd forgotten that you don't know Tibetan. How about making me another pot of milky tea? This pot of yours is too small."

"I'll make one when you've told me." I wasn't going to play along.

"I'll tell you when you've made it."

"I'll make it when you've told me."

"Oh well. OK, I'll tell you. It says this house may never be sold, no matter what happens, unless—now will you make it?"

"Stop going on about making the tea! I'll make it when you've finished what you're saying. Unless what?"

"Unless someone comes along to buy it for twenty-seven silver coins dated the sixty-first year of the Qianlong reign. Then, no matter who it is, we have to sell it to him."

"Twenty-seven—three times nine?"

"Yes, three times three times three. Twenty-seven coins, of the sixty-first year."

"I still don't understand."

"But you're a Han. Don't you know about Qianlong? Don't you know how long the Qianlong emperor reigned? You poor Han people! Let Qimi the Second explain Han history to you. The Qianlong emperor was the fourth emperor of the Manchu Qing dynasty. The three before him were the Shunzhi emperor, the Kangxi emperor, and the Yongzheng emperor. The Qianlong emperor ascended the throne in A.D. 1736, and in Chinese history that year is called the first year of Qianlong. The Qianlong emperor lived for a very long time, and was on the throne for exactly sixty years, dying in A.D. 1795. So there isn't a sixty-first year of the Qianlong reign in Chinese history—that would have been 1796, which in Chinese history is the first year of the Jiaqing emperor. Because that's when the Jiaqing emperor ascended the throne. Now do you understand?"

I thought I did. "You mean that coins with "Sixty-first Year of the Qianlong Reign" on them are fakes? Counterfeit?"

"You don't understand a bloody thing. You're the stupidest guy in the whole world."

Now I may be stupid, but I'm not that stupid.

When I went to her place the next time, I didn't forget to ask her about the coins with "Sixty-first Year of the Qianlong Reign" on them. What she told me was completely different from what he had told me. I didn't know which of them I should believe. That day I didn't leave, I stayed with her. She was a captivating woman.

She said she was thirty, but she honestly didn't look like a woman of thirty, or at least her skin, which was smooth and elastic, didn't look as if it belonged to someone that age. I thought she was deliberately making herself out to be older than she was, but I didn't see why she needed to do that—maybe it was to make me feel easier, but I actually had no sense that I was doing anything wrong, none at all. While I had the chance, I tested her on her Tibetan, and she really couldn't speak it.

ANOTHER WAY OF PUTTING IT

My husband was born in this house. He'll be forty next year. He says this house has been passed down in his family, that it was built over a hundred years ago and is in fact nearly two hundred years old.

His ancestors were great nobles, they were made superintendents of the mint by the eighth Dalai Lama and the officials of the Qing court. You know what "to mint" means? It means to coin money. They made copper coins, and later on they made silver ones.

Ancient Tibetan coins were called *zhangka*, and they were mostly copper, with fewer silver ones, but there were no unified standards; they were like the gold rings you see on sale in the markets in Lhasa nowadays, their size depending on the amount of raw material supplied to the craftsmen who made them. Oh yes, I forgot to tell you, in India I specialize in the study of ancient Tibetan coins. At the university my special subject is economic life during the time of the eighth Dalai Lama. I'm a lecturer.

I'll tell you some more about *zhangka*. After the great Qing dynasty general Fu Kang'an had put down the Gurkha incursions, he and several envoys from the Dalai Lama and the Panchen Lama negotiated the Twenty-nine Articles of the Imperial Regulations, the third one of which specially referred to the standardization of the manufacture of Tibetan coins. This article stipulated that from then on, Tibetan coins should be struck in accordance with government standards and should be inspected by Han officials sent by the Chinese minister in Tibet. Coins should be uniformly minted from pure Han silver, and this should not be adulterated; every *zhangka* should weigh 1.5 *qian*, and six of these pure silver *zhangka* should be equivalent to one ounce of Han silver (six of them would weigh nine *qian*, the extra *qian* going to cover the expense of minting them); on the obverse there should be the Chinese characters for "Precious Tibet, Reign of Qianlong," the edge of the coin should bear the reign title, and the reverse should carry Tibetan script.

The year in which these imperial regulations were formulated was 1792 (the fifty-seventh year of the Qianlong reign), in the winter. The minting of the new silver coins began in the spring of the following year, which is why the only Tibetan silver coins that have come down to us today date from the fifty-eighth year of the Qianlong reign onward. My husband's ancestor was superintendent of the mint at this period, and a trusted retainer of the Dalai Lama.

It would be very easy to become greedy if you were doing this, of course, and I don't know whether he did or not. I do know that their family was very rich, extremely rich. This house is said to have been built at that time.

I know what the silver coins you're asking about are, the ones saying "Sixty-first Year of the Qianlong Reign." You probably don't know that the number of coins that a government needs to have minted annually is planned and subject to a quota: that's the job of the financial experts. Once the quota has been fixed, the mint prepares steel dies in advance, and strikes a small batch of coins in preparation for circulating them on the money market. It took a while for the news of the death of the Qianlong emperor to reach Tibet—until the spring of 1796, in fact. That was how a small amount of money dated sixty-first year came to be circulating among the people. Afterward, the regime of the Dalai Lama managed to collect some of it and melt it down, so the few silver coins that were left have become collector's items, squabbled over by numismatists.

Why did you ask about them? Do you collect old Tibetan coins too? If you're interested, when I come back next time I can bring the one I've got in my collection and show it to you. But to be honest, I'd rather not. There are supposed to be only some forty or fifty of their kind in existence, and they are extremely valuable. They've never made such a mistake again in minting these silver coins.

Besides that, silver coins like this are pressed in dies, and they are very thin: they are made of fine Han silver, which is quite soft. What else would you like to know?

(I've translated what she said into Chinese and put it together into this short passage. The gist of it is as I've said, but it may not be 100 percent accurate, so I hope the reader will forgive me.)

A STORY ABOUT TELLING STORIES

At this point I decided to write a story.

However, there were still some questions I needed to find out more about. I had a consultant ready to hand. A friend of mine is an expert on such things. Big Ox. It isn't a name used to get round a taboo, it's a nickname. Meaning that he's always full of bull. But boasting and telling tall stories is only one minor aspect of Big Ox. Another is that he is at present the greatest collector of ancient Tibetan coins, not only in China but in the world, and no two ways about it. I've already written about him elsewhere; some of the most important aspects of his personality have been amply dealt with, and here I shall omit them.

I ought to have thought of him before, because although he wasn't able to come up with any new explanations about the coins dated sixty-first year of the Qianlong reign, he did know how significant and valuable these small coins were. On my behalf, he searched through handbooks on coins published abroad, as well as in Taiwan and Hong Kong, and he showed me that in Japan, America, Hong Kong, and Taiwan each of them would fetch over one thousand U.S. dollars. The proper price for the genuine article was written there in black and white, and this time I believed him. There are other stories concerning these coins—stories about Big Ox, me, and some other friends, which I also recounted in my biography of Big Ox, "Footloose and Fancy-free." Any readers who are interested can look it up in the literary journal *Spring Wind* (Number 4, 1986). Remember, my name is Ma Yuan, and that piece is my magnum opus.

Big Ox didn't know Qimi the Second. They could have had a lot of opportunities to meet each other, because they both knew me pretty well. But I didn't want them to get to know each other. There's no reason. It was just a fair means of self-defense.

The figure Big Ox came up with was more precise: a total of forty-three such coins in existence. This called Qimi's hoard to mind—twenty-seven. It was a startling figure. He really did seem to be an extraordinary person. Even if what he said was untrue, and the house wasn't his, and even if he hadn't sold it for the twenty-seven silver coins, those coins alone proved that, though he might not be an aristocrat, he was still someone out of the ordinary.

Big Ox also said: "I know that all the original metal dies for silver coins are still preserved in a side hall of the Potala Palace; a friend of mine in the field of religion took me there to see them. They are all registered as key cultural relics. It makes you envious just to look at them. But the die for the sixty-first year of the Qianlong reign was not there. I heard my heart thumping. Pretending to be very casual, I asked my friend whether all the dies were there, and he assured me that they were. He was involved in all the work of making an inventory of the collections in the Potala Palace. It took more than seven years, and every article in the collections is known to him.

"I thought that perhaps it did still exist and had somehow made its way to Eight Corners Road, and I walked up and down the street at least several hundred times in search of it, going into the little shops to ask about it, and all the various roadside stalls, but without any result. You realize that if I could find that die I'd be made."

Because of this, I was even more determined that he shouldn't meet Qimi. But like all men, when I'm with a woman I let down my defenses, and so I told her the whole story, leaving nothing out. She said, "He likes you, too." She meant the dumb servant.

I often went to her small courtyard after that, to chat and drink tea, and after three months my spoken German was greatly improved. I don't know how she managed it, but she never got pregnant. It was really remarkable. And I made friends with the dumb servant and the huge shaggy black dog he had.

She told me she would shortly be returning to India, and when she left, she said she would come back, because of me. I told her that I wanted to write a story for her, and a faintly doubtful look appeared on her lovely smiling face. Though she said, happily enough, that she looked forward to reading it, in my heart I still felt there was a problem.

After that, I sometimes went to the little courtyard to sit awhile with the dumb servant, drinking tea. His milky tea had a strange taste, and I reckoned he must have put shredded coconut into it, because it tasted very much like coconut milk from Hainan Island. The dumb fellow didn't often manage to sit down, as he was always bustling around looking after his flowers. But he would find time to come over for frequent sips of cold tea as he went about his business.

So it was the big black dog who usually kept me company. He would pad silently over and lie at my side, watching me with the kind of relaxed expression an old friend would have. Sometimes I could sit there for several hours at a time.

Were it not for what happened in the end, my story might well have concluded in just such an unexceptional way.

A VERBAL CONTRACT

I was extremely surprised by the first episode connected with this incident. I don't know how Big Ox and Qimi got together, but I immediately assumed that this was a plot that had been going on for a long time behind my back. I have to say that I treated Big Ox shabbily. He may have been a real villain, cheating, swindling, and stealing, but with me he was always straight. I should say he never deceived me in anything. But I'm straying outside the scope of this story.

The problem was that as soon as they saw each other they were thick as thieves, just like old buddies. When they met, by chance, at my house, neither of them told me they knew each other. But it didn't seem as if they had deliberately tried to conceal the fact that they knew each other, and very well at that.

What was interesting was that they started talking about the silver coins from the sixty-first year of the great Qianlong in front of me. Perhaps they were what people mean when they talk about "barefaced robbers." I noticed particularly that old Qimi didn't breathe a word about the twenty-seven treasures he had in his collection, as if it were all nothing to do with him. I could see that Big Ox was completely in the dark about that. They seemed to be exchanging news about the coin market.

Big Ox said, "I need to ask your help with the 'sixty-first year of Qianlong' coins. The money's negotiable, but I definitely need your help."

Qimi the Second said, "Don't worry, you can count on me." Then, he added, "What else do you want?"

"Nothing, nothing," Big Ox answered very firmly.

Qimi was not the sort of guy who gives up when the going gets tough, so he kept up the questions. "Nothing at all?"

This time Big Ox hesitated. "It depends what it is."

"What do you want? What would you like?"

"The die. The die for the 'sixty-first year of Qianlong' coins."

"Is there such a thing? I've lived on Eight Corners Road for more than a hundred years—how come I've never heard of it?"

"I'm absolutely sure there is. Please look for it, and if you find it, I'll give you a hundred silver coins."

"Why would you give me silver coins? What's it to you if I find it? Qimi the Second doesn't take dirty money."

"We'll do an exchange, my hundred coins for the die."

"What does a die look like? I've never seen one."

"It's steel, or iron, about this big (he gestured) and it's hollow, with the pattern inside the same as the pattern on the coins dated sixty-first year of the Qianlong reign. Haven't you ever seen one?"

"I'll see what I can do. So we're agreed, one hundred coins."

"Yes, not a penny less."

Big Ox made a point of asking me to be the middleman, to show that he wouldn't go back on his word, and I was happy to agree. Thus, the verbal contract became a deal with the striking of palms.

It must have been quite a long time after this before I saw the two of them again, and they had probably forgotten all about it, while I was the one who kept thinking about it all the time. Why had I ever gotten involved in this affair? Was I urged by gods and demons? It must have been God's will.

Completely by chance, I noticed a small door next to the deaf-mute servant's room. He lived downstairs, and upstairs there was only one room that was lived in, while two rooms were for the dog. This small door was the only one locked tight, hermetically sealed. The door was so low that only a pygmy could have walked through it without stooping, and it had a large brass lock, a foreign one, now quite green with verdigris. The door had been locked for a long while, and time had left its mark.

I didn't want the deaf-mute servant to know that the door had caught my attention, and I went on drinking my tea very casually. When, casually again, I passed near it, I was very surprised to see that long sealing strips had been pasted all over the door and the frame. They were made of a kind of silky fabric stamped with circles, and although this had half rotted away, the strips were still intact. They had become the same black color as the door, so that if you didn't look carefully, you wouldn't have been able to see them at all.

The big black dog growled as I reached out to touch the strips of silk. It was a scary sound, full of menace, and I dropped my hand to my side at once, and acted natural. The deaf-mute was some distance away, tending his flowers with total concentration, and he didn't turn round.

THE FULL-MOON CONSPIRACY

"Qimi the Second is totally trustworthy, you can ask anyone on Eight Corners Road, and if there is one single person who tells you I'm a liar, may the Buddha give him a horrible death."

"Who's asking you to swear anything? I'd like to ask you if you know your way around that house your ancestor had."

"Of course I do."

"You know all the rooms?"

"Yes, all of them."

"OK then, what about the room downstairs with the small door?"

"That room is locked, my ancestor locked it, and the eighth Dalai Lama sealed it. No one's allowed to touch it. Why do you ask?"

So that was really how it was.

"Why do you ask?"

"Nothing special, I was just asking."

"No, you weren't. Let me think. Let me think." He patted his chest as he spoke and struck an attitude of thought. "I know, even without your telling me. You can't fool old Qimi the Second."

I smiled benignly at him.

We quickly made a secret pact. In three days, there would be the full moon of the Mid-Autumn Festival, and I would go out before it got dark, taking the black dog as big as a donkey, go down to the edge of the Lhasa River, cut across the suspension bridge, and head for the old robbers' haunt of Gumolingka Island, where at the appointed time I would also meet Big Ox.

It was all fixed up.

On the fifteenth of the eighth lunar month, the moon was obscured by clouds, as it is every year.

Because it was so overcast, it got dark earlier than usual. Before I took the big black dog out, I sat with the dumb servant for half an hour, drinking tea. It was very rare for the dog to leave the courtyard, and the outside world was exceedingly strange to him. His mood was very hostile as we crossed Eight Corners Road, and I kept a tight hold on him in case he caused trouble, for it was still very crowded.

He was not used to seeing so many people, of course, because he had been cooped up for so long, and his enormous size and deep, alarming bark meant that the passersby kept well away from us. I realized I'd done something stupid, because the evil hound attracted the attention of all the people out for the evening prayers.

I knew I was too early, and it would probably be a long time before Qimi arrived. Big Ox wouldn't get there early, either. I walked slowly westward with the black dog along the nice, cool embankment at the edge of the river.

The ferry at Oxhide Raft, always so full of people coming and going during the daytime, had stopped running, and all that remained were the stone steps where the passengers would disembark. The empty scene left plenty of room for imagination. Perhaps that was what "poetic" meant?

The dog was romping around on the shingle, charging along, then suddenly pulling up and madly charging off again. The moon had risen and looked uneasy among the clouds that half covered it. They were so thick that there were only a few gaps through which you could see the sky.

Big Ox came first. I recognized his stocky figure at once.

"When did you come?" he said.

"What are you doing here?" I said.

"Didn't you say to come here when it got dark?"

"But I haven't seen you for more than ten days."

"Qimi said you wanted me to come—did he get it wrong, maybe?"

"He sure did."

"Oh well. I'll go back then. What's old Qimi playing at?"

"Don't go, now you're here. It's the Mid-Autumn Festival today, and a bit later we'll be able to enjoy the moon on the riverbank."

But there was no moon. From the time that Big Ox arrived, the black dog had not stayed close to me, and I had not been bothering to pay attention to him. I realized that during that time my mind had been wholly elsewhere. I knew I was waiting for only one thing, and that was Qimi's arrival on the scene. Apart from that, there was nothing I was interested in.

Big Ox sensed the situation and said nothing. We walked onto the suspension bridge, shoulder almost touching shoulder, and for some reason the black dog didn't follow us.

I remember that during the whole of the rest of the evening, the moon only once revealed its round face. I'll testify here and now that the moon had no part in the conspiracy. The moonlit night is innocent.

AN END OR A BEGINNING?

I've borrowed the title of a poem by my friend Bei Dao. You can tell at once.

I told you before that the story of how I met Qimi the Second is very complicated. I got to know him from writing about him, from the process of fabrication and creation. And the end is also the beginning.

It is difficult to tell you about the rest of that evening in any kind of order, and, if it's all right with you, I think I'd better just say truthfully what happened.

The only time the moon showed its face it shone on the deliriously happy Qimi as he lurched across the suspension bridge in jolting steps. You can imagine the sort of mood he was in. He and I and Big Ox walked together to the southern tip of the moonlit island. South of that was the broad, fast-flowing Lhasa River. The moon hid itself once more among the clouds, and didn't emerge again.

"Here it is! That'll be one hundred silver coins."

"You mean the die? Have you got it?"

"One hundred coins. With the middleman on the spot, I'm sure there's no way you'll go back on your word."

Qimi the Second put the die into my hands. When I had looked at it, I passed it on to Big Ox. "That's the one! That's it! Absolutely right!"

"One hundred silver coins."

"Relax. I won't cheat you!"

Big Ox scrutinized it very closely, muttering to himself.

"That's right. It's a pity it's rusty—but it's not too bad. This is the one." Big Ox suddenly raised his head.

"And the other bit?"

"Which bit?" Qimi didn't understand.

"The top half of the die, the top bit with the Tibetan writing on it?"

"You never said anything about that! How was I to know there was a top bit?"

"Shit. Just the bottom bit's no use."

"For what?" Qimi still didn't understand.

"It's no use for anything. You idiot!"

Old Qimi was thoroughly dejected. "Then that's it, it's all over."

Big Ox said, "Think up what else we can do, think!"

"There's nothing we can do; I can't think of anything else. It's all over."

And no matter what else Big Ox said, old Qimi remained silent.

I noticed Big Ox was still clutching the die, and I knew the matter was far from being concluded. Well, perhaps not that far. I heard the dog growling, and he came racing toward me at high speed, racing toward the end of the story.

It was old Qimi who at once realized what this sudden turn of events meant. He snatched the die from Big Ox's hands with an agility that belied his age, then swung his arm. There was a splash. Old Qimi ran off eastward, into the darkness.

The big black dog looked in the direction from which the splash had come and watched the water there awhile, then he turned round and very slowly began to head for home. Big Ox and I followed behind, like bodyguards. Big Ox whispered that he had noted where in the water the die had fallen, and said he would definitely try to fish it up.

I said that the Lhasa River was too cold and flowed too rapidly for him to be able to do that without professional divers. So he said he'd hire one, regardless of expense.

I knew he had no money at all to hire anyone.

For the sake of the majority of my readers, I'd like to give some more information in addition to this ending. I never went to that small courtyard again, even after I found out that she was back, and I never again saw the aged dumb retainer or the big black dog he kept.

I often see old Qimi wandering around on Eight Corners Road. His clothes are ragged, and he looks very preoccupied. He doesn't seem to recognize me anymore, as if he had never known me. Only Big Ox still often comes round to my place, to cadge a meal and show off the coins he's just got hold of. But we never mention what happened on that night of the Mid-Autumn Festival.

Translated by Caroline Mason

ACKNOWLEDGMENT OF COPYRIGHTS

wudao (*Sorrowful Dance*) (Taipei, 1991). Copyright © 1995 by Yuan-Liou Publishing Co., Ltd., Taiwan. Translation copyright © 1997 by Beatrice Spade.

"The Brothers Shu" (Shunong huozhe nanfang shenghuo) appeared in *Zhongshan* 3 (1989). Anthologized in *Hongfen* (*Rouge*) (Taipei, 1991). Copyright © 1995 by Yuan-Liou Publishing Co., Ltd., Taiwan. Translation copyright © 1997 by Grove/Atlantic, Inc.

Can Xue

"The Hut on the Mountain" (Shanshang de xiaowu) was anthologized in *Huangni jie* (Yellow Mud Street), (Taipei, 1987). Reprint permission © 1997 by Northwestern University Press.

Bei Cun

"The Big Drugstore" (Da yaofang) appeared in *Jintian* (Today) 4 (1992). Copyright © 1994 by Bei Cun. Translation Copyright © 1997 by Caroline Mason.

Sun Ganlu

"I Am a Young Drunkard" (Wo shi shaonian jiutanzi) appeared in *Renmin wenxue* (People's Literature) 1 & 2 (1987). Copyright © 1994 by Sun Ganlu. Translation copyright © 1997 by Kristina M. Torgeson.

Ma Yuan

"More Ways Than One to Make a Kite" (Die zhiyao de sanzhong fangfa) appeared in *Xizang wenxue* 3 (1985). Copyright © 1997 by Ma Yuan. Translation copyright © 1997 by Zhu Hong.

"A Wandering Spirit" (*Youshen*) appeared in *Shanghai wenxue* (Shanghai Literary Monthly) 1 (1987). Copyright © 1997 by Ma Yuan. Translation copyright © 1997 by Caroline Mason.

CONTRIBUTORS

The Editor

Jing Wang is Associate Professor of Chinese Literature at Duke University. She is the author of *The Story of Stone*, which won the Joseph Levenson Prize in 1994, and *High Culture Fever: Politics, Aesthetics, and Ideologies in Deng's China.*

The Authors

Ge Fei (1964–) teaches Chinese literature at his alma mater, East China Normal University, in Shanghai. His writing career began in 1986 with the publication of "Remembering Mr. Wu You." The most stylistically refined of all the avant-gardists, Ge Fei is also known to be a writer who has the knack of subverting metaphysics through fiction. Ge Fei is fond of summer thunderstorms and has spoken on many occasions of his desire to re-create the subtle sensations those summer storms engraved on his mind when he was little. Writing fiction offers him the possibility of revisiting those haunting sites in his childhood memories. The motif of mnemonic return maps out a fictional space where philosophical inquiry is indistinguishable from the pursuit of the pure form of storytelling. Since the early 1990s, Ge Fei has been publishing full-length novels.

Yu Hua (1960–) is a freelance writer in Beijing. Writing against conventions of all sorts, he is one of the most "indecent" and controversial avant-gardists. Yu has denounced the "real," as defined by realism, and gone in search of a fictional reality that borders on total disorder. One of his obsessions is to deconstruct violence. His meticulous efforts at peeling away the trappings of humanity and civilization result in a frantic and radical experimentation, not only with the form of narration but with the stories themselves. Arguing that his stories exhibit a world that has never been narrated before, Yu Hua delivers some of the most improbable and shocking story lines that Chinese readers have ever encountered.

Su Tong (1963–) is the best-known Chinese avant-garde writer in the West, thanks to film director Zhang Yimou's adaptation of his novella *Raise the Red Lantern* and to Howard Goldblatt's translation of his novel *Rice*. Su Tong's stories have high entertainment value because they are replete with the familiar ingredients of popular fiction: history mixed with doses of mystery and sexual violence. His famous stories set in Maple Village illustrate his deep fascination with genealogy. He tells stories of decadent families in the south and relishes the storyteller's privilege of blurring the boundary between the mythical and the historical. The most commercial of all the avant-gardists, Su Tong continues to write fiction in the 1990s. He is now a professional writer affiliated with the Writers' Association of Jiangsu Province.

Can Xue (1953–) is one of the pioneers of avant-garde fiction. During the Cultural Revolution, her father was imprisoned, and her mother and all her siblings were sent to the countryside for labor reform. She herself lived alone in a small dark cell during those years. She had only an elementary school education. After the Cultural Revolution, she was self-employed as a seamstress. She started writing in 1983, and her first work appeared in 1985. Nineteen eighty-six marked her most prolific period. Her fiction depicts a viciously tautological mental world ruled by her female protagonists' psychotic vision.

Bei Cun (1965–) is a true member of the avant-garde, as Su Tong says, because his experiment with language pushes to extremes the possibilities of narration. He never finishes telling a story. He leads his readers deeper and deeper into a maze wherein the same characters and the same episodes are being reinvented and repositioned in proliferating simulacra of the parent tale. One of the few uncompromising Experimentalists who still upholds an elitist, avant-gardist stance in the 1990s, he is the editor of *Fujian wenyi* (Fujian literary monthly).

Sun Ganlu (1959–) is reputed to be the most undecipherable avant-gardist. He succeeds in deconstructing meaning altogether. What his fictional world presents is a self-referential system of riddlelike signifiers. His stories read more like prose poetry strung together by fables, fragmentary images, and extravagant verbal play. Writing is, for him, a process of gaining self-sufficiency through the meticulous construction of loss of control. Sun is now a professional writer affiliated with the Shanghai Writers' Association.

Ma Yuan (1953–), a pioneer of the avant-garde, writes about Tibet with a passion that is rarely found in Han Chinese writers. His prominence is not entirely due to his fascination with outlandish Tibetan myths and rituals. Ma Yuan was the trendsetter of a new mode of storytelling in post-Mao China, one that privileges the narrator's voice over what he or she is narrating. After Ma, all the taboos on fiction writing disappeared, and the search for an idiosyncratic style became the writer's legitimate pursuit. Ma Yuan graduated from the Chinese department of Liaoning University in 1978. He went to Tibet in 1982 and worked there as a journalist until 1987. He is now a freelance writer.

The Translators

Eva Shan Chou is the author of *Reconsidering Tu Fu* and of several articles on poetry that have appeared in the *Harvard Journal of Asiatic Studies* and in other periodicals. Her current research is on Lu Xun. She teaches in the English department of Baruch College, City University of New York.

Michael S. Duke is Professor of Chinese in the Department of Asian Studies at the University of British Columbia. He is the author of *Blooming and Contending: Chinese Lit-*

erature in the Post-Mao Era and *The Iron House: A Memoir of the Chinese Democracy Movement and the Tiananmen Massacre*, and he is the translator of Su Tong, *Raise the Red Lantern: Three Novellas* and of other works of modern Chinese fiction.

Howard Goldblatt teaches modern Chinese literature at the University of Colorado, Boulder. He edits the journal *Modern Chinese Literature* and is a translator of Chinese fiction including Mo Yan's *Red Sorghum* and *The Garlic Ballads*, and Su Tong's *Rice*.

Ronald R. Janssen teaches modern and postmodern literature and criticism at Hofstra University. His article on the French surrealist André Breton is forthcoming in *Breton: The American Years*.

Andrew F. Jones is Assistant Professor of Chinese Literature at the University of Washington. He is the author of *Like a Knife: Ideology and Genre in Contemporary Chinese Popular Music* and the translator of Yu Hua, *The Past and the Punishments*.

Denis C. Mair, with a master's degree in Chinese from Ohio State University, has translated autobiographies by Feng Yulan and Yan Jiaqi. While working for Foreign Languages Press in Beijing, he translated works by Tie Ning and Wang Meng. He is Chinese editor for the Pacific Rim literary magazine *Temple*.

Victor H. Mair is Professor of Chinese Language and Literature in the Department of Asian and Middle Eastern Studies at the University of Pennsylvania. He is the translator of Lao-tzu, *Tao Te Ching*, *Wandering on the Way: Early Taoist Tales and Parables of Chuang Tzu*, and *Tun-huang: Popular Narratives*. He also is the editor of *The Columbia Anthology of Traditional Chinese Literature*.

Caroline Mason is a freelance translator and language trainer in the northeast of England. After graduating in Chinese from London University, she went on to study at Harvard University and in Taiwan. She was a lecturer in East Asian studies at the University of Durham in England for fourteen years.

Beatrice Spade currently teaches history at the University of Southern Colorado. Her interest in modern Chinese literature grew while teaching at the Institute of Modern American Literature, Shandong University, from 1982 to 1986.

Kristina M. Torgeson is a Ph.D. candidate in modern Chinese literature at Columbia University. She is the editor and translator of Wei Jingsheng, *The Courage to Stand Alone: Prison Letters and Other Writings* and, with Amy D. Dooling, *Writing Women in Modern China: An Anthology of Women's Literature from the Early Twentieth Century*.

Jian Zhang is Associate Chairperson of the Communication and Arts Department at the Brentwood Campus of Suffolk Community College, State University of New York.

Zhu Hong is Visiting Professor in the Department of Modern Foreign Languages and Literatures at Boston University. She is the translator of several works, including *A Higher Kind of Loyalty*, *The Chinese Western*, *The Serenity of Whiteness*, and *The Stubborn Porridge*.